LEVEL UP

GENE LUEN YANG   **THIEN PHAM**

First Second
New York & London

Dedicated to our brothers Jon and Thinh, both of whom work in the medical field, for being the good Asian sons.

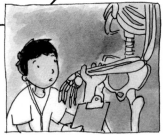

Published by First Second
First Second is an imprint of Roaring Brook Press,
a division of Holtzbrinck Publishing Holdings Limited Partnership
175 Fifth Avenue, New York, New York 10010
All rights reserved

Distributed in Canada by H. B. Fenn and Company Ltd.
Distributed in the United Kingdom by Macmillan Children's Books, a division of Pan Macmillan.

Cataloging-in-Publication Data is on file with the Library of Congress
Paperback ISBN: 978-1-59643-235-2
Hardcover ISBN: 978-1-59643-714-2

First Second books are available for special promotions and premiums.
For details, contact: Director of Special Markets, Holtzbrinck Publishers.

Book design by Marion Vitus
Printed in China

FIRST
EDITION

First Edition 2011

BY ART
WE LIVE

Paperback: 1 3 5 7 9 8 6 4 2
Hardcover: 1 3 5 7 9 8 6 4 2

http://www.jaderibboncampaign.com/

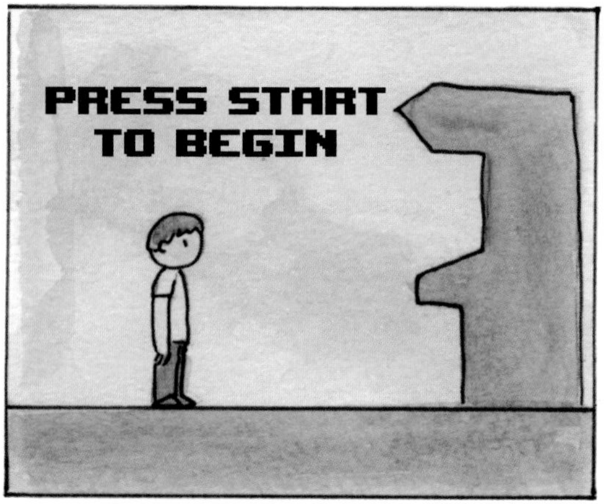
PRESS START
TO BEGIN

I saw my first arcade video game when I was six.

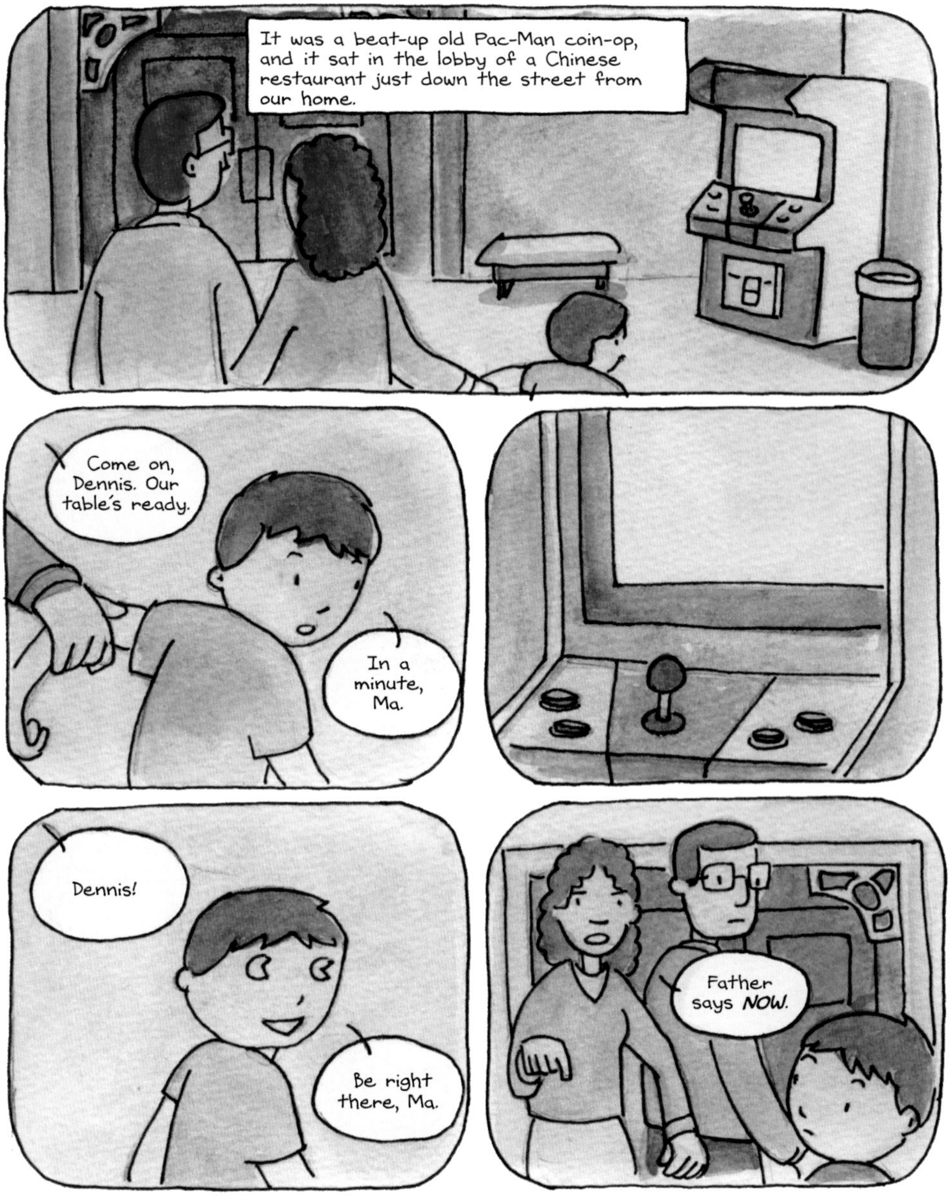
It was a beat-up old Pac-Man coin-op, and it sat in the lobby of a Chinese restaurant just down the street from our home.
Come on, Dennis. Our table's ready.
In a minute, Ma.
Dennis!
Be right there, Ma.
Father says *NOW*.

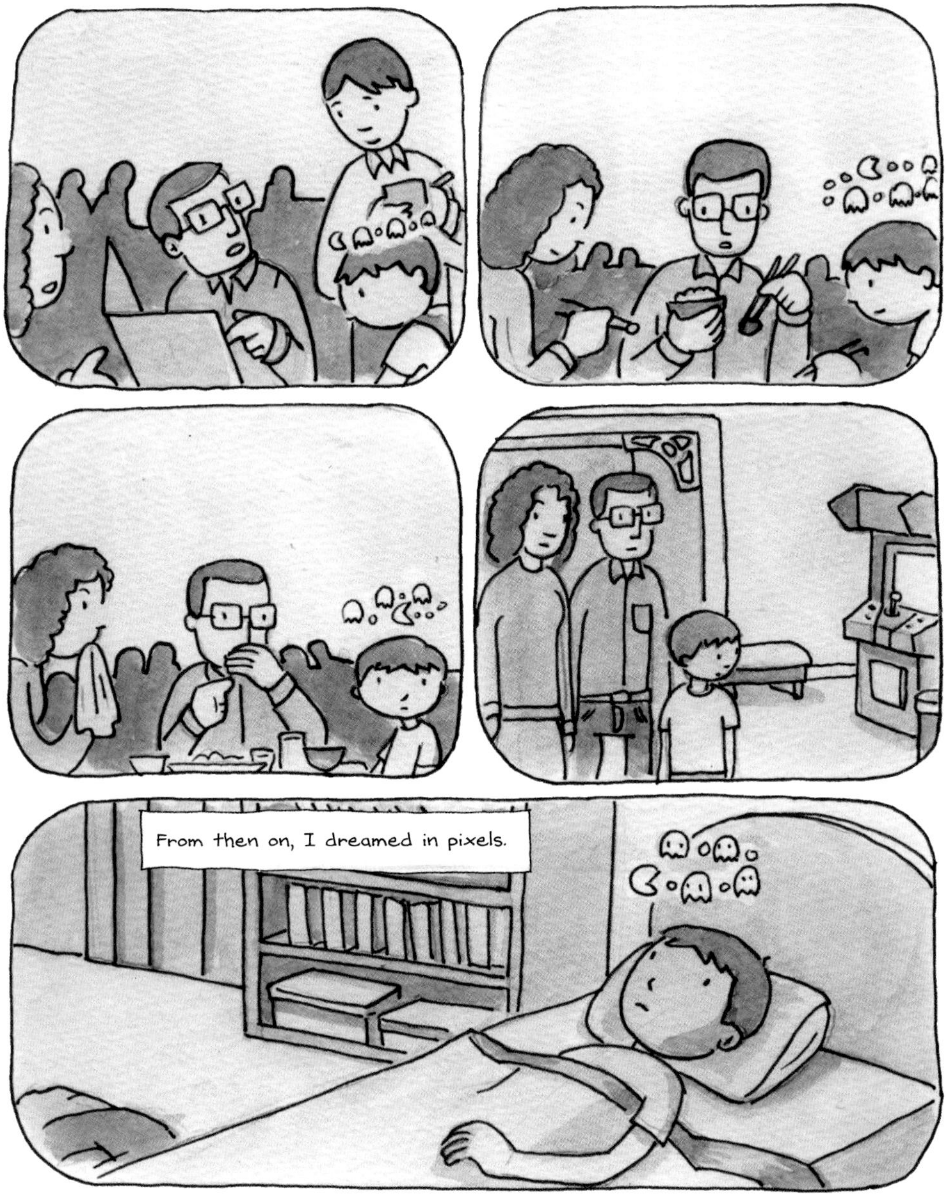
From then on, I dreamed in pixels.

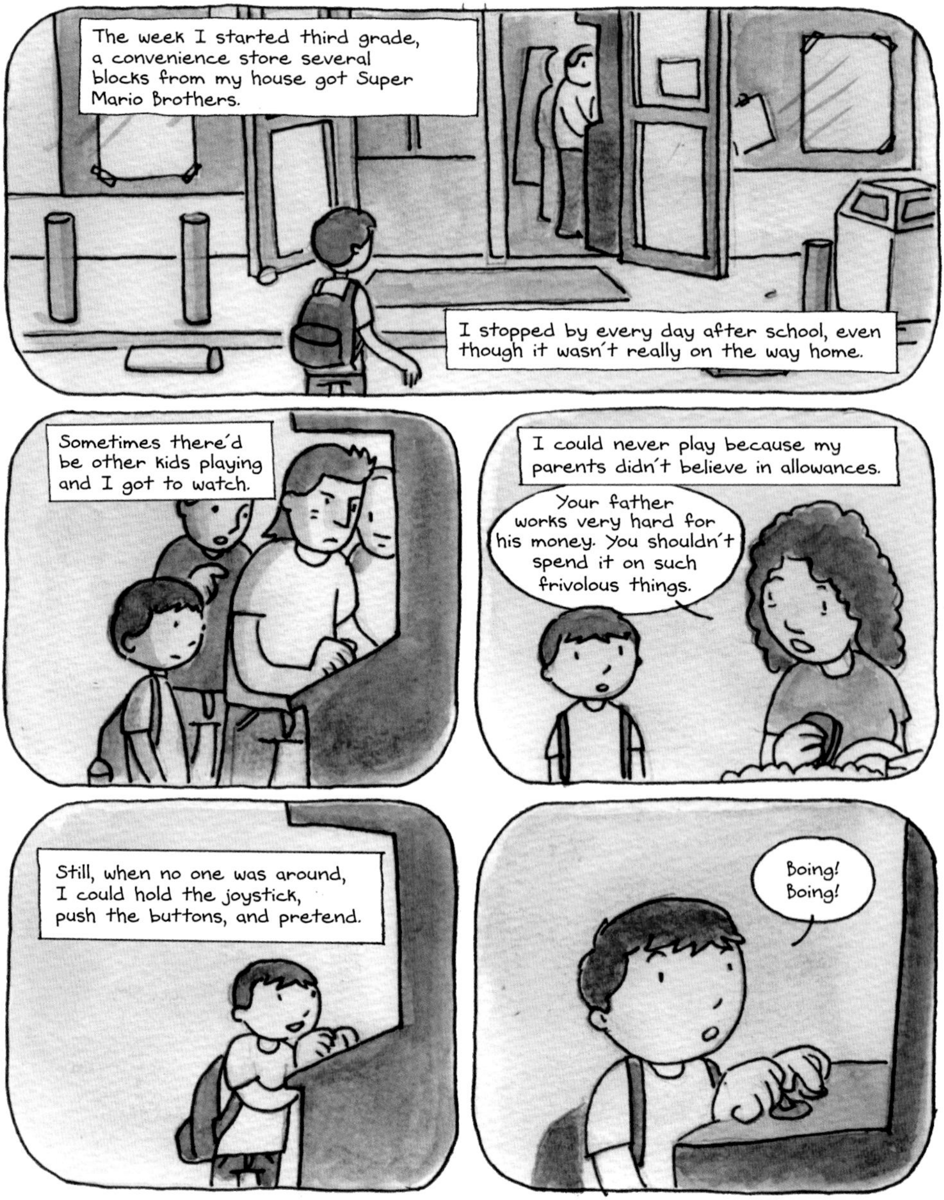
The week I started third grade, a convenience store several blocks from my house got Super Mario Brothers.
I stopped by every day after school, even though it wasn't really on the way home.
Sometimes there'd be other kids playing and I got to watch.
I could never play because my parents didn't believe in allowances.
Your father works very hard for his money. You shouldn't spend it on such frivolous things.
Still, when no one was around, I could hold the joystick, push the buttons, and pretend.
Boing! Boing!

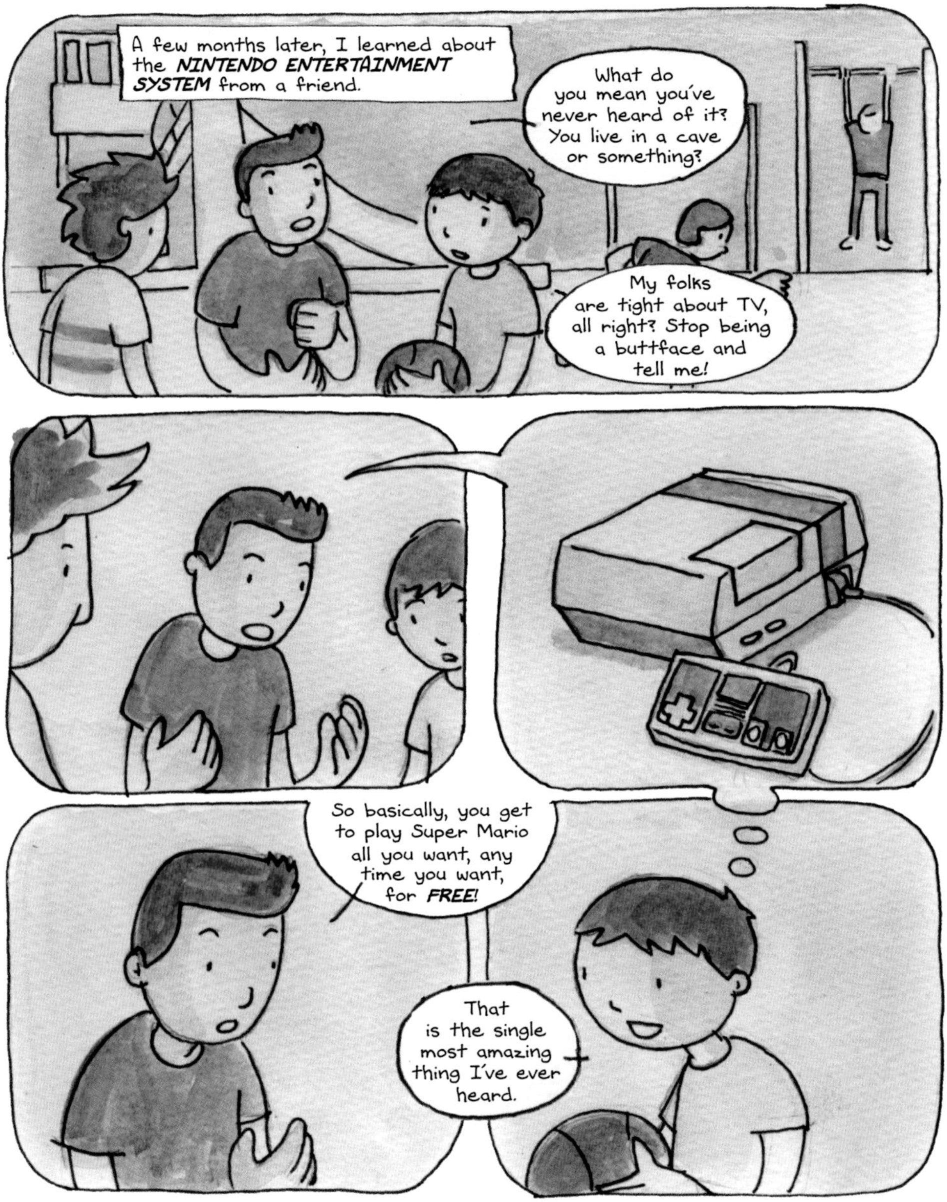
A few months later, I learned about the **NINTENDO ENTERTAINMENT SYSTEM** from a friend.
What do you mean you've never heard of it? You live in a cave or something?
My folks are tight about TV, all right? Stop being a buttface and tell me!
So basically, you get to play Super Mario all you want, any time you want, for **FREE!**
That is the single most amazing thing I've ever heard.

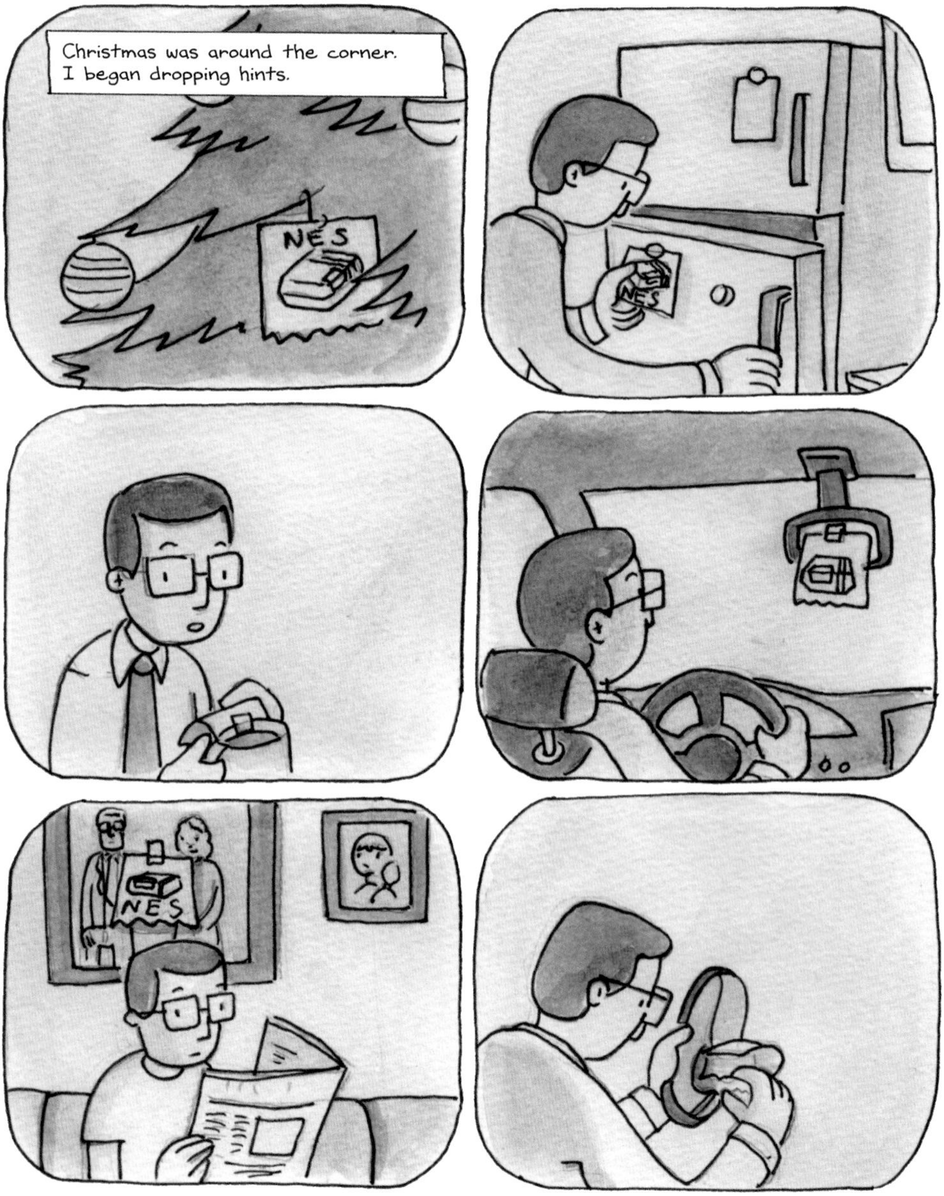
Christmas was around the corner.
I began dropping hints.
NES
NES
NES

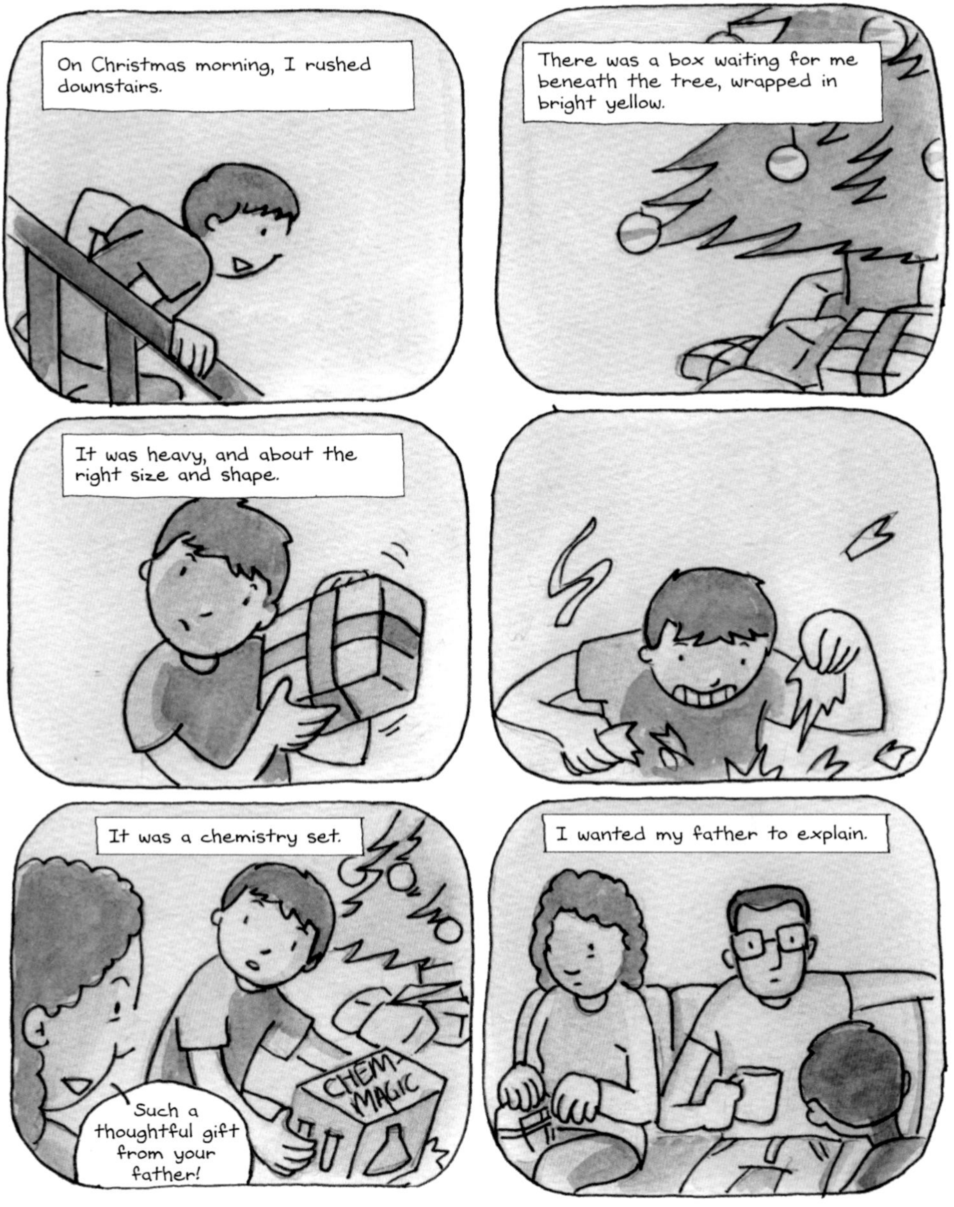
On Christmas morning, I rushed downstairs.
There was a box waiting for me beneath the tree, wrapped in bright yellow.
It was heavy, and about the right size and shape.
It was a chemistry set.
Such a thoughtful gift from your father!
CHEM-MAGIC
I wanted my father to explain.

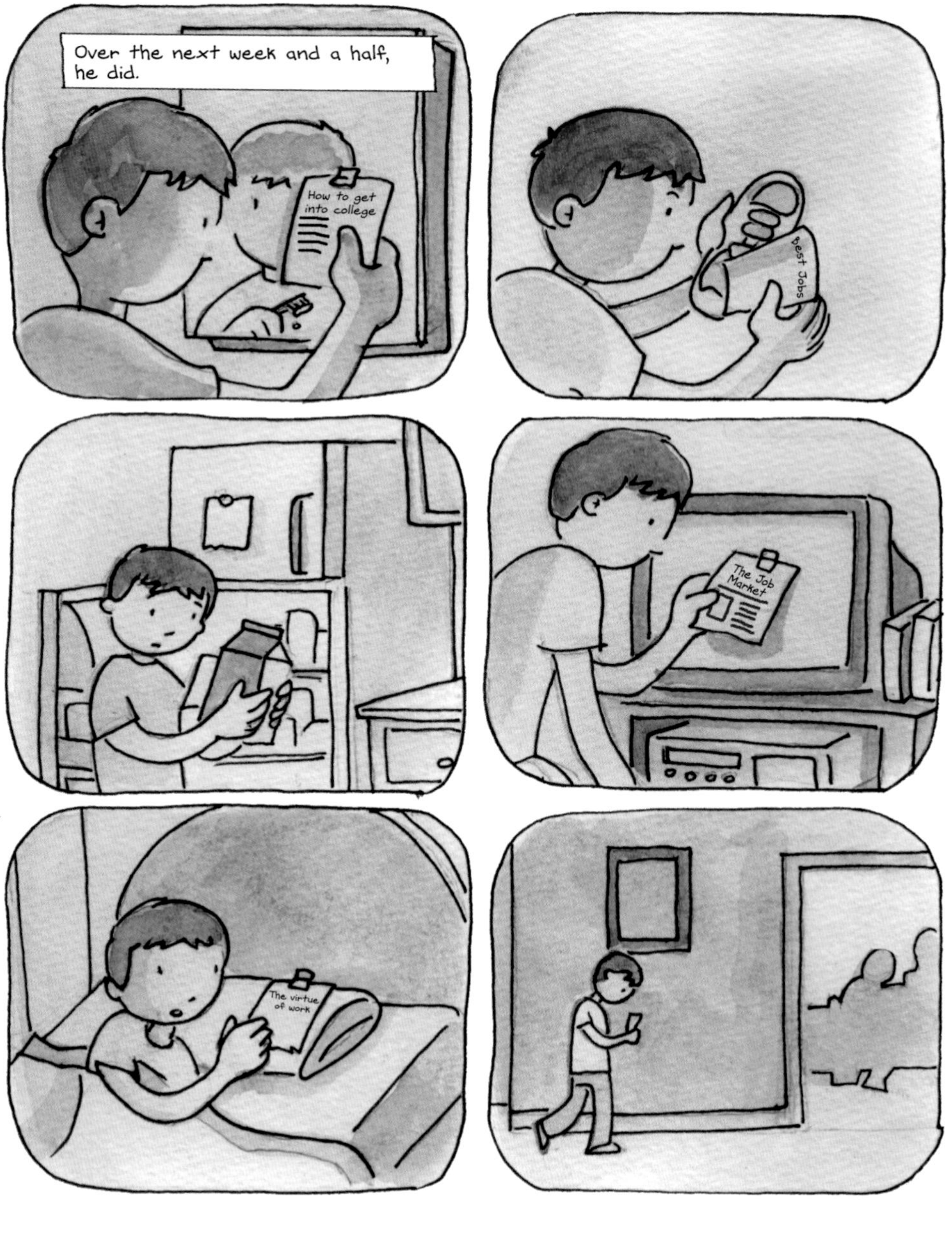
Over the next week and a half, he did.
How to get into college
Best Jobs
The Job Market
The virtue of work

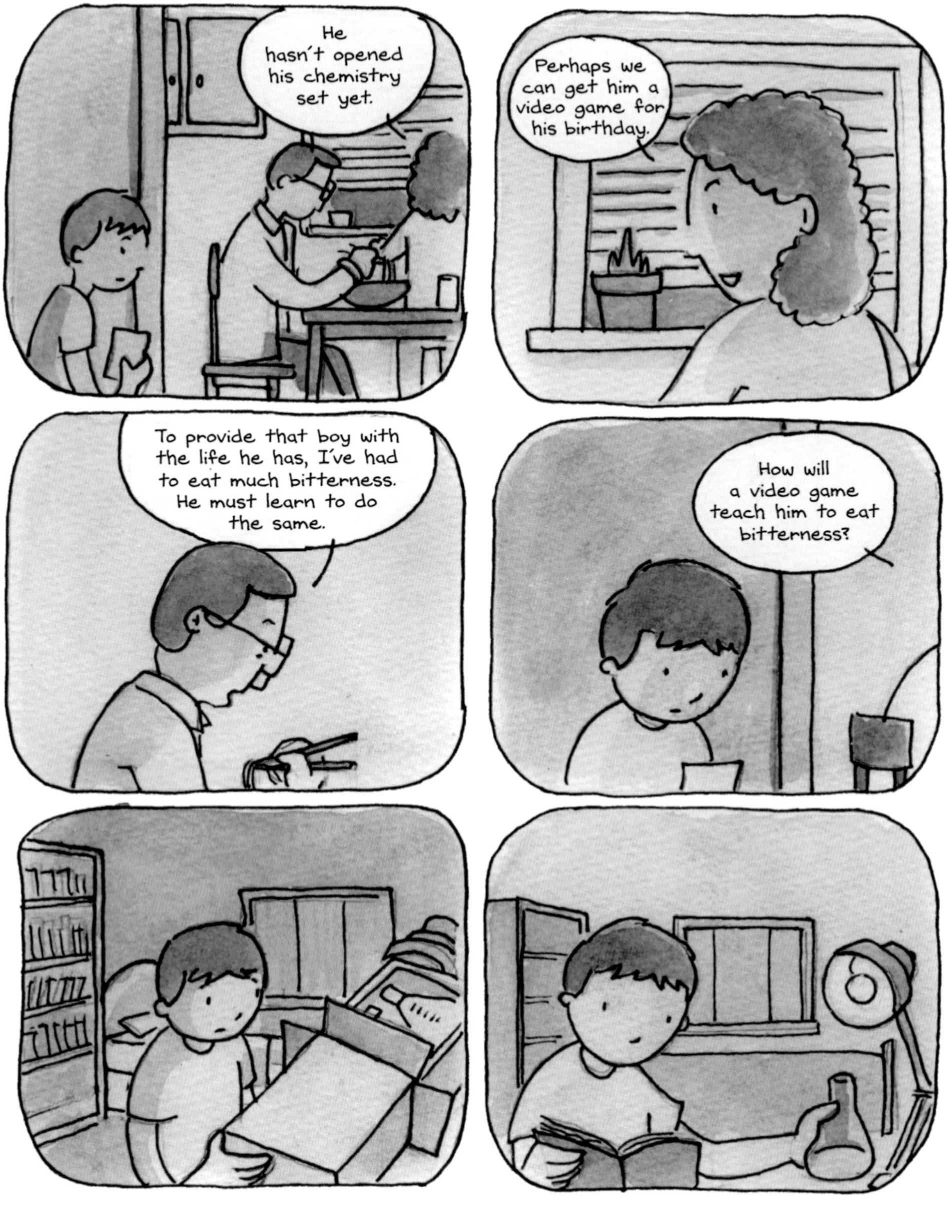
He hasn´t opened his chemistry set yet.
Perhaps we can get him a video game for his birthday.
To provide that boy with the life he has, I´ve had to eat much bitterness. He must learn to do the same.
How will a video game teach him to eat bitterness?

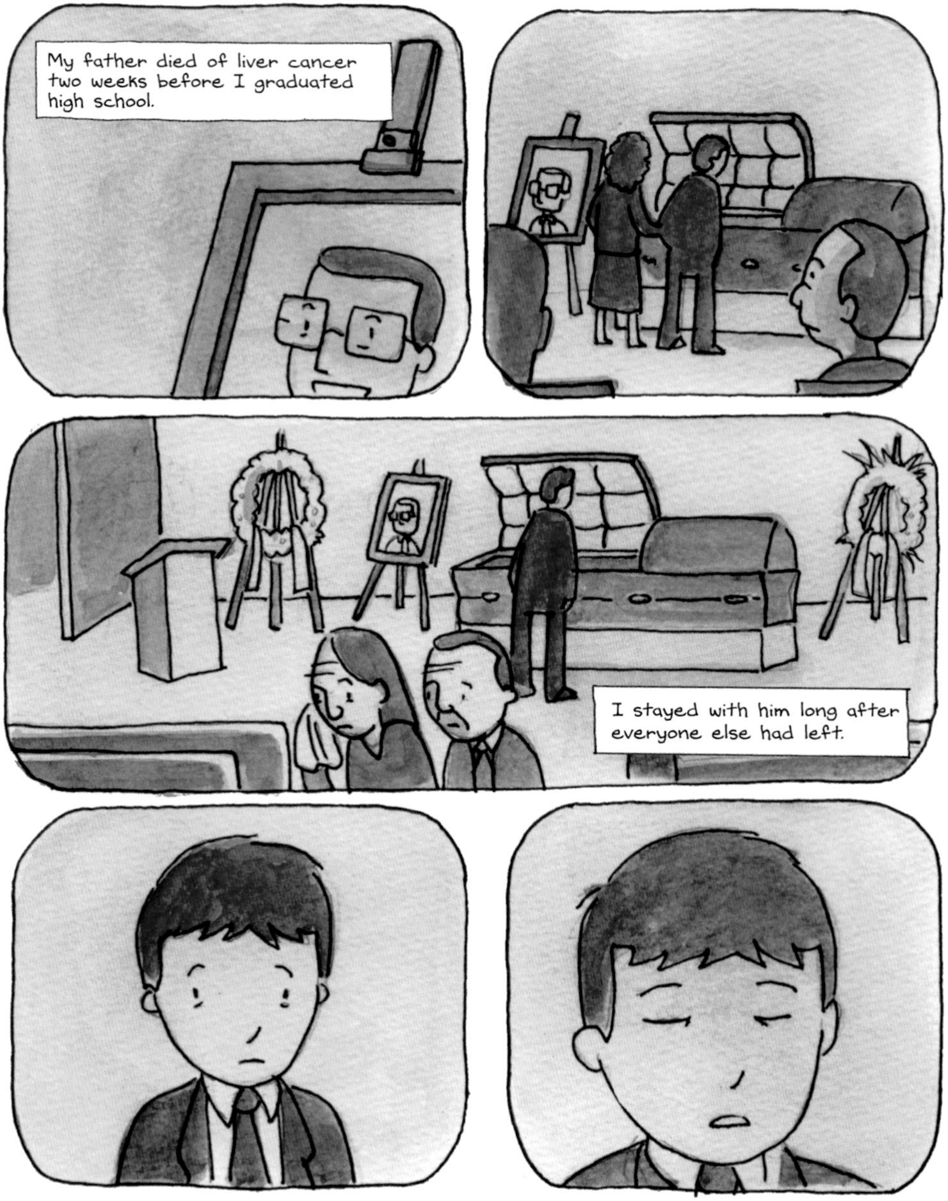
My father died of liver cancer two weeks before I graduated high school.
I stayed with him long after everyone else had left.

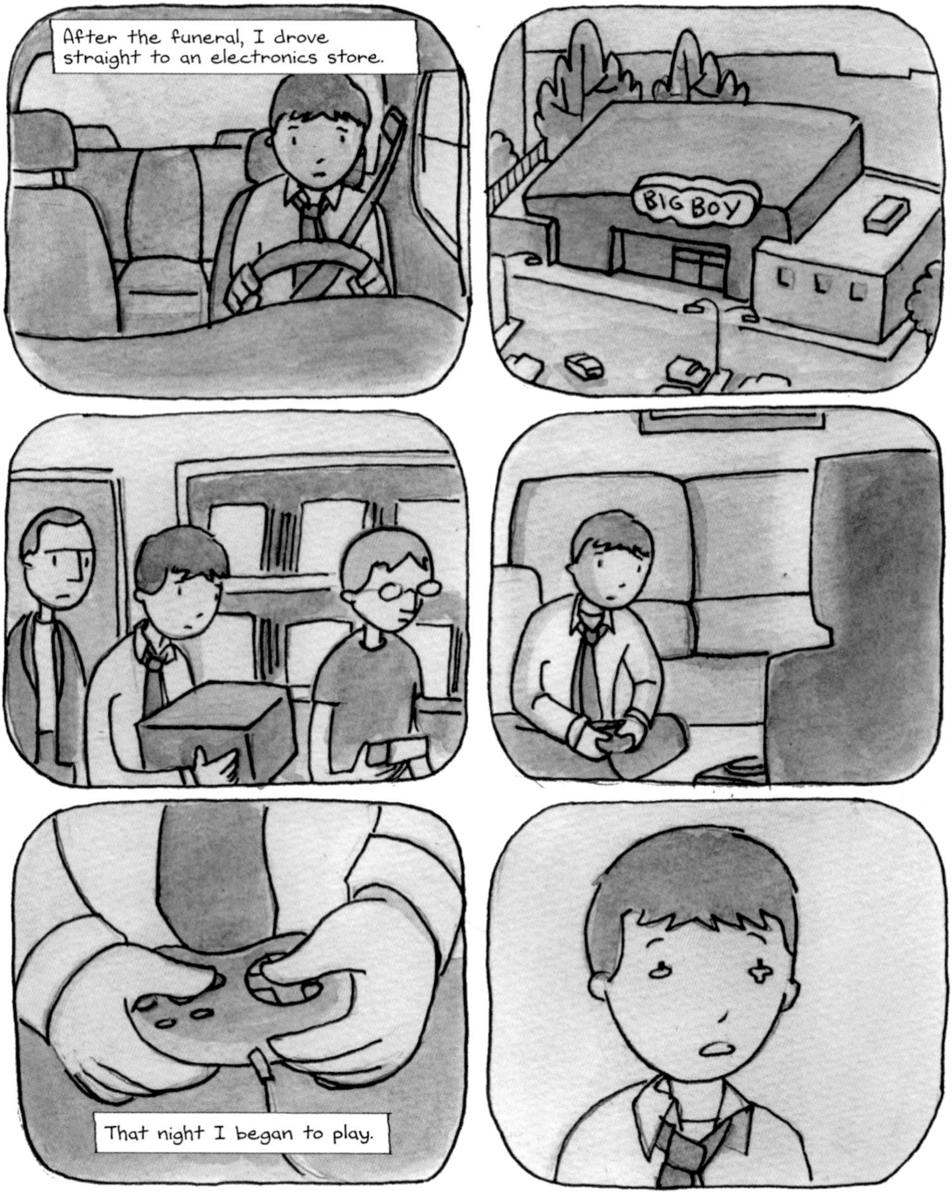
After the funeral, I drove straight to an electronics store.
BIG BOY
That night I began to play.

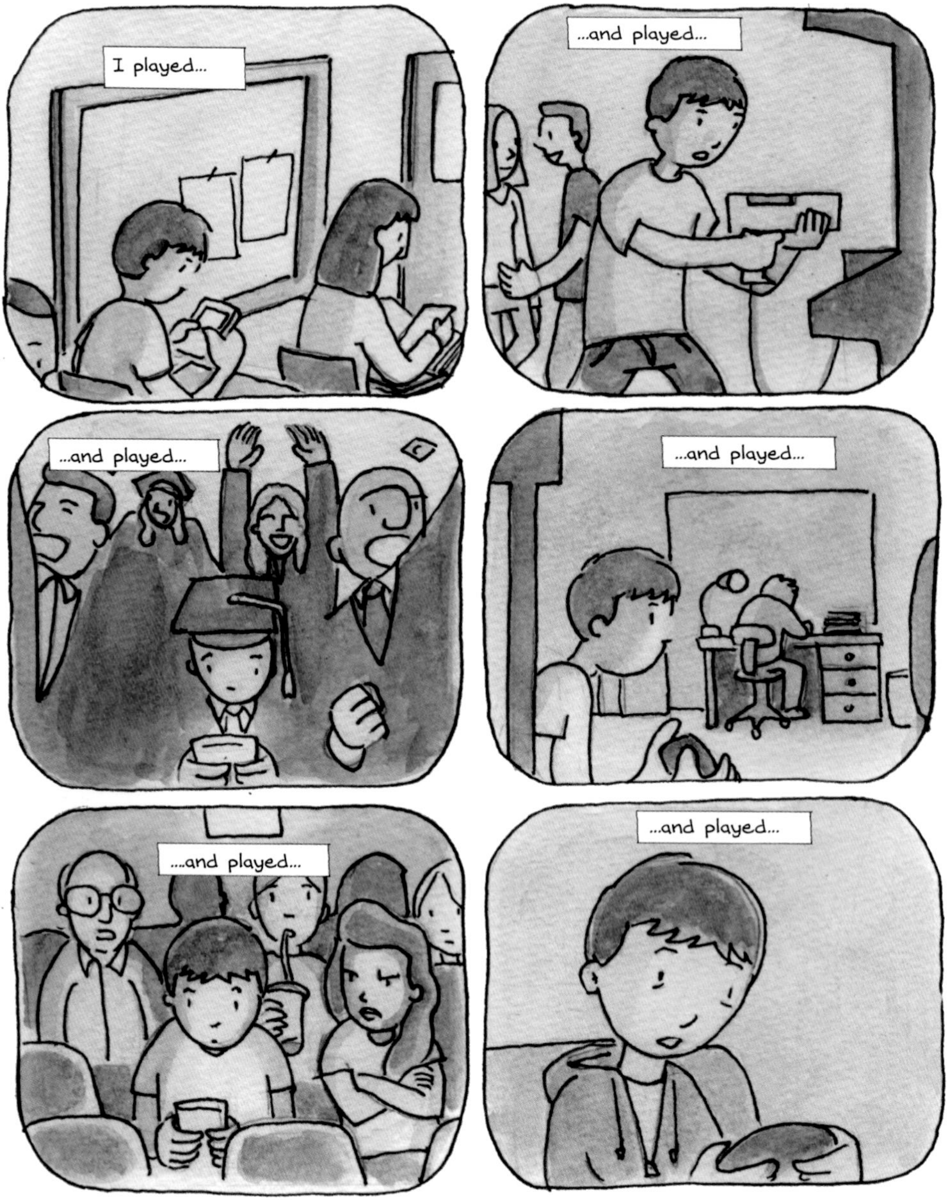
I played...
...and played...
...and played...
...and played...
....and played...
...and played...

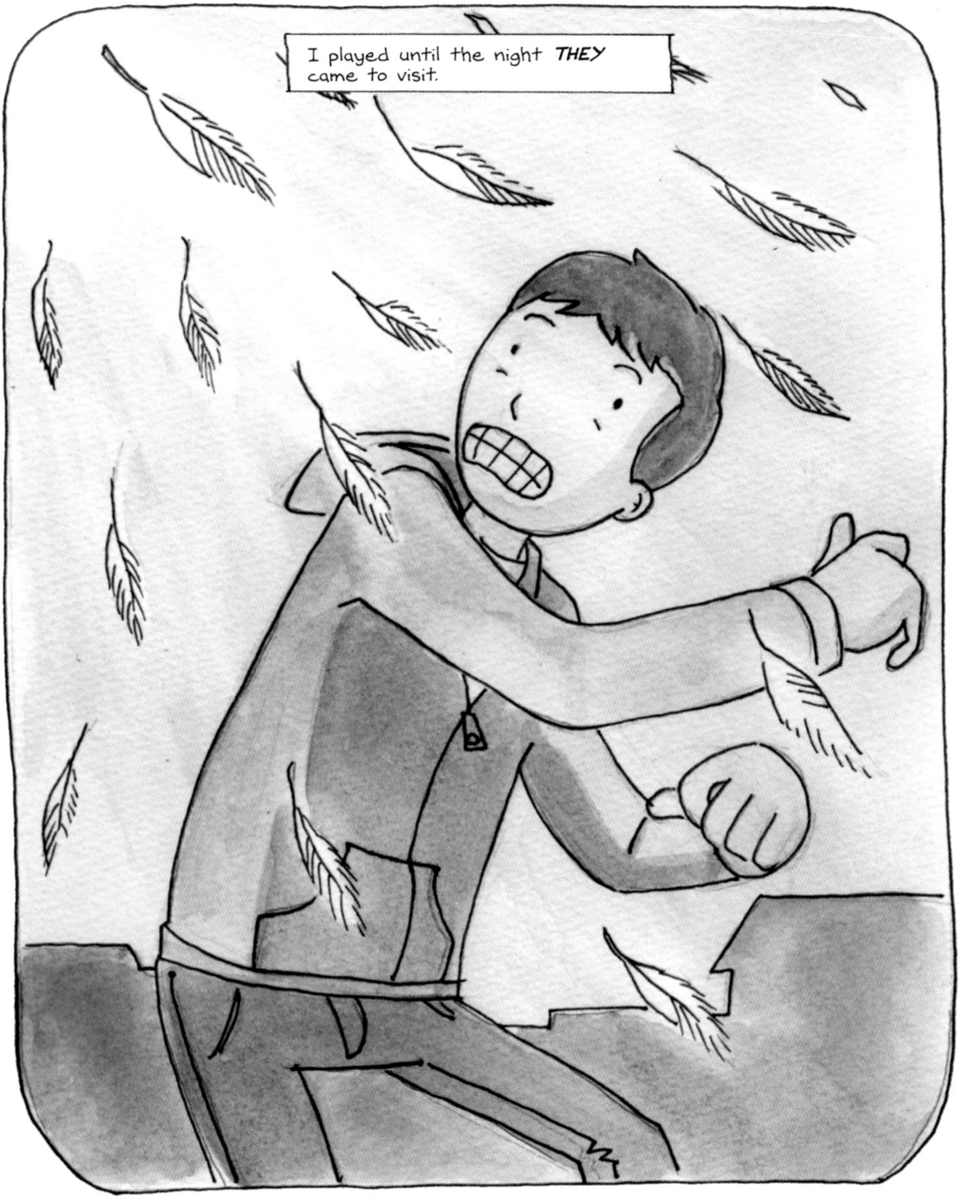
I played until the night THEY came to visit.

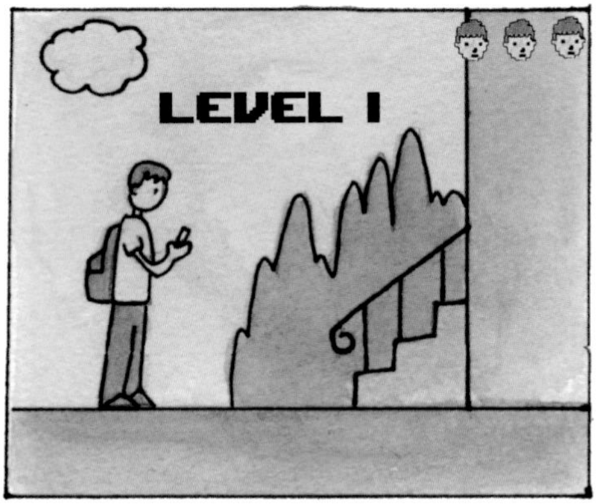
LEVEL 1

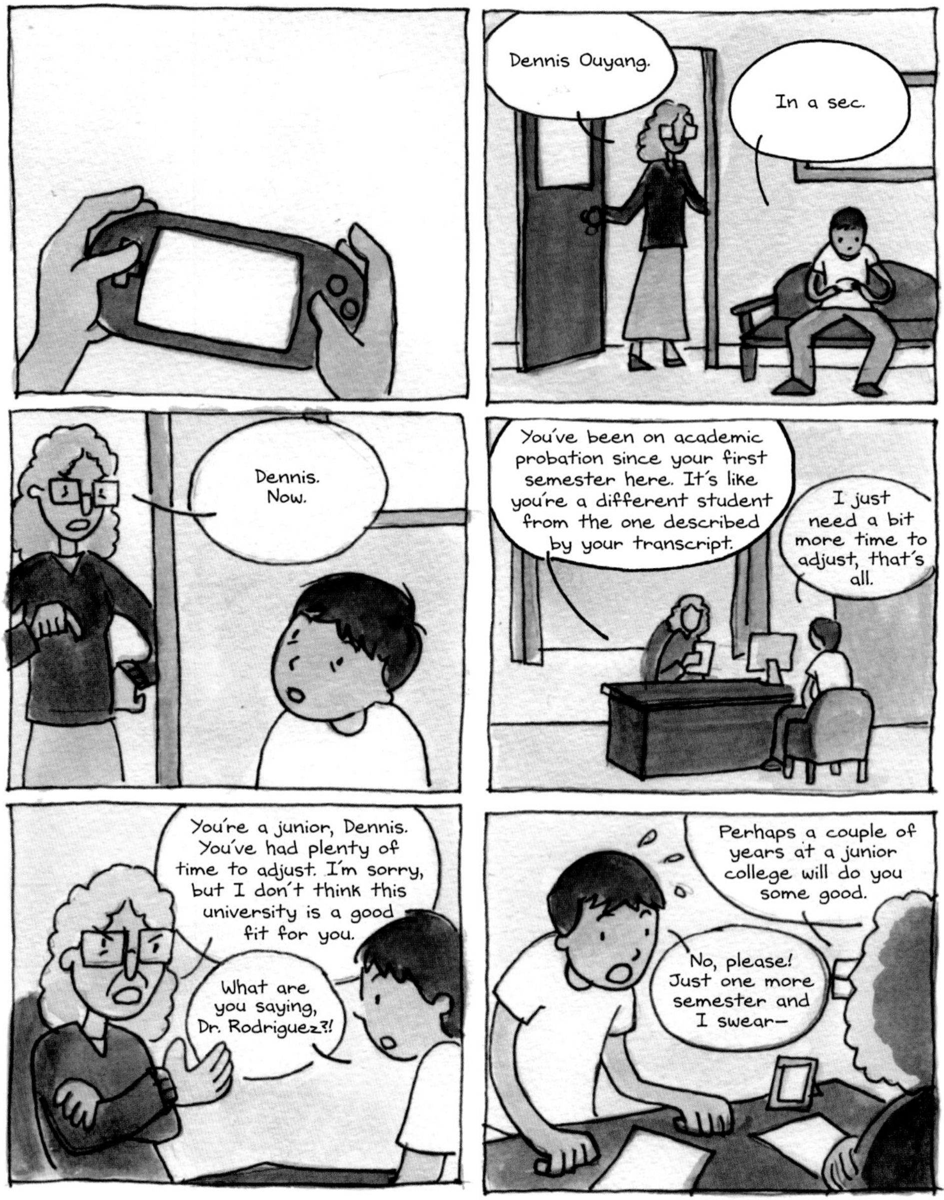
Dennis Ouyang.
In a sec.
Dennis. Now.
You've been on academic probation since your first semester here. It's like you're a different student from the one described by your transcript.
I just need a bit more time to adjust, that's all.
You're a junior, Dennis. You've had plenty of time to adjust. I'm sorry, but I don't think this university is a good fit for you.
What are you saying, Dr. Rodriguez?!
Perhaps a couple of years at a junior college will do you some good.
No, please! Just one more semester and I swear—

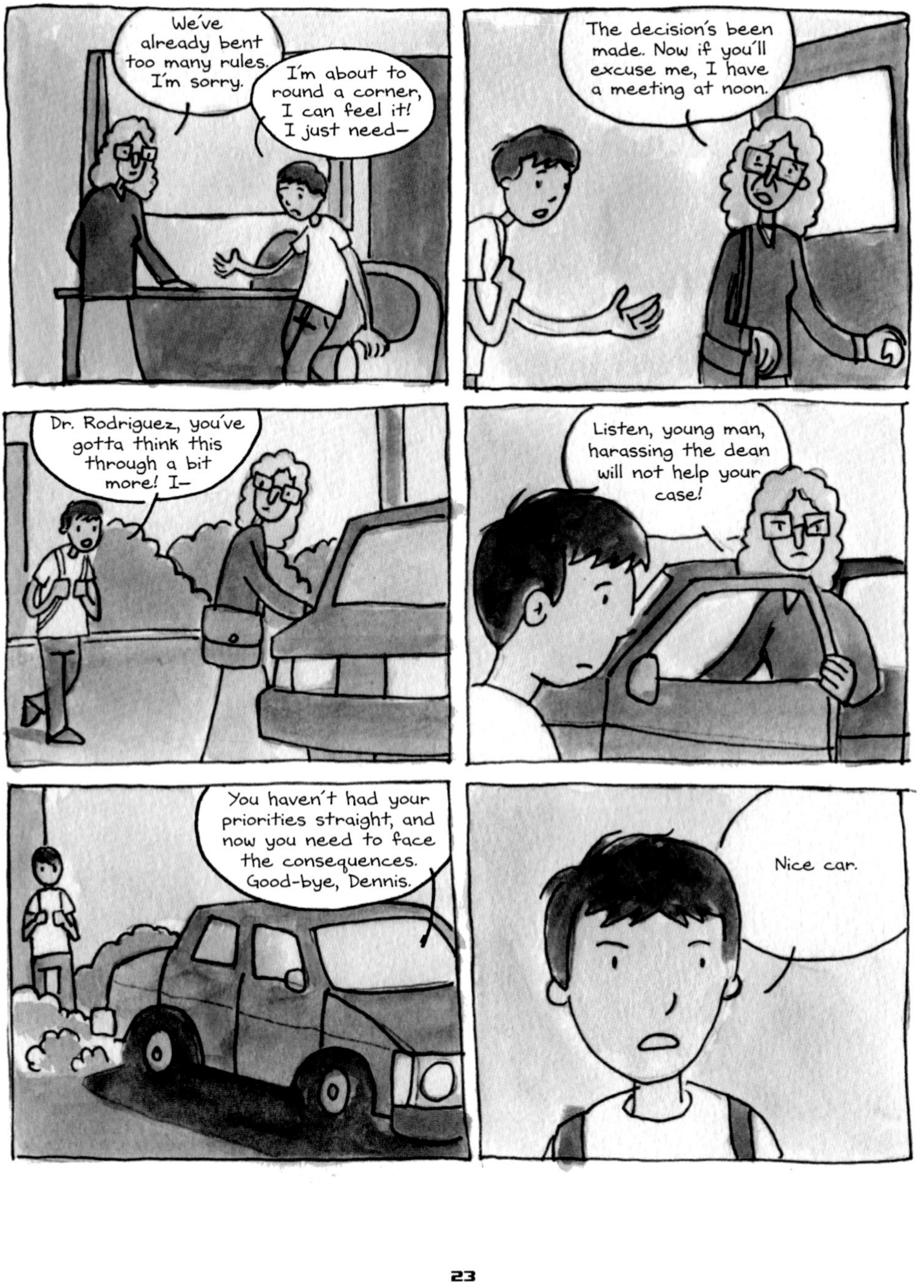
We've already bent too many rules. I'm sorry.
I'm about to round a corner, I can feel it! I just need—
The decision's been made. Now if you'll excuse me, I have a meeting at noon.
Dr. Rodriguez, you've gotta think this through a bit more! I—
Listen, young man, harassing the dean will not help your case!
You haven't had your priorities straight, and now you need to face the consequences. Good-bye, Dennis.
Nice car.

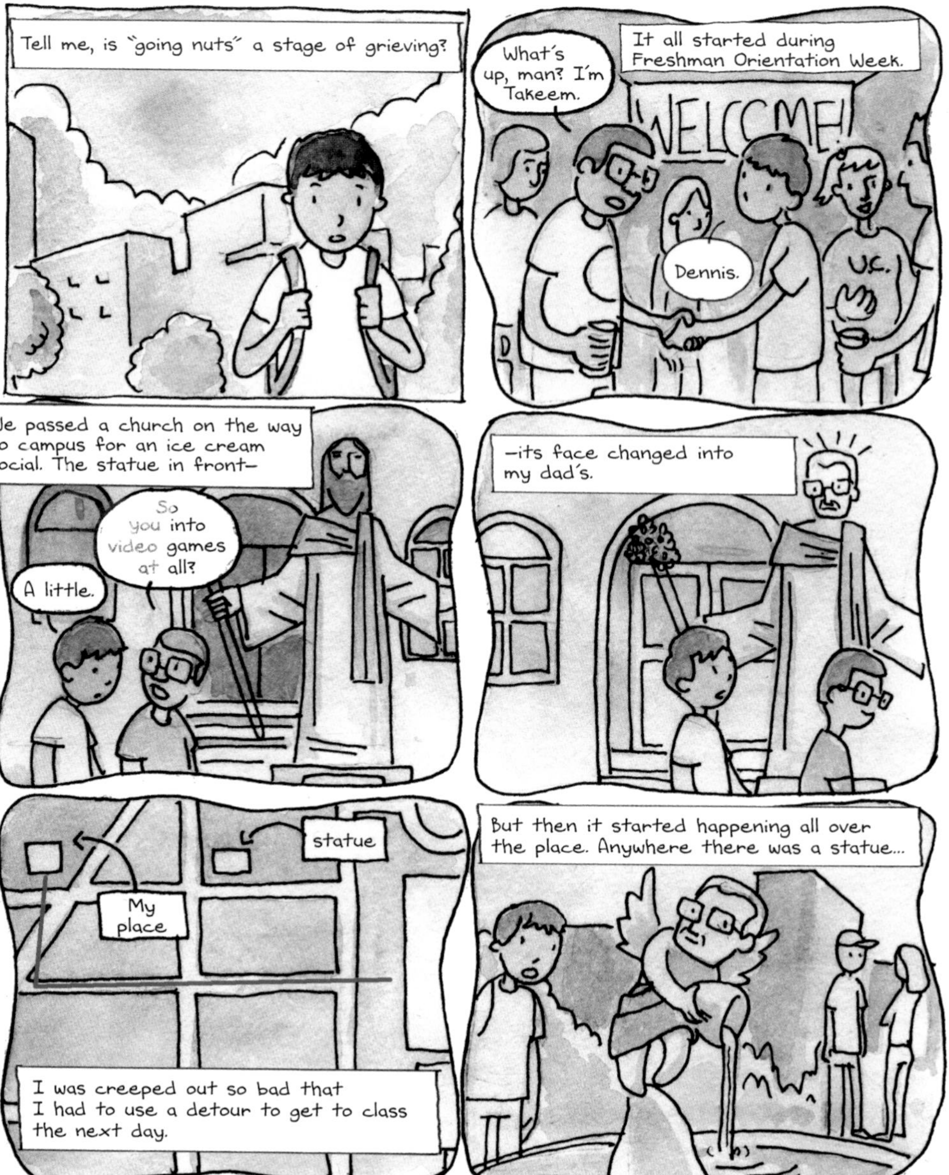
Tell me, is "going nuts" a stage of grieving?
It all started during Freshman Orientation Week.
What's up, man? I'm Takeem.
WELCOME!
Dennis.
U.C.
We passed a church on the way to campus for an ice cream social. The statue in front–
So you into video games at all?
A little.
–its face changed into my dad's.
statue
My place
I was creeped out so bad that I had to use a detour to get to class the next day.
But then it started happening all over the place. Anywhere there was a statue...

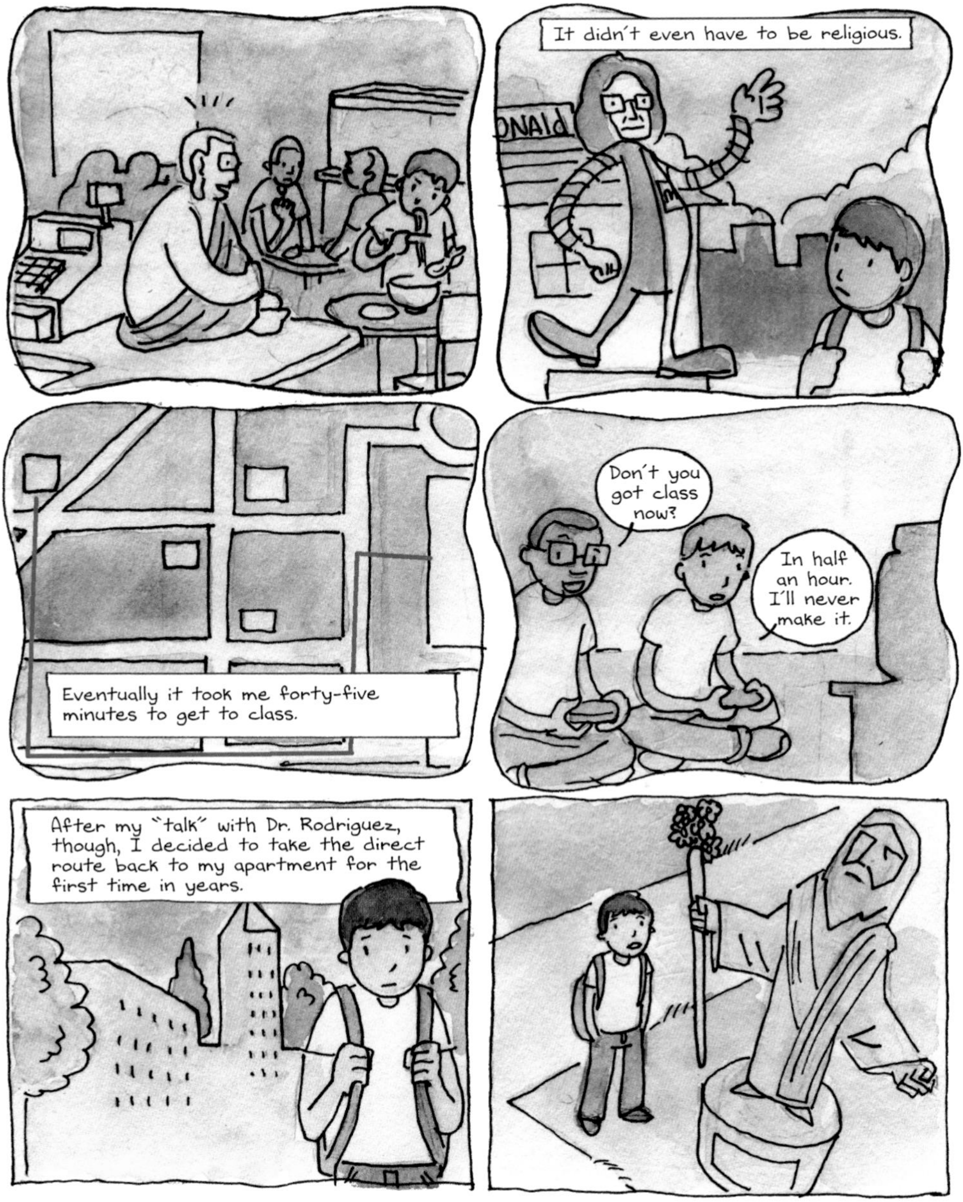

It didn't even have to be religious.
ONAld
Eventually it took me forty-five minutes to get to class.
Don't you got class now?
In half an hour. I'll never make it.
After my "talk" with Dr. Rodriguez, though, I decided to take the direct route back to my apartment for the first time in years.

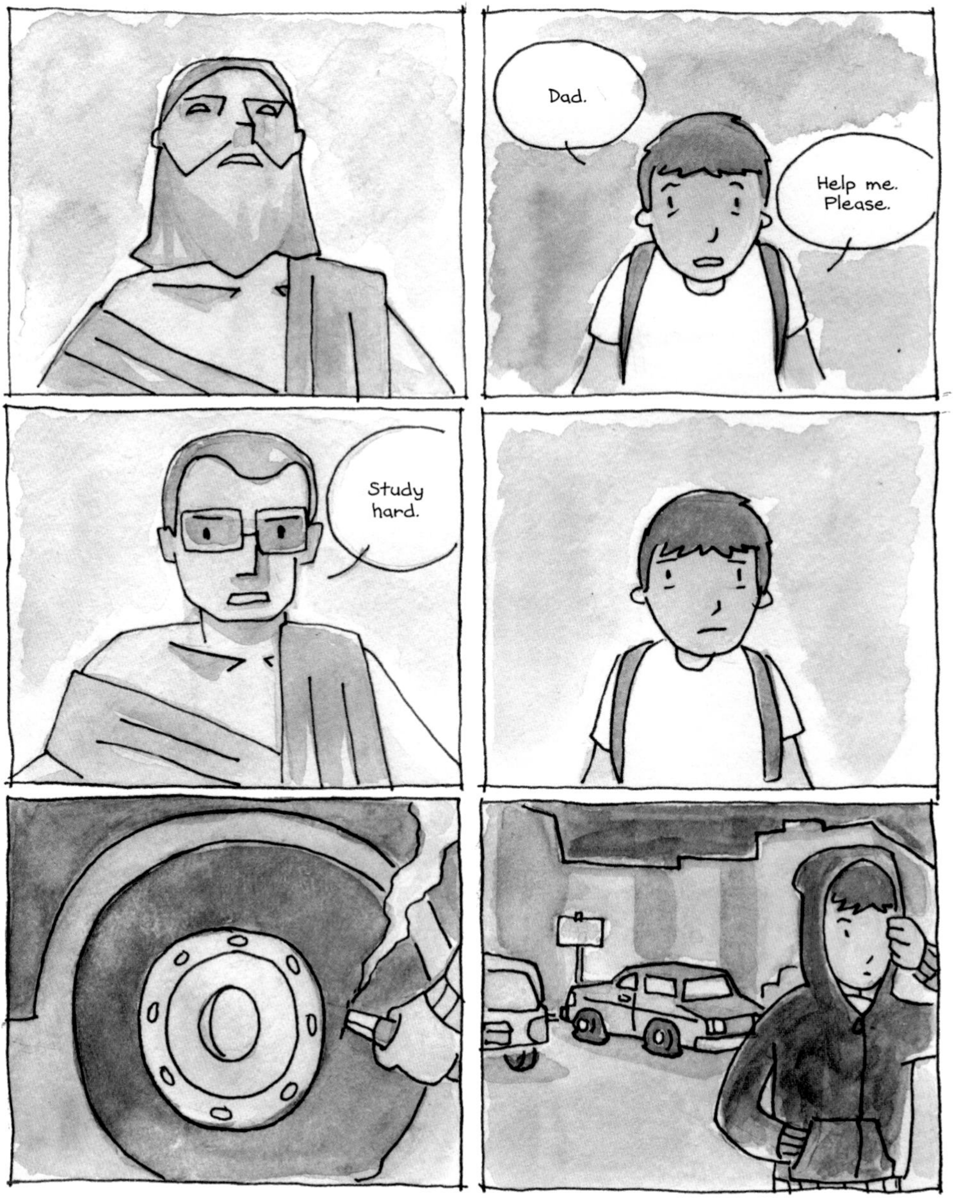
Dad.
Help me. Please.
Study hard.

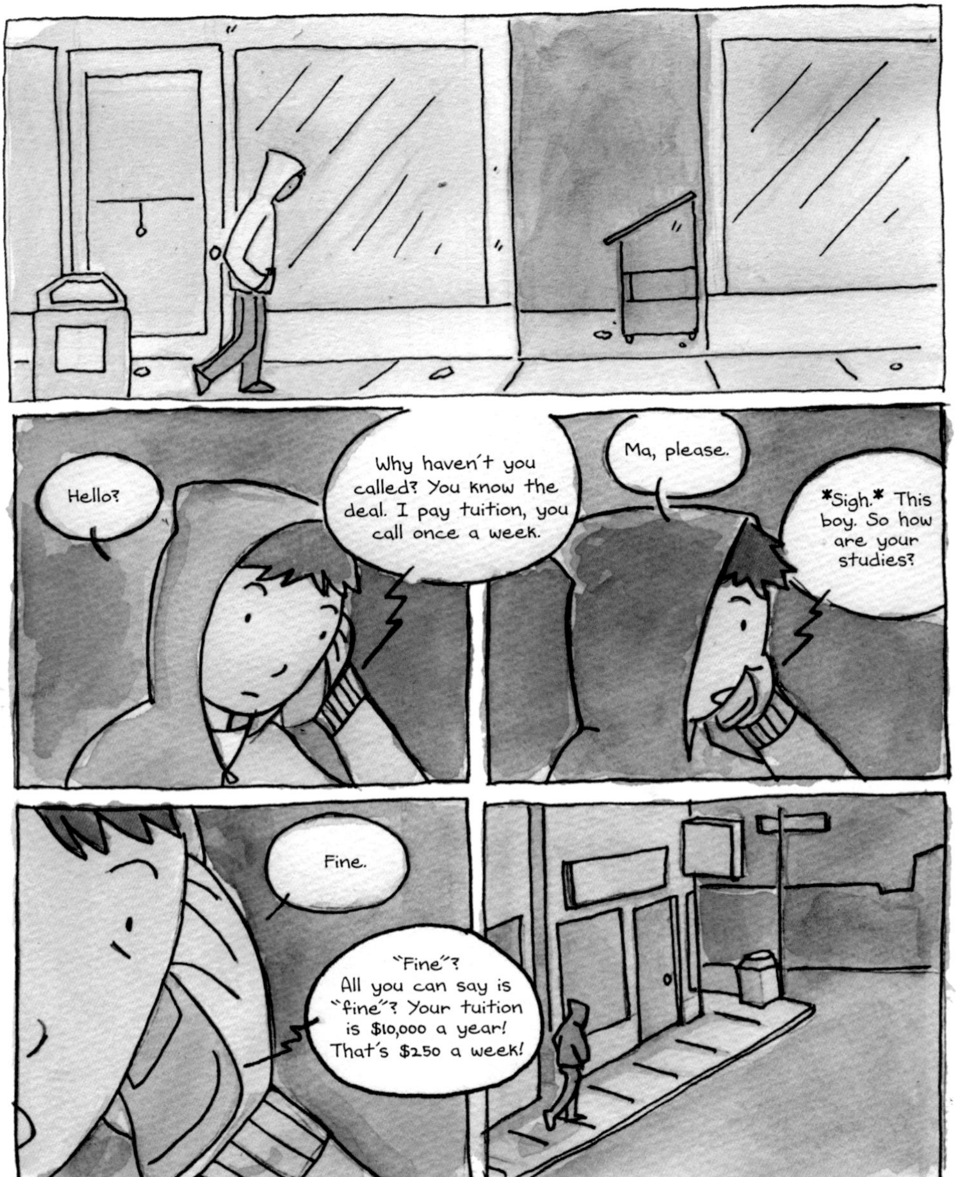
Hello?
Why haven't you called? You know the deal. I pay tuition, you call once a week.
Ma, please.
Sigh. This boy. So how are your studies?
Fine.
"Fine"? All you can say is "fine"? Your tuition is $10,000 a year! That's $250 a week!

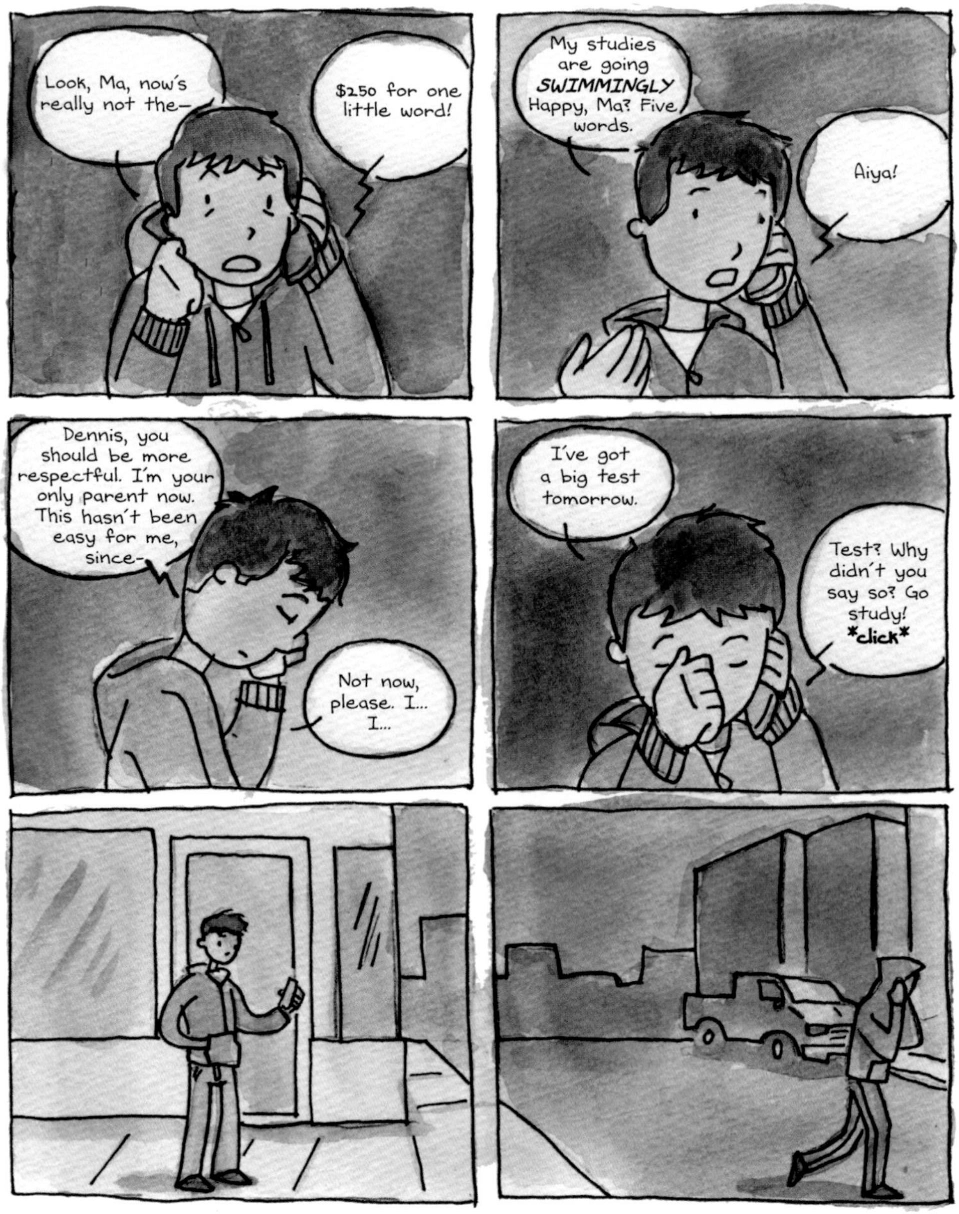
Look, Ma, now's really not the–
$250 for one little word!
My studies are going SWIMMINGLY Happy, Ma? Five words.
Aiya!
Dennis, you should be more respectful. I'm your only parent now. This hasn't been easy for me, since–
Not now, please. I... I...
I've got a big test tomorrow.
Test? Why didn't you say so? Go study! *click*

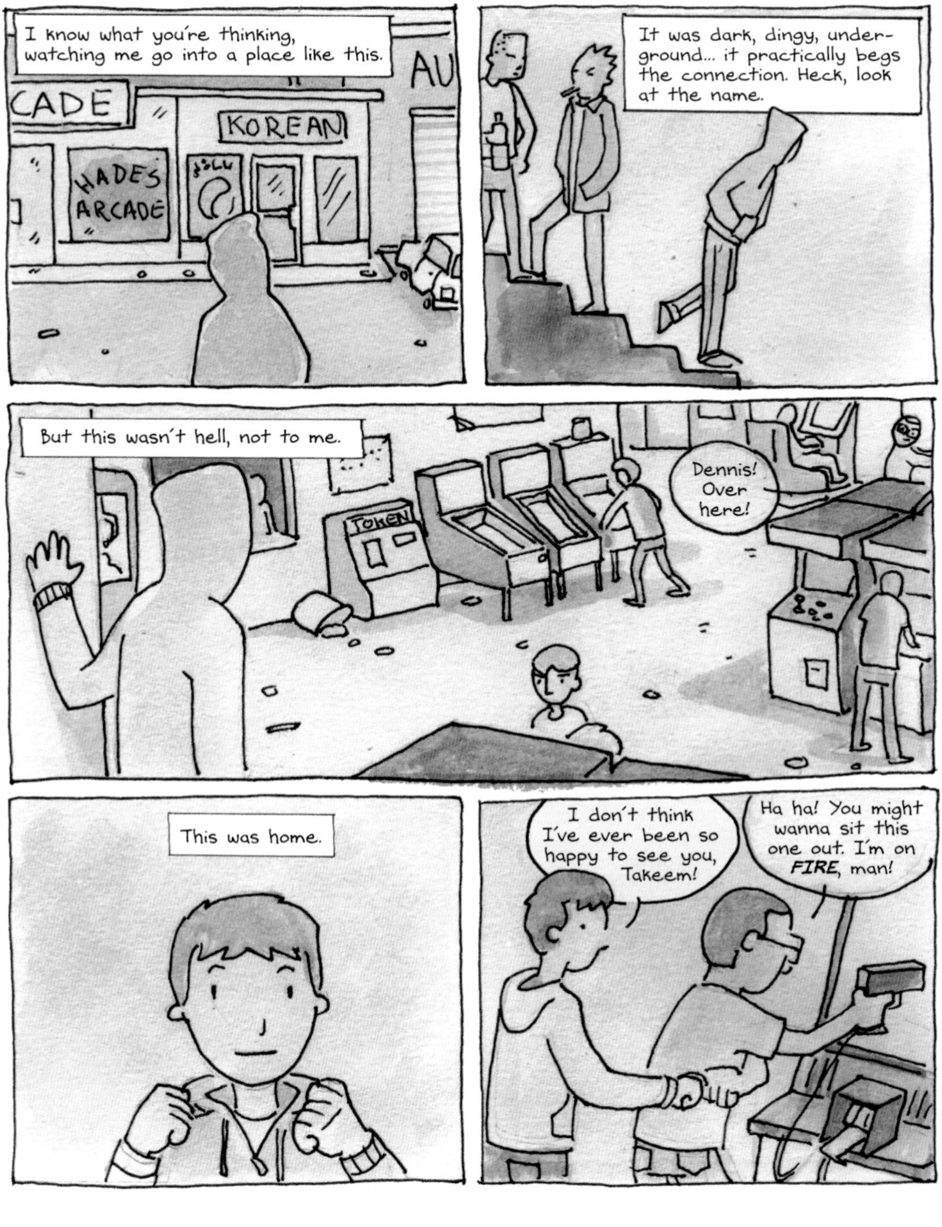
I know what you're thinking, watching me go into a place like this.
CADE
AU
KOREAN
HADES ARCADE
It was dark, dingy, underground... it practically begs the connection. Heck, look at the name.
But this wasn't hell, not to me.
TOKEN
Dennis! Over here!
This was home.
I don't think I've ever been so happy to see you, Takeem!
Ha ha! You might wanna sit this one out. I'm on *FIRE*, man!

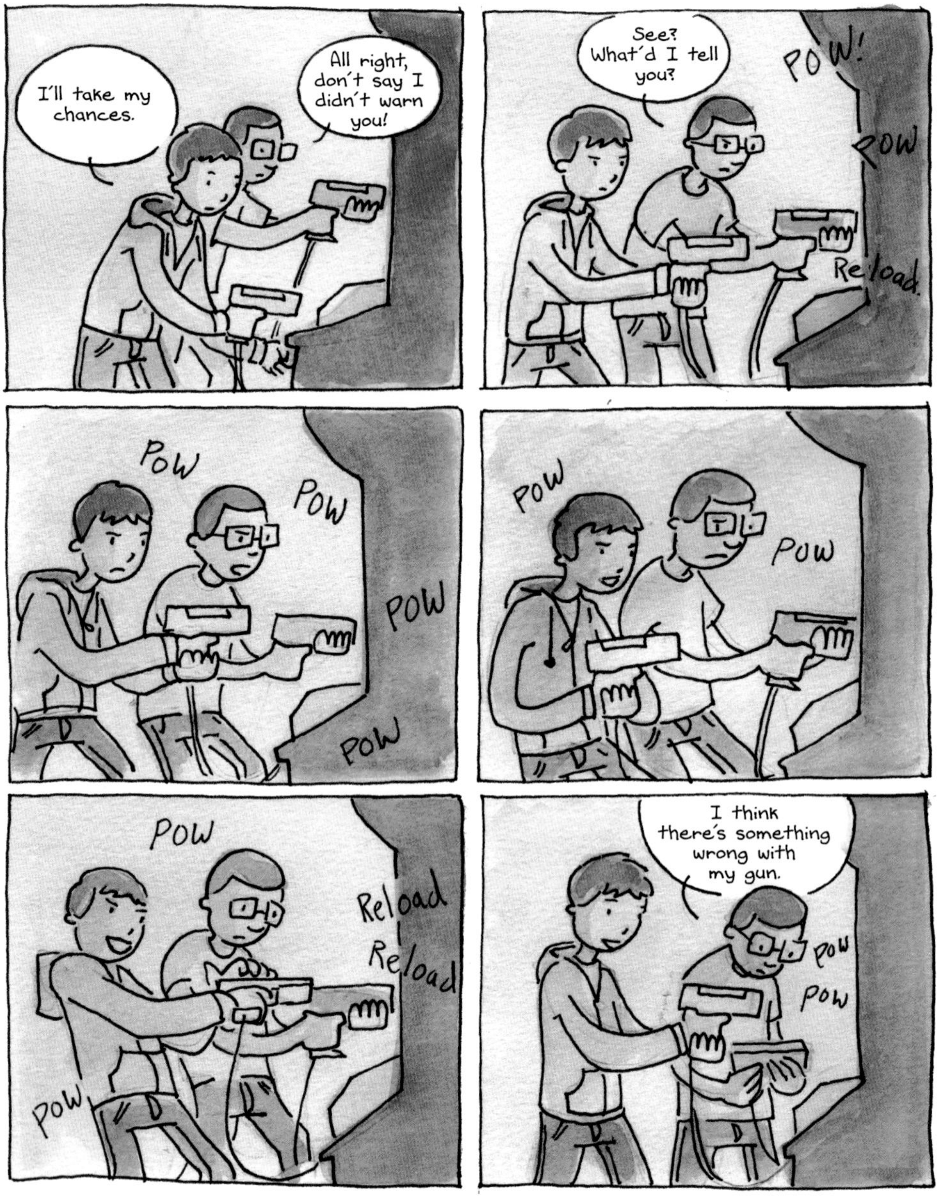
I'll take my chances.
All right, don't say I didn't warn you!
See? What'd I tell you?
POW!
POW
Reload.
POW
POW
POW
POW
POW
POW
POW
Reload
Reload
POW
I think there's something wrong with my gun.
POW
POW

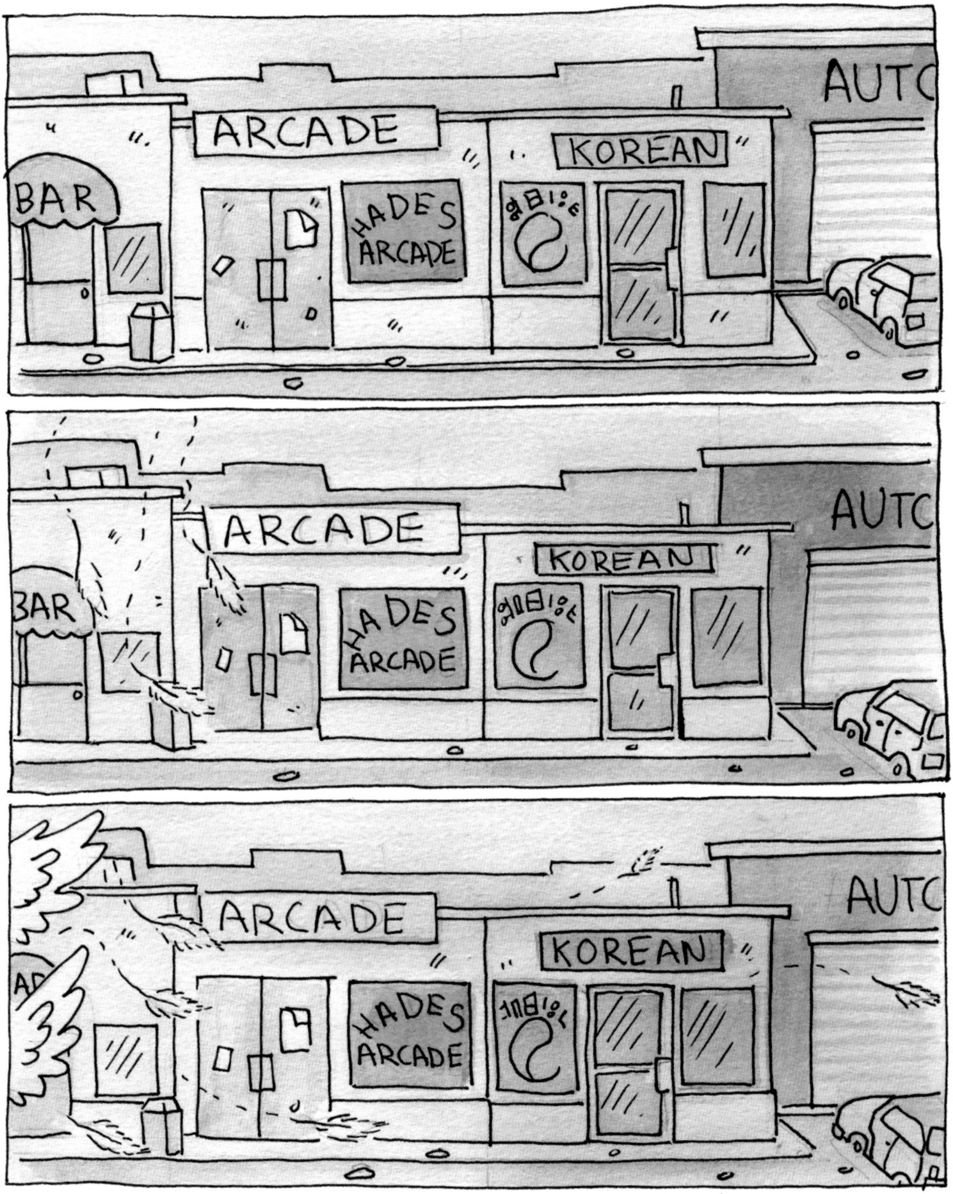
BAR
ARCADE
HADES ARCADE
KOREAN
ARCADE
HADES ARCADE
KOREAN
ARCADE
HADES ARCADE
KOREAN

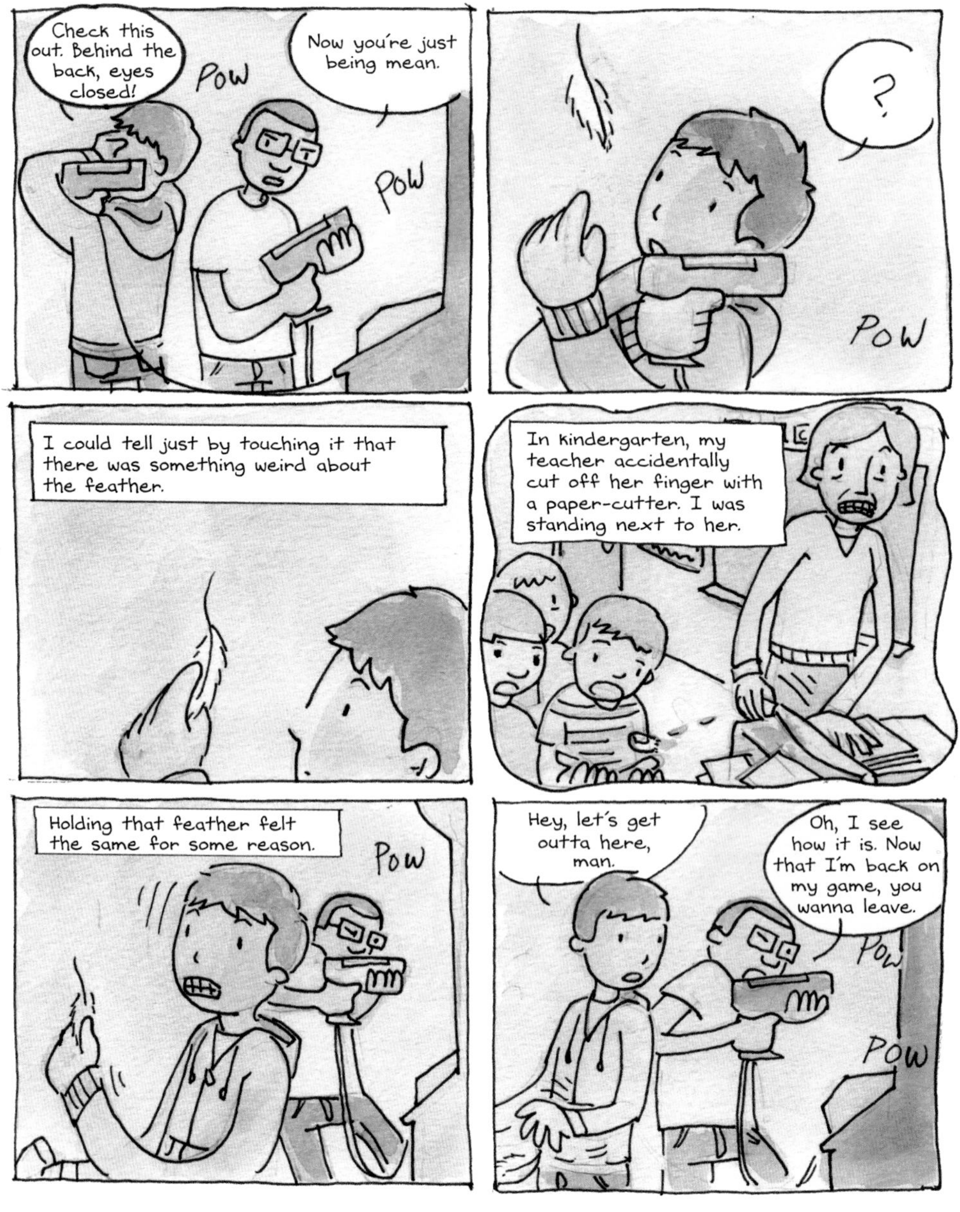
Check this out. Behind the back, eyes closed!
POW
Now you're just being mean.
POW
?
POW
I could tell just by touching it that there was something weird about the feather.
In kindergarten, my teacher accidentally cut off her finger with a paper-cutter. I was standing next to her.
Holding that feather felt the same for some reason.
POW
Hey, let's get outta here, man.
Oh, I see how it is. Now that I'm back on my game, you wanna leave.
POW
POW

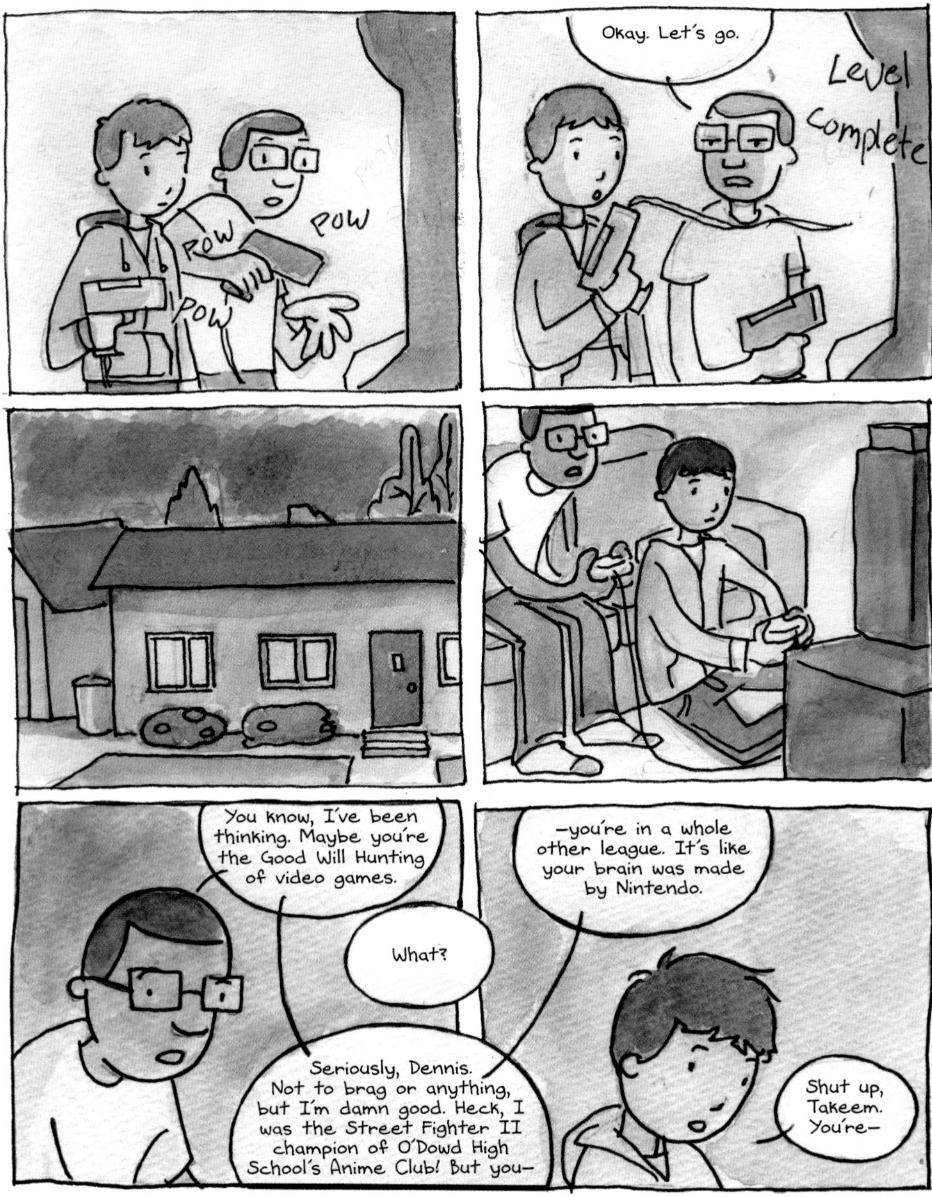
POW
POW
POW
Okay. Let's go.
Level complete
You know, I've been thinking. Maybe you're the Good Will Hunting of video games.
What?
Seriously, Dennis. Not to brag or anything, but I'm damn good. Heck, I was the Street Fighter II champion of O'Dowd High School's Anime Club! But you—
—you're in a whole other league. It's like your brain was made by Nintendo.
Shut up, Takeem. You're—

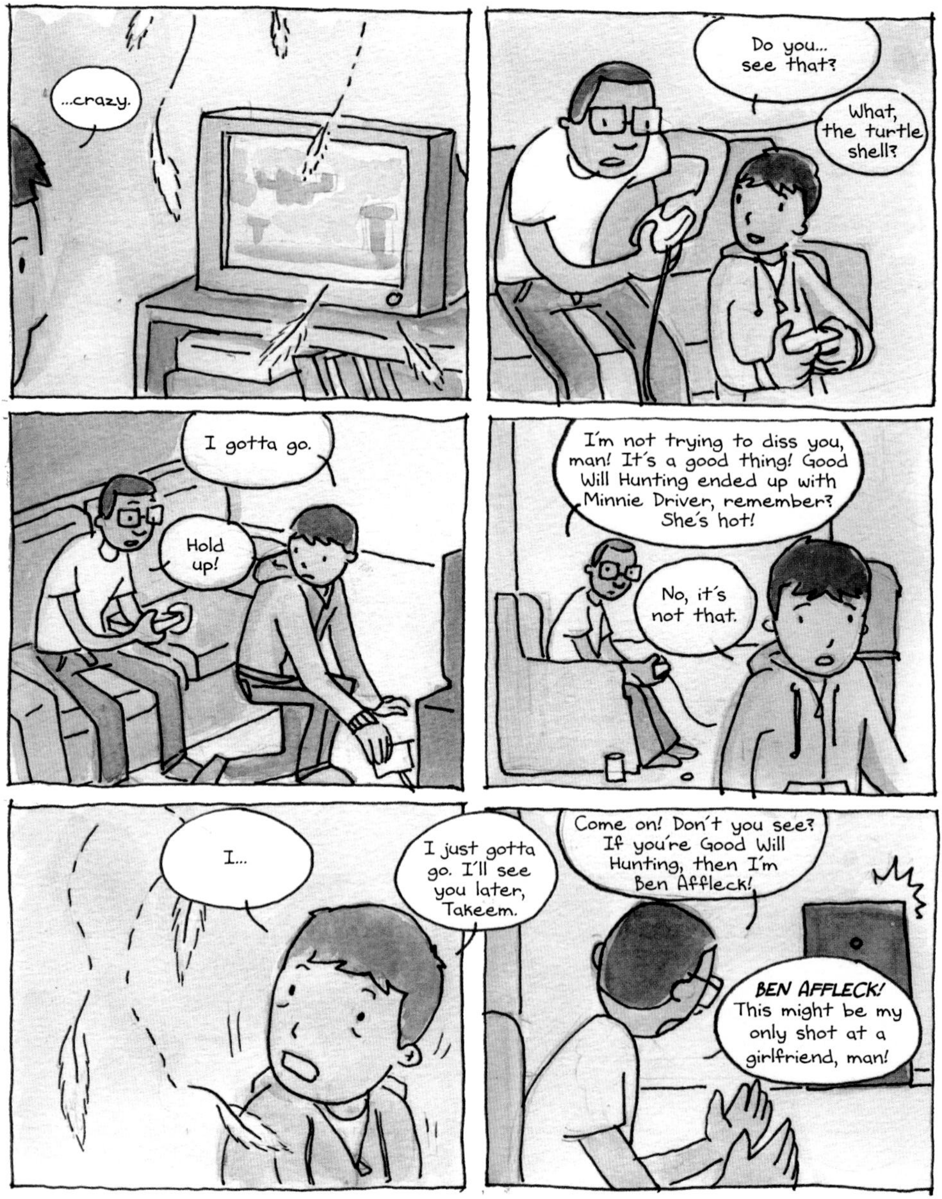

...crazy.
Do you... see that?
What, the turtle shell?
I gotta go.
Hold up!
I'm not trying to diss you, man! It's a good thing! Good Will Hunting ended up with Minnie Driver, remember? She's hot!
No, it's not that.
I...
I just gotta go. I'll see you later, Takeem.
Come on! Don't you see? If you're Good Will Hunting, then I'm Ben Affleck!
BEN AFFLECK! This might be my only shot at a girlfriend, man!

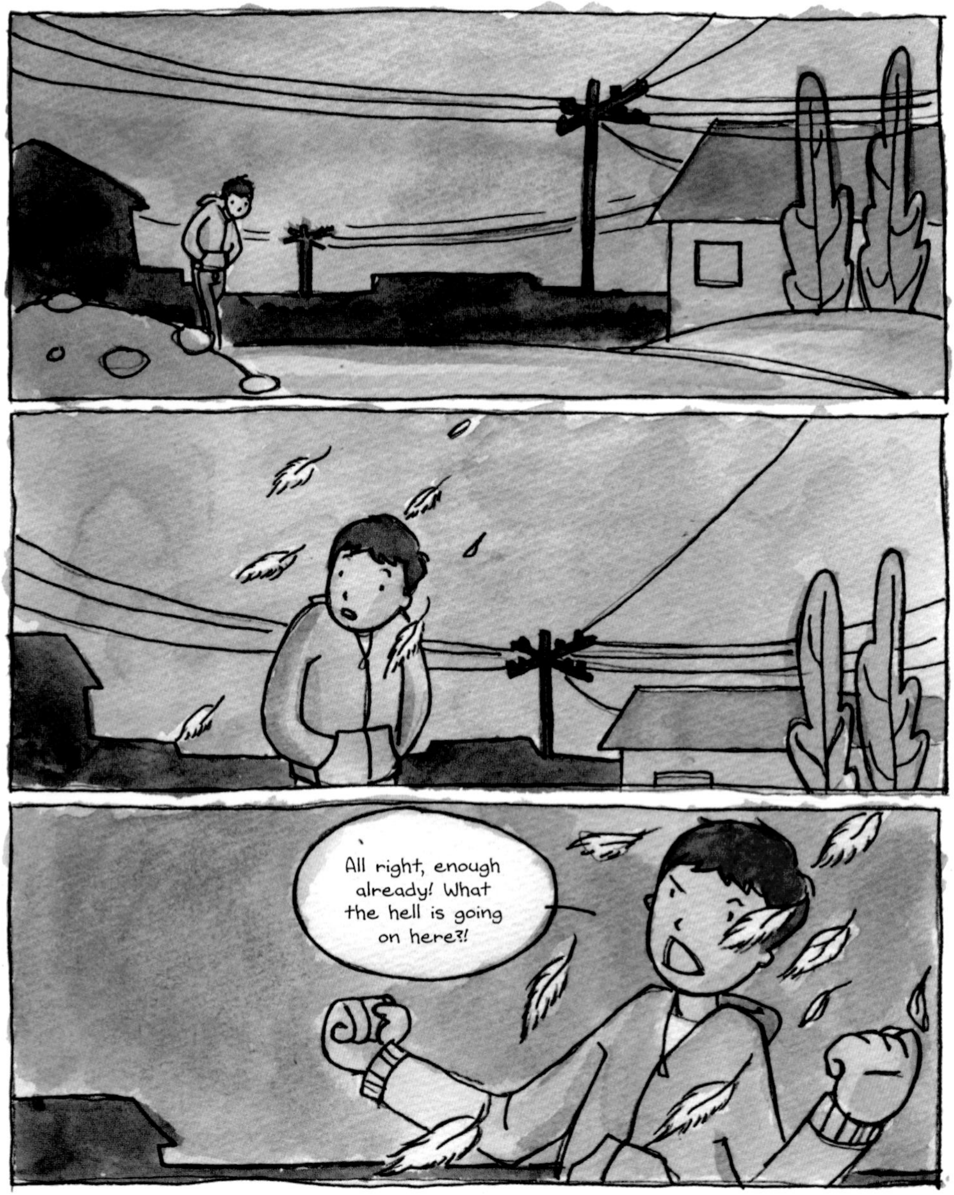
All right, enough already! What the hell is going on here?!

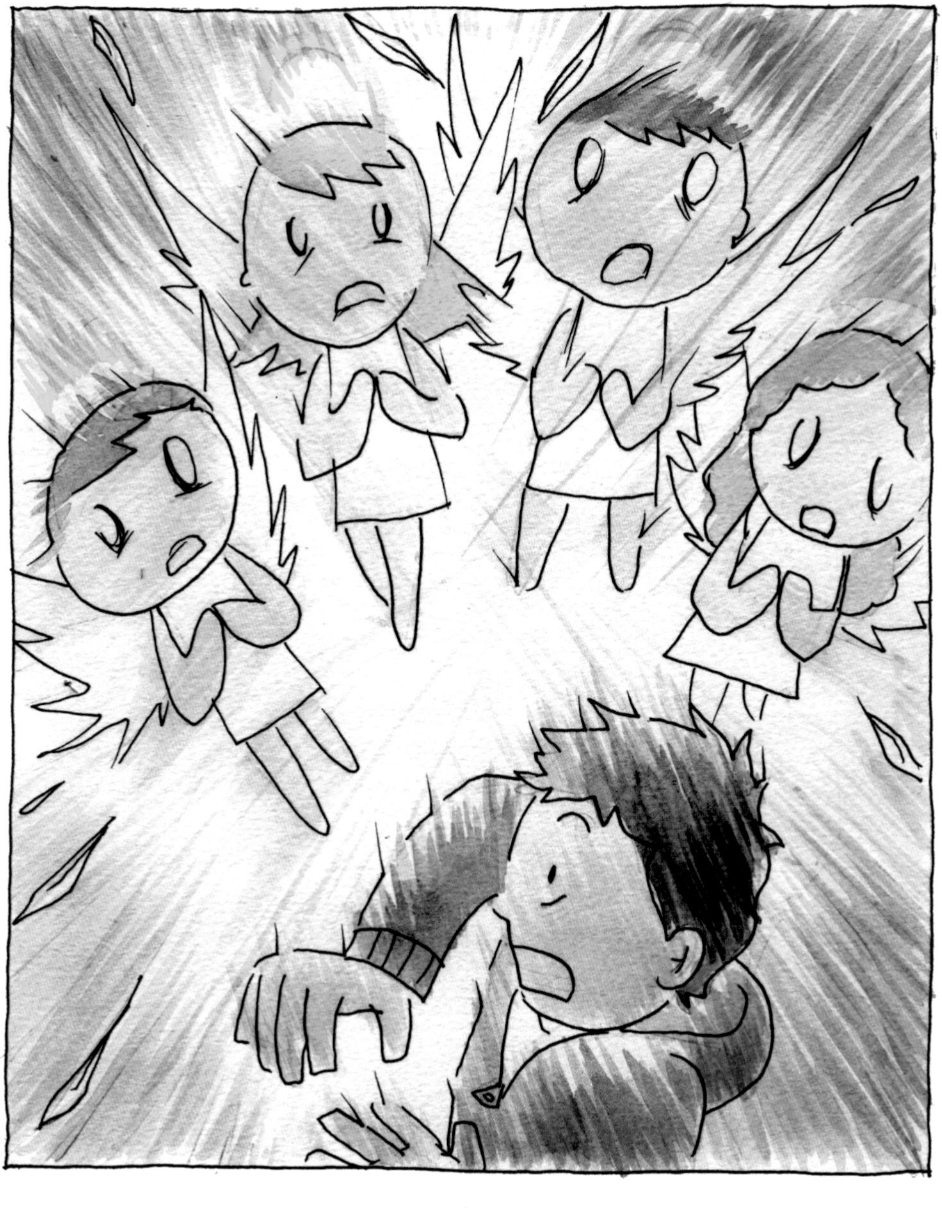

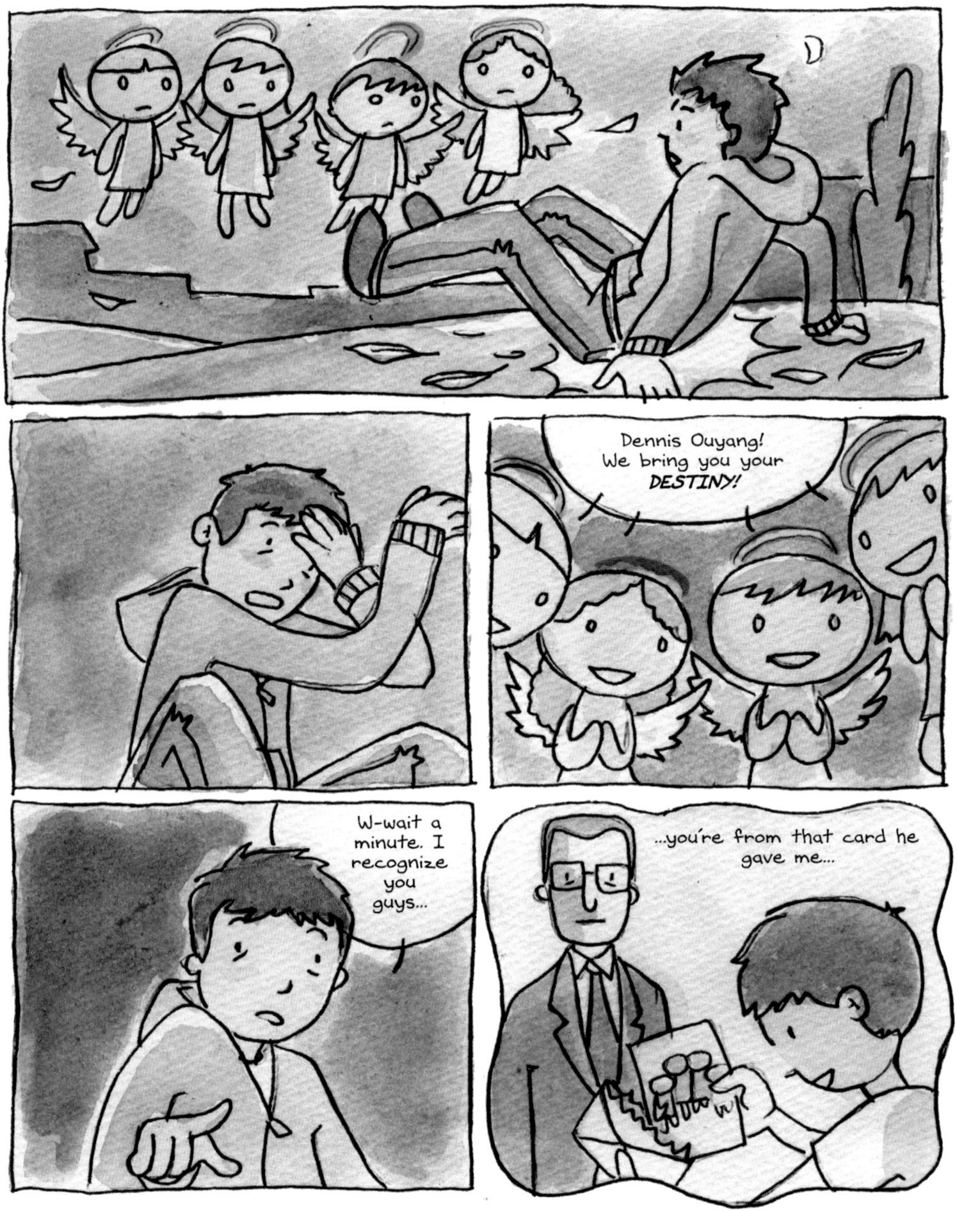
Dennis Ouyang! We bring you your DESTINY!
W-wait a minute. I recognize you guys...
...you're from that card he gave me...

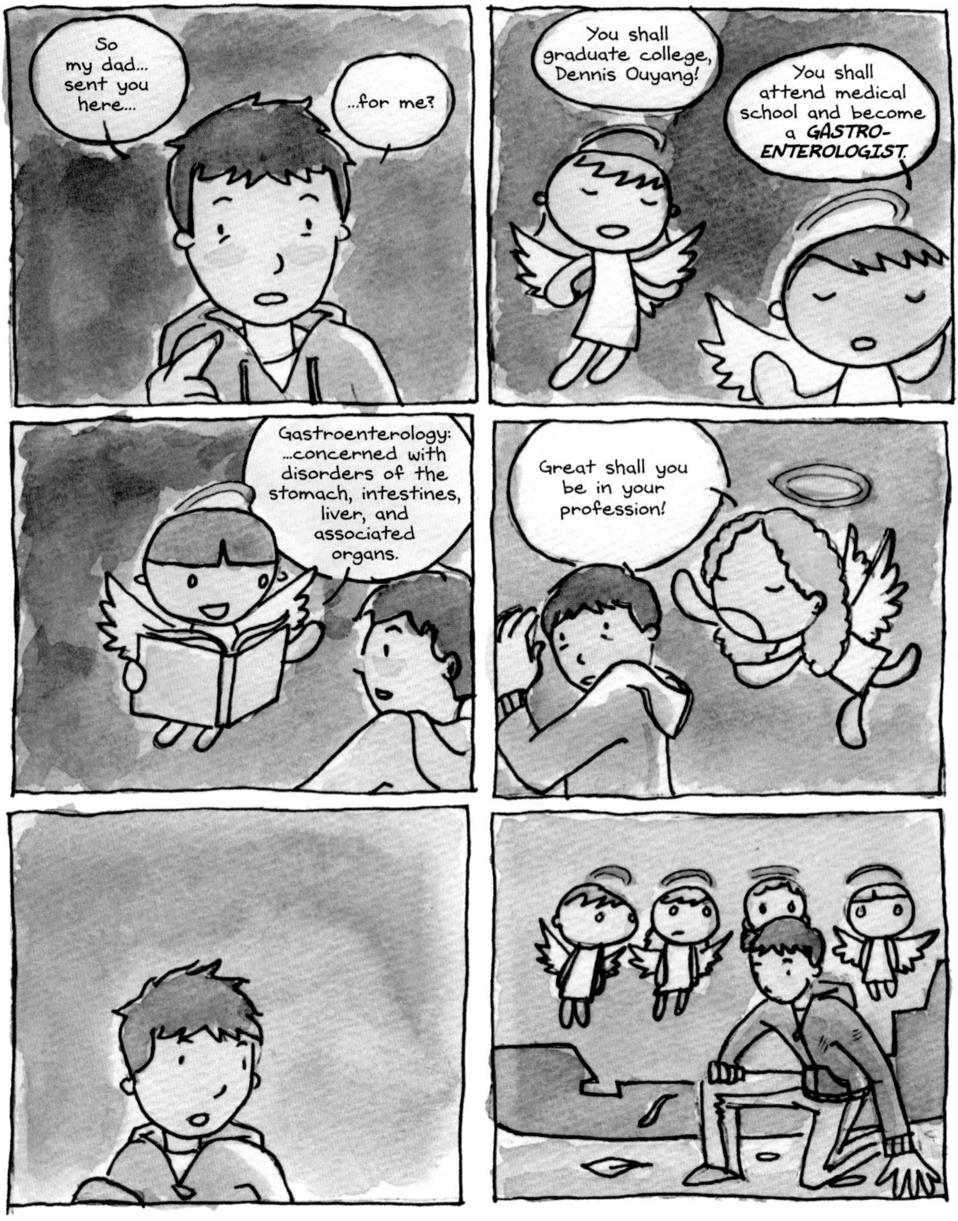
So my dad... sent you here...
...for me?
You shall graduate college, Dennis Ouyang!
You shall attend medical school and become a GASTRO-ENTEROLOGIST.
Gastroenterology: ...concerned with disorders of the stomach, intestines, liver, and associated organs.
Great shall you be in your profession!

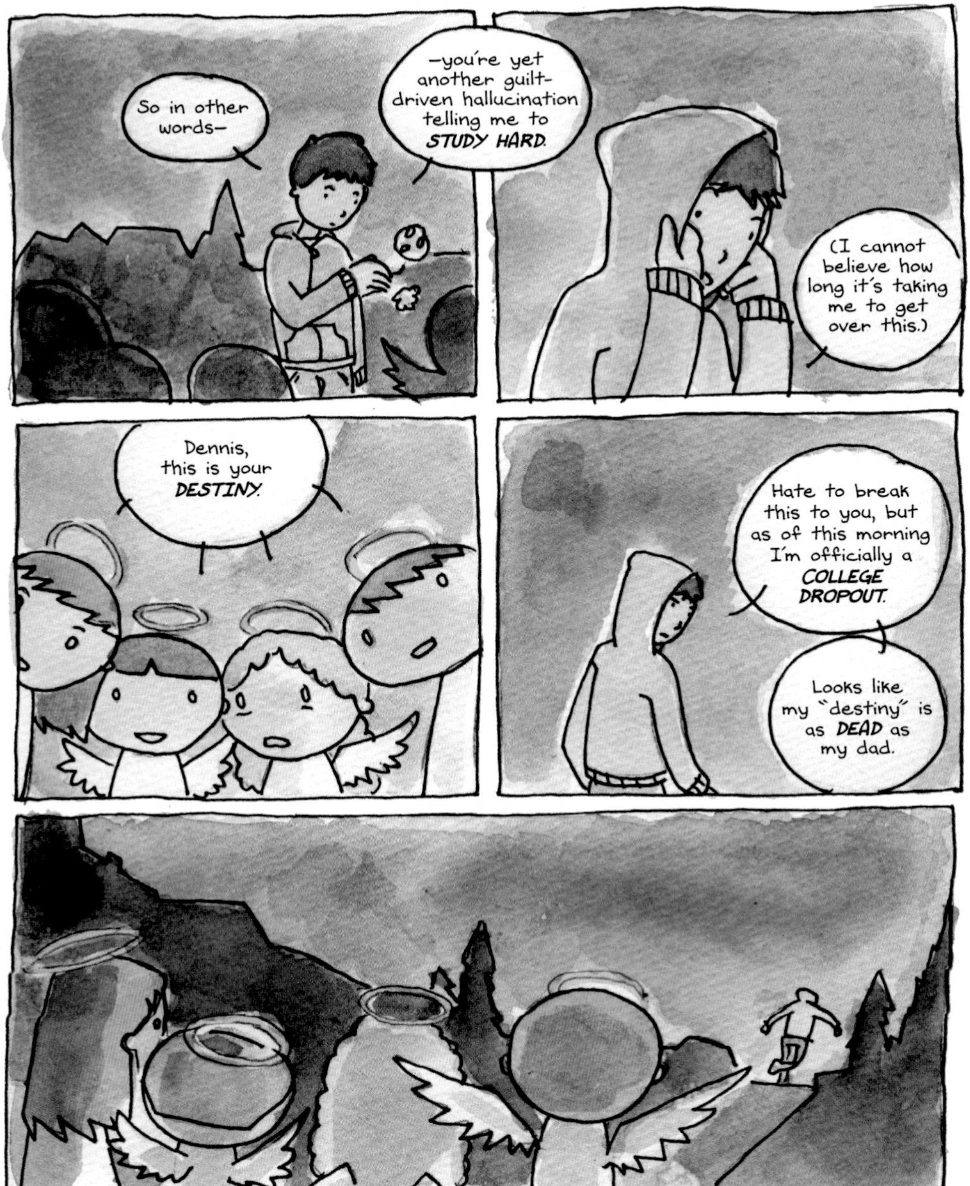
So in other words—
—you're yet another guilt-driven hallucination telling me to STUDY HARD.
(I cannot believe how long it's taking me to get over this.)
Dennis, this is your DESTINY.
Hate to break this to you, but as of this morning I'm officially a COLLEGE DROPOUT.
Looks like my "destiny" is as DEAD as my dad.

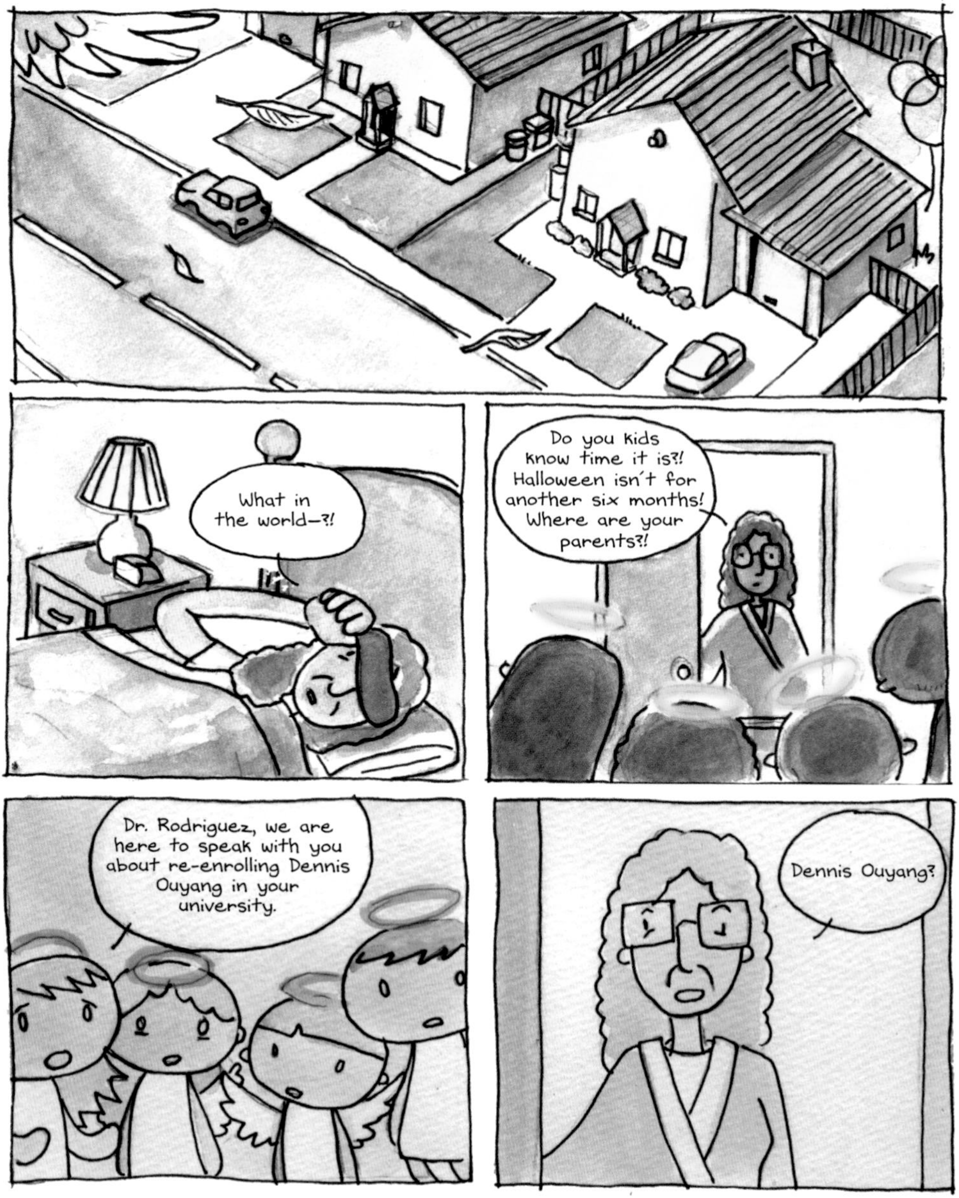

What in the world—?!
Do you kids know time it is?! Halloween isn't for another six months! Where are your parents?!
Dr. Rodriguez, we are here to speak with you about re-enrolling Dennis Ouyang in your university.
Dennis Ouyang?

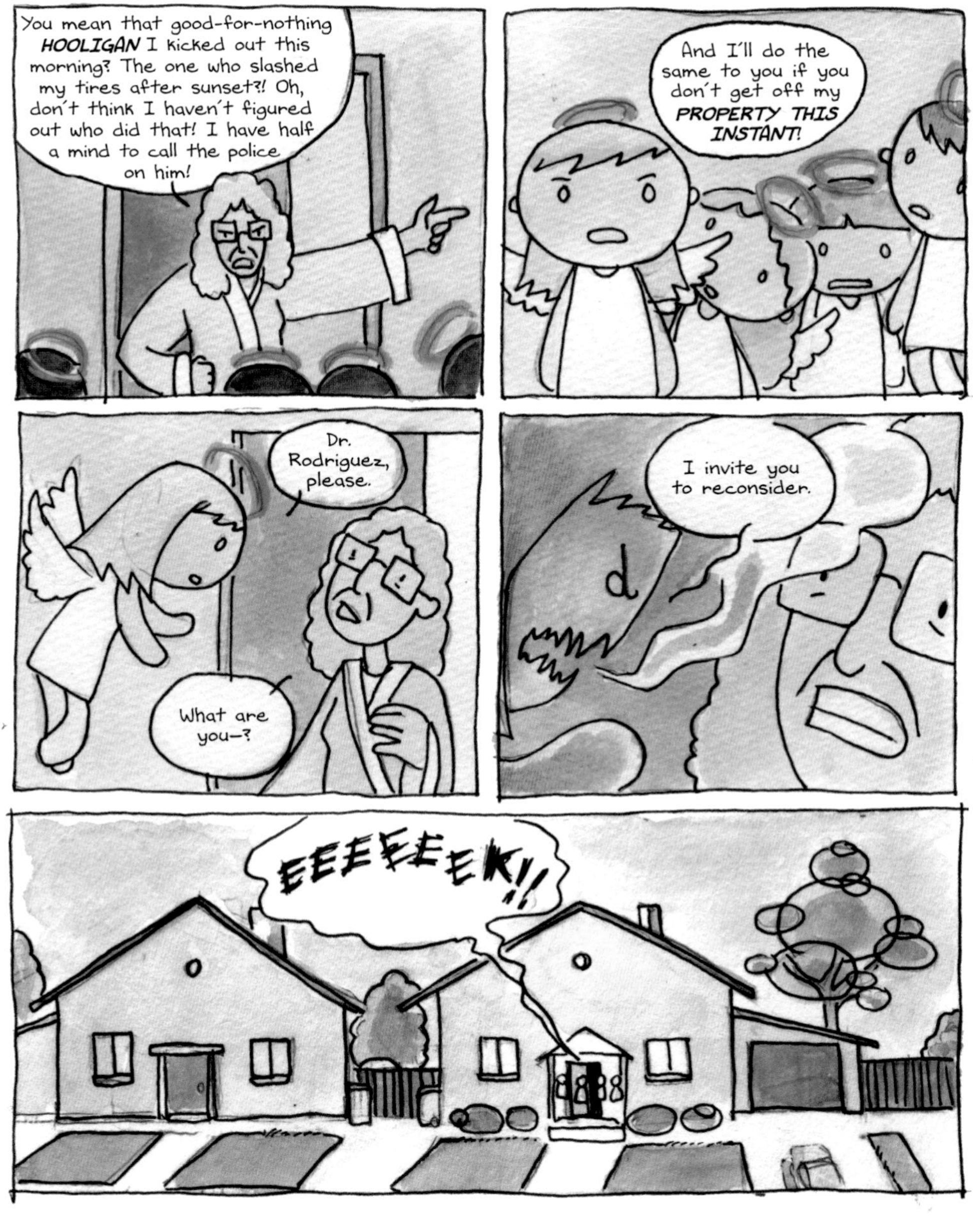

You mean that good-for-nothing **HOOLIGAN** I kicked out this morning? The one who slashed my tires after sunset?! Oh, don't think I haven't figured out who did that! I have half a mind to call the police on him!
And I'll do the same to you if you don't get off my **PROPERTY THIS INSTANT!**
Dr. Rodriguez, please.
What are you–?
I invite you to reconsider.
EEEEEEEK!!

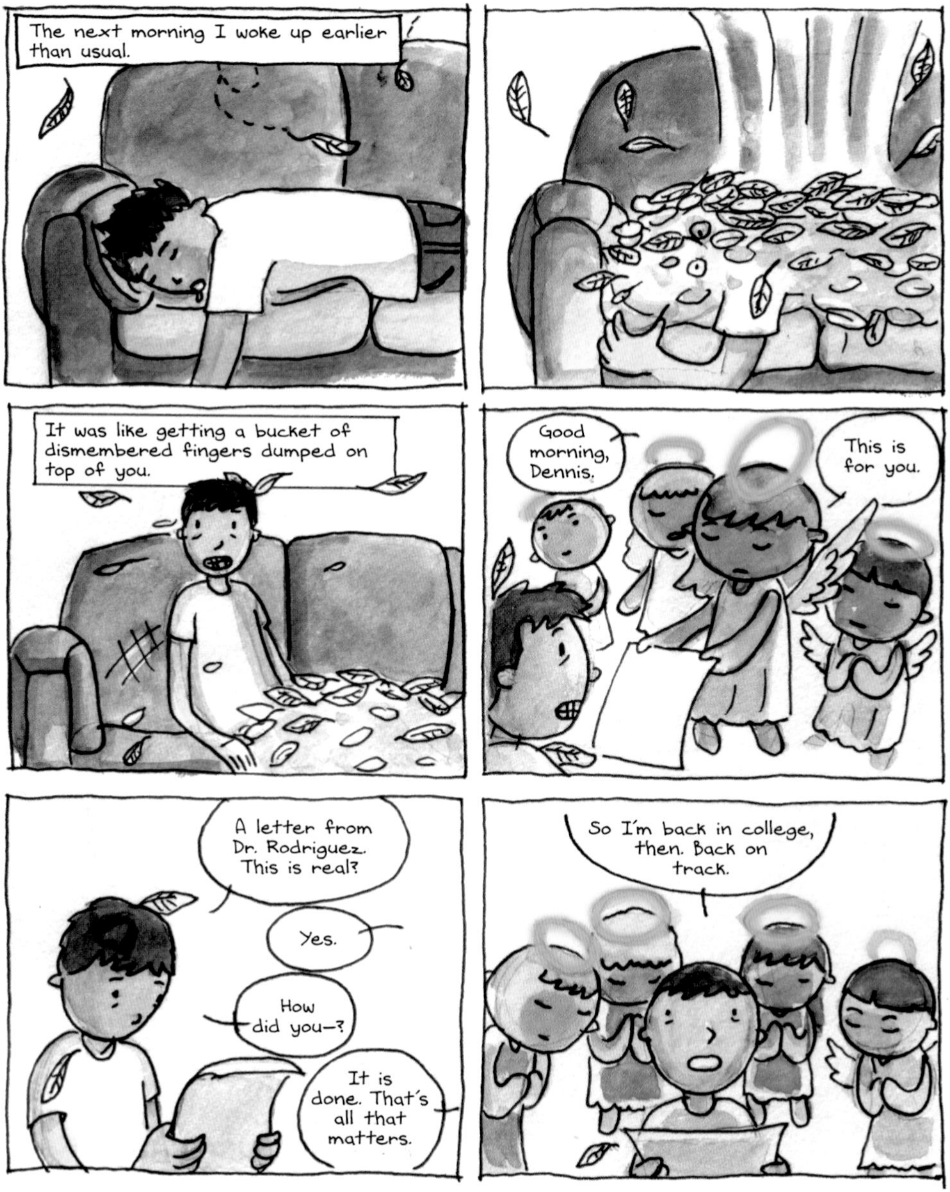
The next morning I woke up earlier than usual.
It was like getting a bucket of dismembered fingers dumped on top of you.
Good morning, Dennis.
This is for you.
A letter from Dr. Rodriguez. This is real?
Yes.
How did you—?
It is done. That's all that matters.
So I'm back in college, then. Back on track.

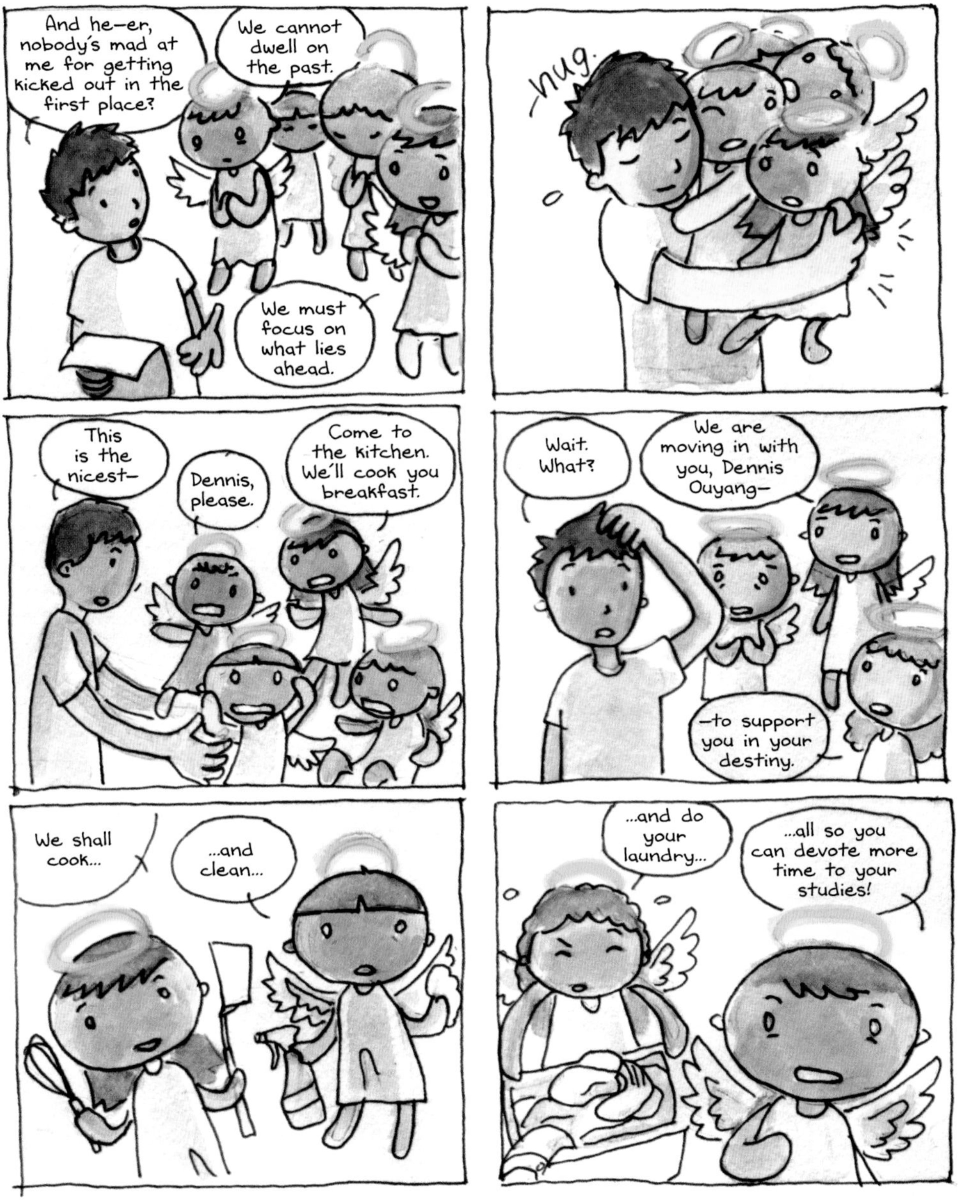
And he—er, nobody's mad at me for getting kicked out in the first place?
We cannot dwell on the past.
We must focus on what lies ahead.
-hug.
This is the nicest—
Dennis, please.
Come to the kitchen. We'll cook you breakfast.
Wait. What?
We are moving in with you, Dennis Ouyang—
—to support you in your destiny.
We shall cook...
...and clean...
...and do your laundry...
...all so you can devote more time to your studies!

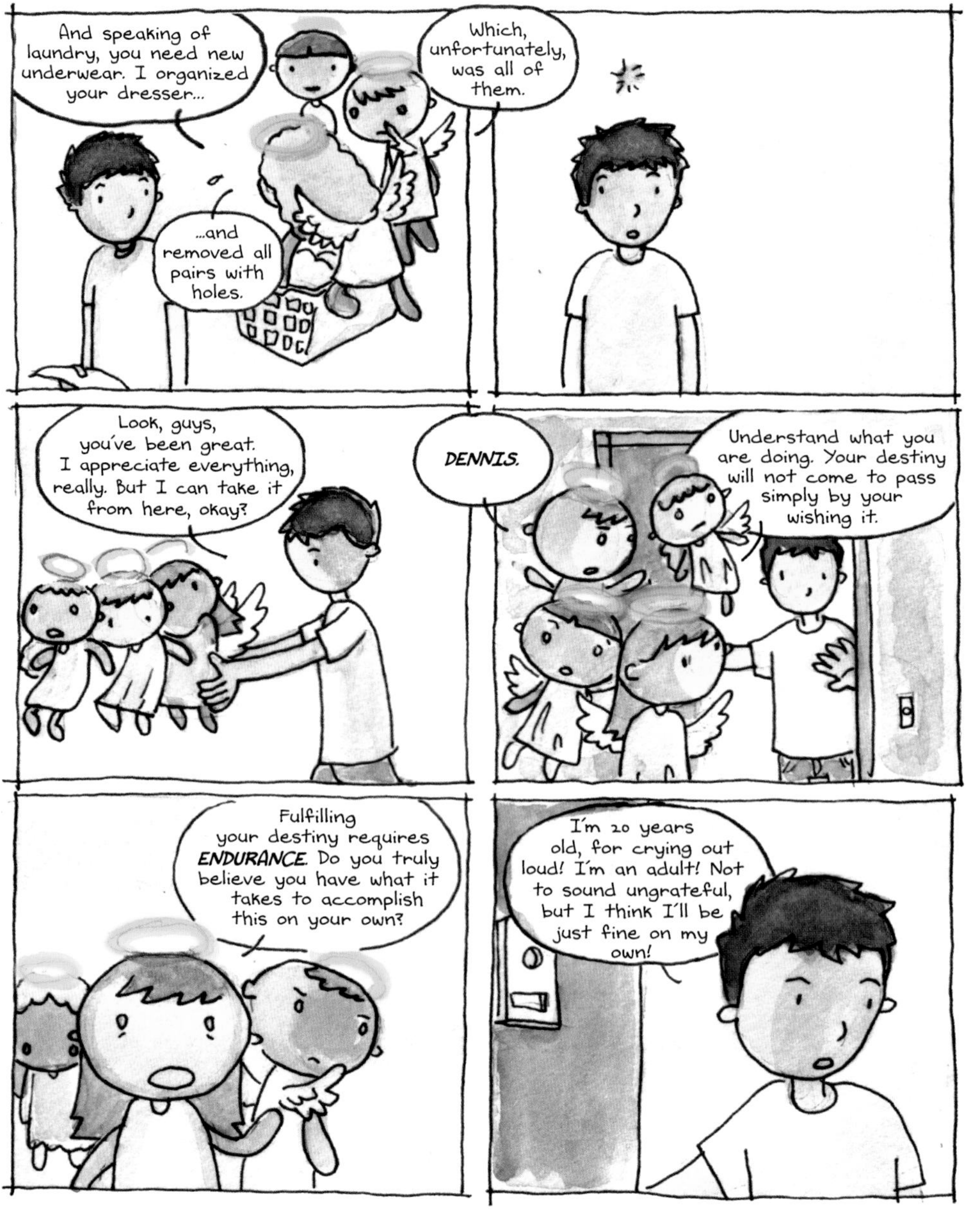
And speaking of laundry, you need new underwear. I organized your dresser...
...and removed all pairs with holes.
Which, unfortunately, was all of them.
Look, guys, you've been great. I appreciate everything, really. But I can take it from here, okay?
DENNIS.
Understand what you are doing. Your destiny will not come to pass simply by your wishing it.
Fulfilling your destiny requires ENDURANCE. Do you truly believe you have what it takes to accomplish this on your own?
I'm 20 years old, for crying out loud! I'm an adult! Not to sound ungrateful, but I think I'll be just fine on my own!

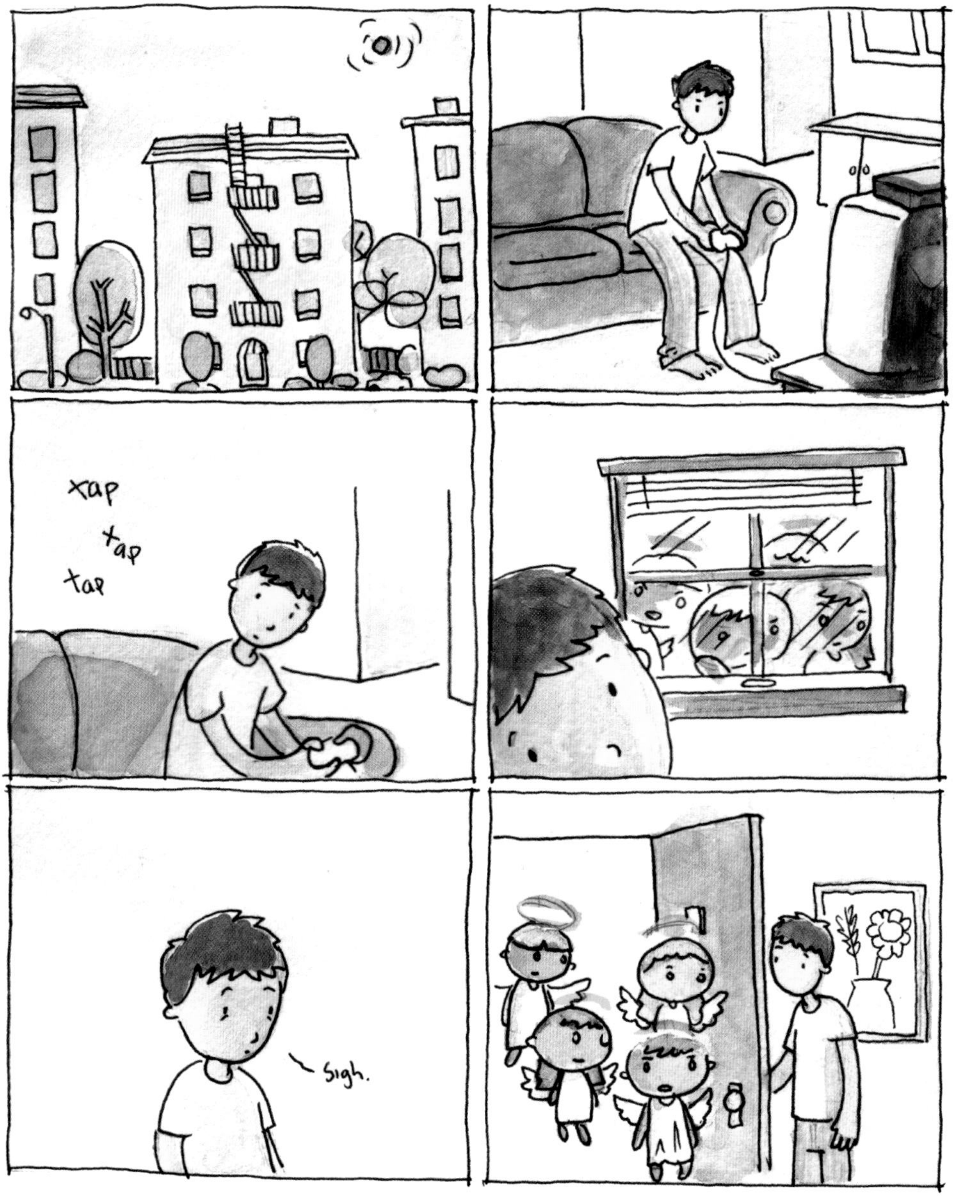
tap
tap
tap
Sigh.

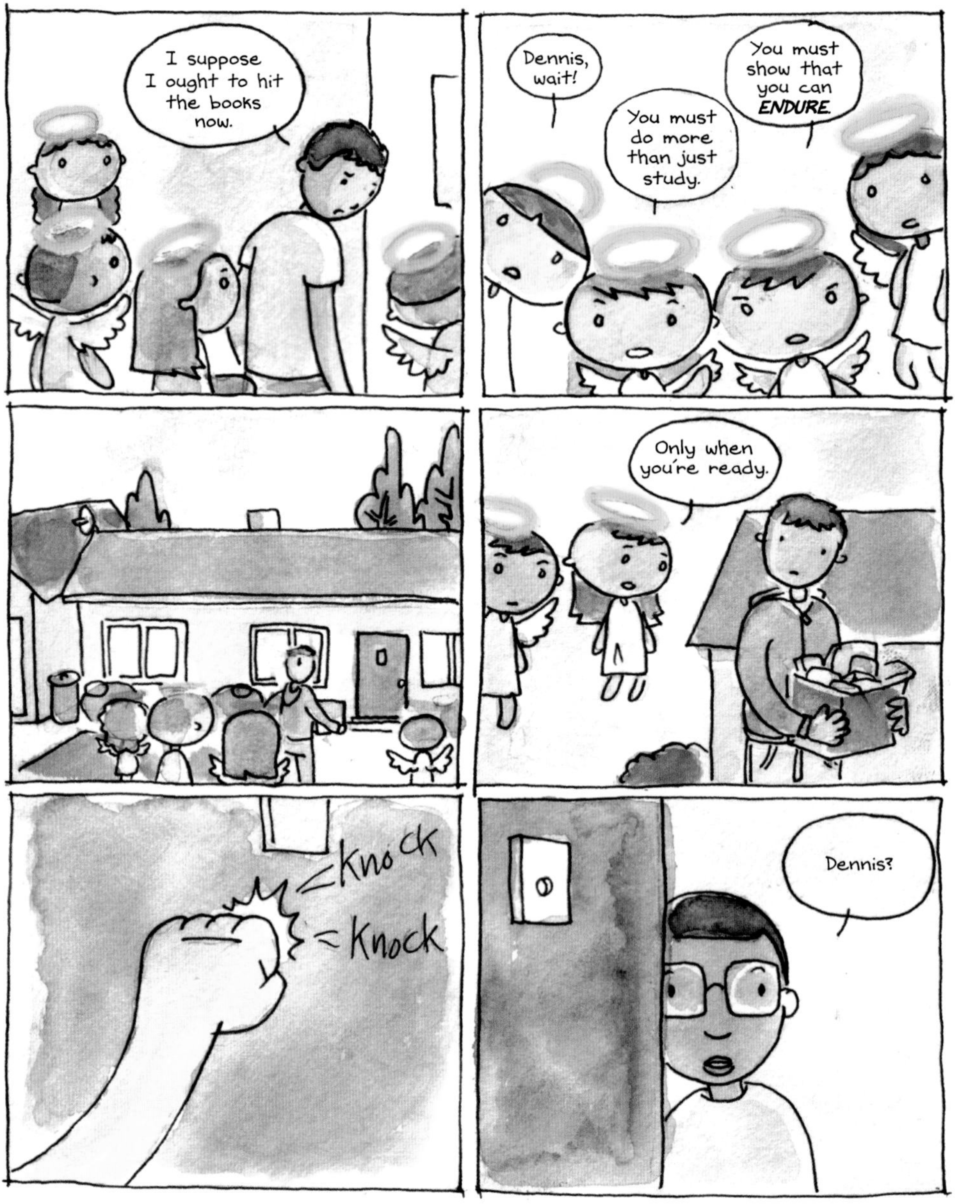
I suppose I ought to hit the books now.
Dennis, wait!
You must do more than just study.
You must show that you can ENDURE.
Only when you're ready.
Knock
Knock
Dennis?

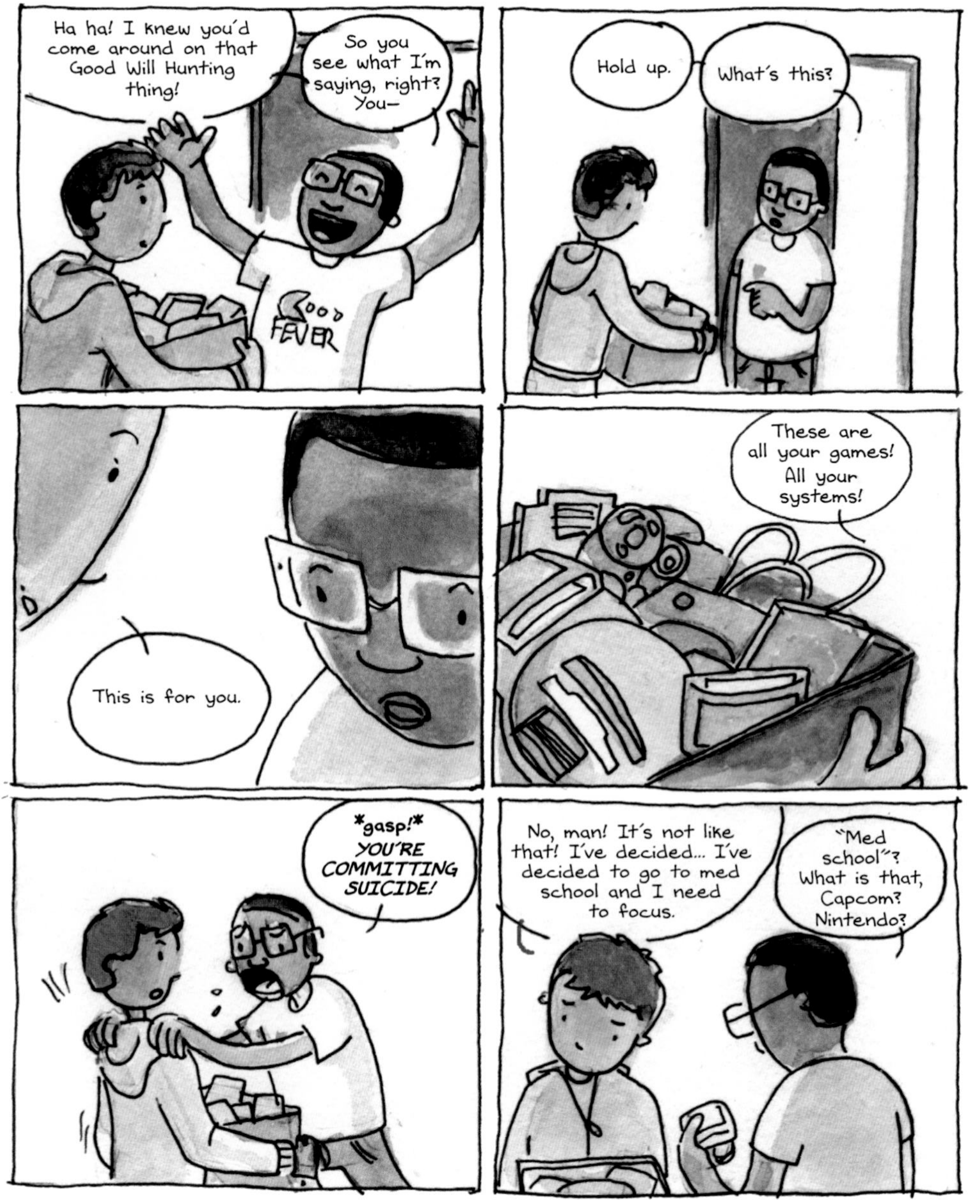
Ha ha! I knew you'd come around on that Good Will Hunting thing!
So you see what I'm saying, right? You—
GOOD FEVER
Hold up.
What's this?
This is for you.
These are all your games! All your systems!
gasp! YOU'RE COMMITTING SUICIDE!
No, man! It's not like that! I've decided... I've decided to go to med school and I need to focus.
"Med school"? What is that, Capcom? Nintendo?

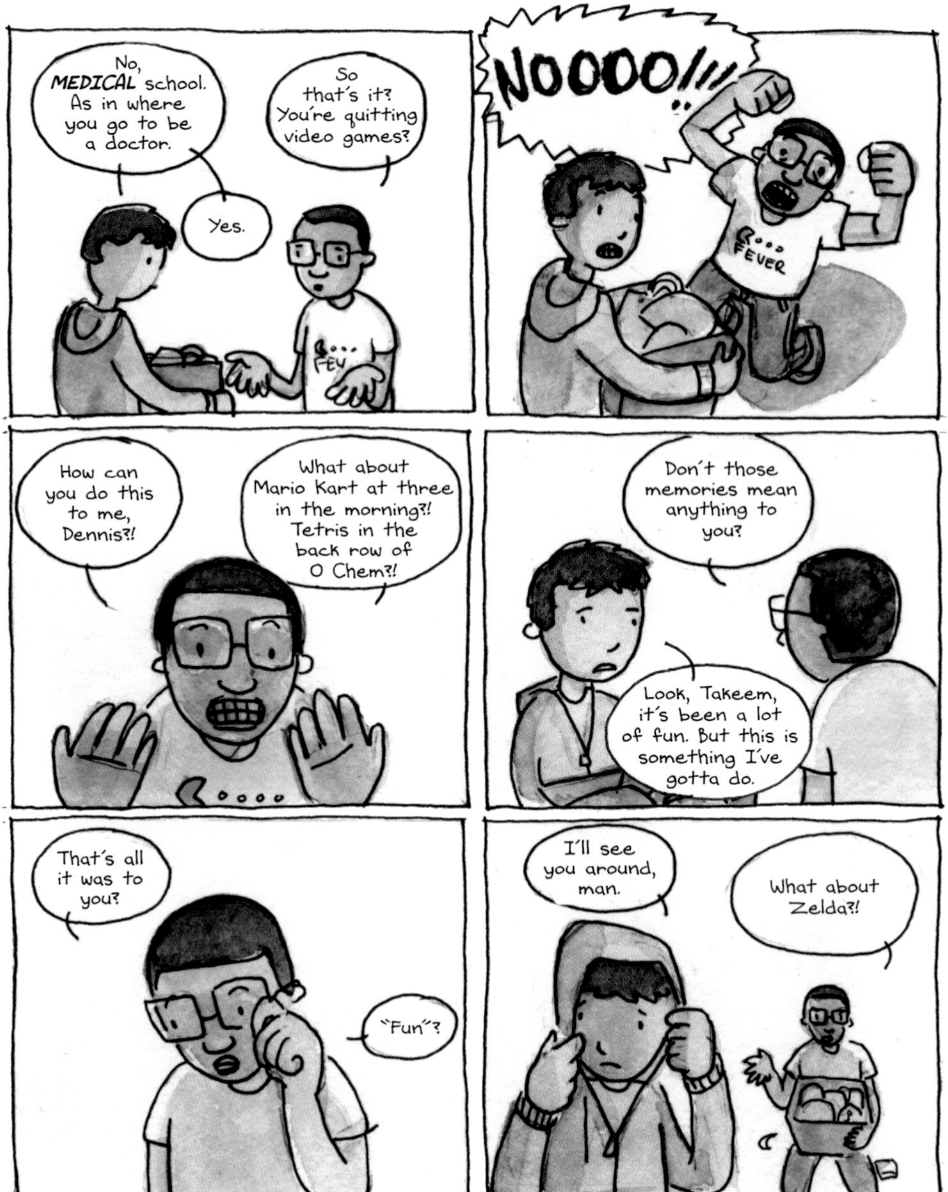
No, MEDICAL school. As in where you go to be a doctor.
So that's it? You're quitting video games?
Yes.
NOOOO!!!
FEVER
How can you do this to me, Dennis?!
What about Mario Kart at three in the morning?! Tetris in the back row of O Chem?!
Don't those memories mean anything to you?
Look, Takeem, it's been a lot of fun. But this is something I've gotta do.
That's all it was to you?
"Fun"?
I'll see you around, man.
What about Zelda?!

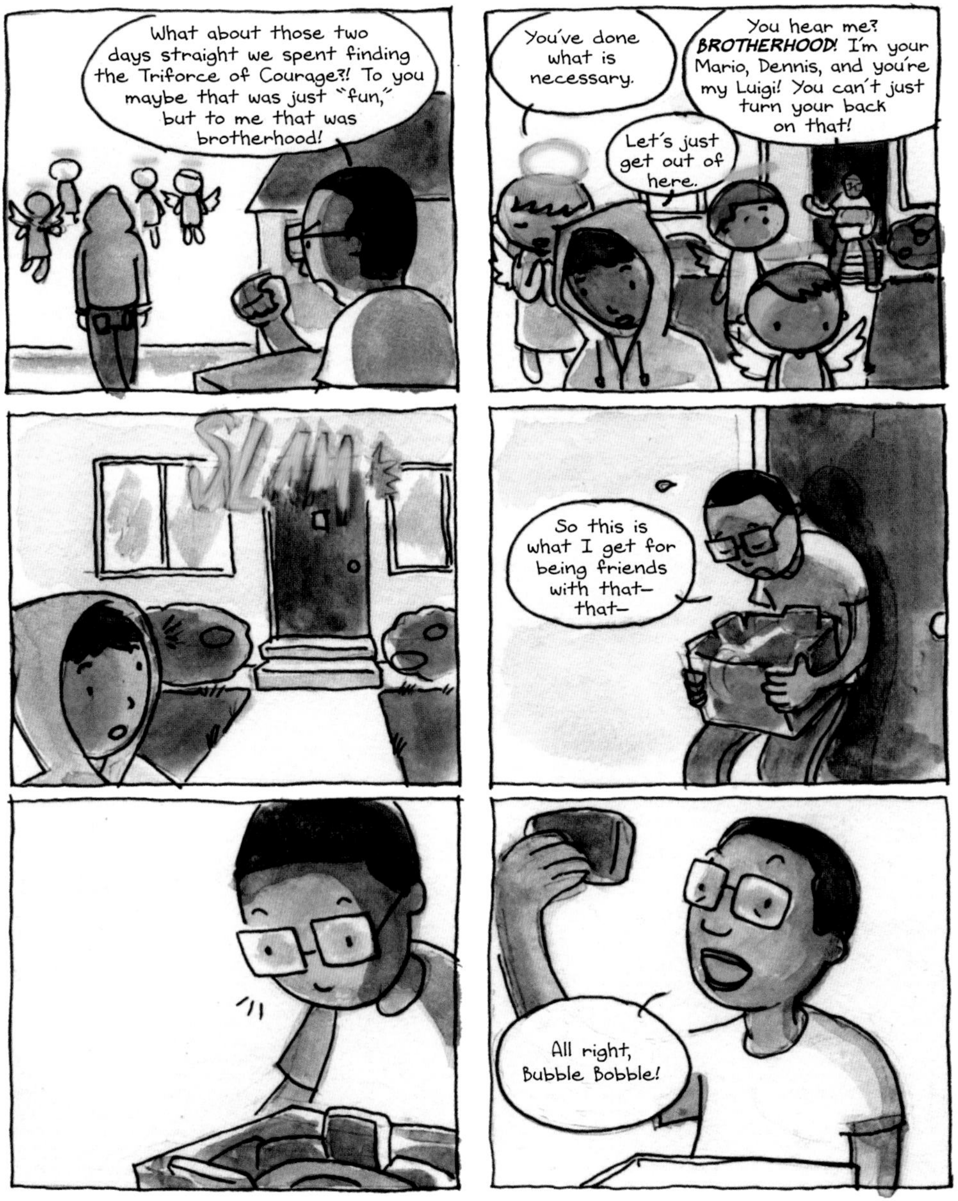
What about those two days straight we spent finding the Triforce of Courage?! To you maybe that was just "fun," but to me that was brotherhood!
You've done what is necessary.
You hear me? **BROTHERHOOD!** I'm your Mario, Dennis, and you're my Luigi! You can't just turn your back on that!
Let's just get out of here.
SLAM
So this is what I get for being friends with that— that—
All right, Bubble Bobble!

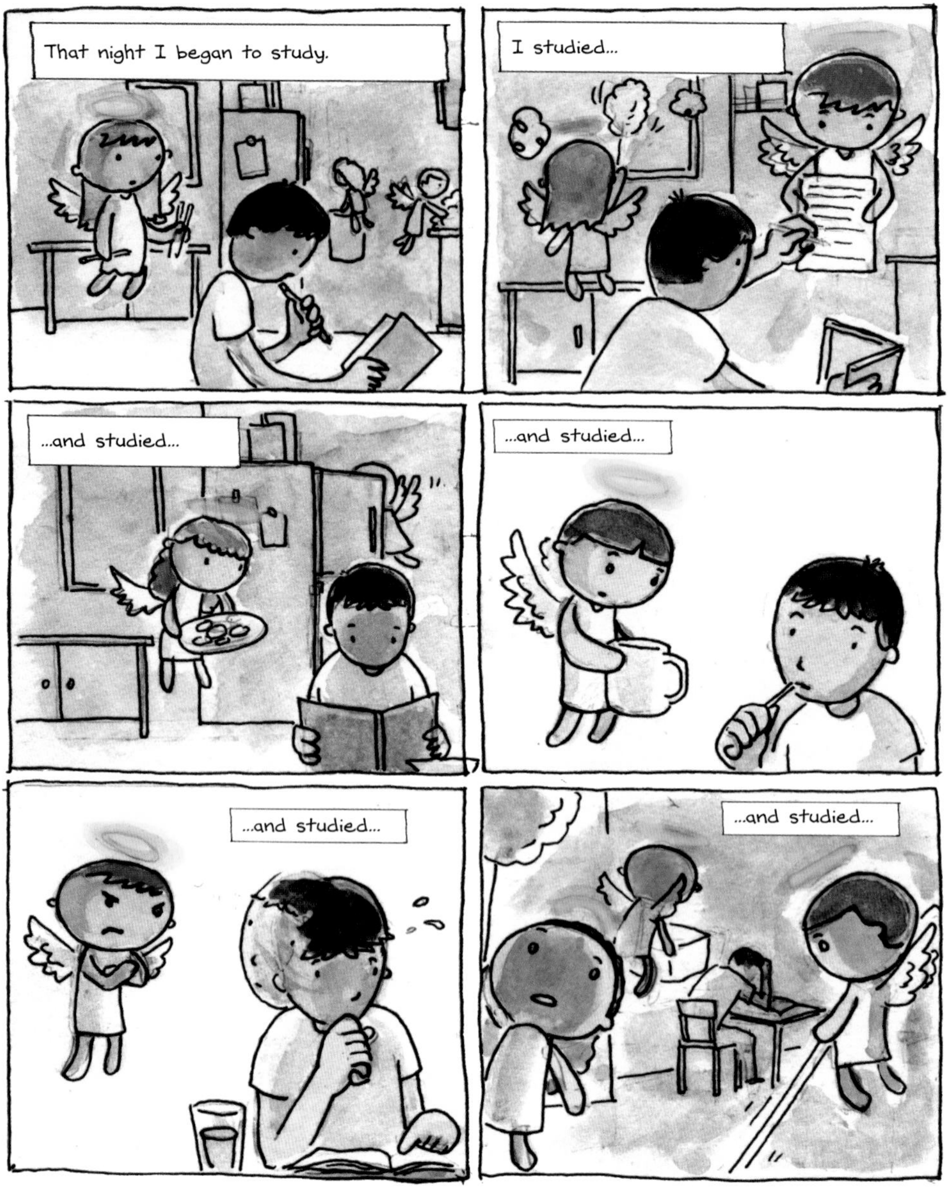
That night I began to study.
I studied...
...and studied...
...and studied...
...and studied...
...and studied...

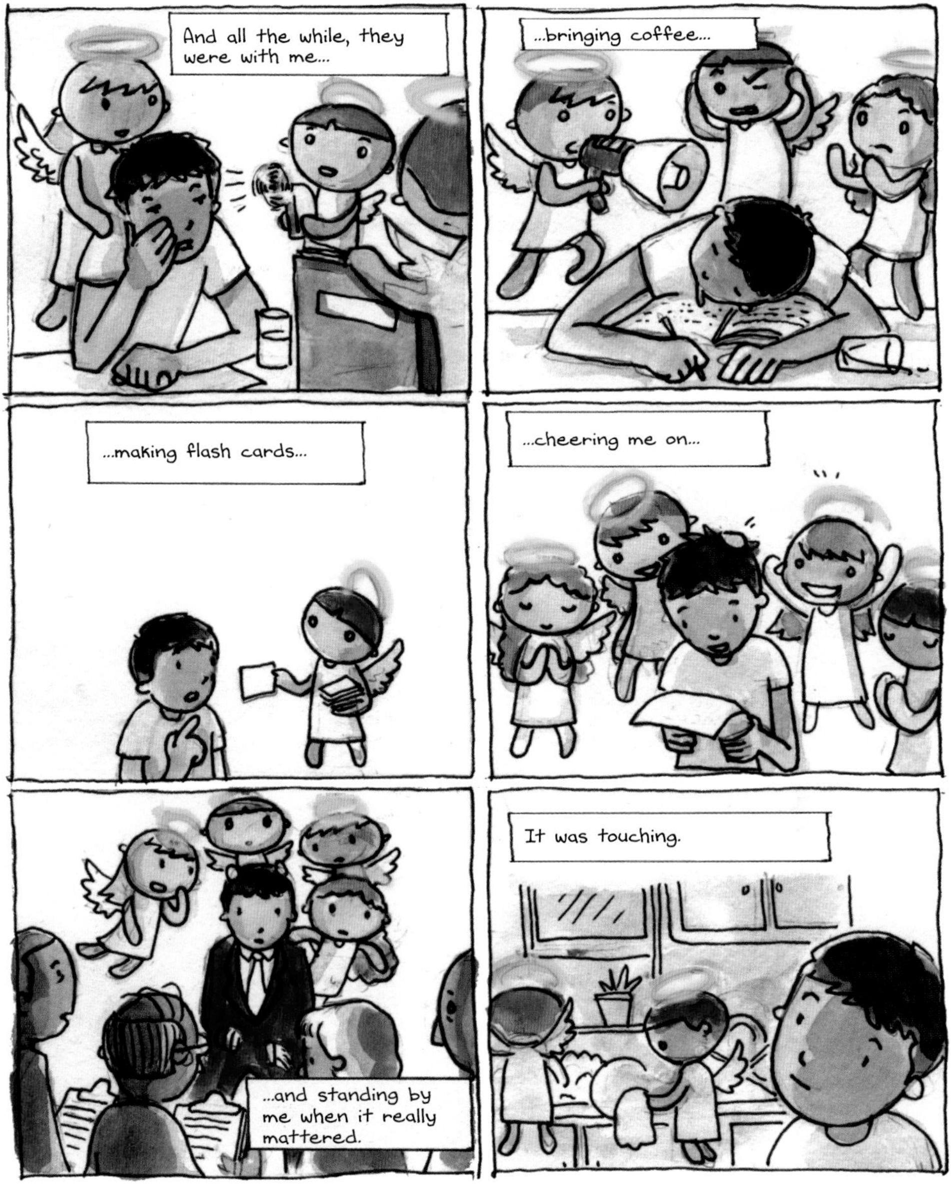
And all the while, they were with me...
...bringing coffee...
...making flash cards...
...cheering me on...
...and standing by me when it really mattered.
It was touching.

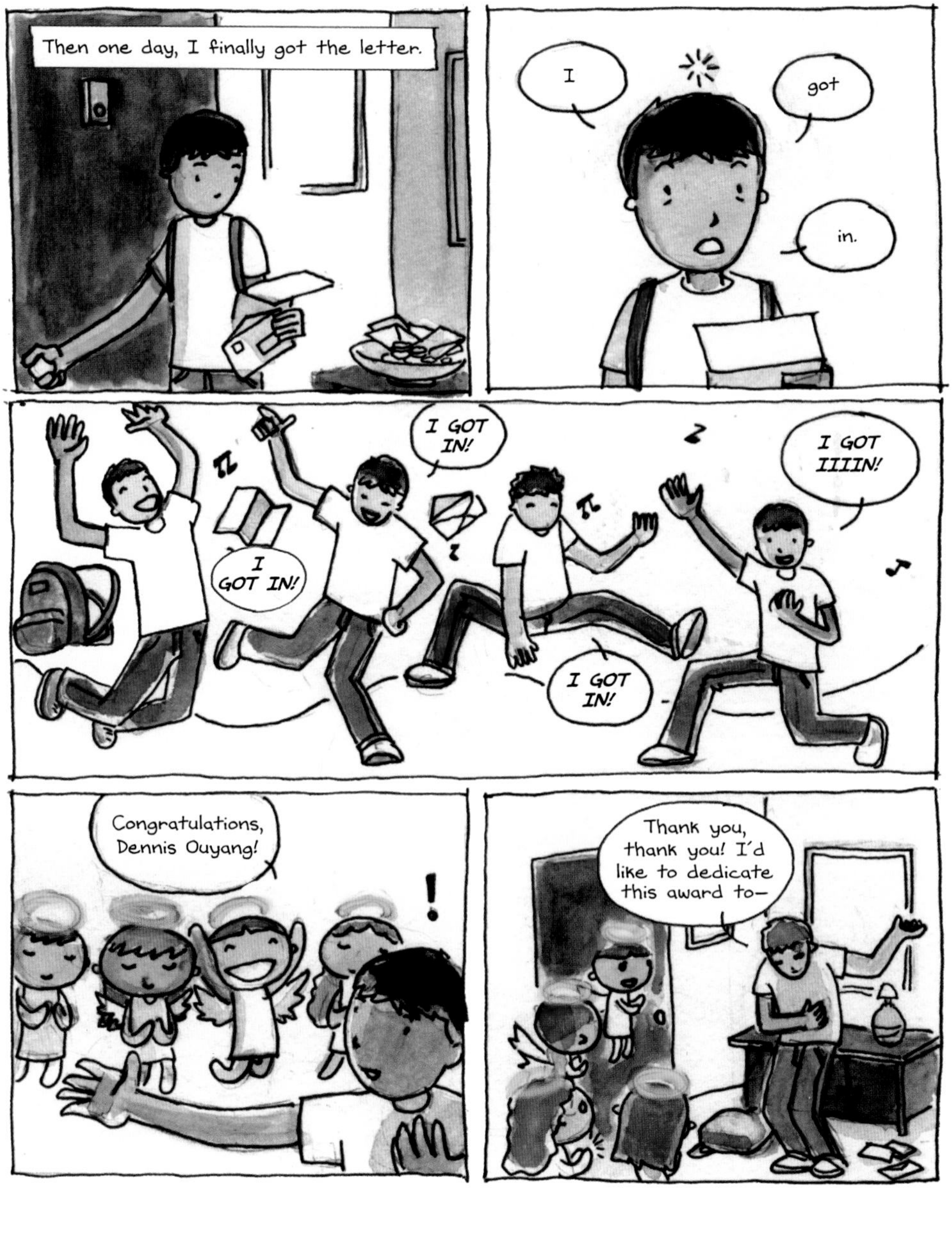
Then one day, I finally got the letter.
I
got
in.
I GOT IN!
I GOT IN!
I GOT IN!
I GOT IIIIN!
Congratulations, Dennis Ouyang!
!
Thank you, thank you! I'd like to dedicate this award to—

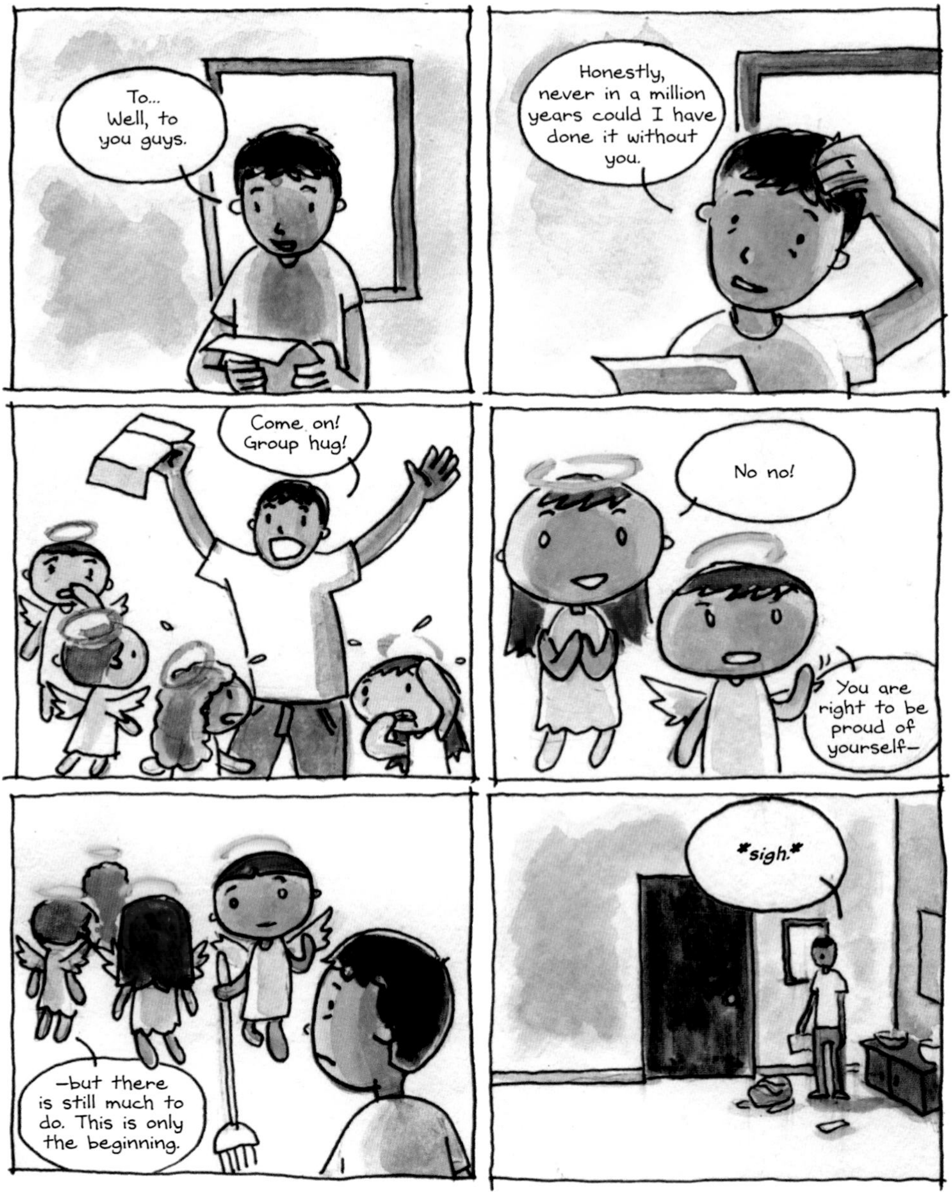
To... Well, to you guys.
Honestly, never in a million years could I have done it without you.
Come on! Group hug!
No no!
You are right to be proud of yourself—
—but there is still much to do. This is only the beginning.
sigh.

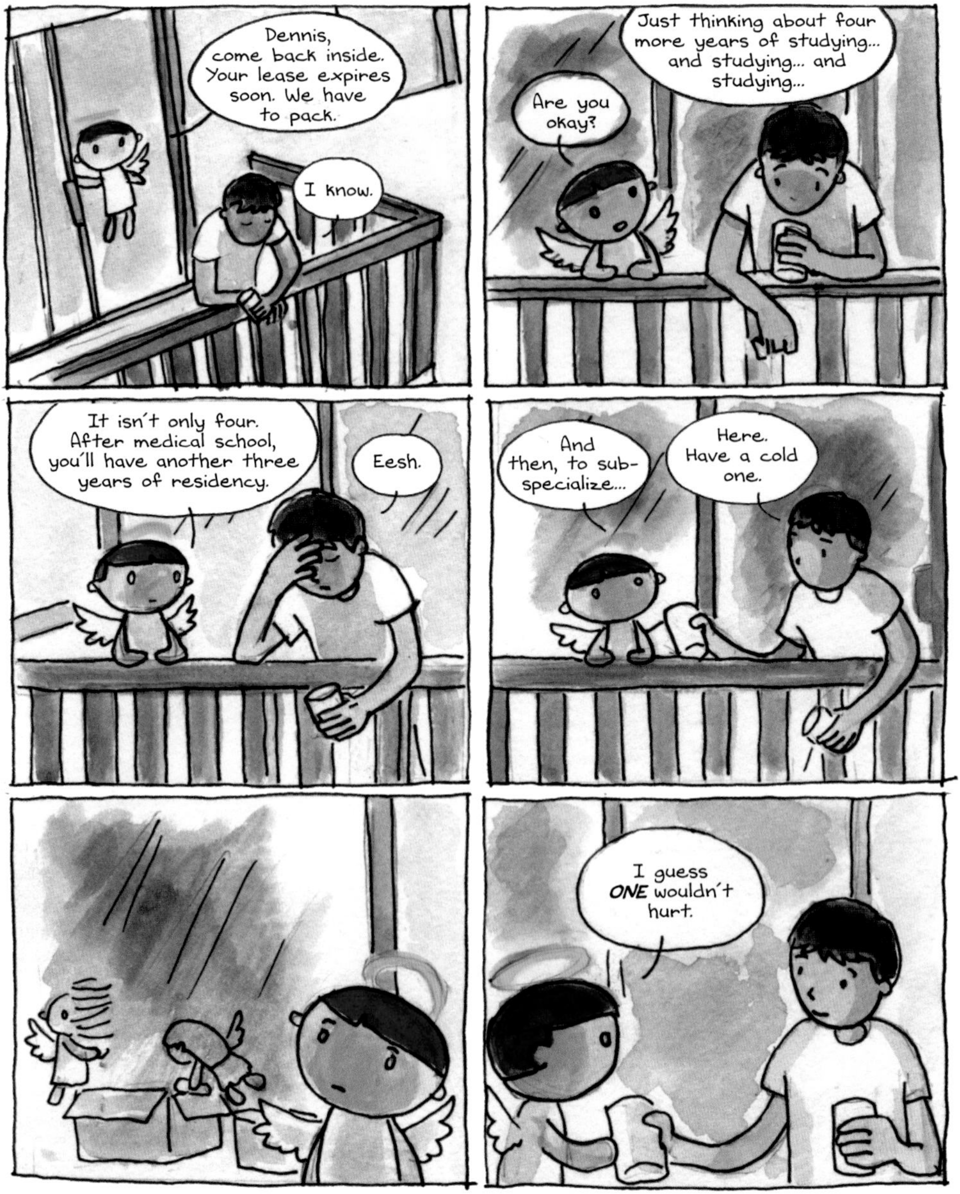
Dennis, come back inside. Your lease expires soon. We have to pack.
I know.
Are you okay?
Just thinking about four more years of studying... and studying... and studying...
It isn't only four. After medical school, you'll have another three years of residency.
Eesh.
And then, to sub-specialize...
Here. Have a cold one.
I guess ***ONE*** wouldn't hurt.

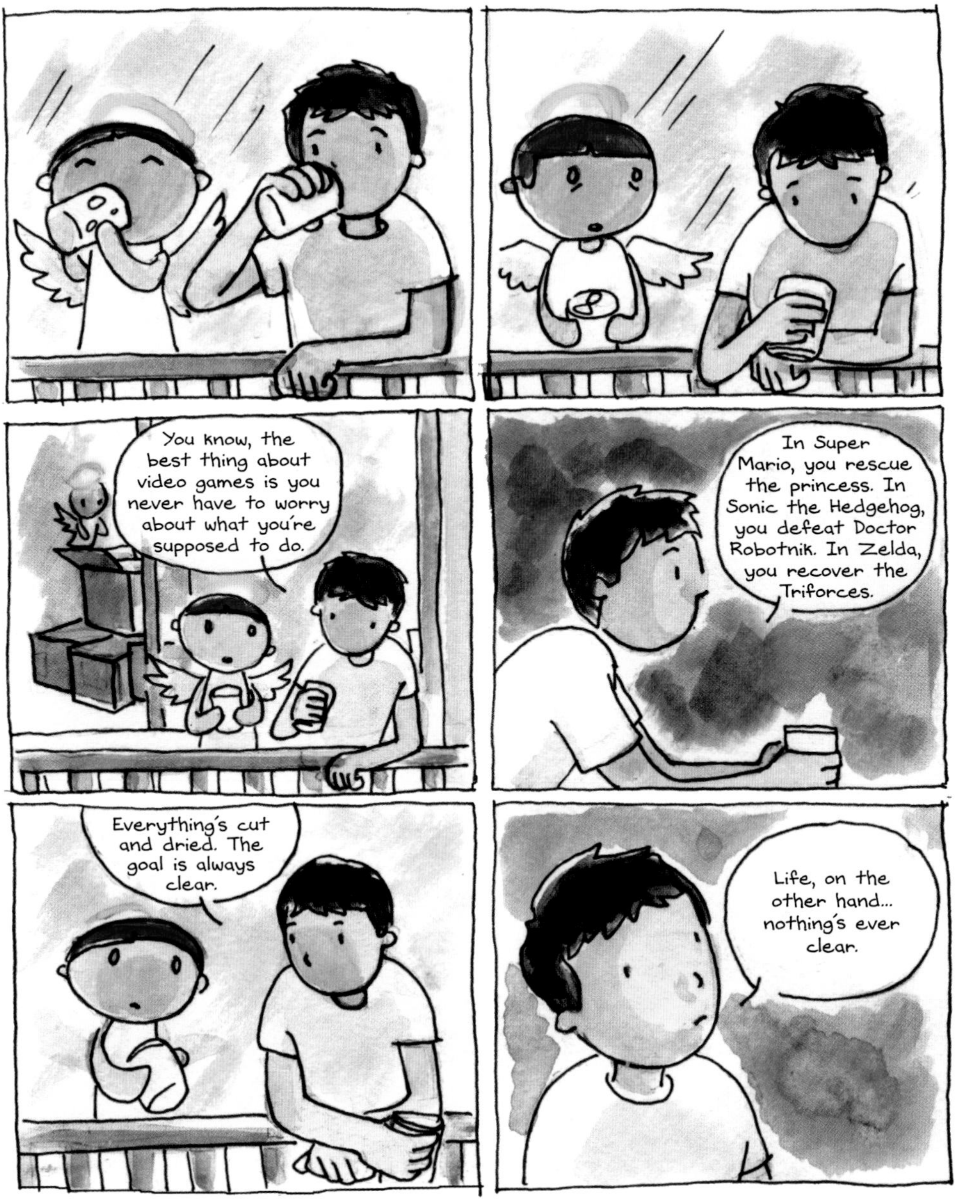
You know, the best thing about video games is you never have to worry about what you're supposed to do.
In Super Mario, you rescue the princess. In Sonic the Hedgehog, you defeat Doctor Robotnik. In Zelda, you recover the Triforces.
Everything's cut and dried. The goal is always clear.
Life, on the other hand... nothing's ever clear.

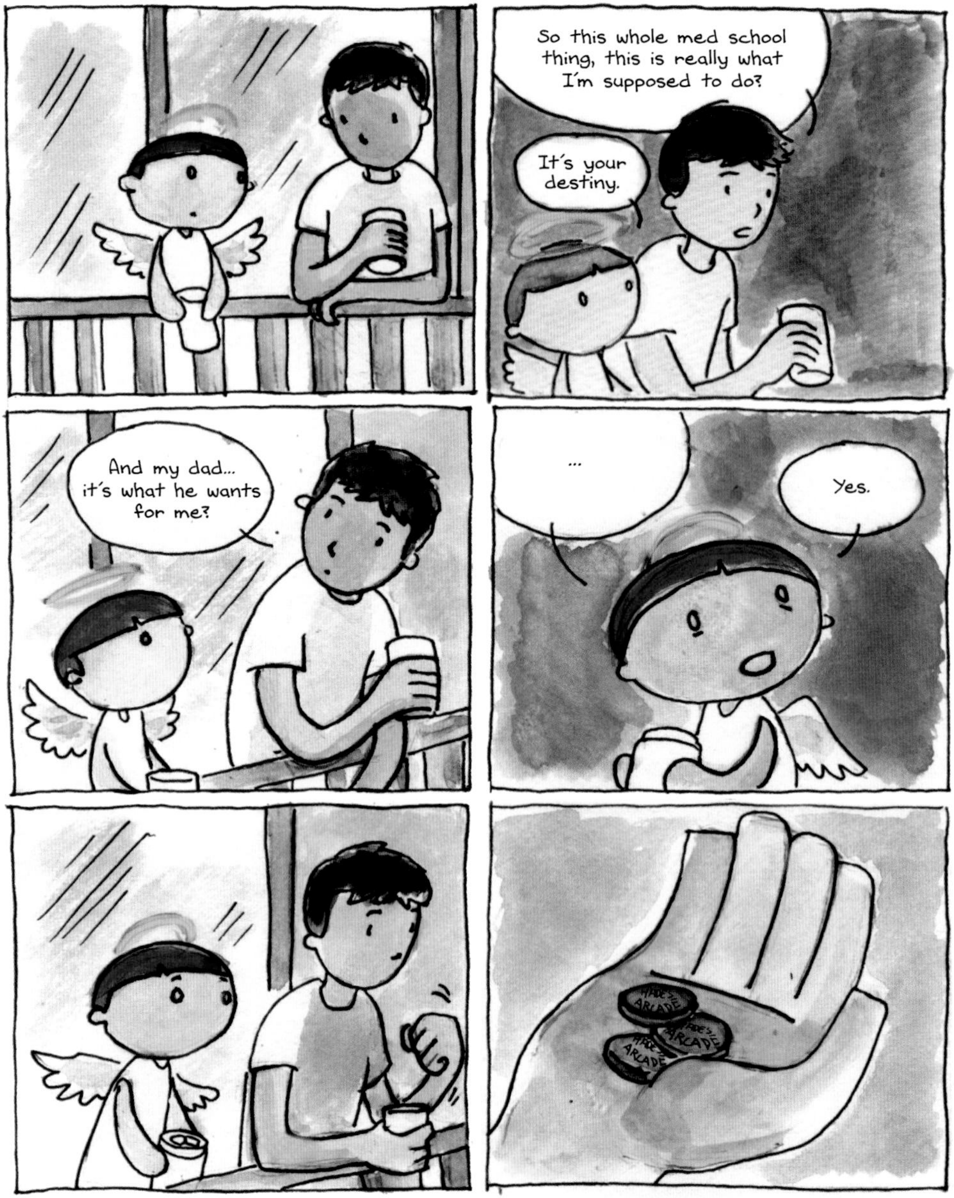
So this whole med school thing, this is really what I'm supposed to do?
It's your destiny.
And my dad... it's what he wants for me?
...
Yes.

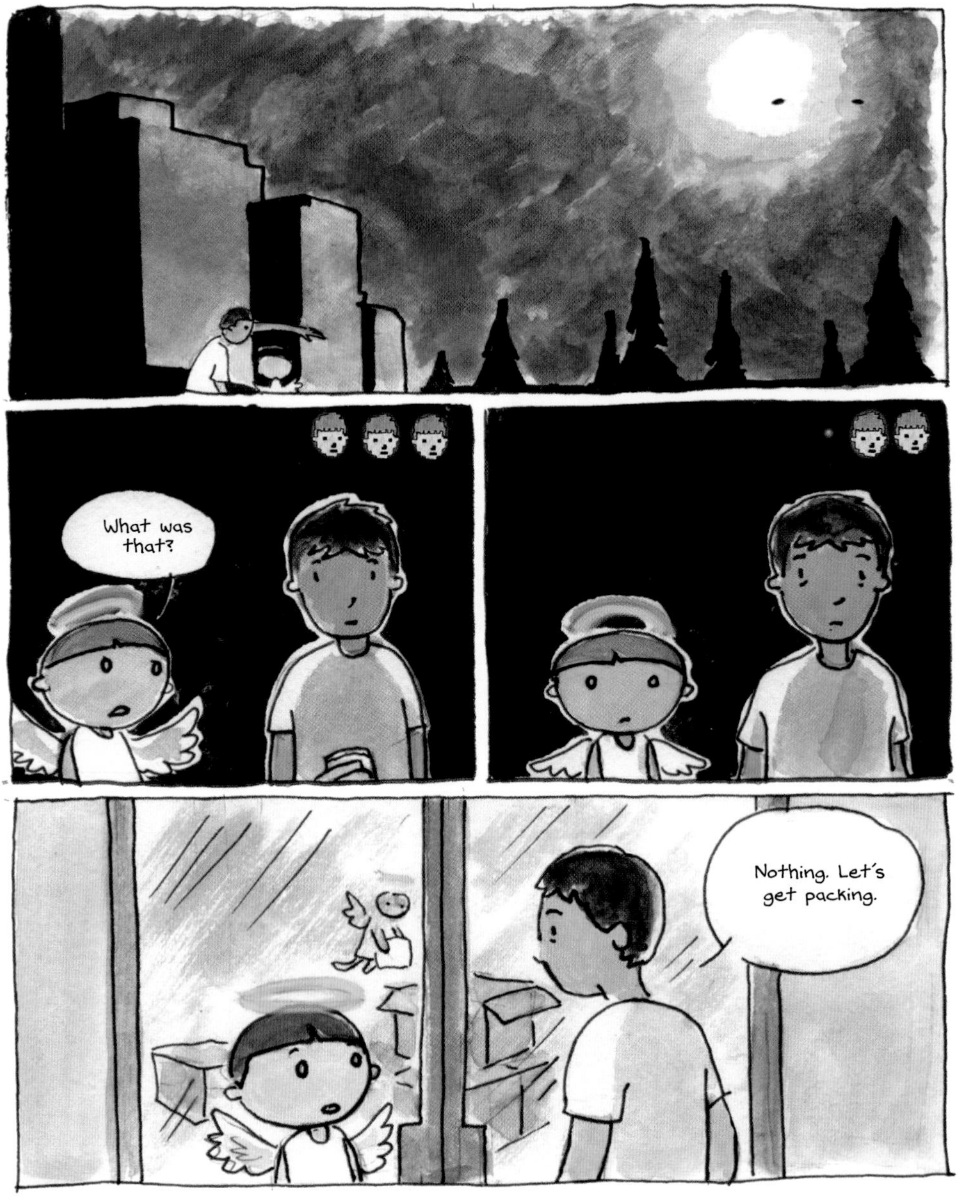
What was that?
Nothing. Let´s get packing.

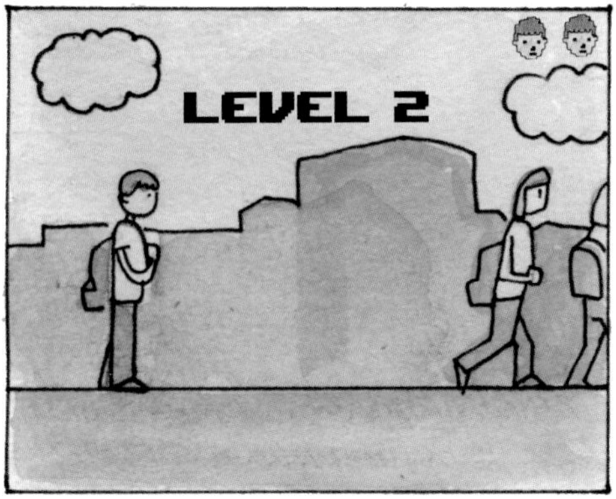
LEVEL 2

On the morning of my first day of med school,
everything was *BEAUTIFUL*.

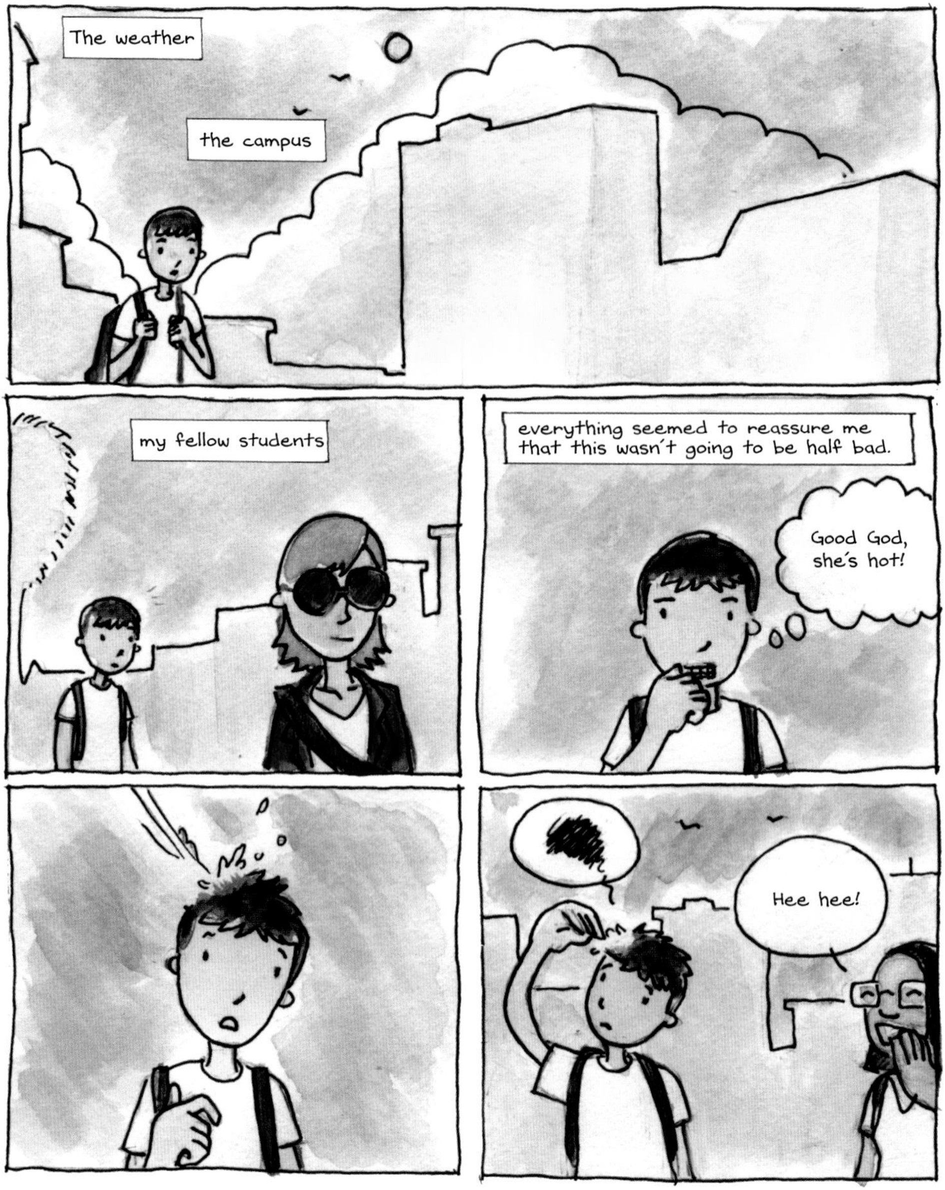
The weather
the campus
my fellow students
everything seemed to reassure me that this wasn´t going to be half bad.
Good God, she´s hot!
Hee hee!

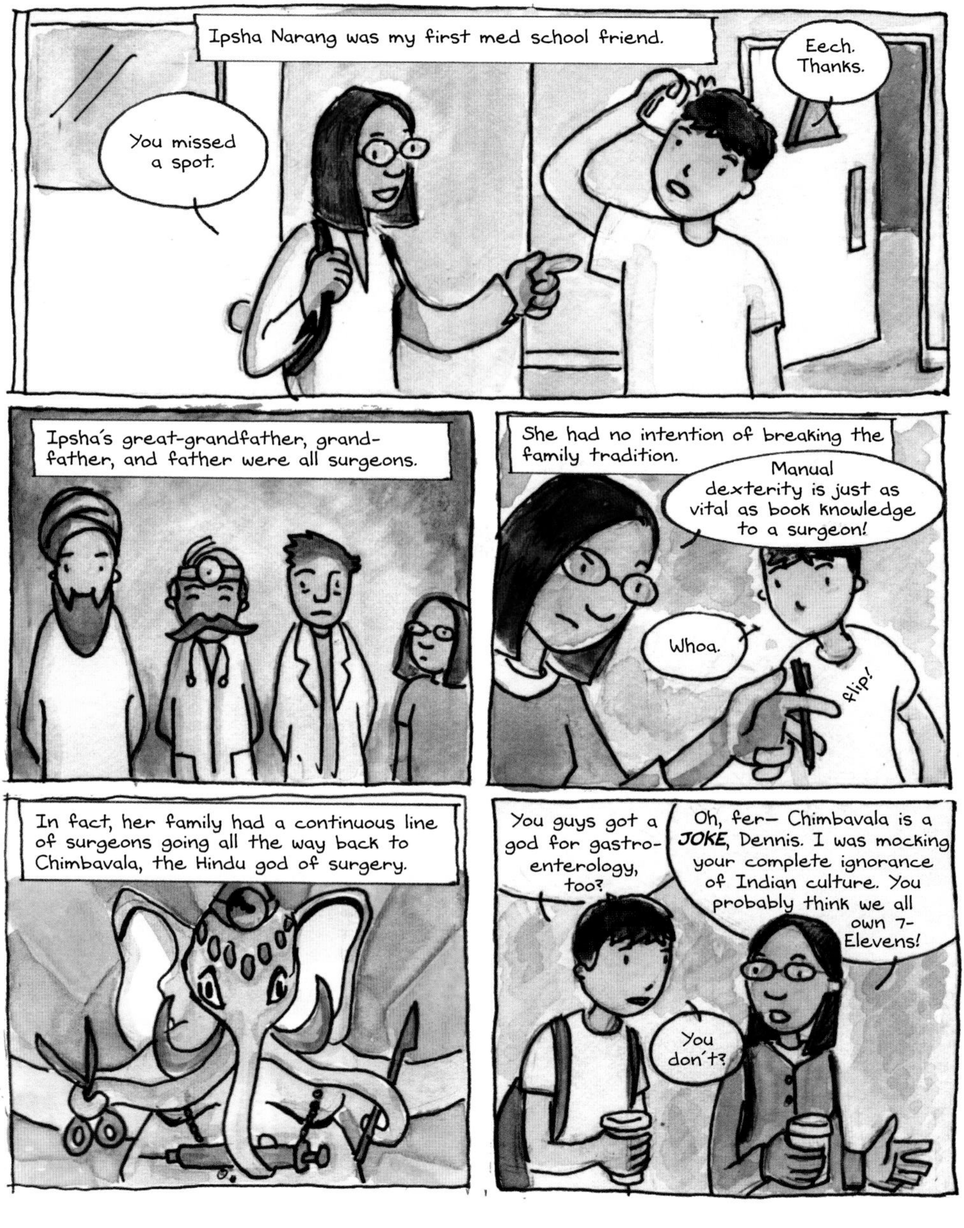

Ipsha Narang was my first med school friend.
You missed a spot.
Eech. Thanks.
Ipsha's great-grandfather, grandfather, and father were all surgeons.
She had no intention of breaking the family tradition.
Manual dexterity is just as vital as book knowledge to a surgeon!
Whoa.
flip!
In fact, her family had a continuous line of surgeons going all the way back to Chimbavala, the Hindu god of surgery.
You guys got a god for gastroenterology, too?
Oh, fer— Chimbavala is a JOKE, Dennis. I was mocking your complete ignorance of Indian culture. You probably think we all own 7-Elevens!
You don't?

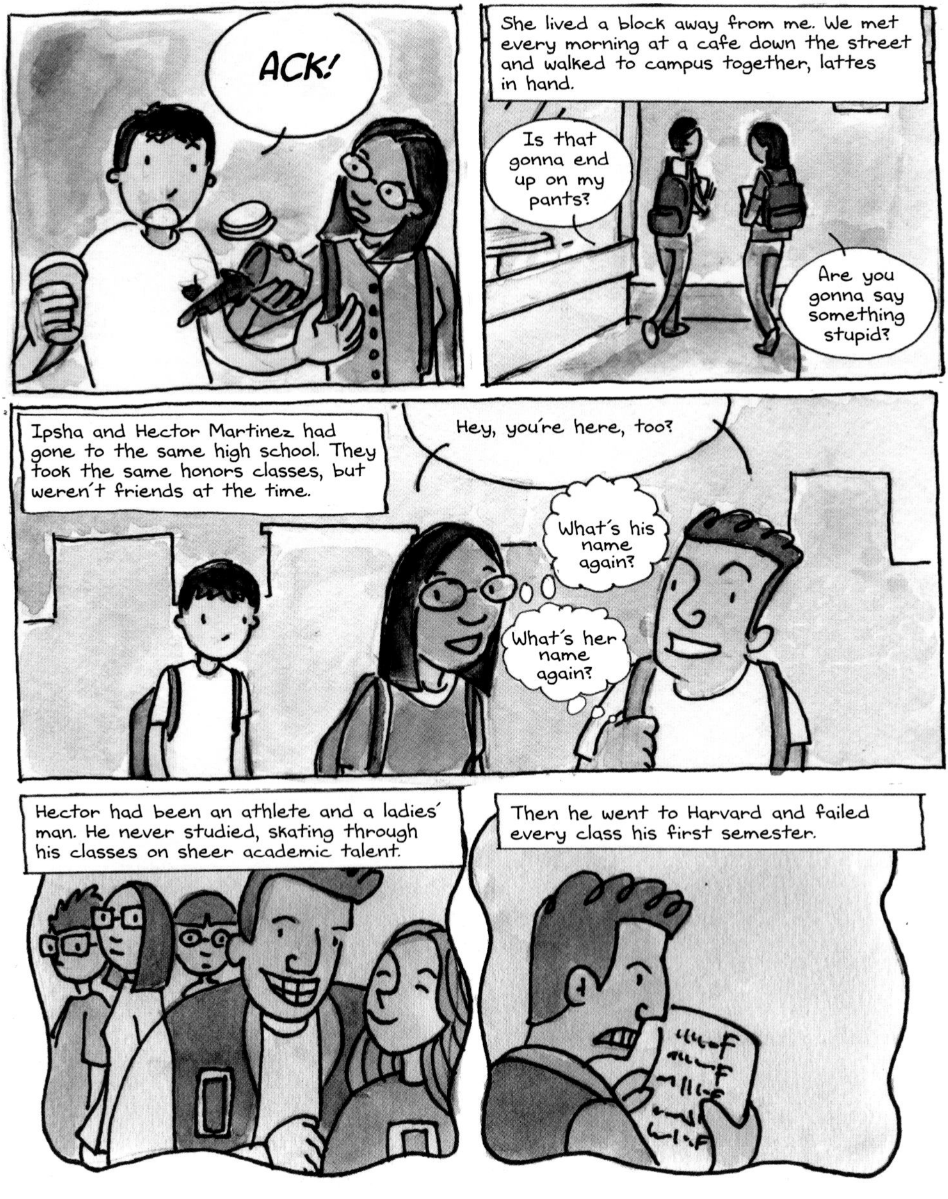
ACK!
She lived a block away from me. We met every morning at a cafe down the street and walked to campus together, lattes in hand.
Is that gonna end up on my pants?
Are you gonna say something stupid?
Ipsha and Hector Martinez had gone to the same high school. They took the same honors classes, but weren't friends at the time.
Hey, you're here, too?
What's his name again?
What's her name again?
Hector had been an athlete and a ladies' man. He never studied, skating through his classes on sheer academic talent.
Then he went to Harvard and failed every class his first semester.

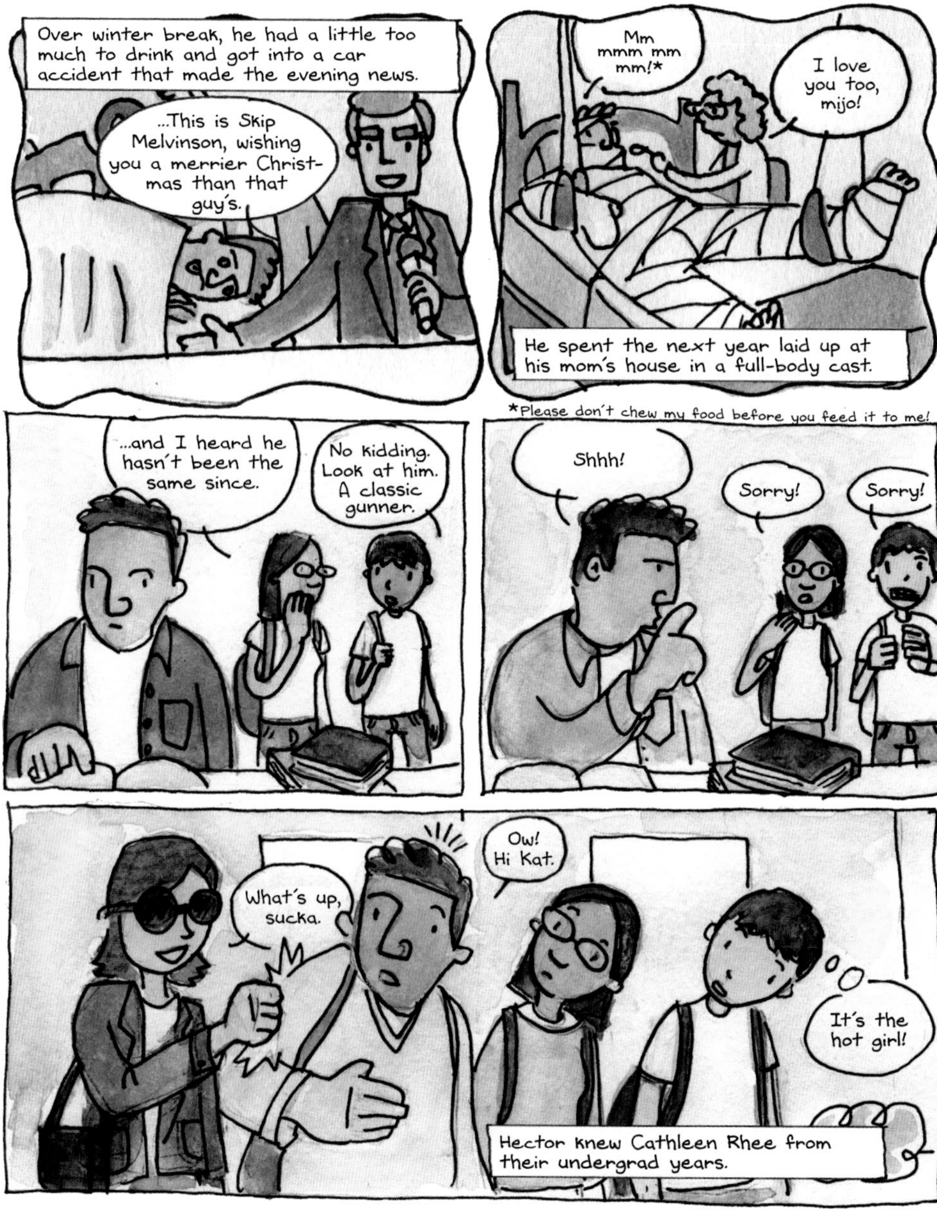
Over winter break, he had a little too much to drink and got into a car accident that made the evening news.
...This is Skip Melvinson, wishing you a merrier Christmas than that guy's.
Mm mmm mm mm!*
I love you too, mijo!
He spent the next year laid up at his mom's house in a full-body cast.
*Please don't chew my food before you feed it to me!
...and I heard he hasn't been the same since.
No kidding. Look at him. A classic gunner.
Shhh!
Sorry!
Sorry!
What's up, sucka.
Ow! Hi Kat.
It's the hot girl!
Hector knew Cathleen Rhee from their undergrad years.

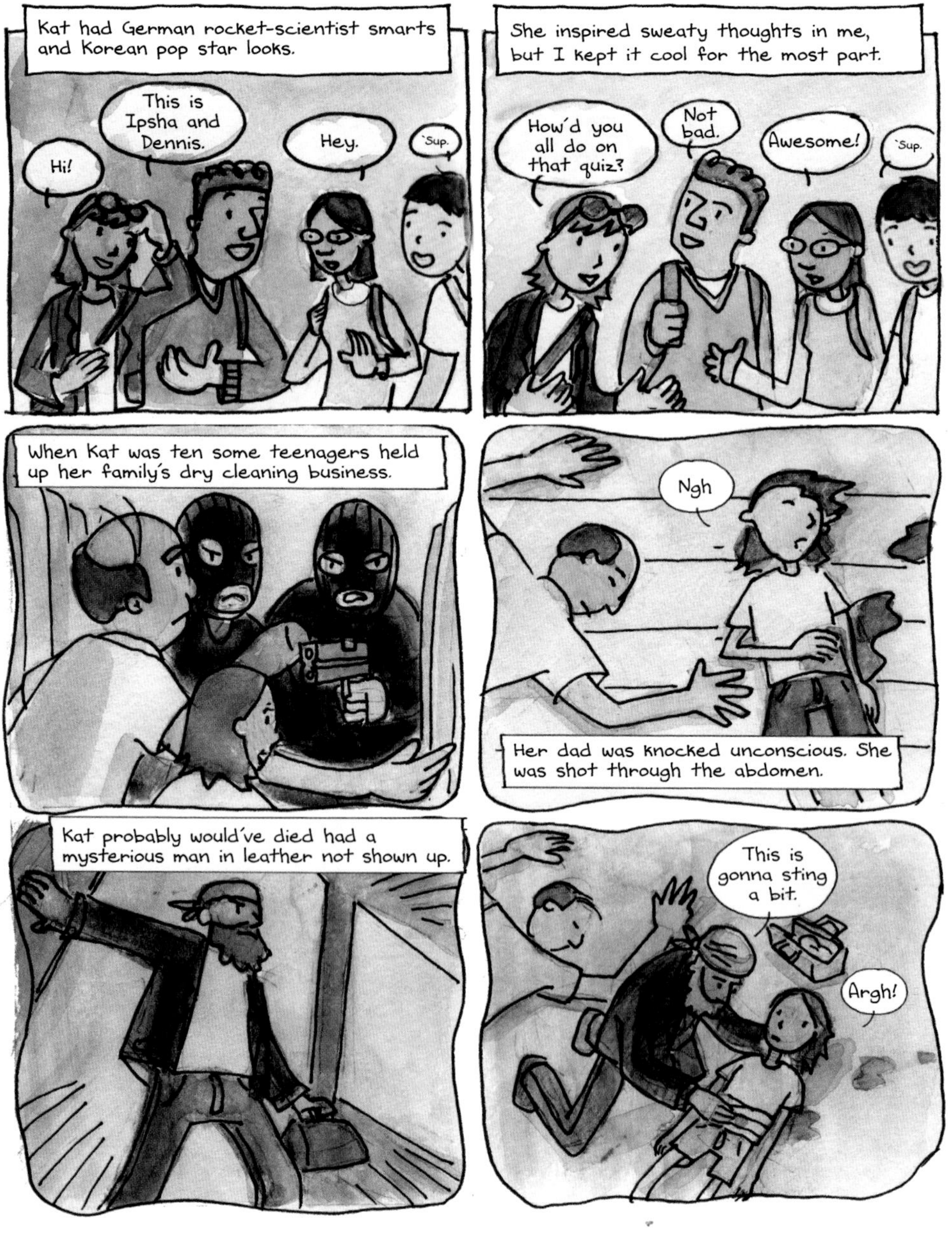
Kat had German rocket-scientist smarts and Korean pop star looks.
Hi!
This is Ipsha and Dennis.
Hey.
`Sup.
She inspired sweaty thoughts in me, but I kept it cool for the most part.
How'd you all do on that quiz?
Not bad.
Awesome!
`Sup.
When Kat was ten some teenagers held up her family's dry cleaning business.
Ngh
Her dad was knocked unconscious. She was shot through the abdomen.
Kat probably would've died had a mysterious man in leather not shown up.
This is gonna sting a bit.
Argh!

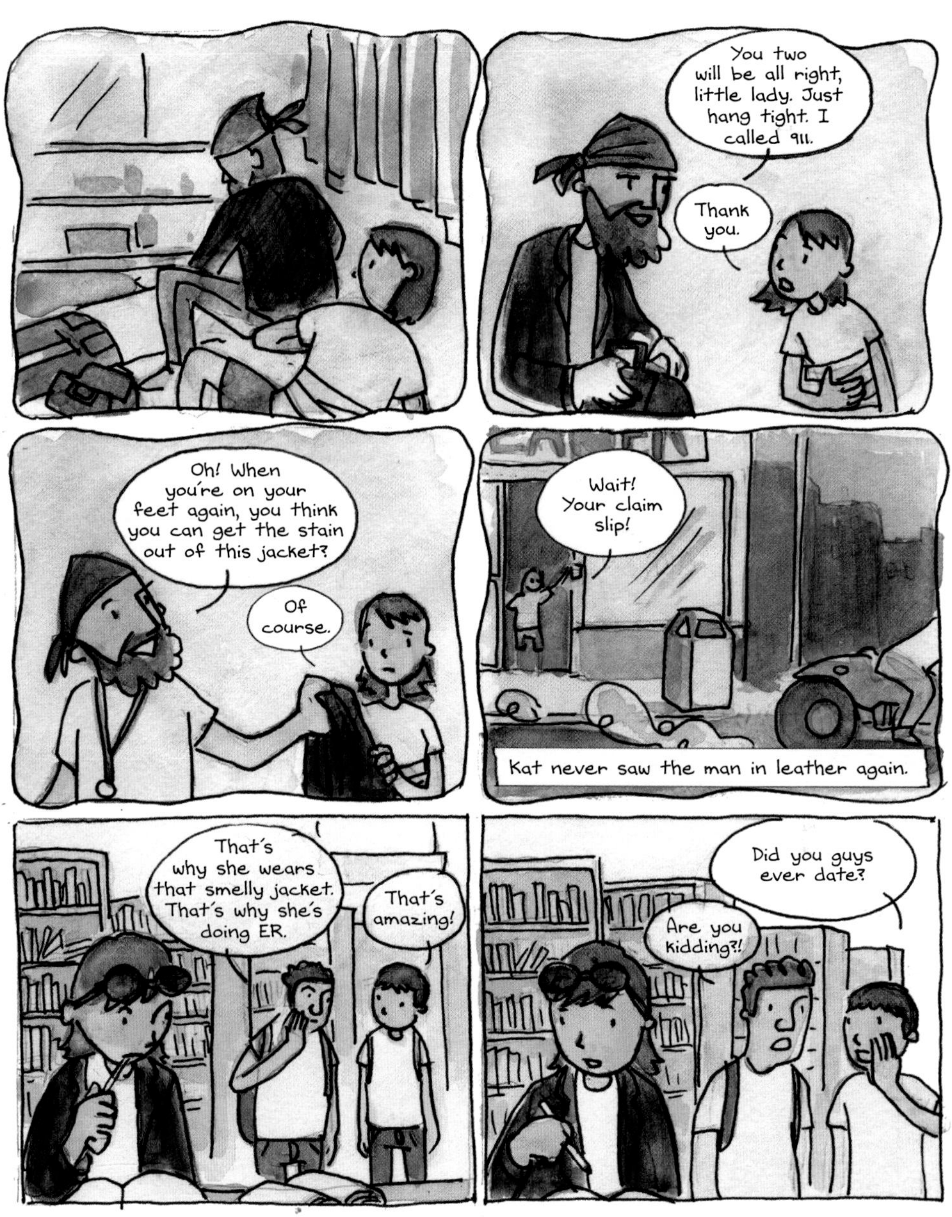

You two will be all right, little lady. Just hang tight. I called 911.
Thank you.
Oh! When you're on your feet again, you think you can get the stain out of this jacket?
Of course.
Wait! Your claim slip!
Kat never saw the man in leather again.
That's why she wears that smelly jacket. That's why she's doing ER.
That's amazing!
Did you guys ever date?
Are you kidding?!

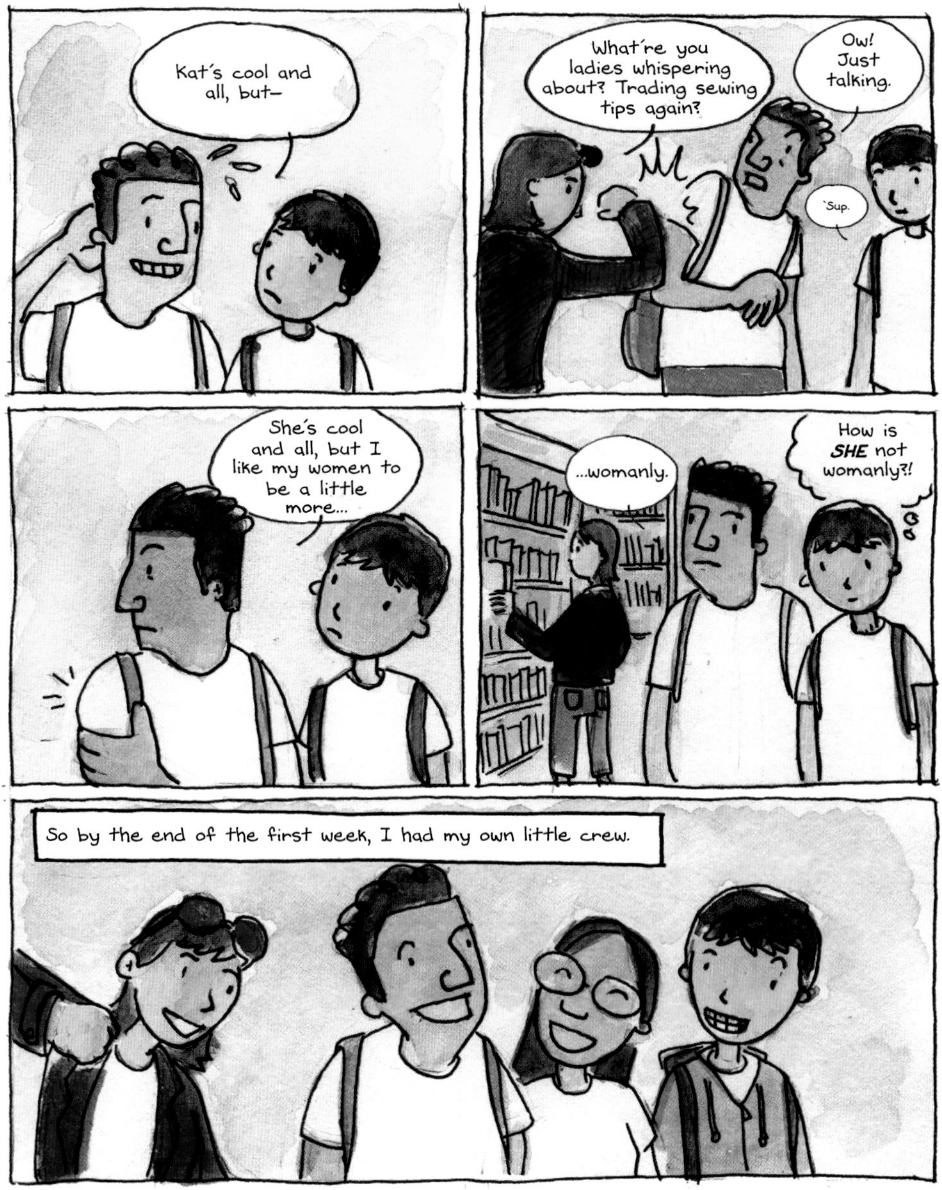
Kat's cool and all, but—
What're you ladies whispering about? Trading sewing tips again?
Ow! Just talking.
'Sup.
She's cool and all, but I like my women to be a little more...
...womanly.
How is **SHE** not womanly?!
So by the end of the first week, I had my own little crew.

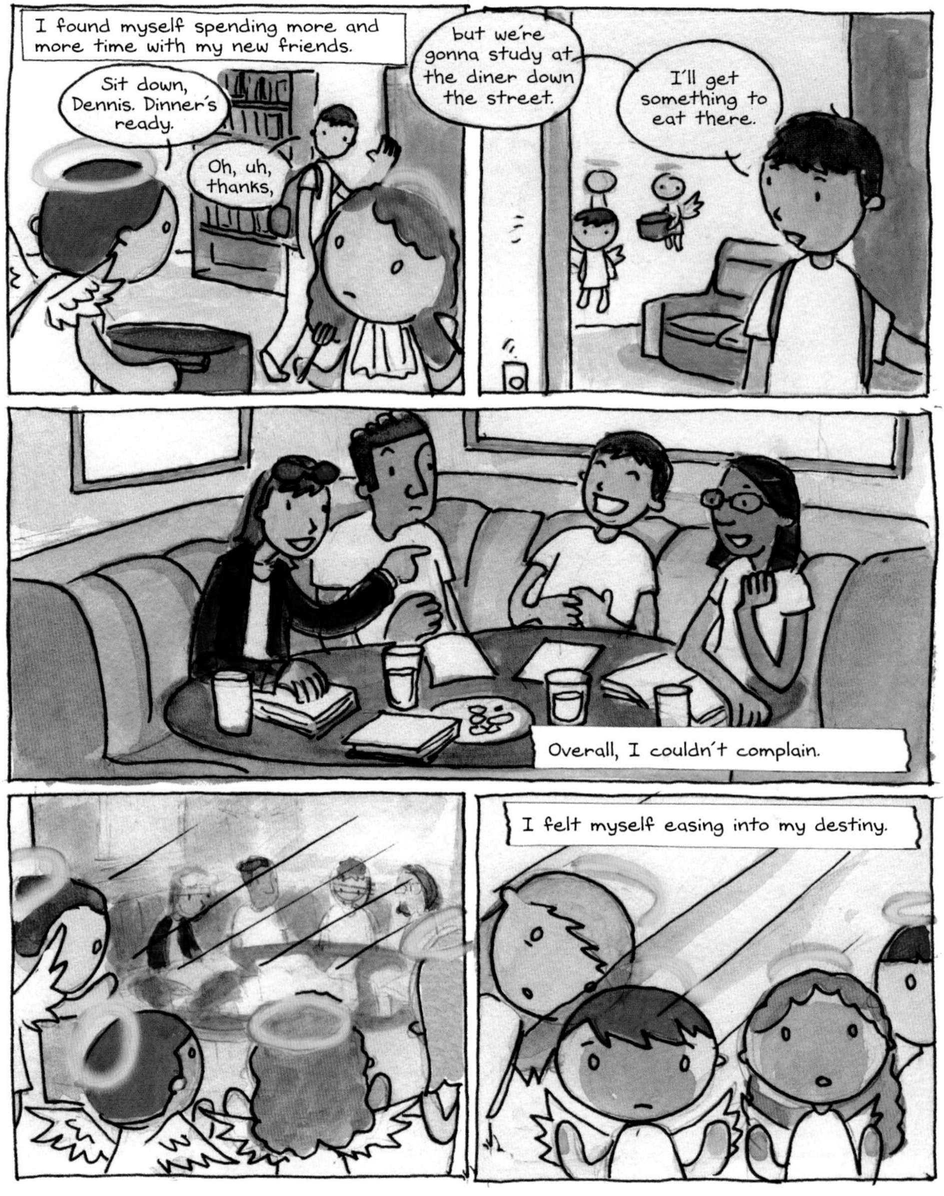
I found myself spending more and more time with my new friends.
Sit down, Dennis. Dinner's ready.
Oh, uh, thanks,
but we're gonna study at the diner down the street.
I'll get something to eat there.
Overall, I couldn't complain.
I felt myself easing into my destiny.

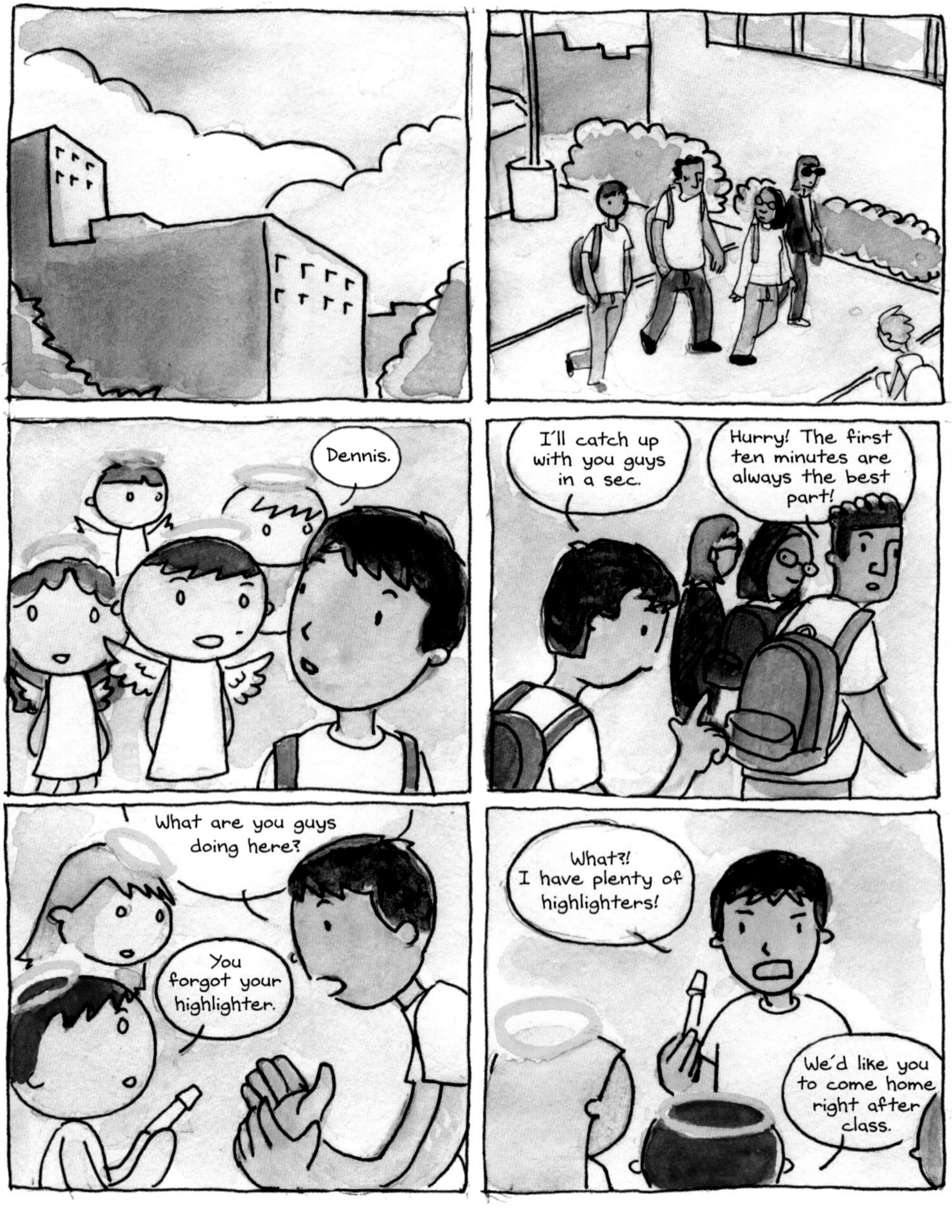
Dennis.
I'll catch up with you guys in a sec.
Hurry! The first ten minutes are always the best part!
What are you guys doing here?
You forgot your highlighter.
What?! I have plenty of highlighters!
We'd like you to come home right after class.

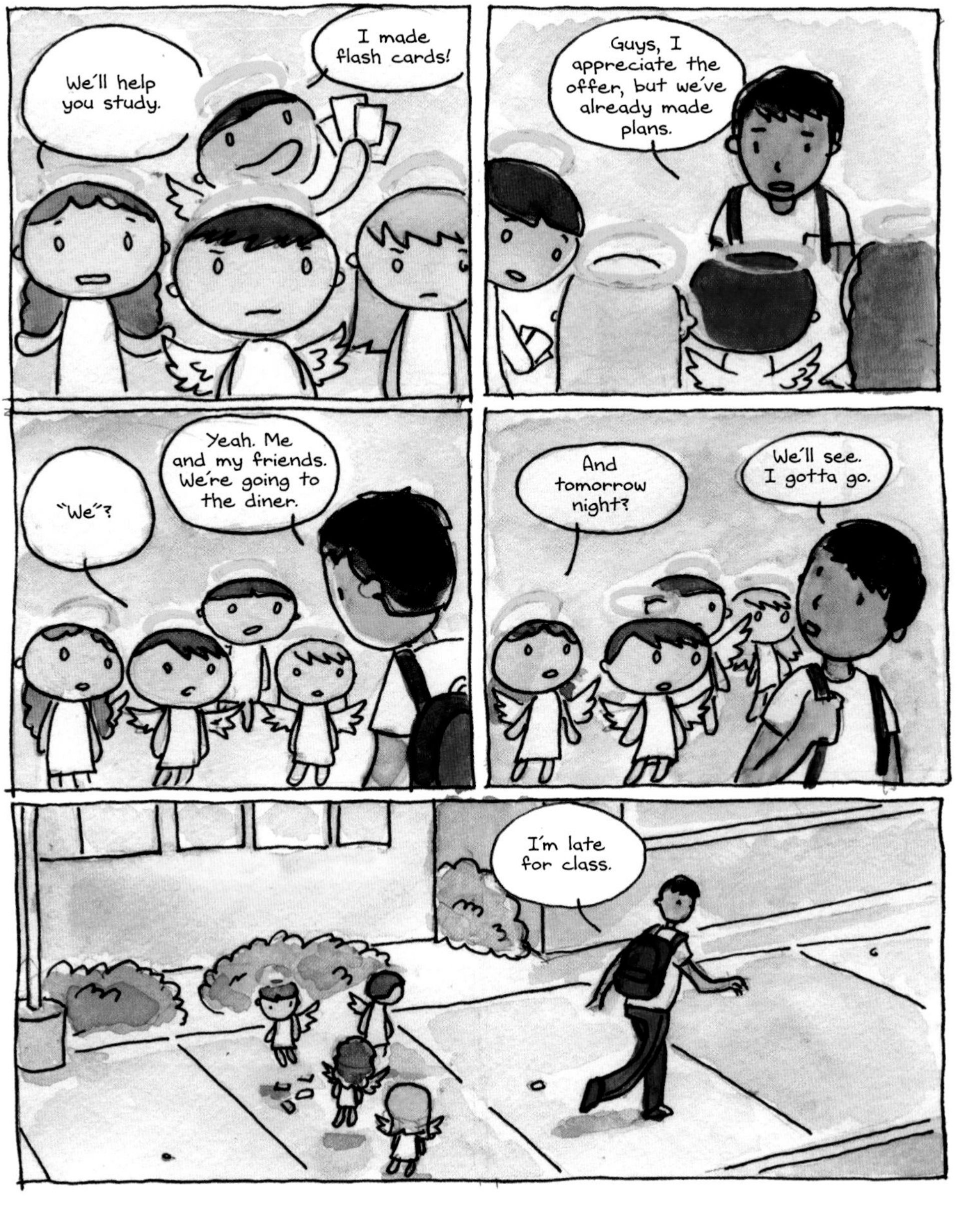
We'll help you study.
I made flash cards!
Guys, I appreciate the offer, but we've already made plans.
"We"?
Yeah. Me and my friends. We're going to the diner.
And tomorrow night?
We'll see. I gotta go.
I'm late for class.

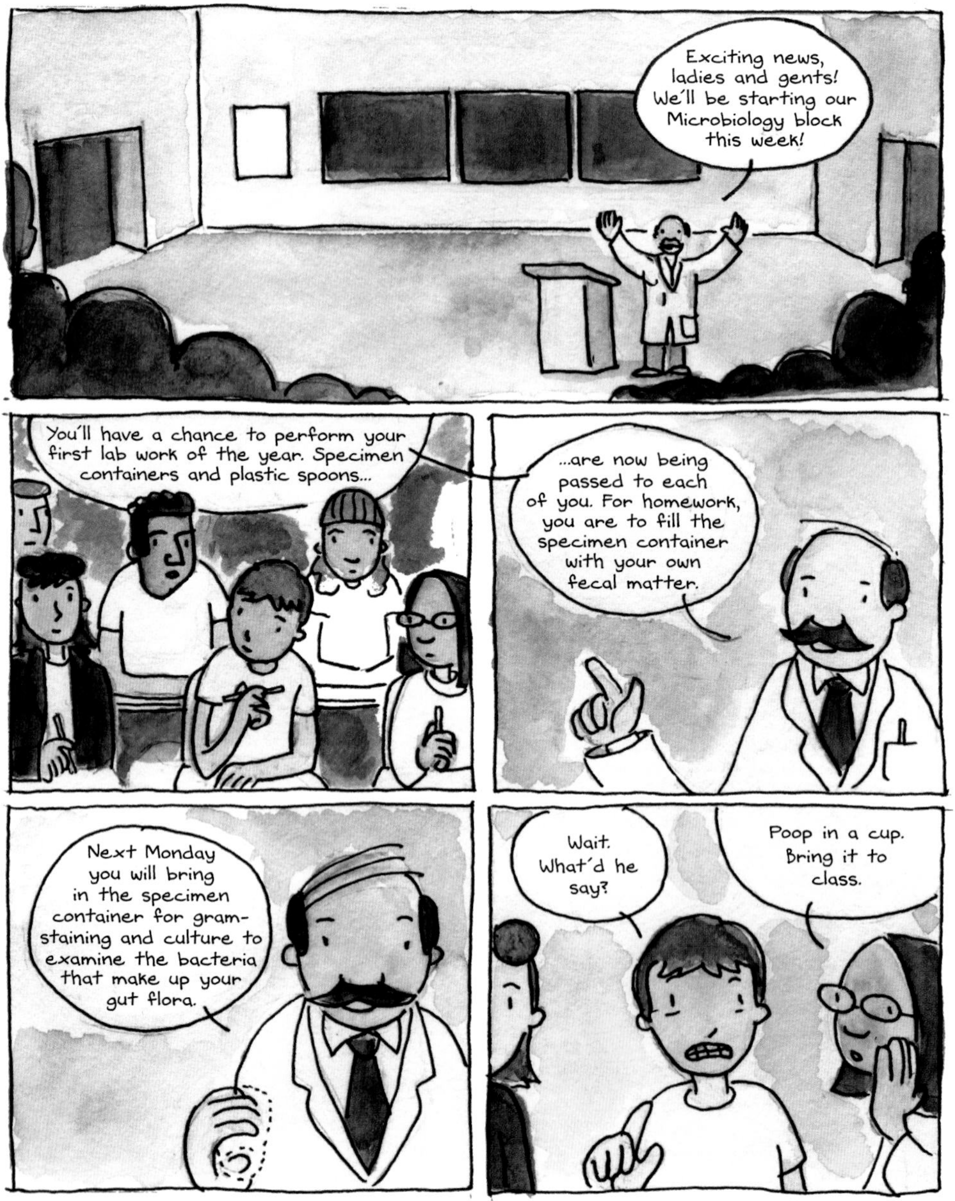
Exciting news, ladies and gents! We'll be starting our Microbiology block this week!
You'll have a chance to perform your first lab work of the year. Specimen containers and plastic spoons...
...are now being passed to each of you. For homework, you are to fill the specimen container with your own fecal matter.
Next Monday you will bring in the specimen container for gram-staining and culture to examine the bacteria that make up your gut flora.
Wait. What'd he say?
Poop in a cup. Bring it to class.

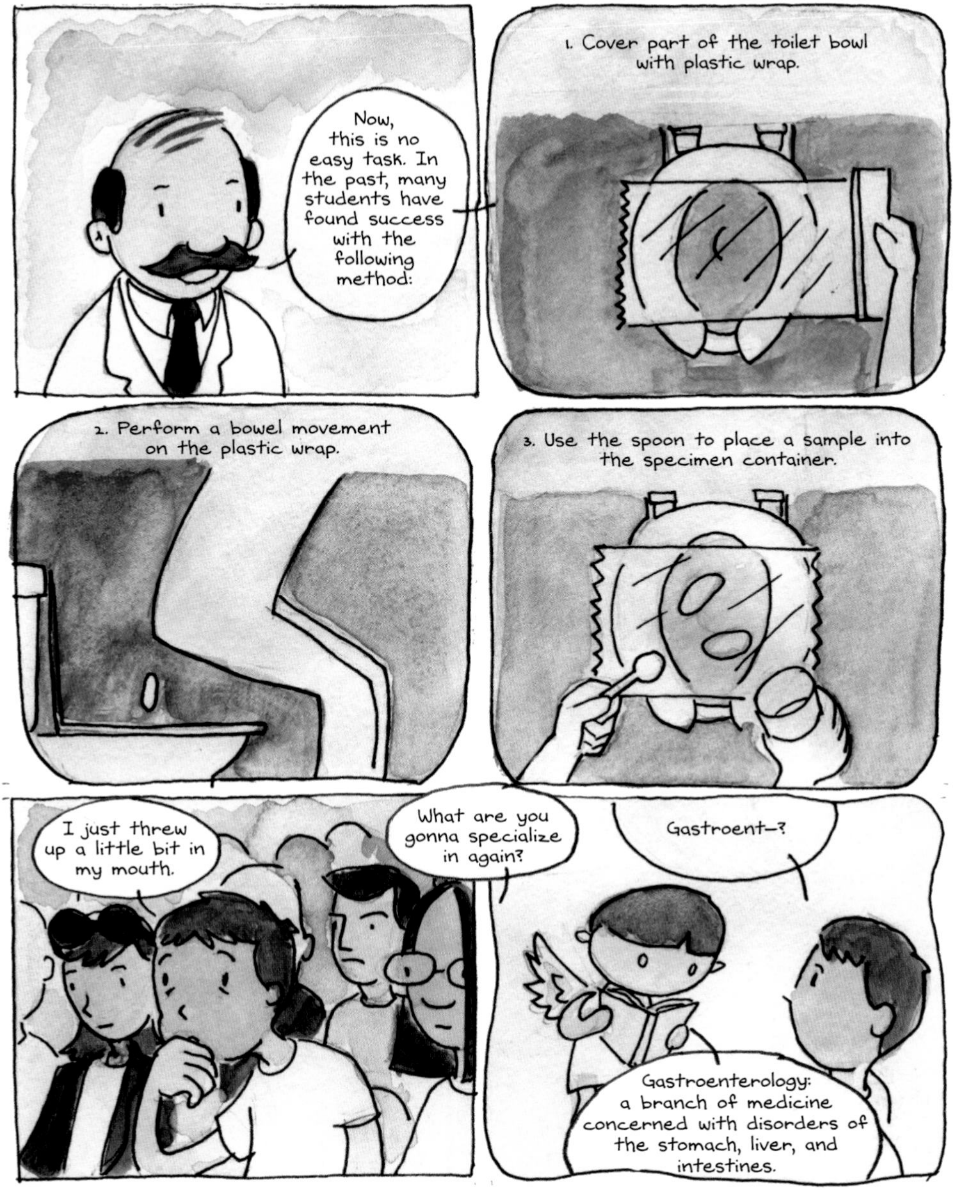
Now, this is no easy task. In the past, many students have found success with the following method:
1. Cover part of the toilet bowl with plastic wrap.
2. Perform a bowel movement on the plastic wrap.
3. Use the spoon to place a sample into the specimen container.
I just threw up a little bit in my mouth.
What are you gonna specialize in again?
Gastroent—?
Gastroenterology: a branch of medicine concerned with disorders of the stomach, liver, and intestines.

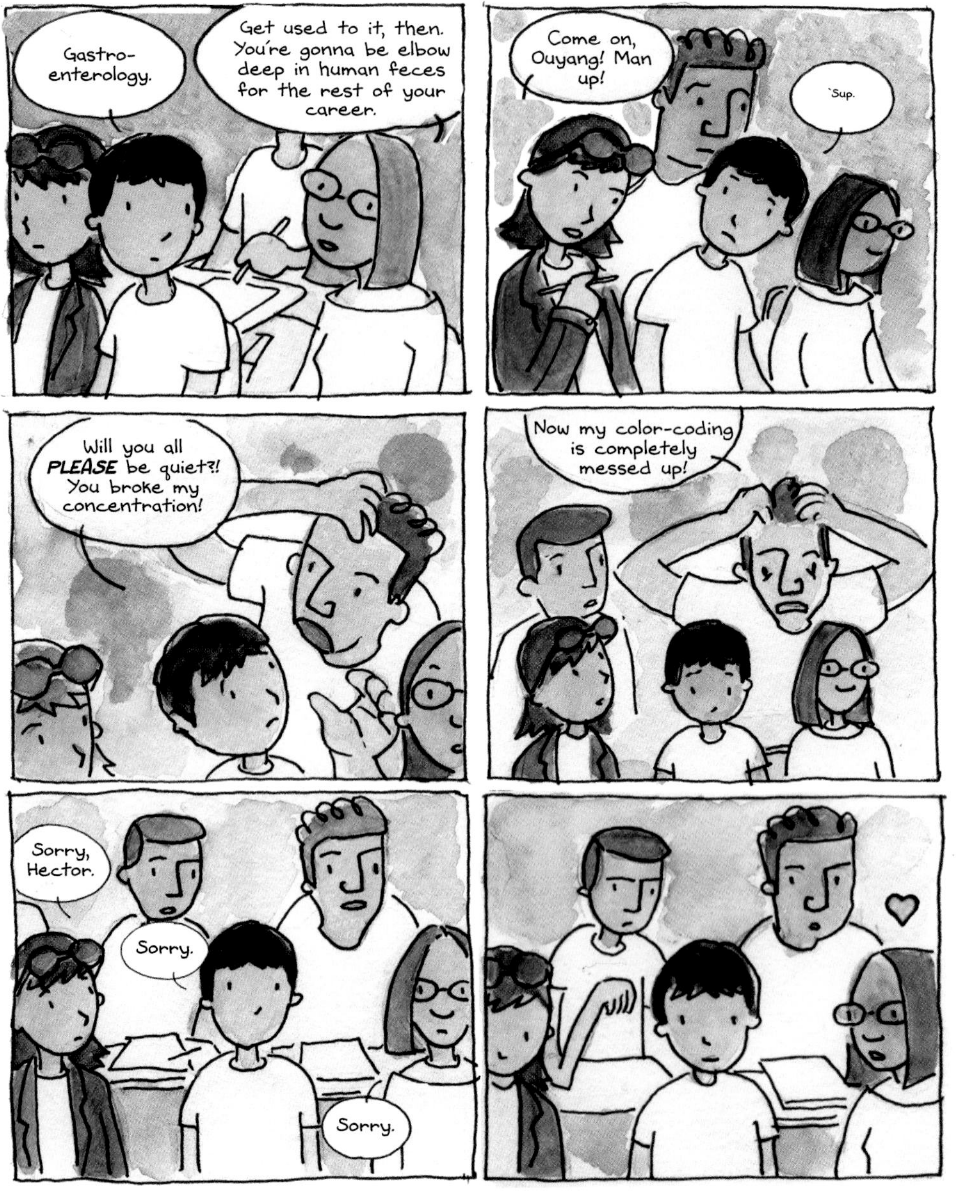
Gastro-enterology.
Get used to it, then. You're gonna be elbow deep in human feces for the rest of your career.
Come on, Ouyang! Man up!
`Sup.
Will you all **PLEASE** be quiet?! You broke my concentration!
Now my color-coding is completely messed up!
Sorry, Hector.
Sorry.
Sorry.

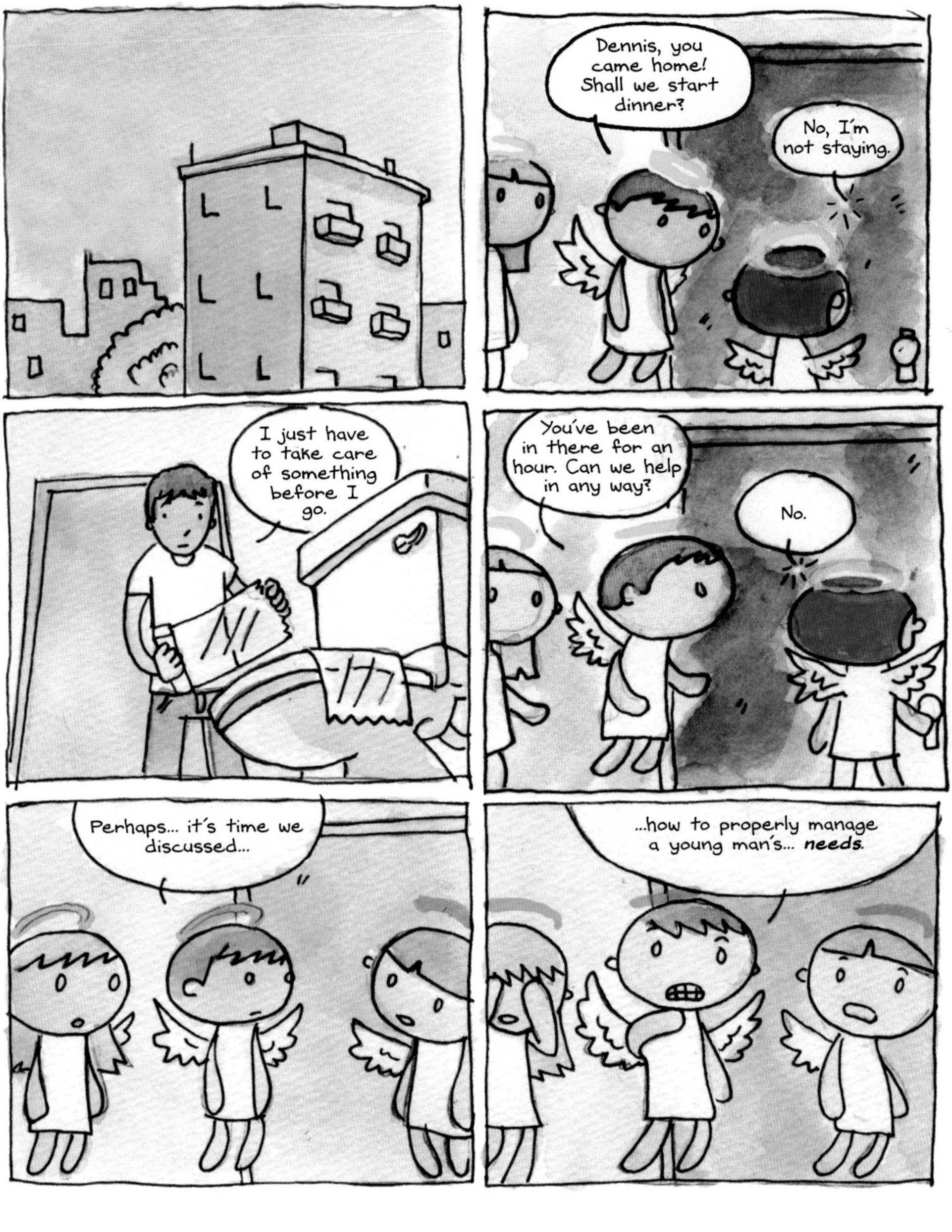
Dennis, you came home! Shall we start dinner?
No, I´m not staying.
I just have to take care of something before I go.
You´ve been in there for an hour. Can we help in any way?
No.
Perhaps... it´s time we discussed...
...how to properly manage a young man´s... **needs**.

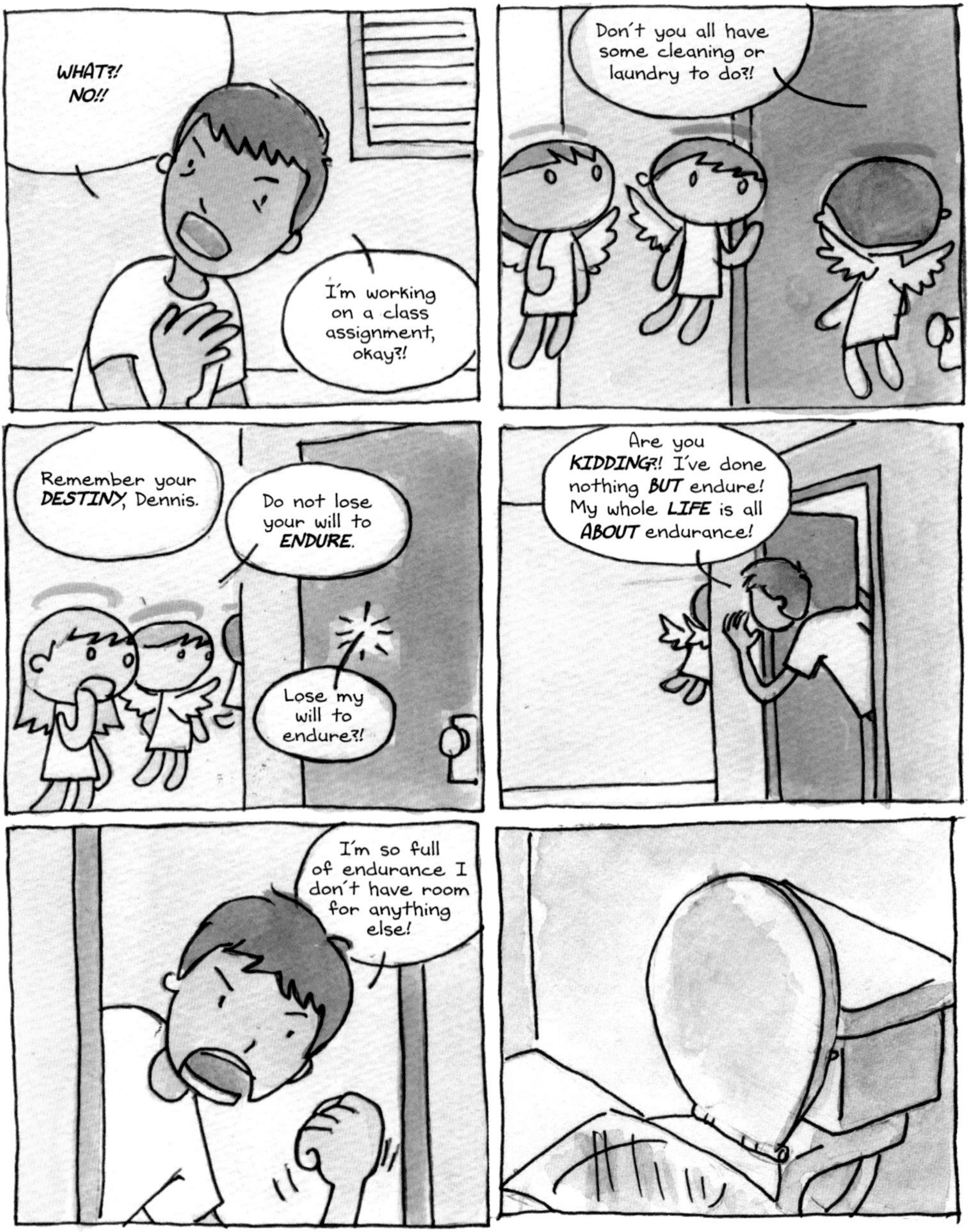
WHAT?! NO!!
I'm working on a class assignment, okay?!
Don't you all have some cleaning or laundry to do?!
Remember your DESTINY, Dennis.
Do not lose your will to ENDURE.
Lose my will to endure?!
Are you KIDDING?! I've done nothing BUT endure! My whole LIFE is all ABOUT endurance!
I'm so full of endurance I don't have room for anything else!

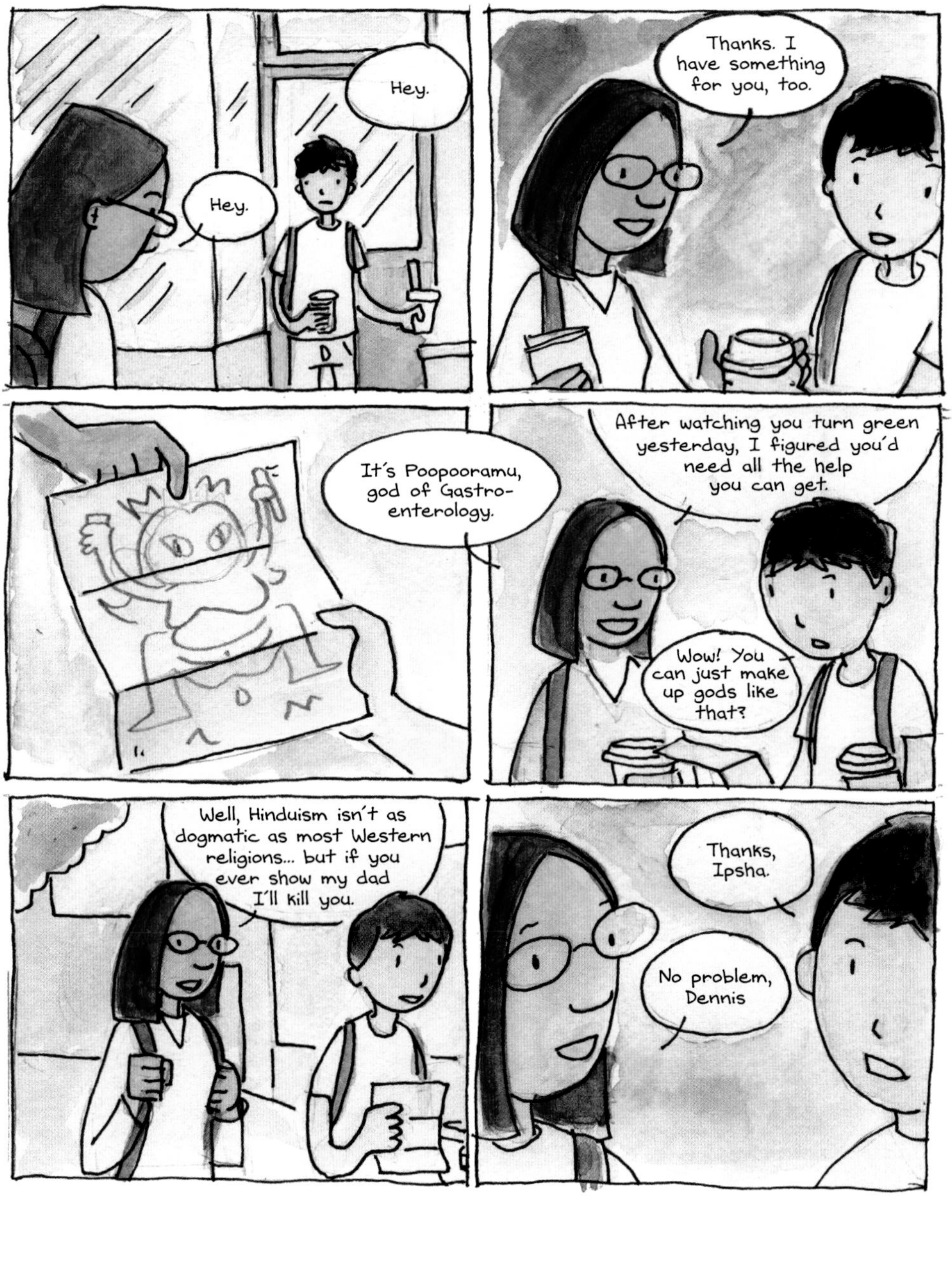
Hey.
Hey.
Thanks. I have something for you, too.
It´s Poopooramu, god of Gastro-enterology.
After watching you turn green yesterday, I figured you´d need all the help you can get.
Wow! You can just make up gods like that?
Well, Hinduism isn´t as dogmatic as most Western religions... but if you ever show my dad I´ll kill you.
Thanks, Ipsha.
No problem, Dennis

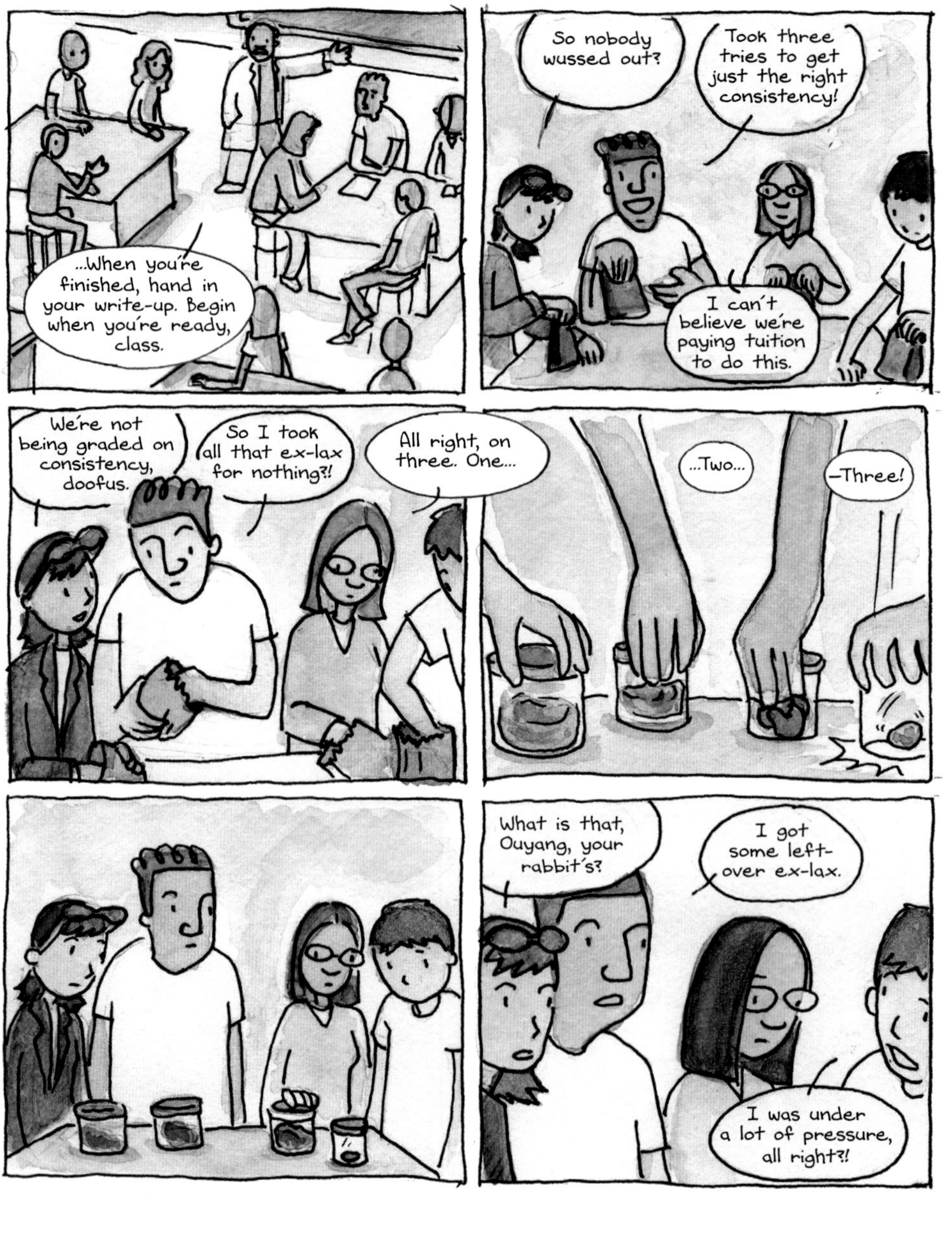
...When you're finished, hand in your write-up. Begin when you're ready, class.
So nobody wussed out?
Took three tries to get just the right consistency!
I can't believe we're paying tuition to do this.
We're not being graded on consistency, doofus.
So I took all that ex-lax for nothing?!
All right, on three. One...
...Two...
—Three!
What is that, Ouyang, your rabbit's?
I got some left-over ex-lax.
I was under a lot of pressure, all right?!

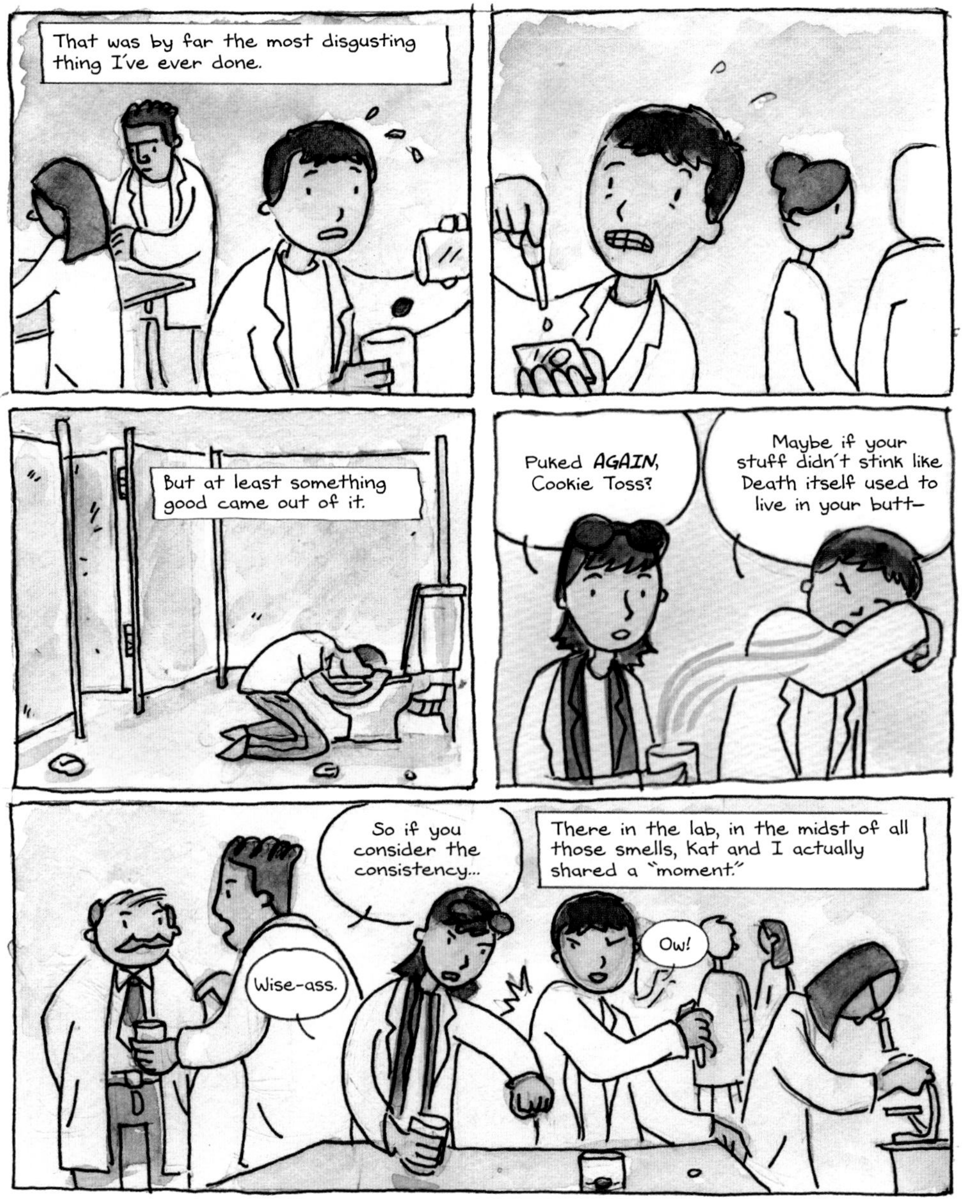

That was by far the most disgusting thing I've ever done.
But at least something good came out of it.
Puked **AGAIN**, Cookie Toss?
Maybe if your stuff didn't stink like Death itself used to live in your butt—
So if you consider the consistency...
There in the lab, in the midst of all those smells, Kat and I actually shared a "moment."
Wise-ass.
Ow!

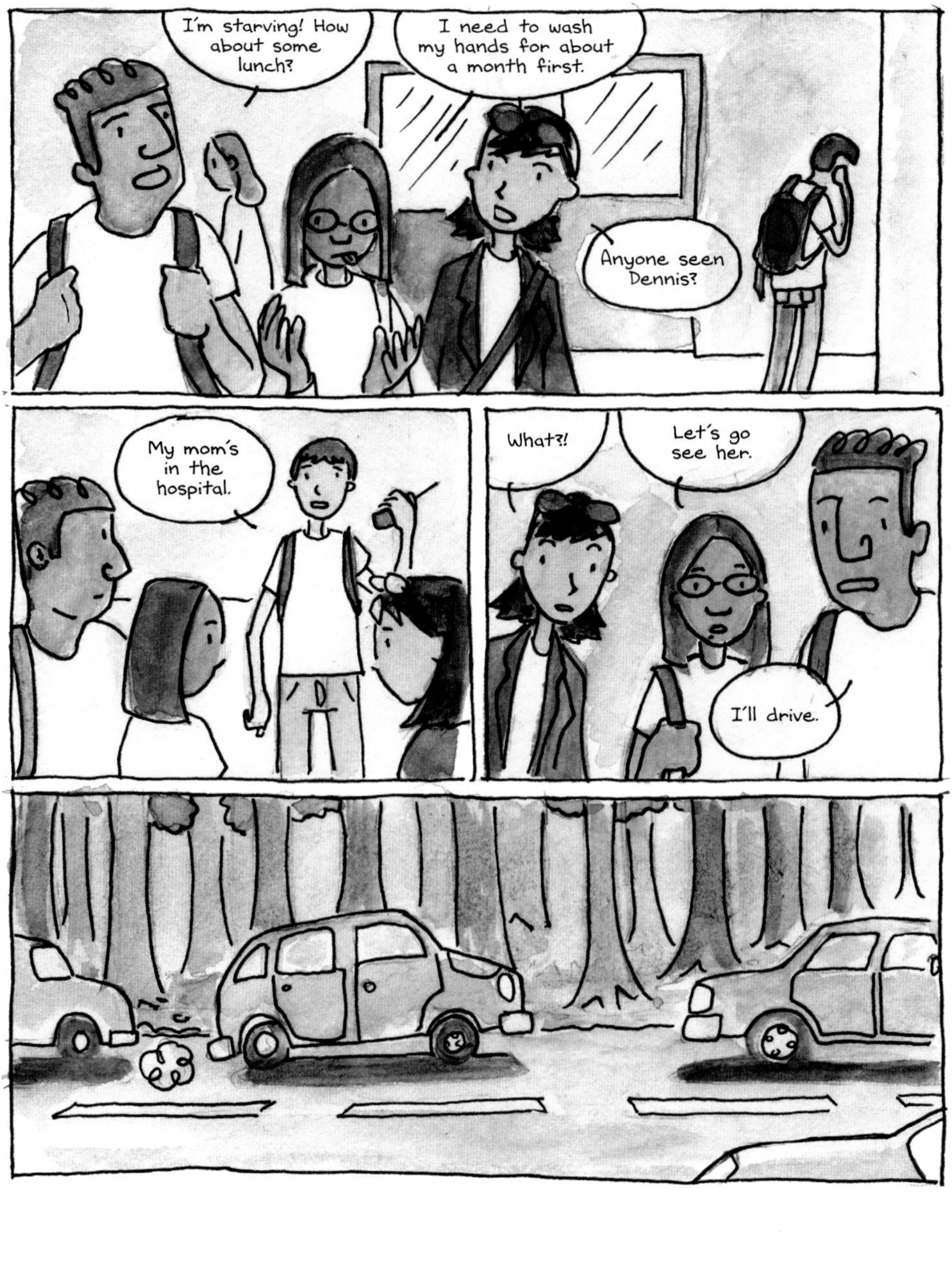
I'm starving! How about some lunch?
I need to wash my hands for about a month first.
Anyone seen Dennis?
My mom's in the hospital.
What?!
Let's go see her.
I'll drive.

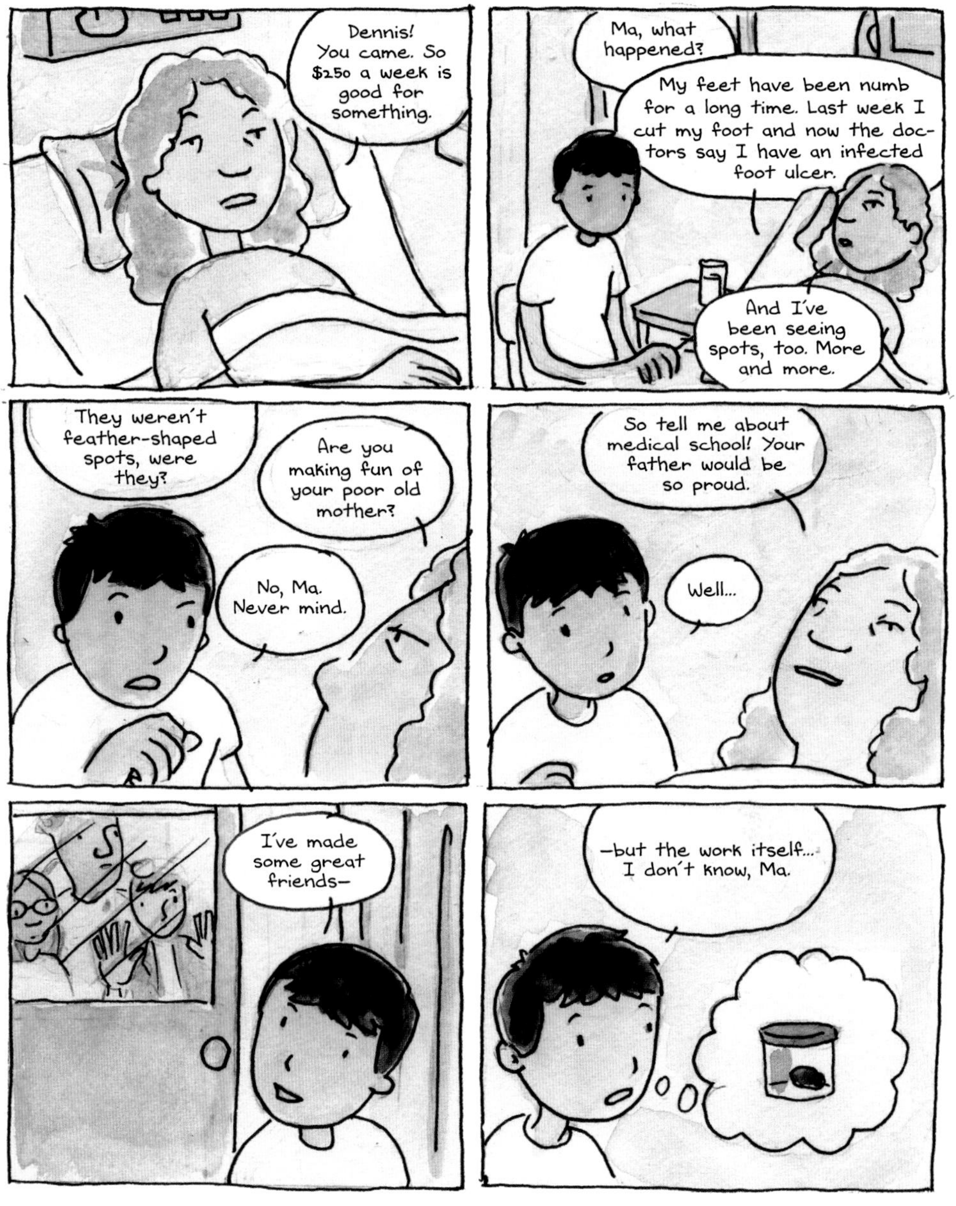
Dennis! You came. So $250 a week is good for something.
Ma, what happened?
My feet have been numb for a long time. Last week I cut my foot and now the doctors say I have an infected foot ulcer.
And I've been seeing spots, too. More and more.
They weren't feather-shaped spots, were they?
Are you making fun of your poor old mother?
No, Ma. Never mind.
So tell me about medical school! Your father would be so proud.
Well...
I've made some great friends—
—but the work itself... I don't know, Ma.

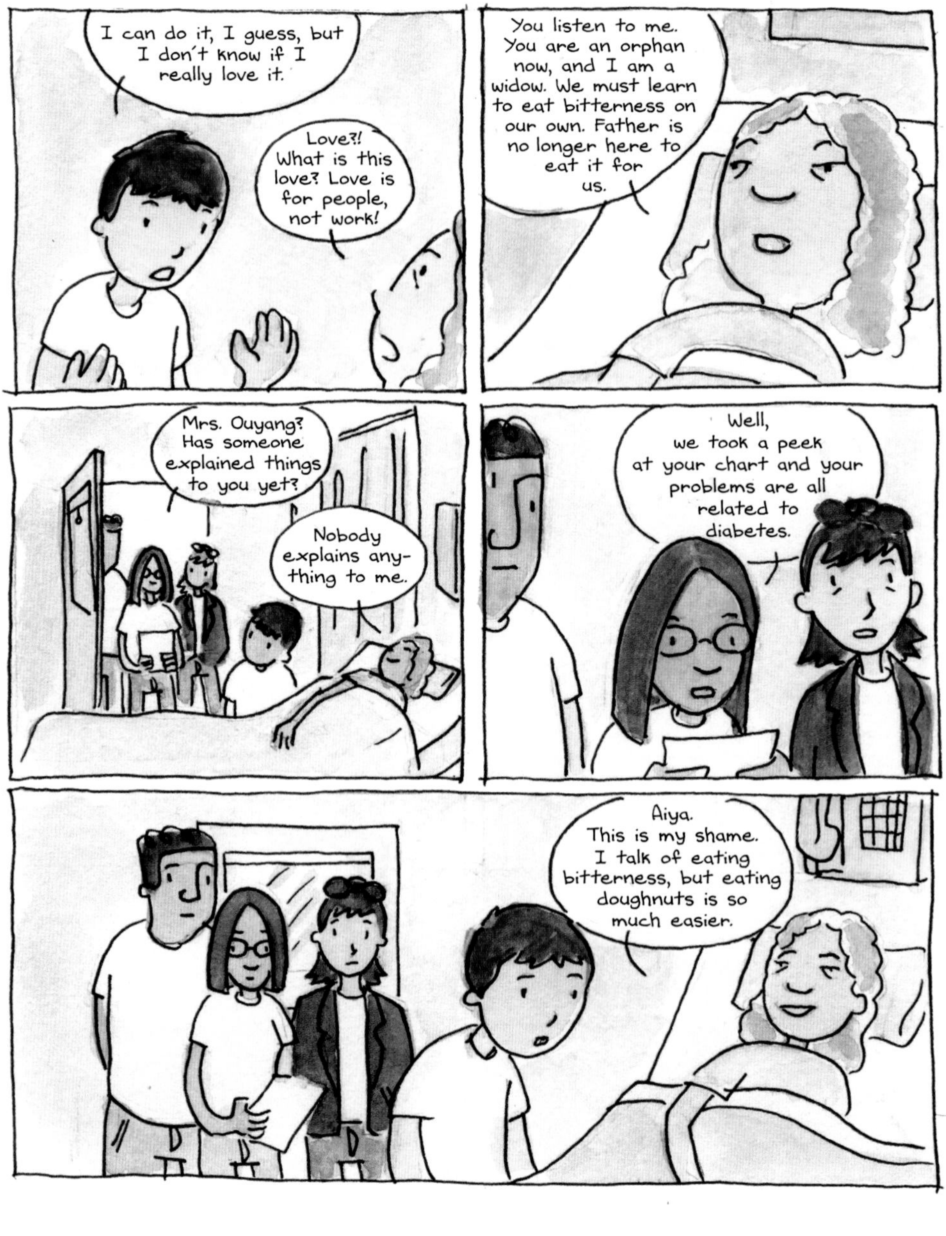
I can do it, I guess, but I don't know if I really love it.
Love?! What is this love? Love is for people, not work!
You listen to me. You are an orphan now, and I am a widow. We must learn to eat bitterness on our own. Father is no longer here to eat it for us.
Mrs. Ouyang? Has someone explained things to you yet?
Nobody explains anything to me.
Well, we took a peek at your chart and your problems are all related to diabetes.
Aiya. This is my shame. I talk of eating bitterness, but eating doughnuts is so much easier.

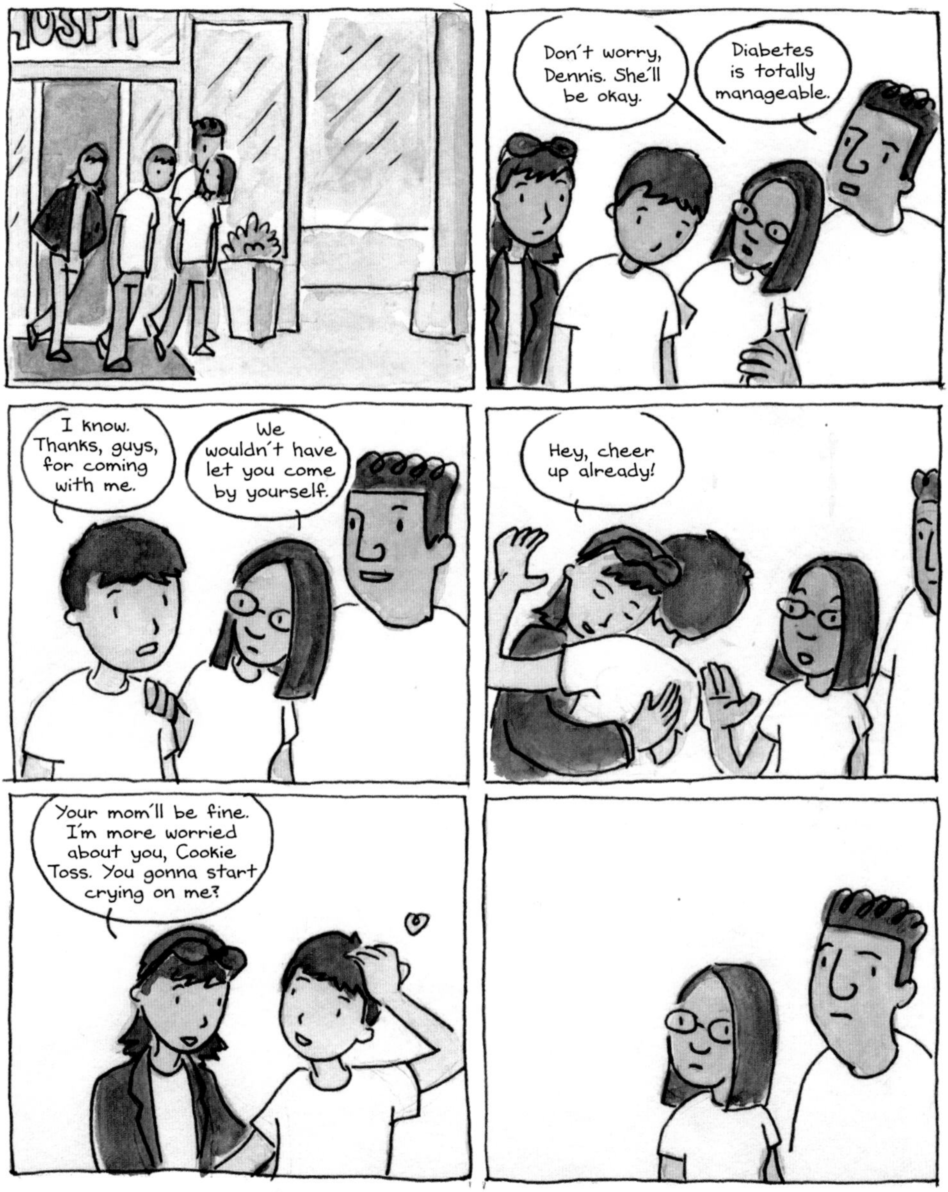

HOSPIT
Don't worry, Dennis. She'll be okay.
Diabetes is totally manageable.
I know. Thanks, guys, for coming with me.
We wouldn't have let you come by yourself.
Hey, cheer up already!
Your mom'll be fine. I'm more worried about you, Cookie Toss. You gonna start crying on me?

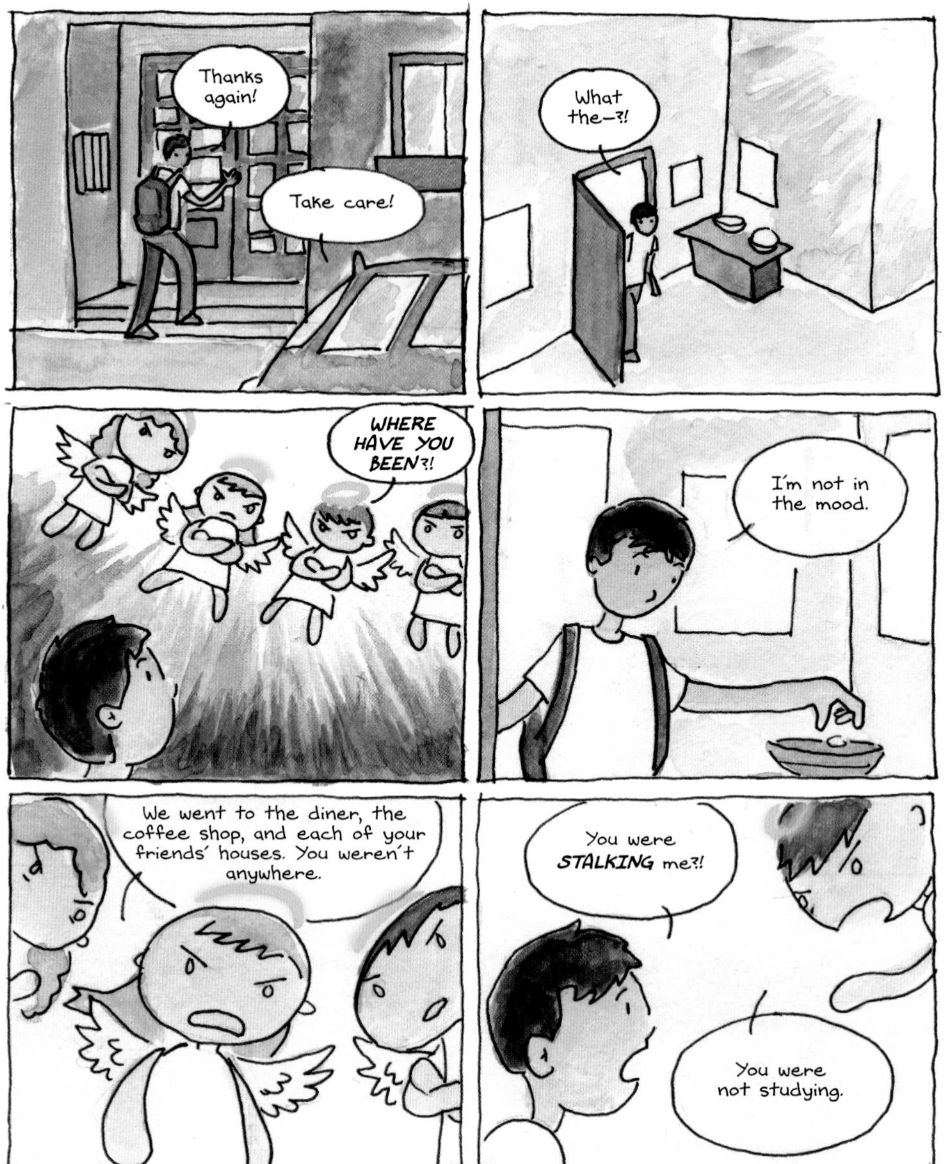
Thanks again!
Take care!
What the–?!
WHERE HAVE YOU BEEN?!
I'm not in the mood.
We went to the diner, the coffee shop, and each of your friends' houses. You weren't anywhere.
You were STALKING me?!
You were not studying.

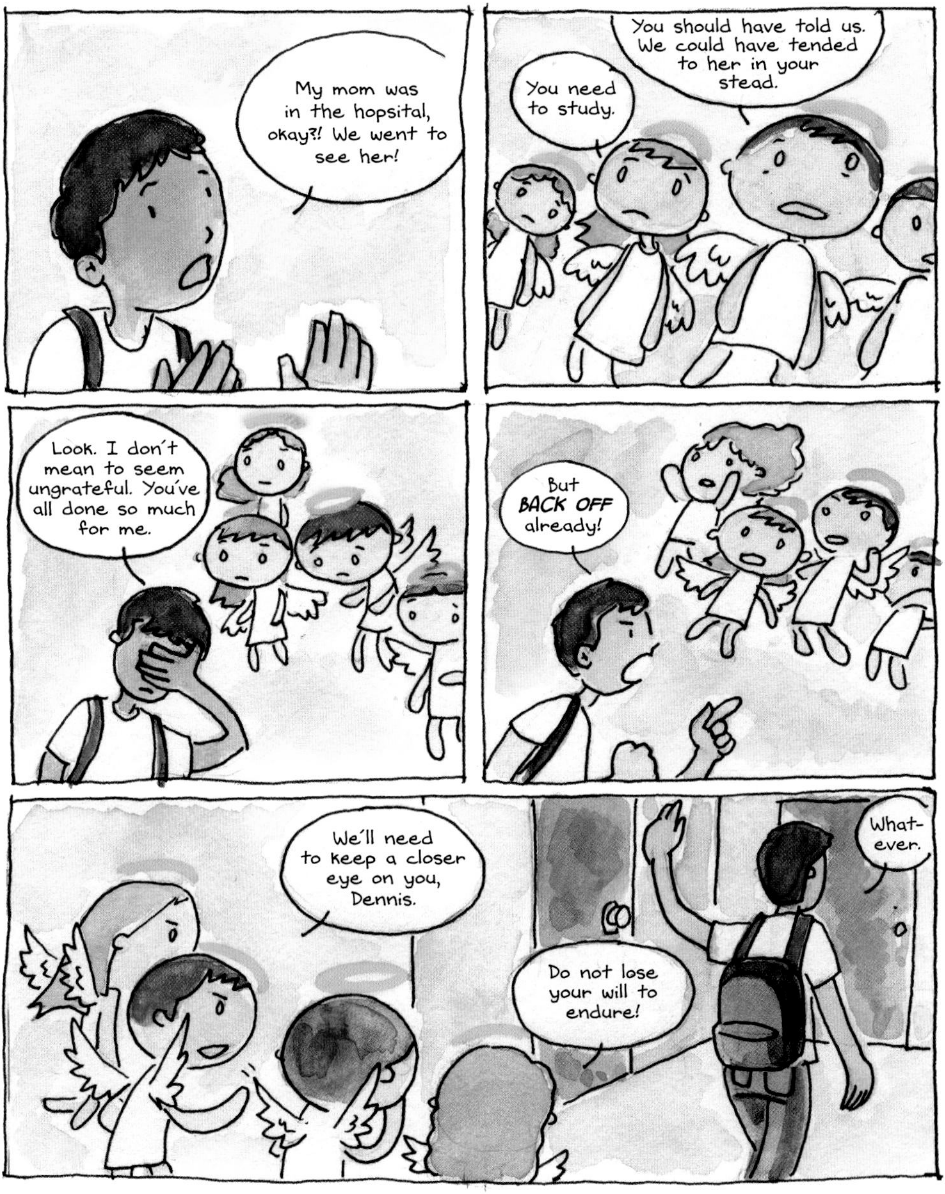
My mom was in the hopsital, okay?! We went to see her!
You should have told us. We could have tended to her in your stead.
You need to study.
Look. I don't mean to seem ungrateful. You've all done so much for me.
But BACK OFF already!
We'll need to keep a closer eye on you, Dennis.
Do not lose your will to endure!
What-ever.

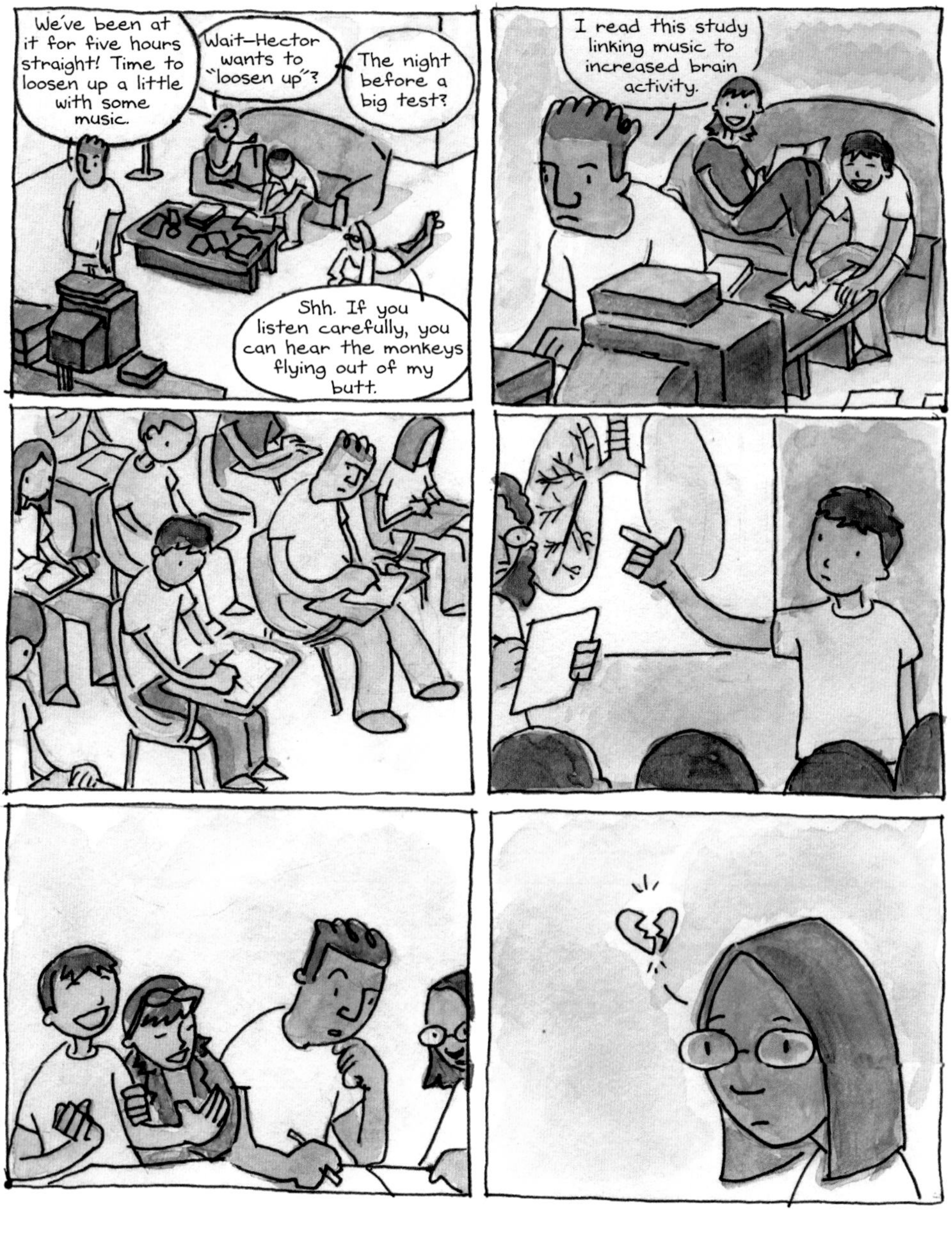
We've been at it for five hours straight! Time to loosen up a little with some music.
Wait—Hector wants to "loosen up"?
The night before a big test?
Shh. If you listen carefully, you can hear the monkeys flying out of my butt.
I read this study linking music to increased brain activity.

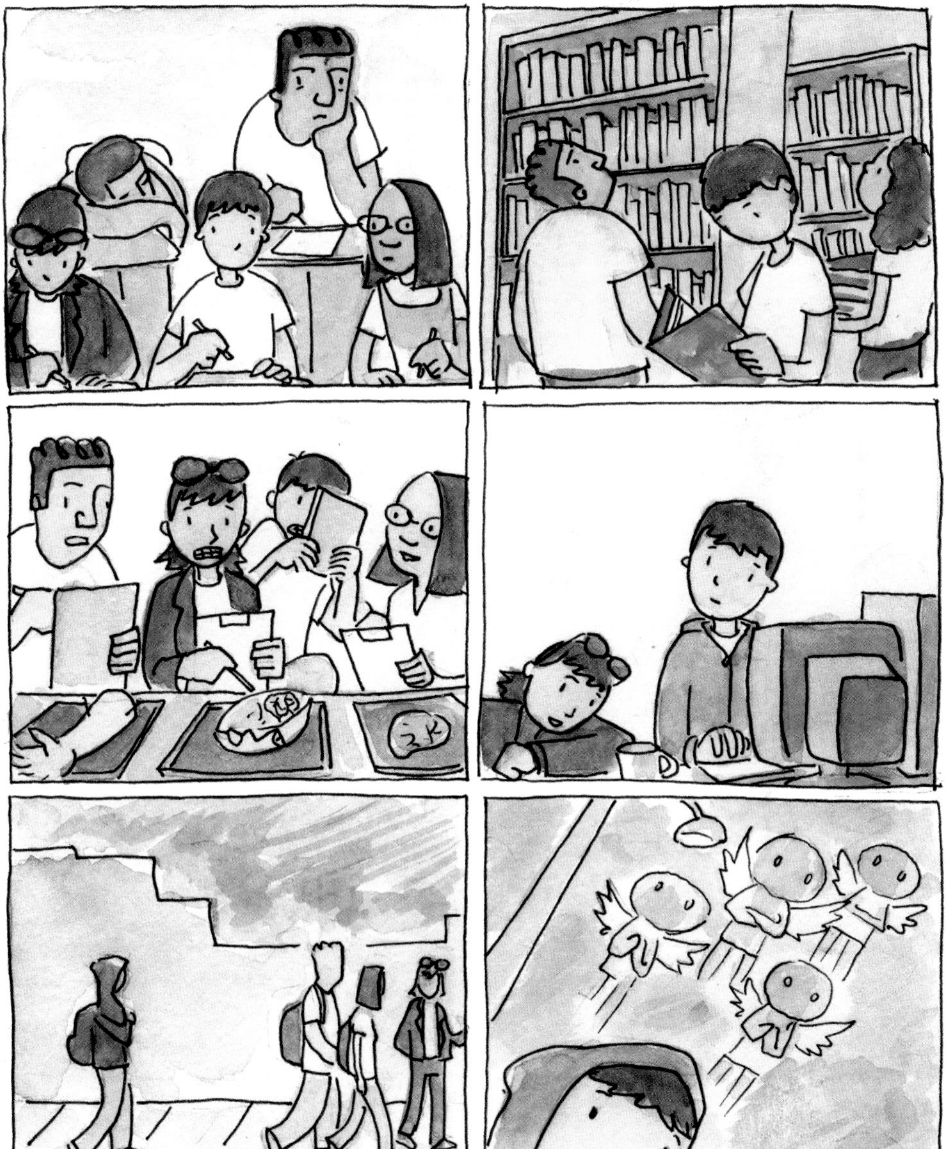

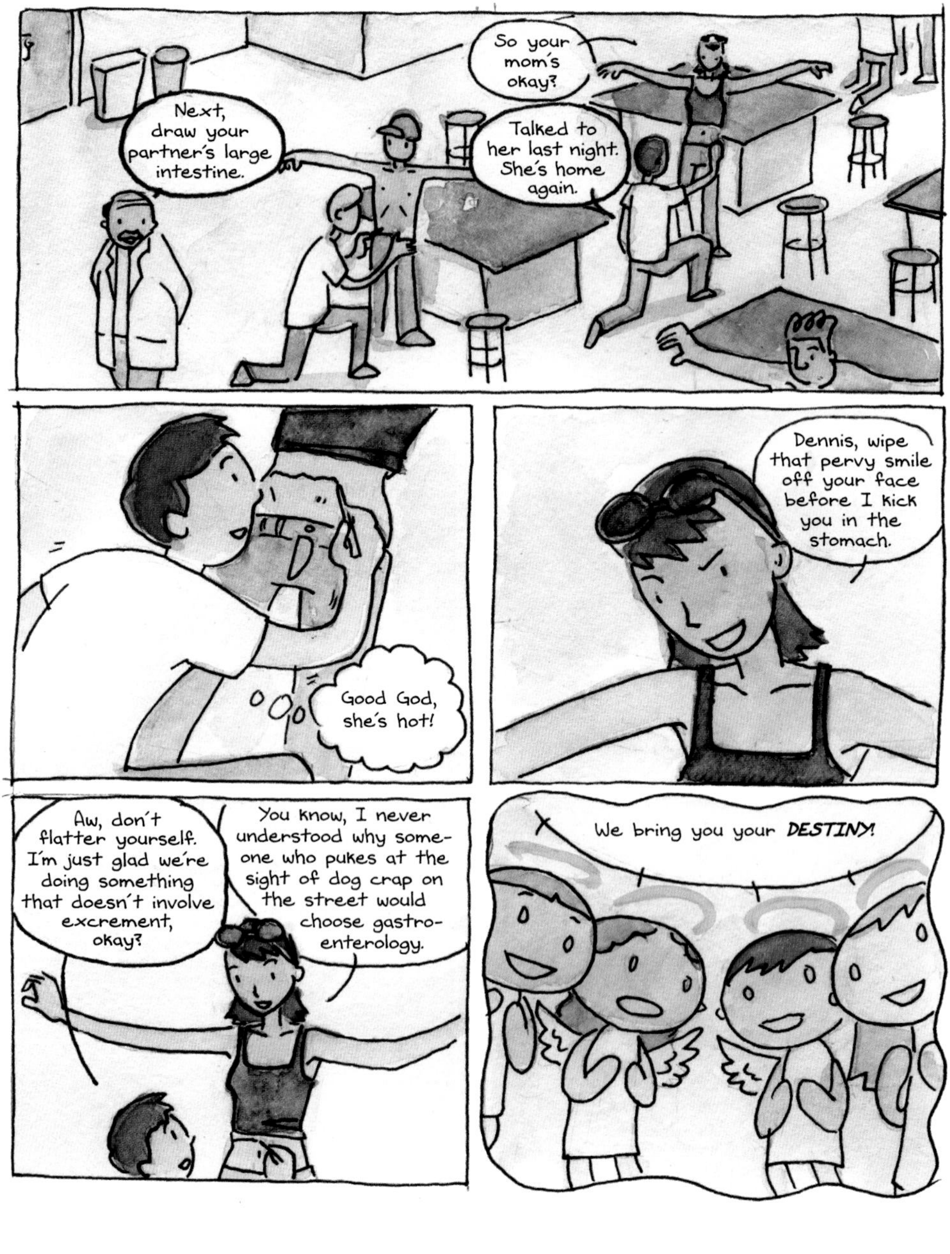
Next, draw your partner's large intestine.
So your mom's okay?
Talked to her last night. She's home again.
Good God, she's hot!
Dennis, wipe that pervy smile off your face before I kick you in the stomach.
Aw, don't flatter yourself. I'm just glad we're doing something that doesn't involve excrement, okay?
You know, I never understood why someone who pukes at the sight of dog crap on the street would choose gastroenterology.
We bring you your ***DESTINY!***

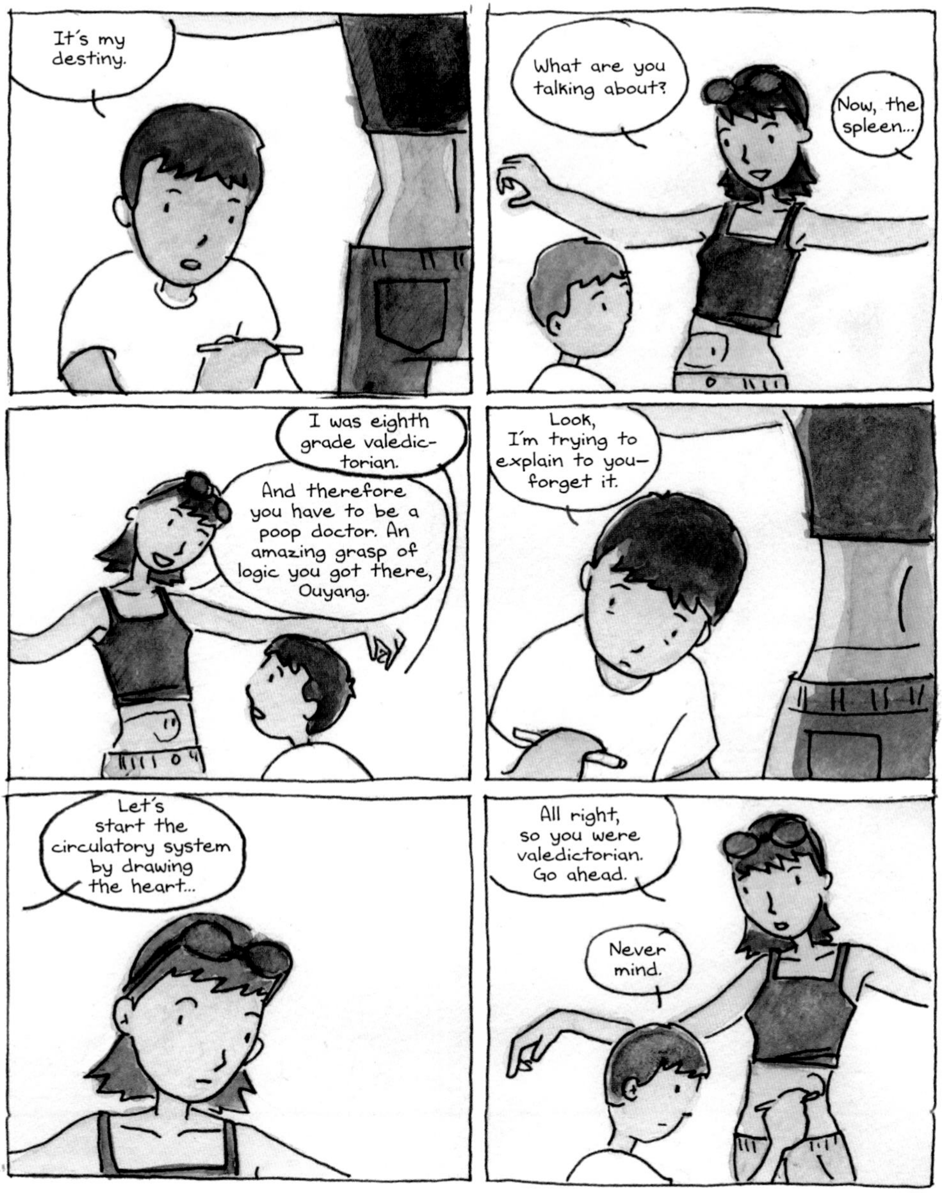
It's my destiny.
What are you talking about?
Now, the spleen...
I was eighth grade valedictorian.
And therefore you have to be a poop doctor. An amazing grasp of logic you got there, Ouyang.
Look, I'm trying to explain to you— forget it.
Let's start the circulatory system by drawing the heart...
All right, so you were valedictorian. Go ahead.
Never mind.

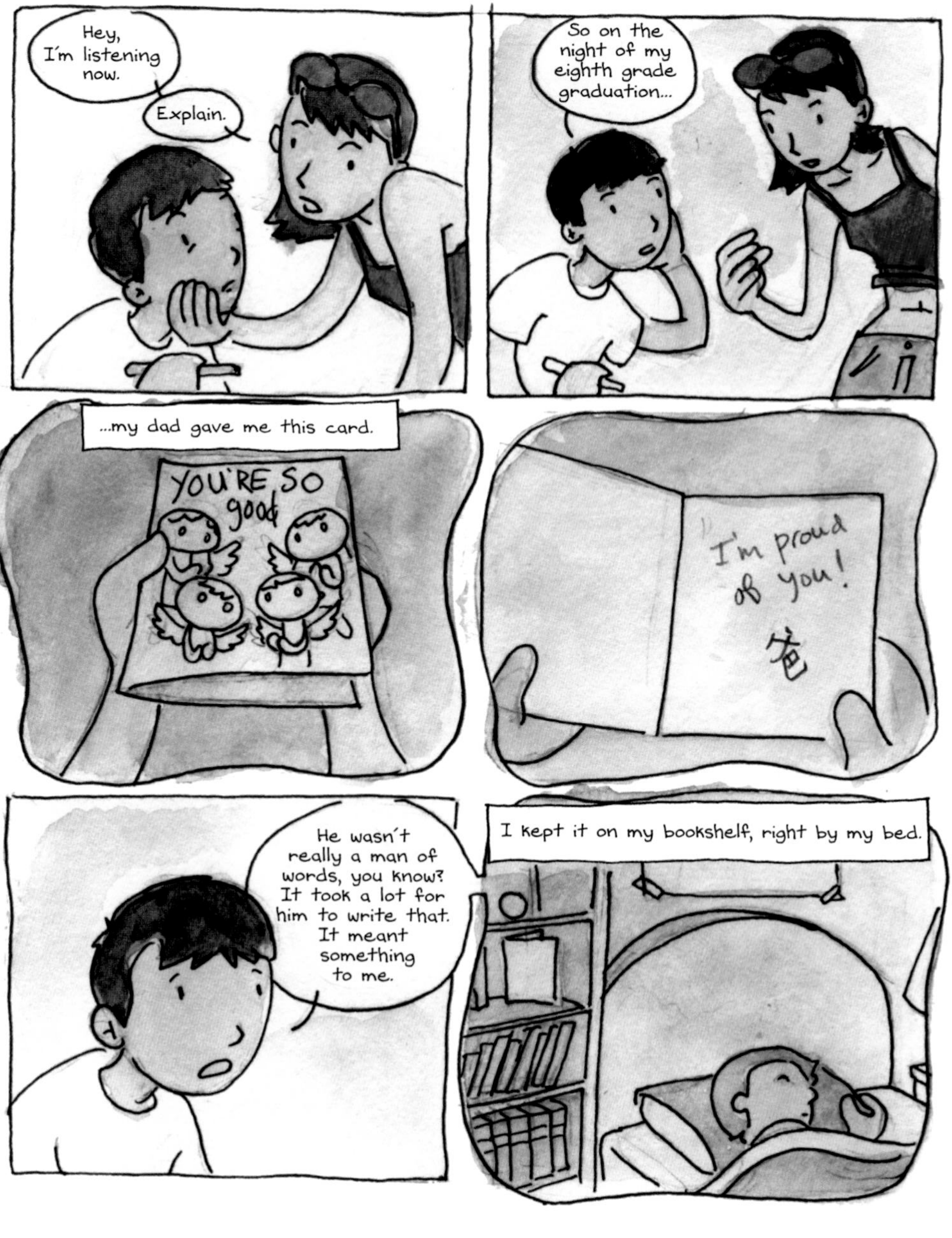
Hey, I'm listening now.
Explain.
So on the night of my eighth grade graduation...
...my dad gave me this card.
YOU'RE SO good
I'm proud of you!
爸
He wasn't really a man of words, you know? It took a lot for him to write that. It meant something to me.
I kept it on my bookshelf, right by my bed.

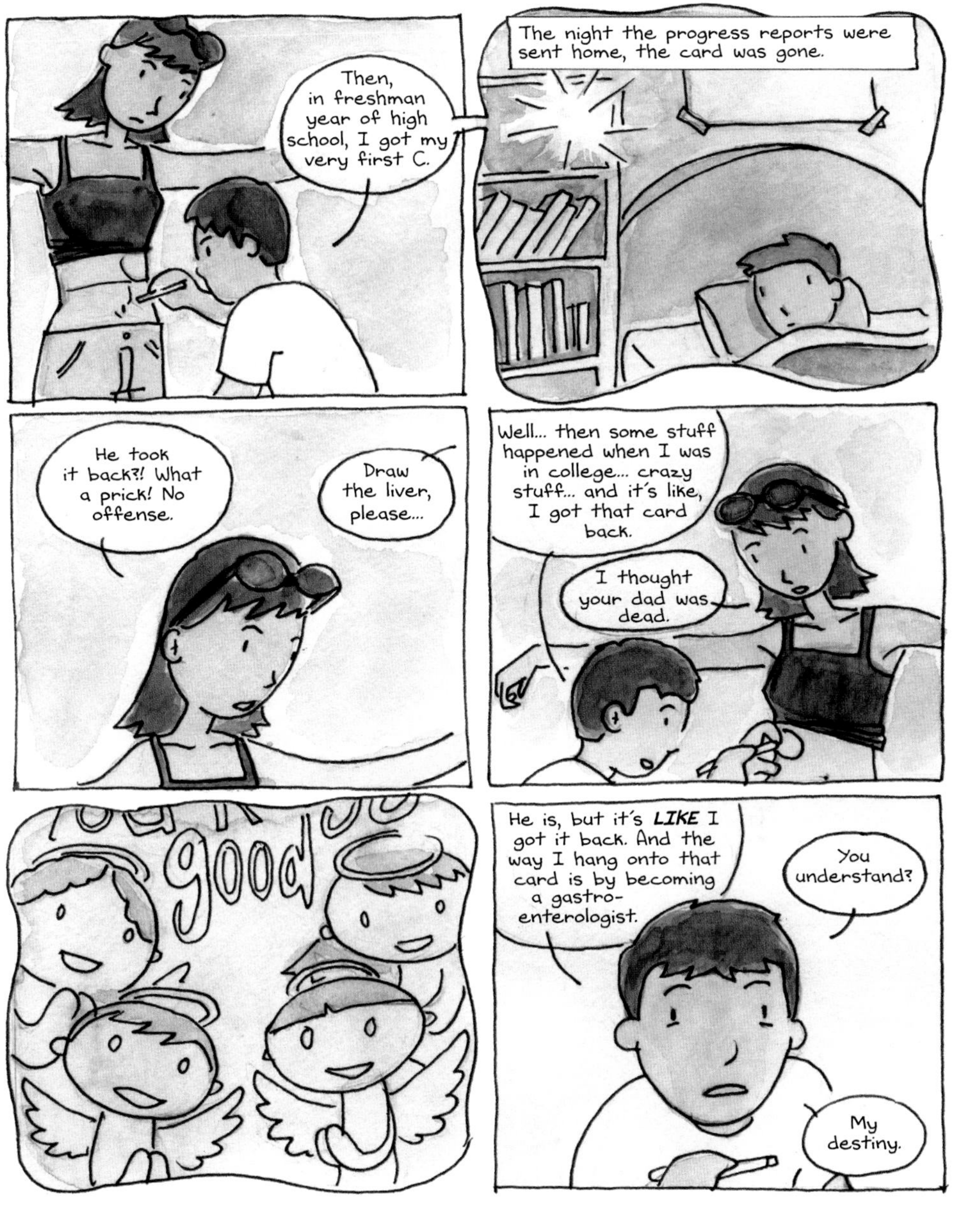
Then, in freshman year of high school, I got my very first C.
The night the progress reports were sent home, the card was gone.
He took it back?! What a prick! No offense.
Draw the liver, please...
Well... then some stuff happened when I was in college... crazy stuff... and it's like, I got that card back.
I thought your dad was dead.
good
He is, but it's **LIKE** I got it back. And the way I hang onto that card is by becoming a gastro-enterologist.
You understand?
My destiny.

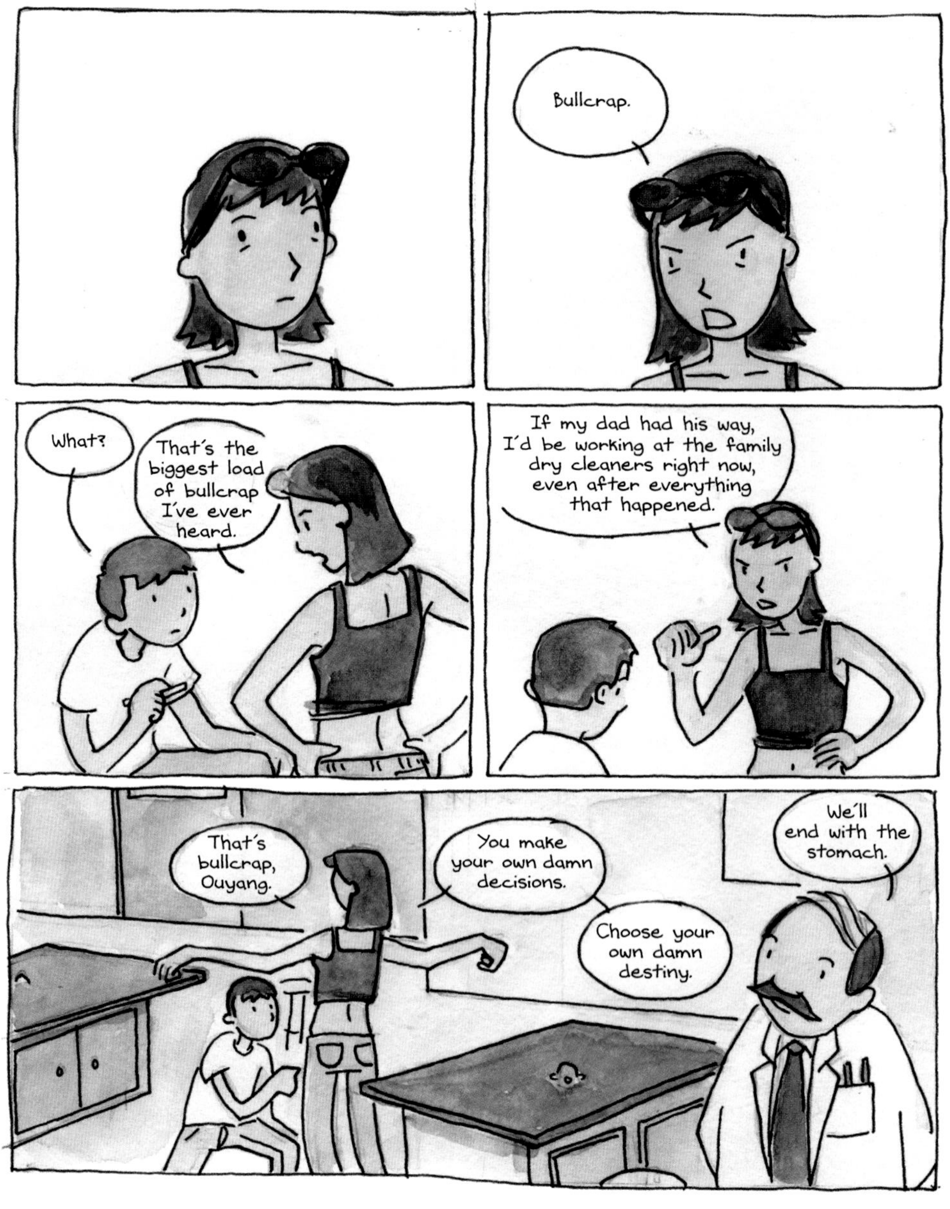
Bullcrap.
What?
That's the biggest load of bullcrap I've ever heard.
If my dad had his way, I'd be working at the family dry cleaners right now, even after everything that happened.
That's bullcrap, Ouyang.
You make your own damn decisions.
Choose your own damn destiny.
We'll end with the stomach.

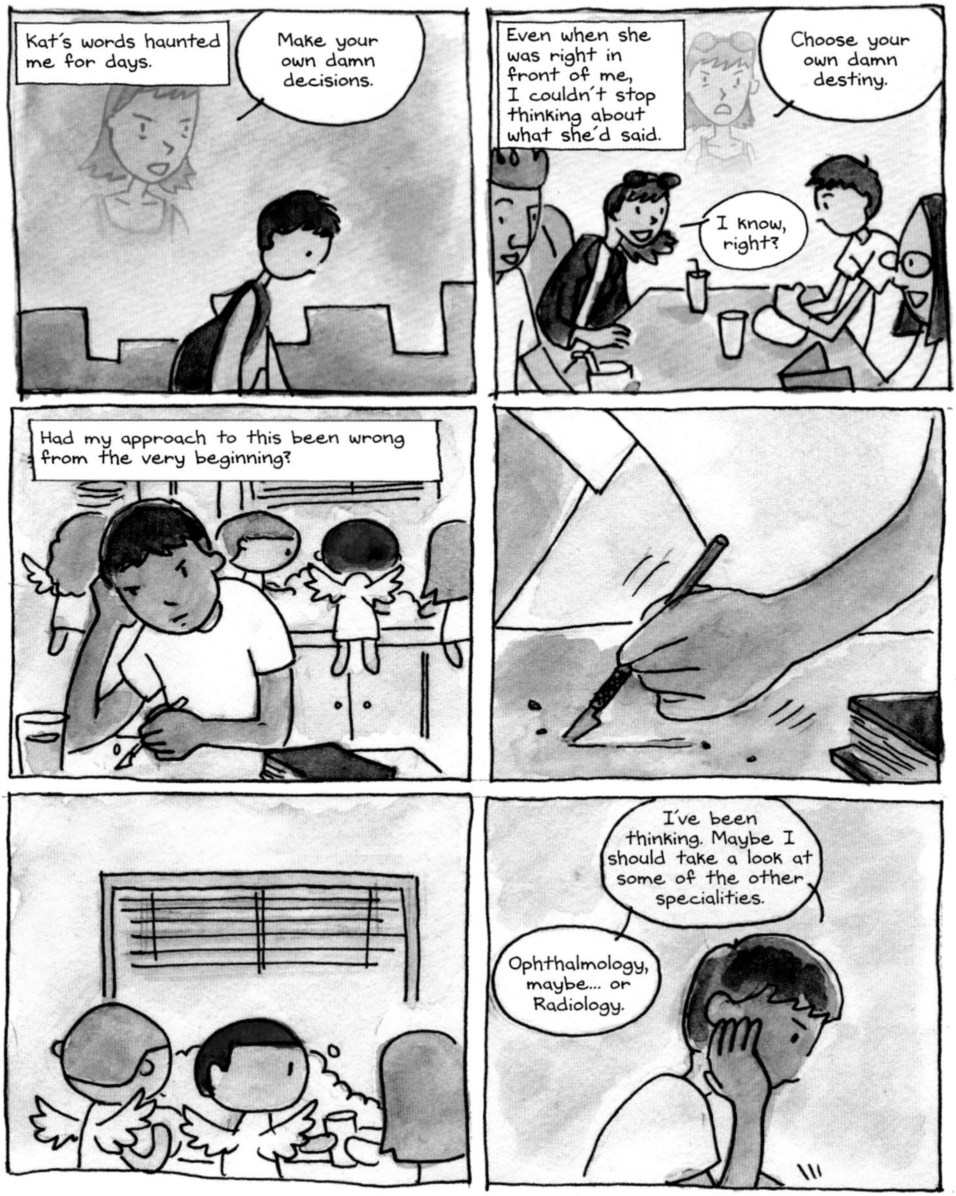

Kat's words haunted me for days.
Make your own damn decisions.
Even when she was right in front of me, I couldn't stop thinking about what she'd said.
Choose your own damn destiny.
I know, right?
Had my approach to this been wrong from the very beginning?
I've been thinking. Maybe I should take a look at some of the other specialities.
Ophthalmology, maybe... or Radiology.

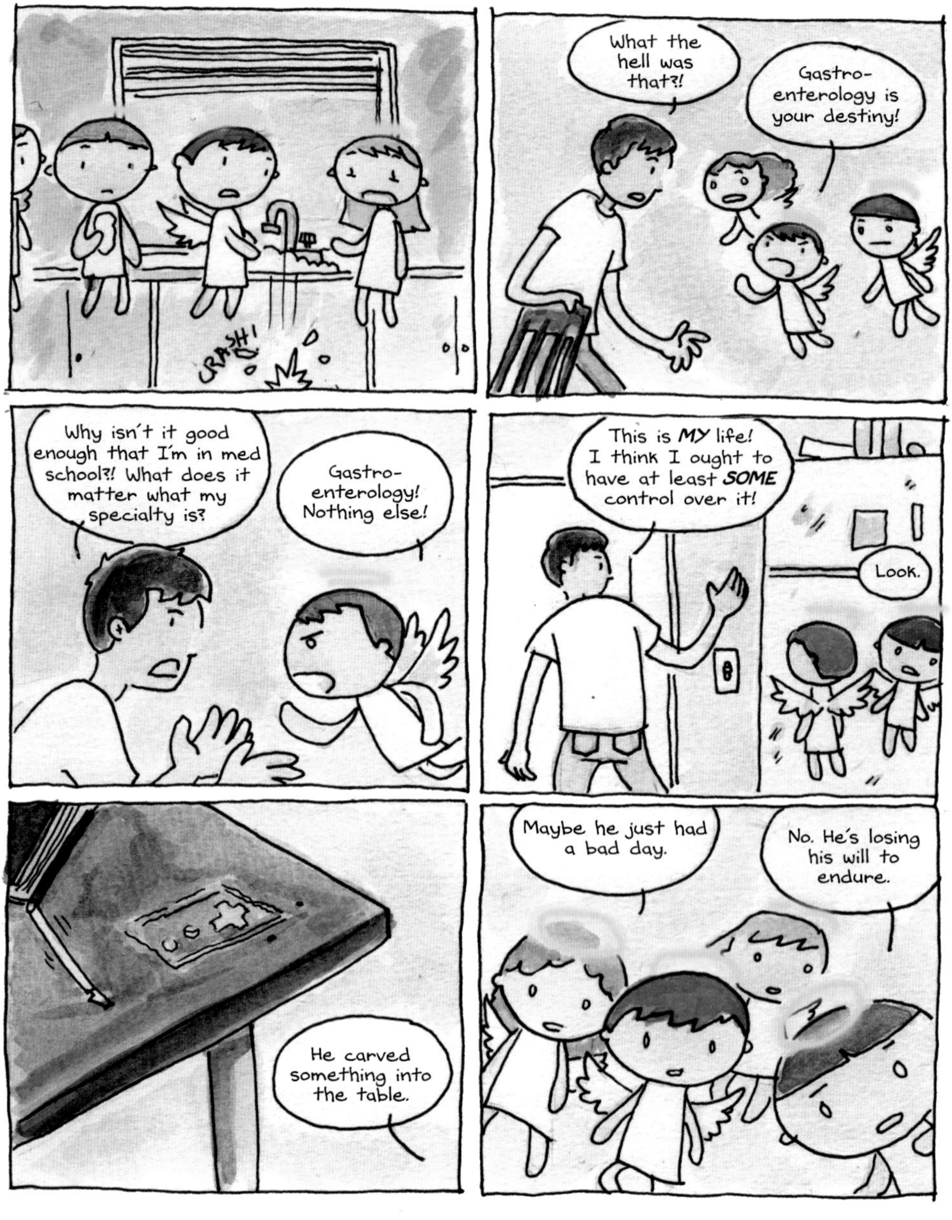
CRASH!
What the hell was that?!
Gastro-enterology is your destiny!
Why isn't it good enough that I'm in med school?! What does it matter what my specialty is?
Gastro-enterology! Nothing else!
This is **MY** life! I think I ought to have at least **SOME** control over it!
Look.
He carved something into the table.
Maybe he just had a bad day.
No. He's losing his will to endure.

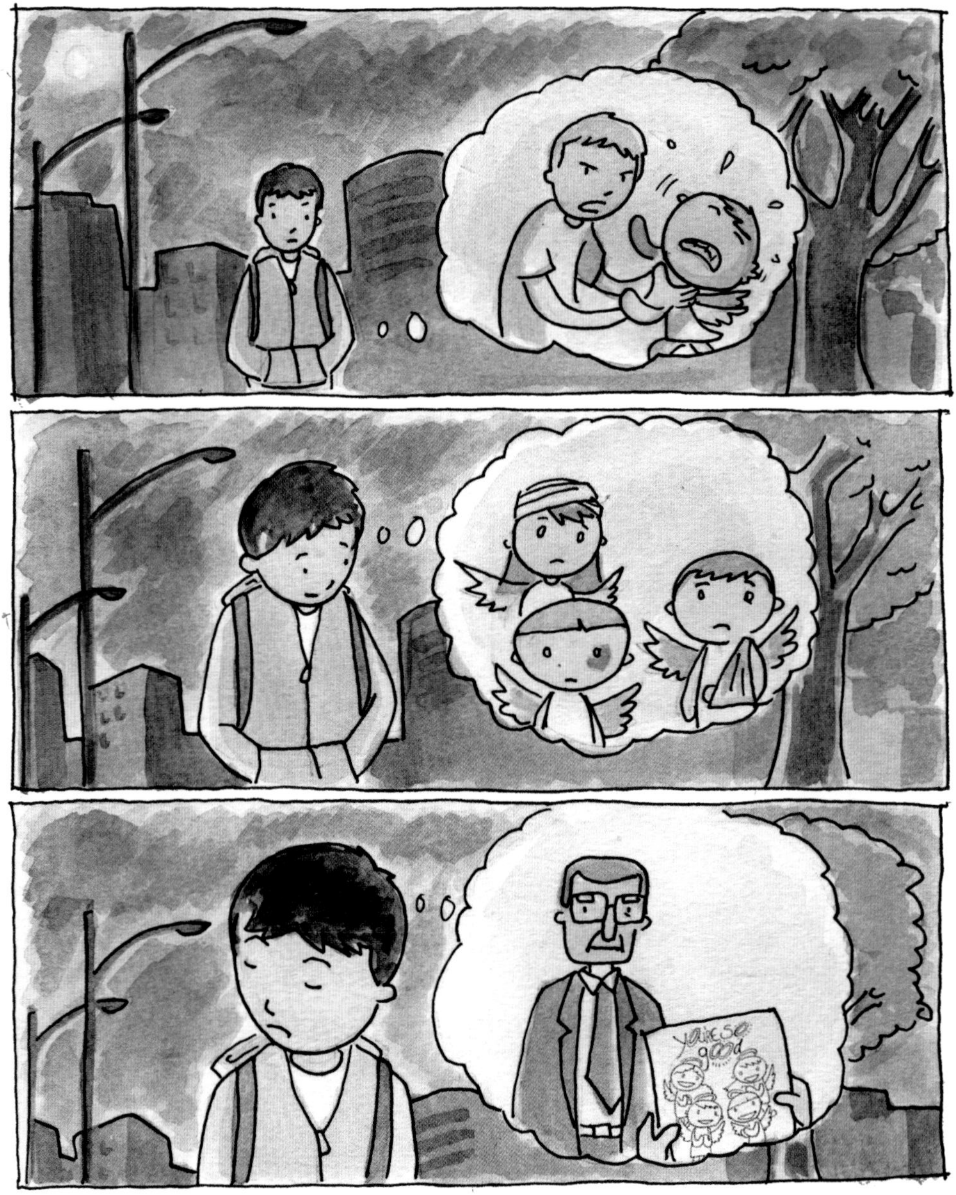
youRE SO good

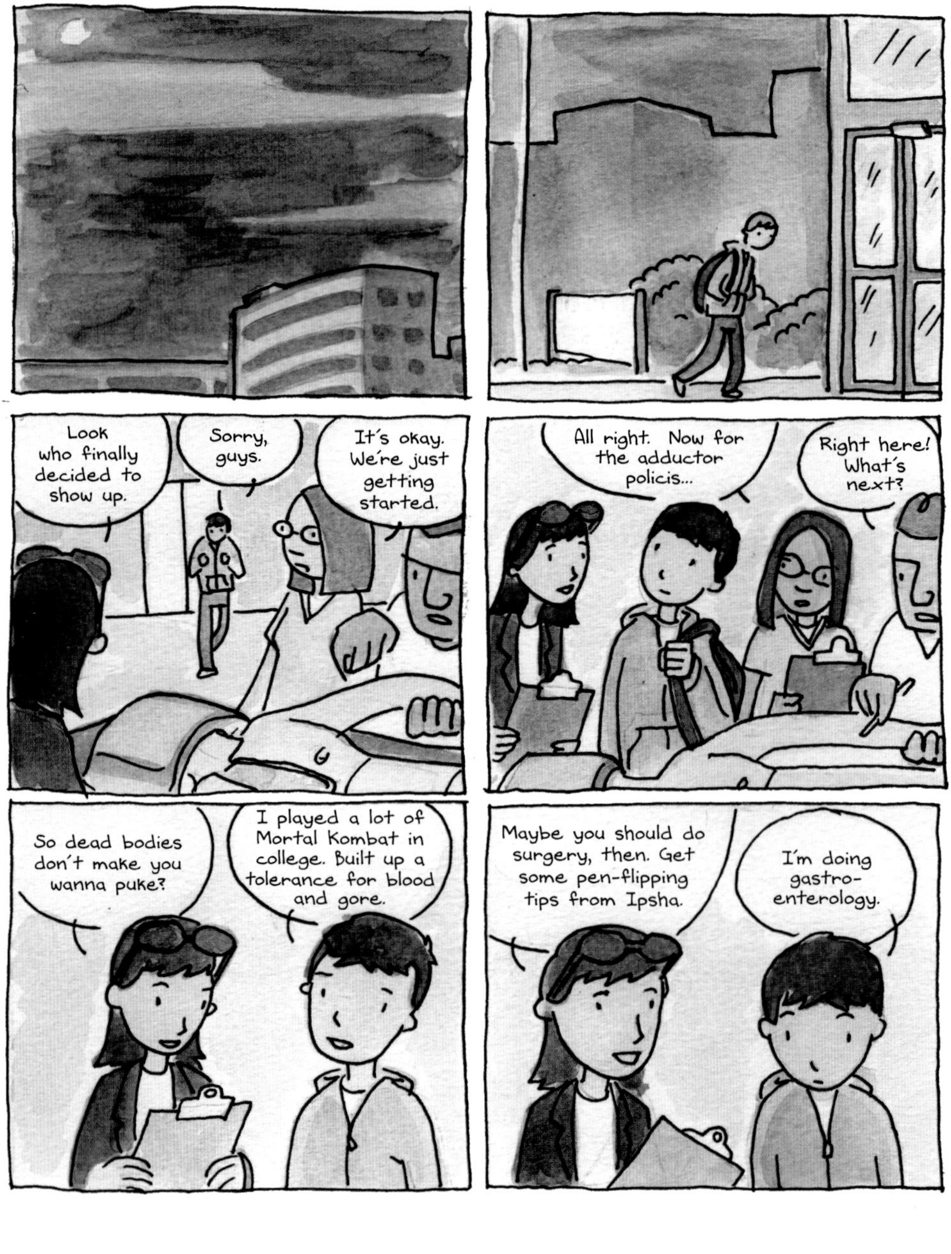
Look who finally decided to show up.
Sorry, guys.
It's okay. We're just getting started.
All right. Now for the adductor policis...
Right here! What's next?
So dead bodies don't make you wanna puke?
I played a lot of Mortal Kombat in college. Built up a tolerance for blood and gore.
Maybe you should do surgery, then. Get some pen-flipping tips from Ipsha.
I'm doing gastro-enterology.

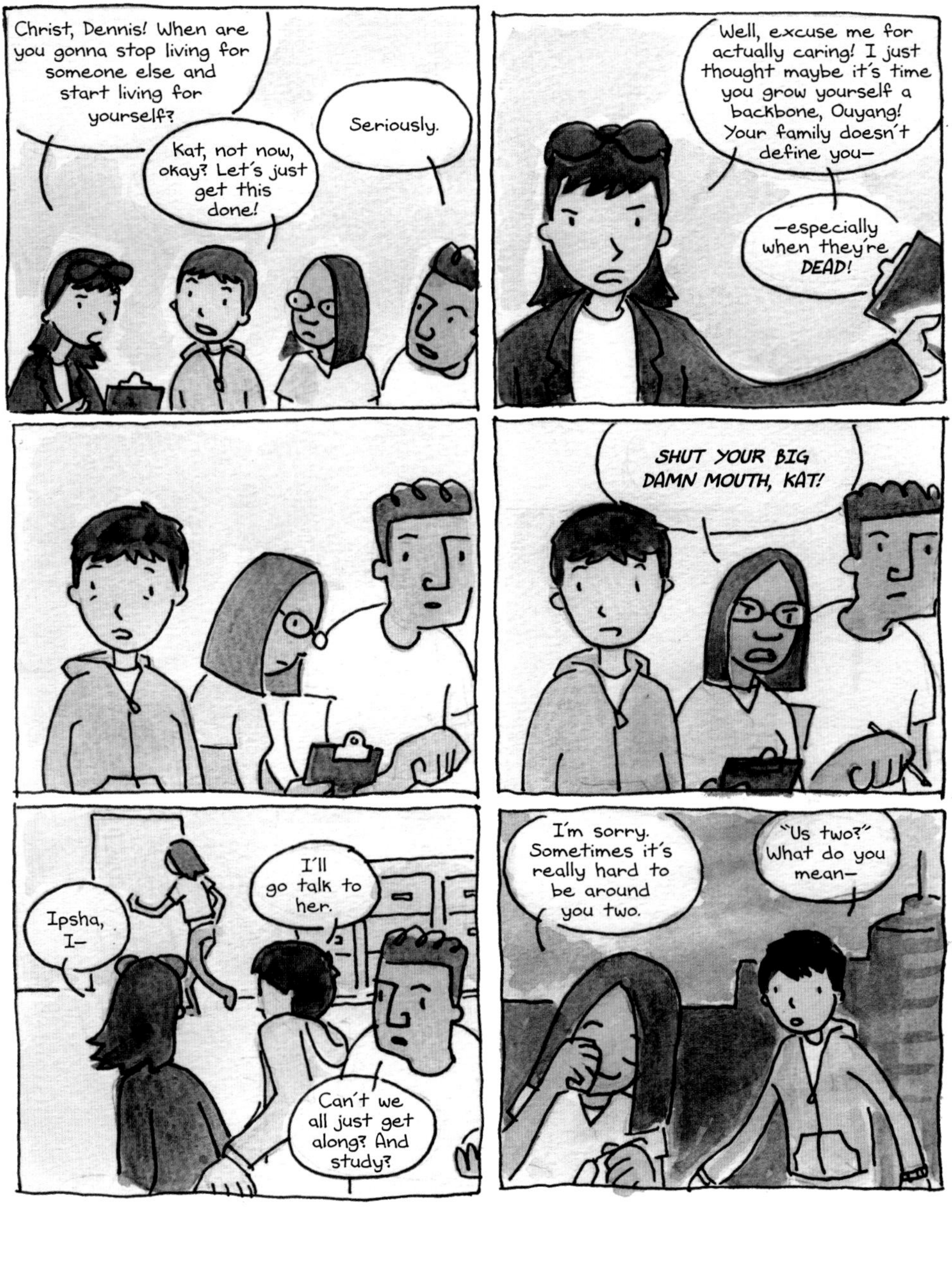
Christ, Dennis! When are you gonna stop living for someone else and start living for yourself?
Kat, not now, okay? Let's just get this done!
Seriously.
Well, excuse me for actually caring! I just thought maybe it's time you grow yourself a backbone, Ouyang! Your family doesn't define you—
—especially when they're DEAD!
SHUT YOUR BIG DAMN MOUTH, KAT!
Ipsha, I—
I'll go talk to her.
Can't we all just get along? And study?
I'm sorry. Sometimes it's really hard to be around you two.
"Us two?" What do you mean—

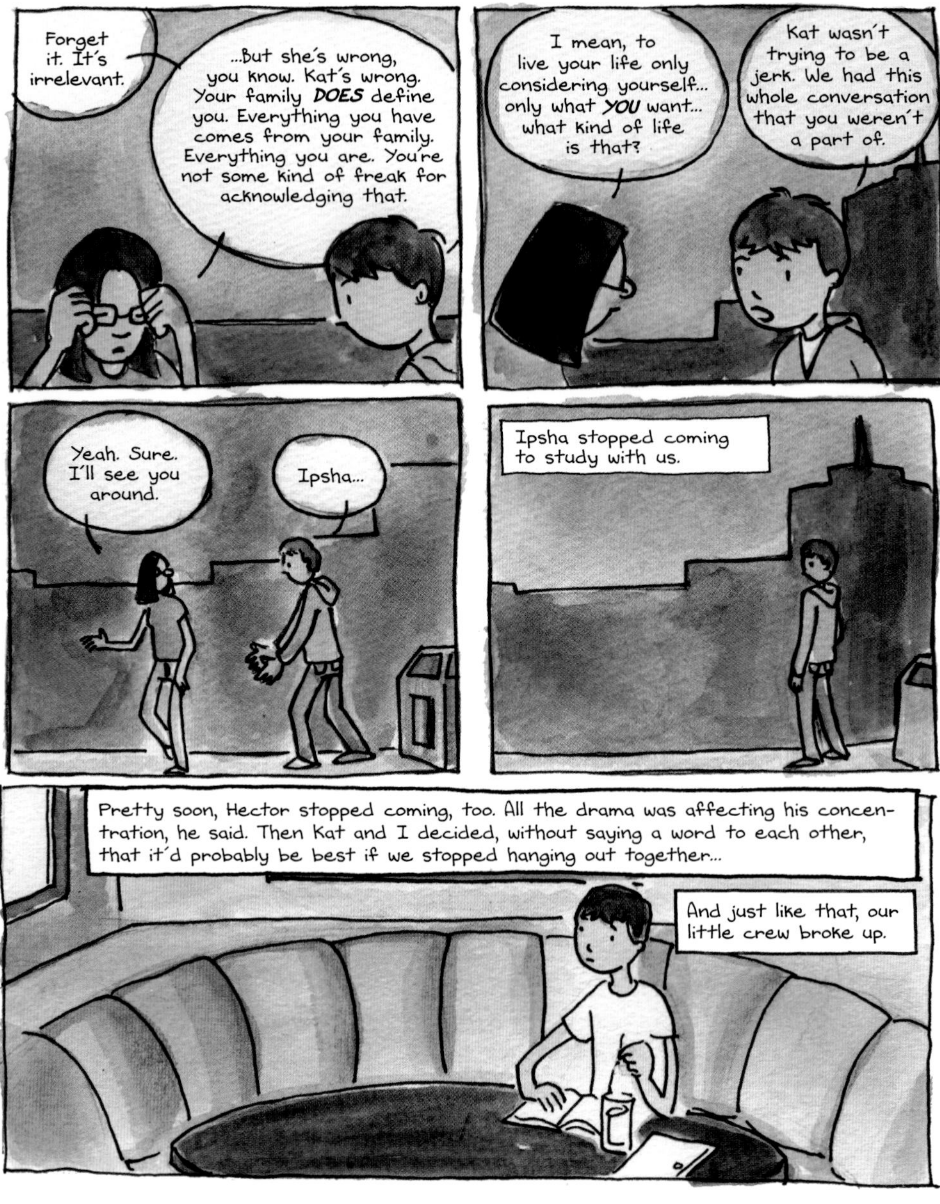
Forget it. It's irrelevant.
...But she's wrong, you know. Kat's wrong. Your family **DOES** define you. Everything you have comes from your family. Everything you are. You're not some kind of freak for acknowledging that.
I mean, to live your life only considering yourself... only what **YOU** want... what kind of life is that?
Kat wasn't trying to be a jerk. We had this whole conversation that you weren't a part of.
Yeah. Sure. I'll see you around.
Ipsha...
Ipsha stopped coming to study with us.
Pretty soon, Hector stopped coming, too. All the drama was affecting his concentration, he said. Then Kat and I decided, without saying a word to each other, that it'd probably be best if we stopped hanging out together...
And just like that, our little crew broke up.

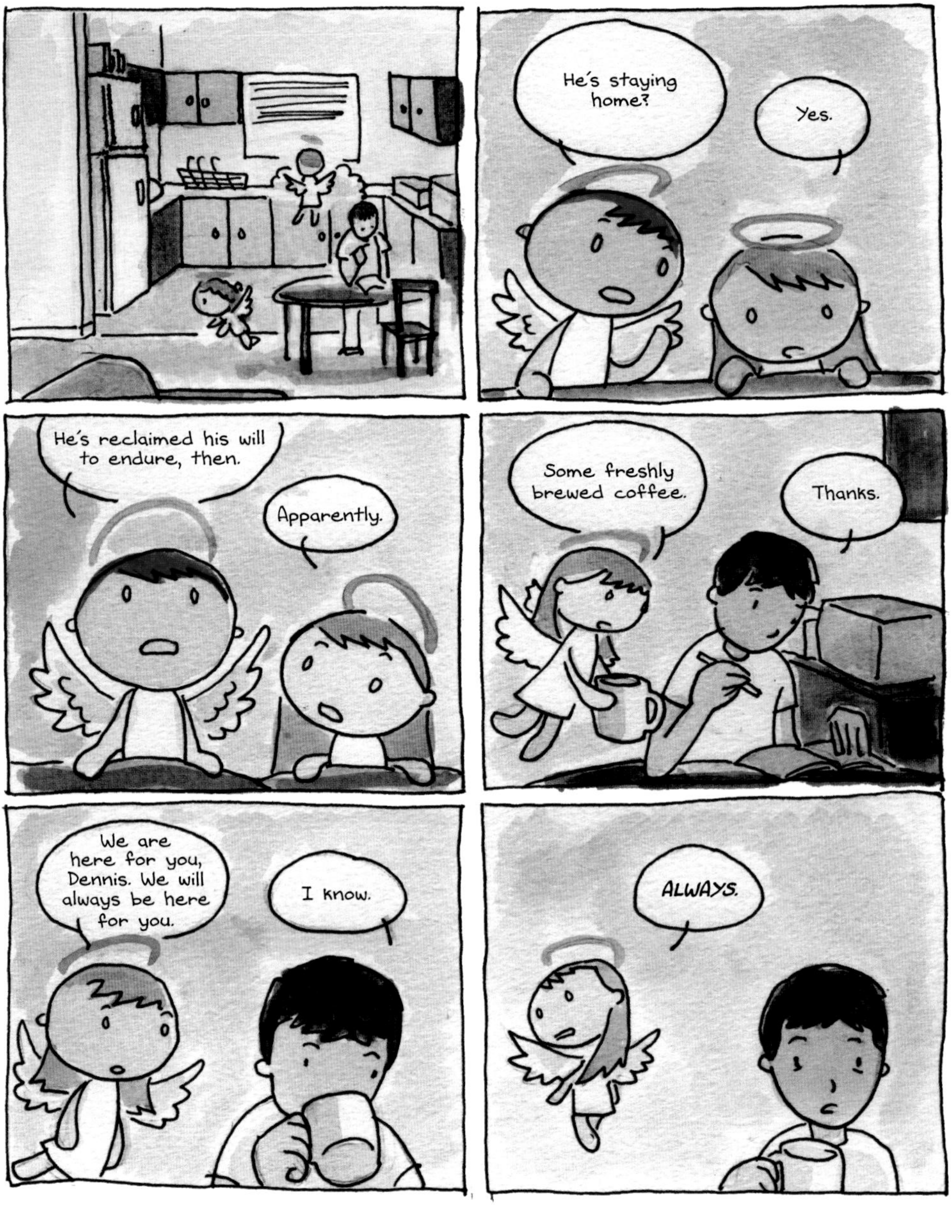
He's staying home?
Yes.
He's reclaimed his will to endure, then.
Apparently.
Some freshly brewed coffee.
Thanks.
We are here for you, Dennis. We will always be here for you.
I know.
ALWAYS.

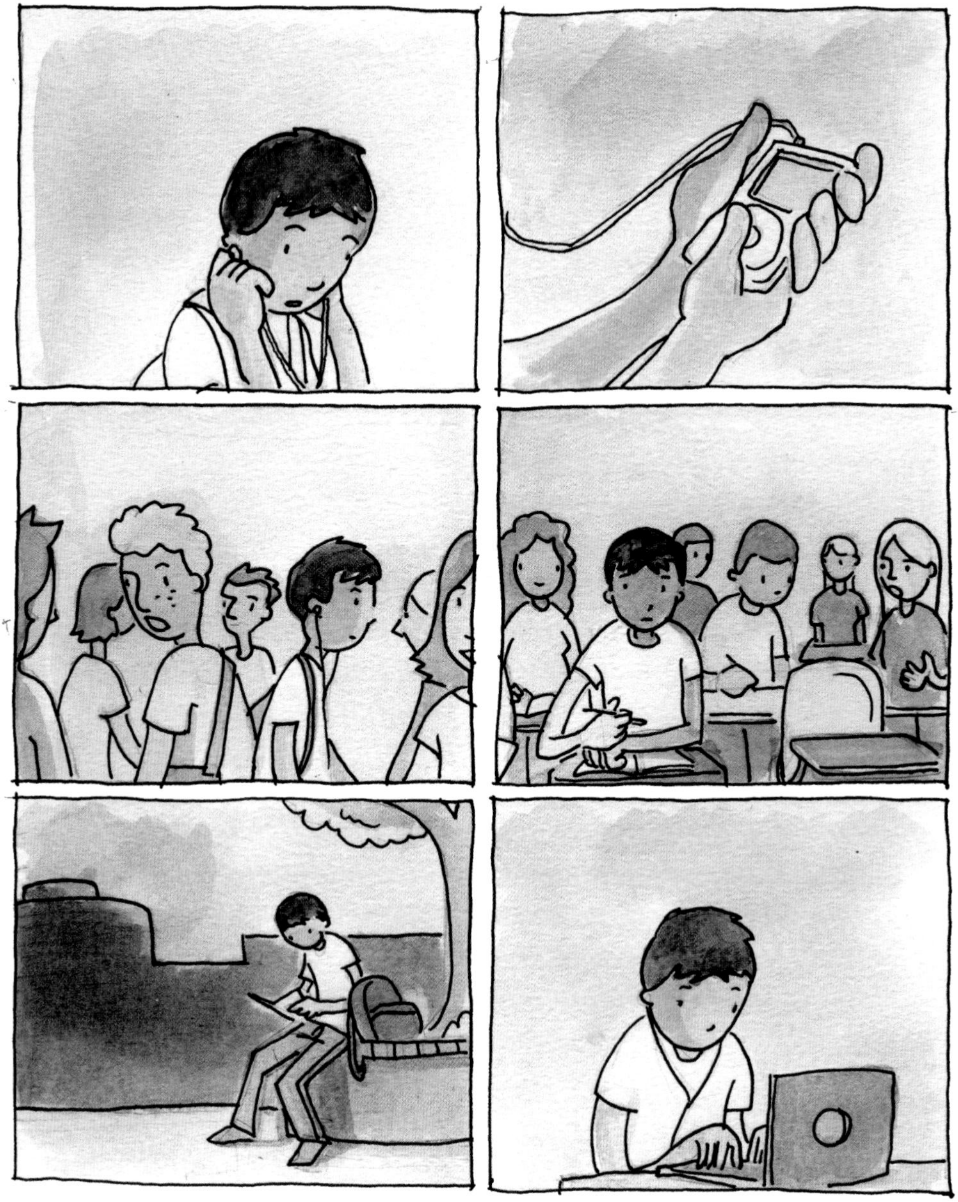

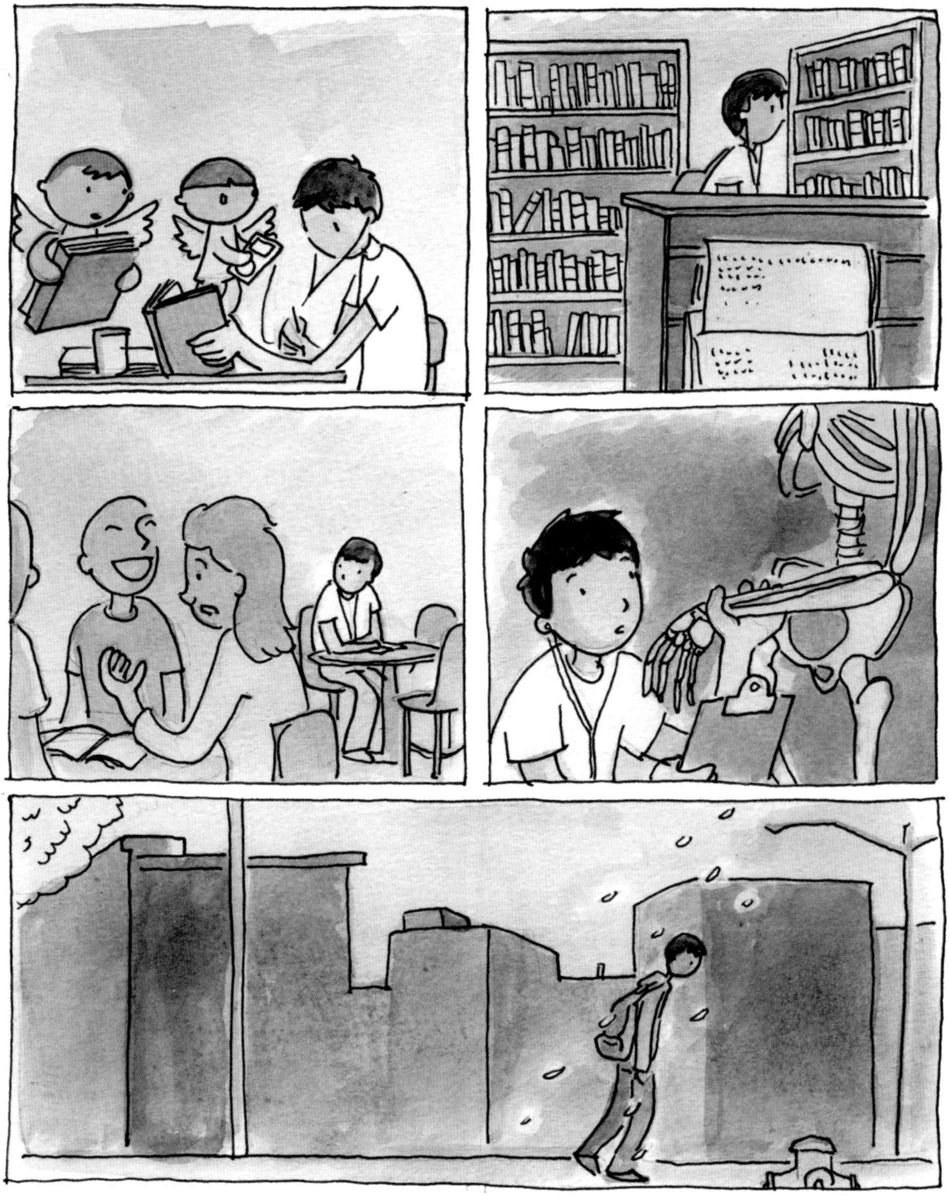

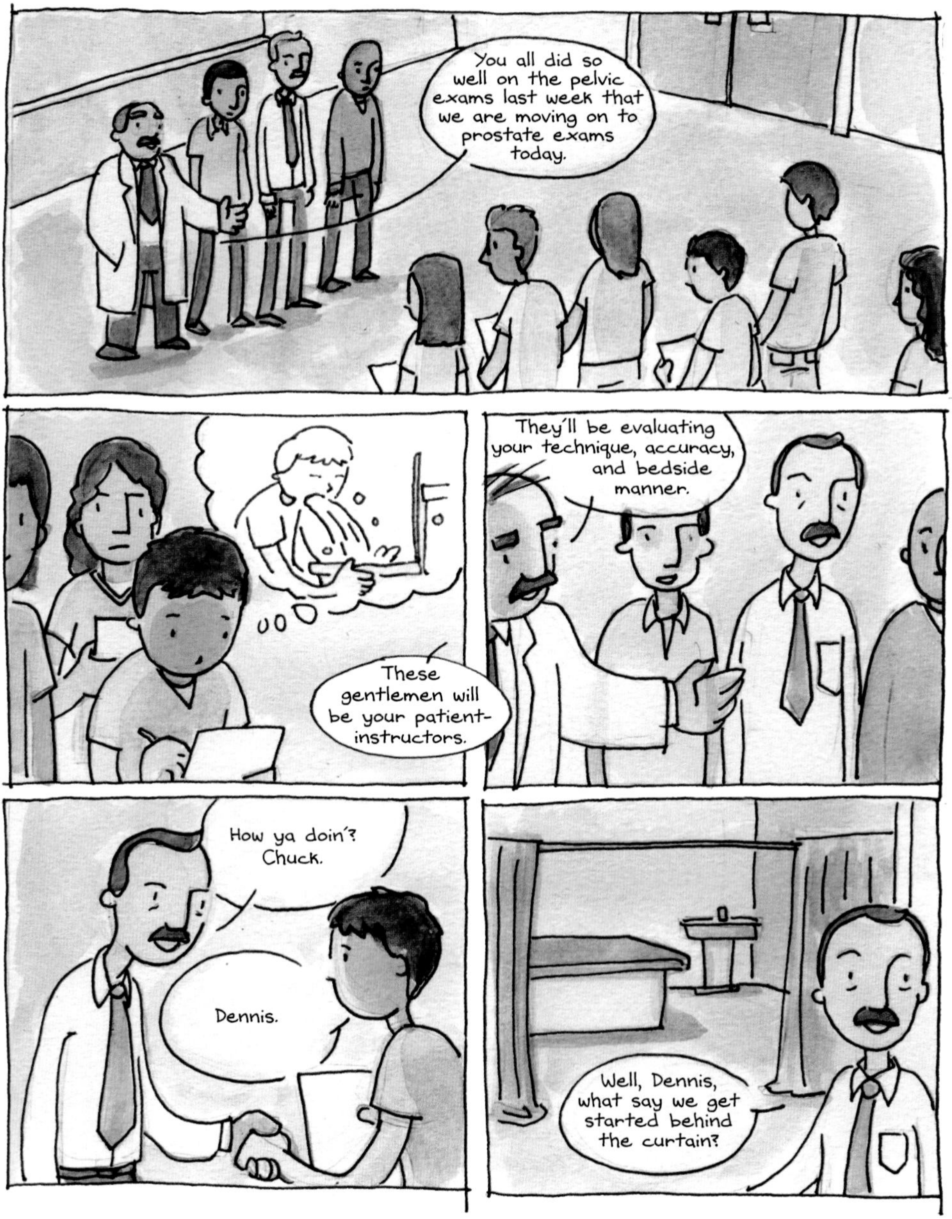
You all did so well on the pelvic exams last week that we are moving on to prostate exams today.
These gentlemen will be your patient-instructors.
They'll be evaluating your technique, accuracy, and bedside manner.
How ya doin'? Chuck.
Dennis.
Well, Dennis, what say we get started behind the curtain?

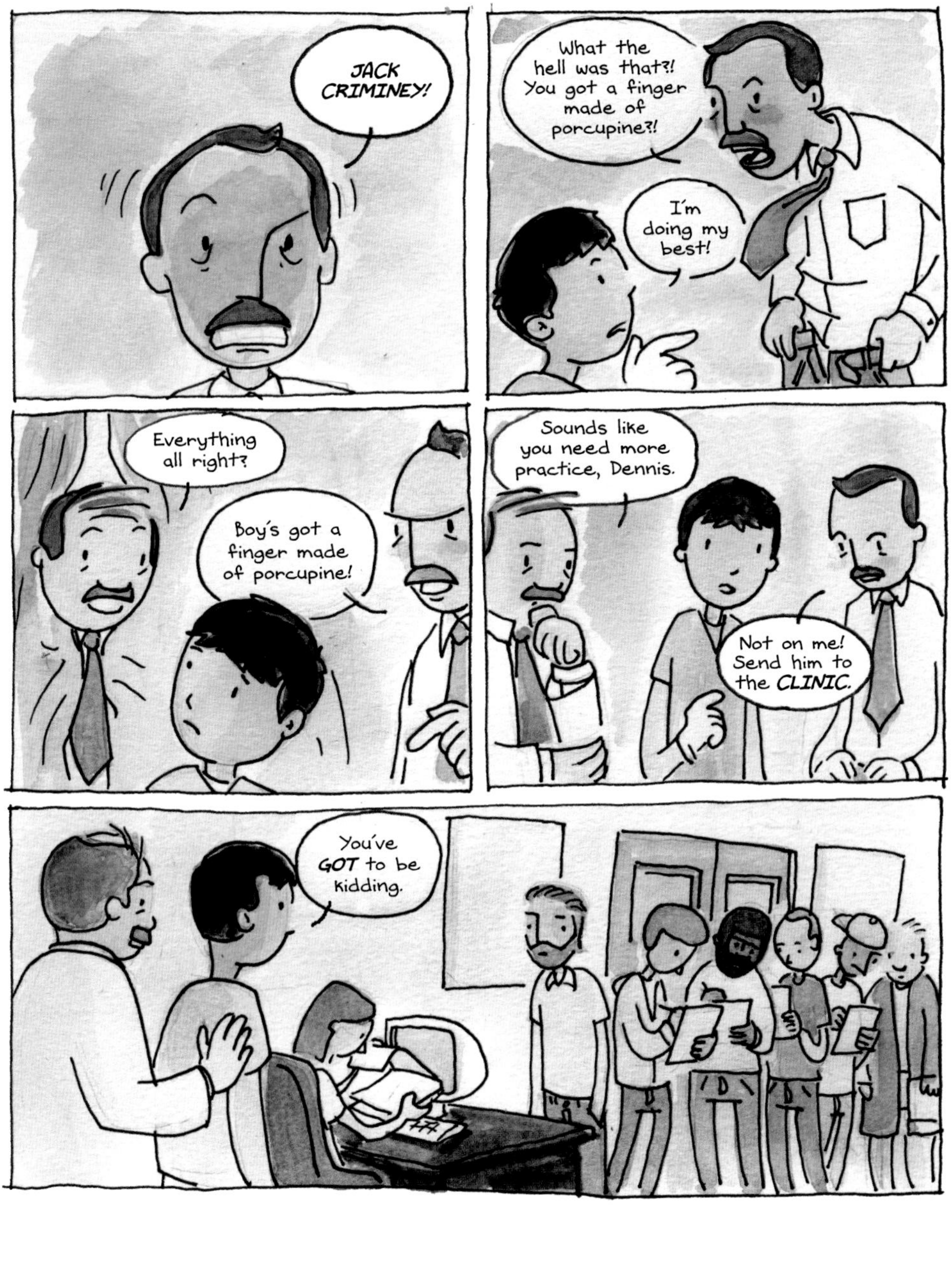
JACK CRIMINEY!
What the hell was that?! You got a finger made of porcupine?!
I'm doing my best!
Everything all right?
Boy's got a finger made of porcupine!
Sounds like you need more practice, Dennis.
Not on me! Send him to the CLINIC.
You've GOT to be kidding.

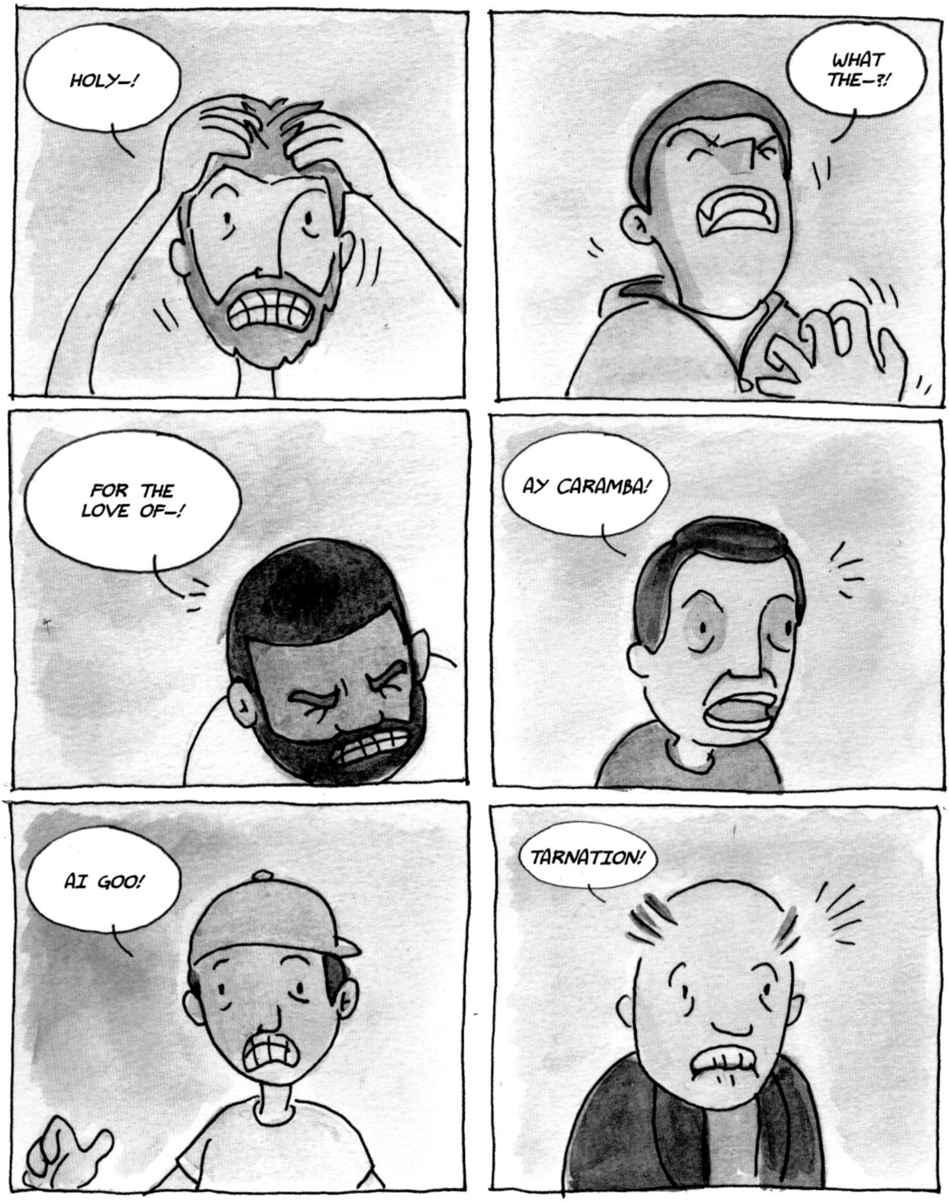
HOLY–!
WHAT THE–?!
FOR THE LOVE OF–!
AY CARAMBA!
AI GOO!
TARNATION!

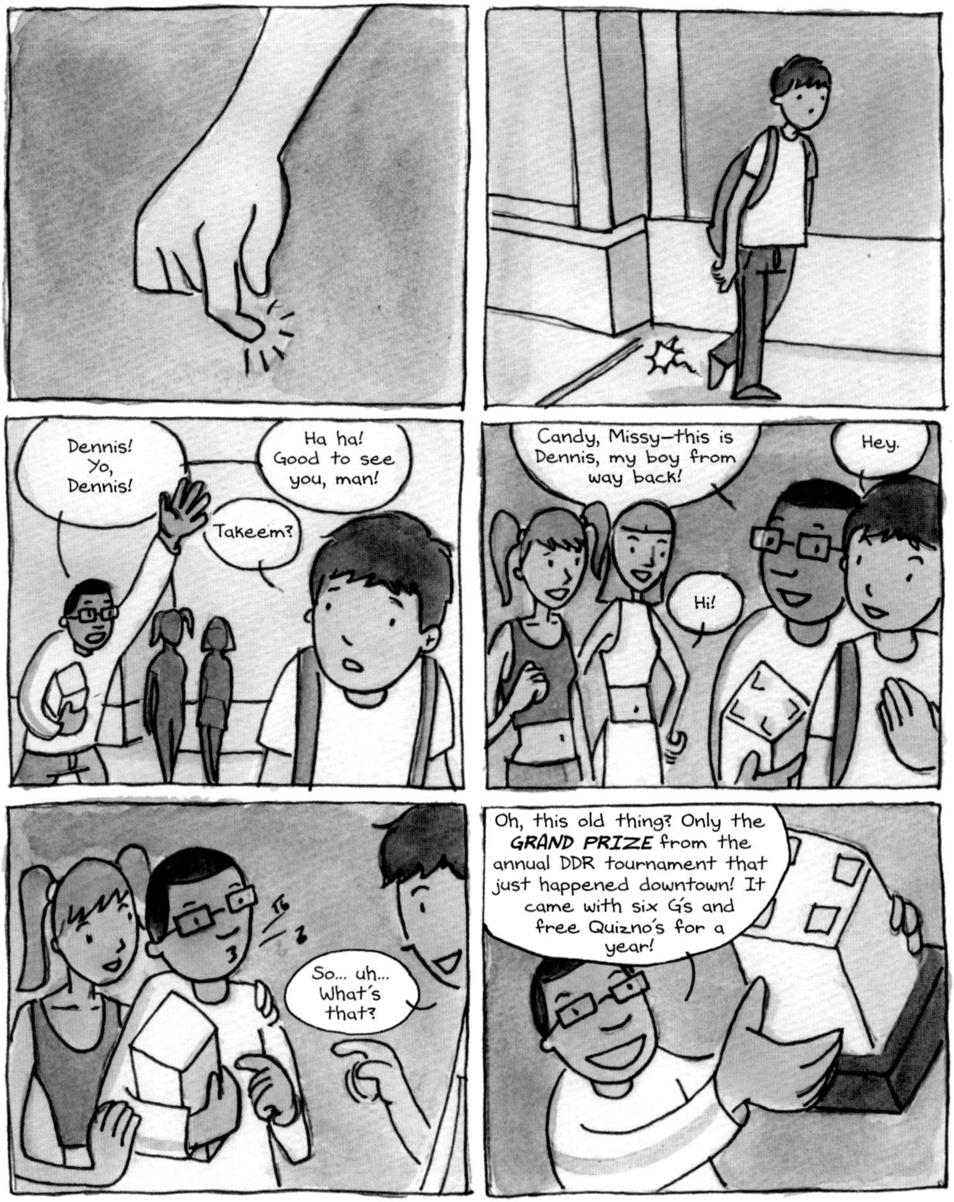
Dennis! Yo, Dennis!
Ha ha! Good to see you, man!
Takeem?
Candy, Missy—this is Dennis, my boy from way back!
Hey.
Hi!
So... uh... What's that?
Oh, this old thing? Only the **GRAND PRIZE** from the annual DDR tournament that just happened downtown! It came with six G's and free Quizno's for a year!

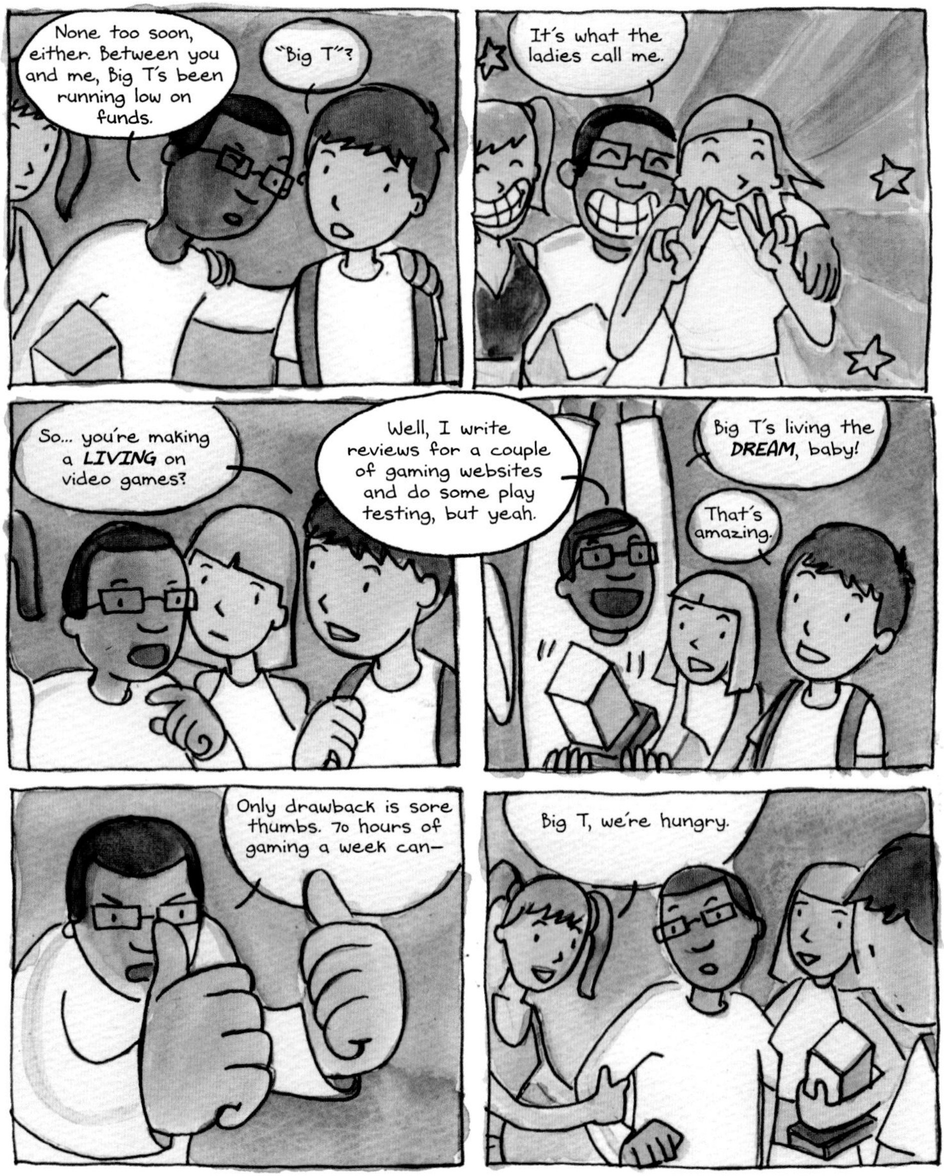
None too soon, either. Between you and me, Big T's been running low on funds.
"Big T"?
It's what the ladies call me.
So... you're making a **LIVING** on video games?
Well, I write reviews for a couple of gaming websites and do some play testing, but yeah.
Big T's living the **DREAM**, baby!
That's amazing.
Only drawback is sore thumbs. 70 hours of gaming a week can—
Big T, we're hungry.

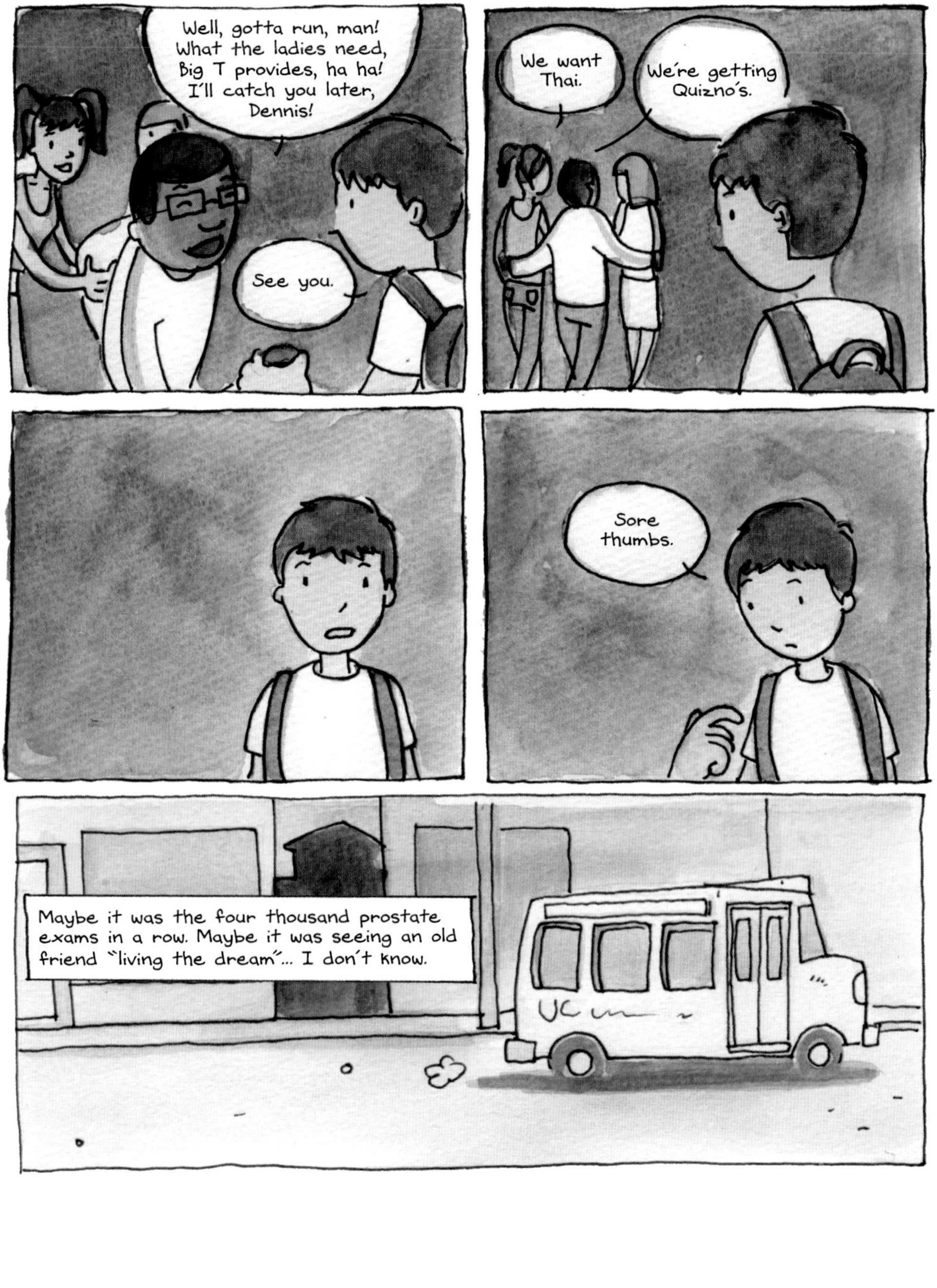
Well, gotta run, man! What the ladies need, Big T provides, ha ha! I'll catch you later, Dennis!
See you.
We want Thai.
We're getting Quizno's.
Sore thumbs.
Maybe it was the four thousand prostate exams in a row. Maybe it was seeing an old friend "living the dream"... I don't know.
UC

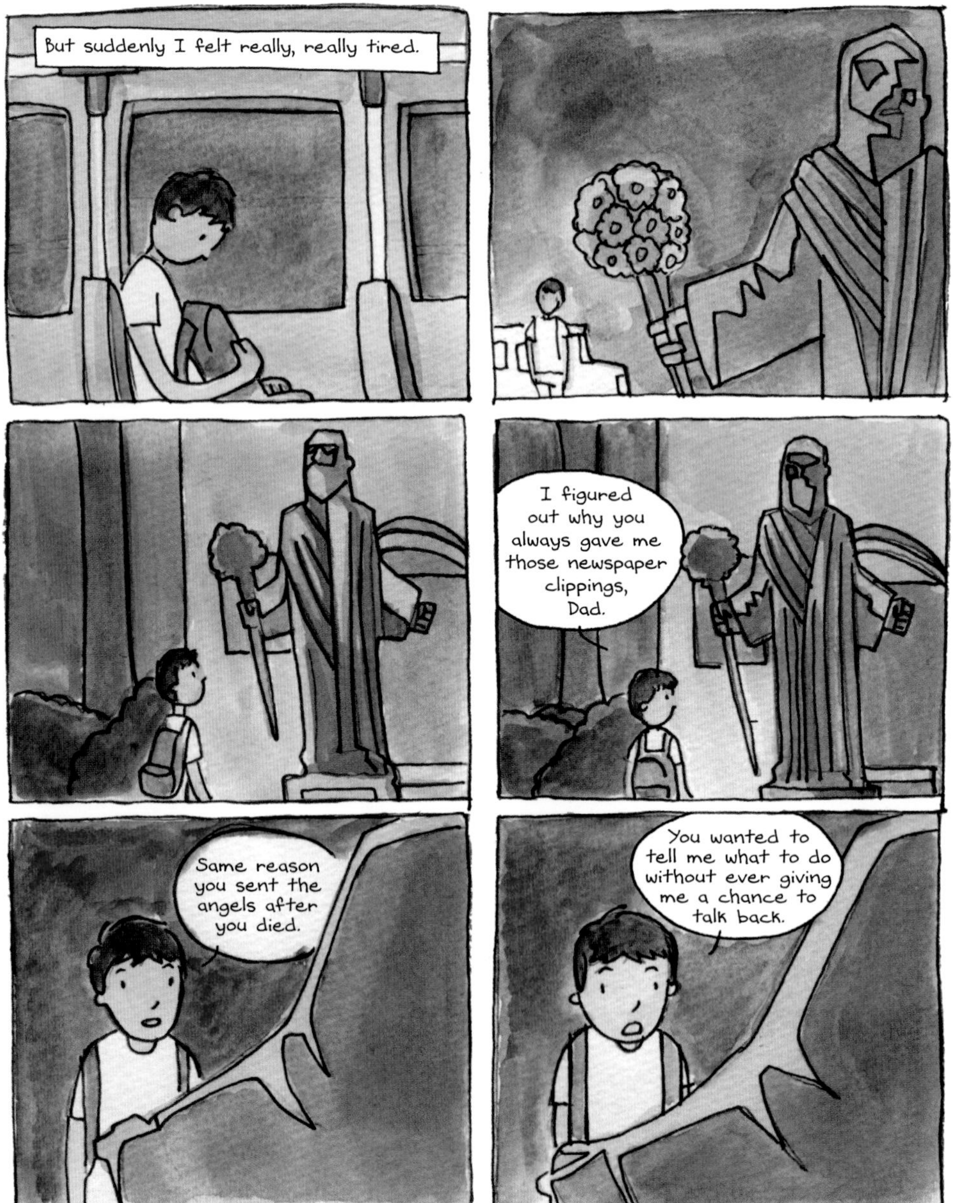

But suddenly I felt really, really tired.
I figured out why you always gave me those newspaper clippings, Dad.
Same reason you sent the angels after you died.
You wanted to tell me what to do without ever giving me a chance to talk back.

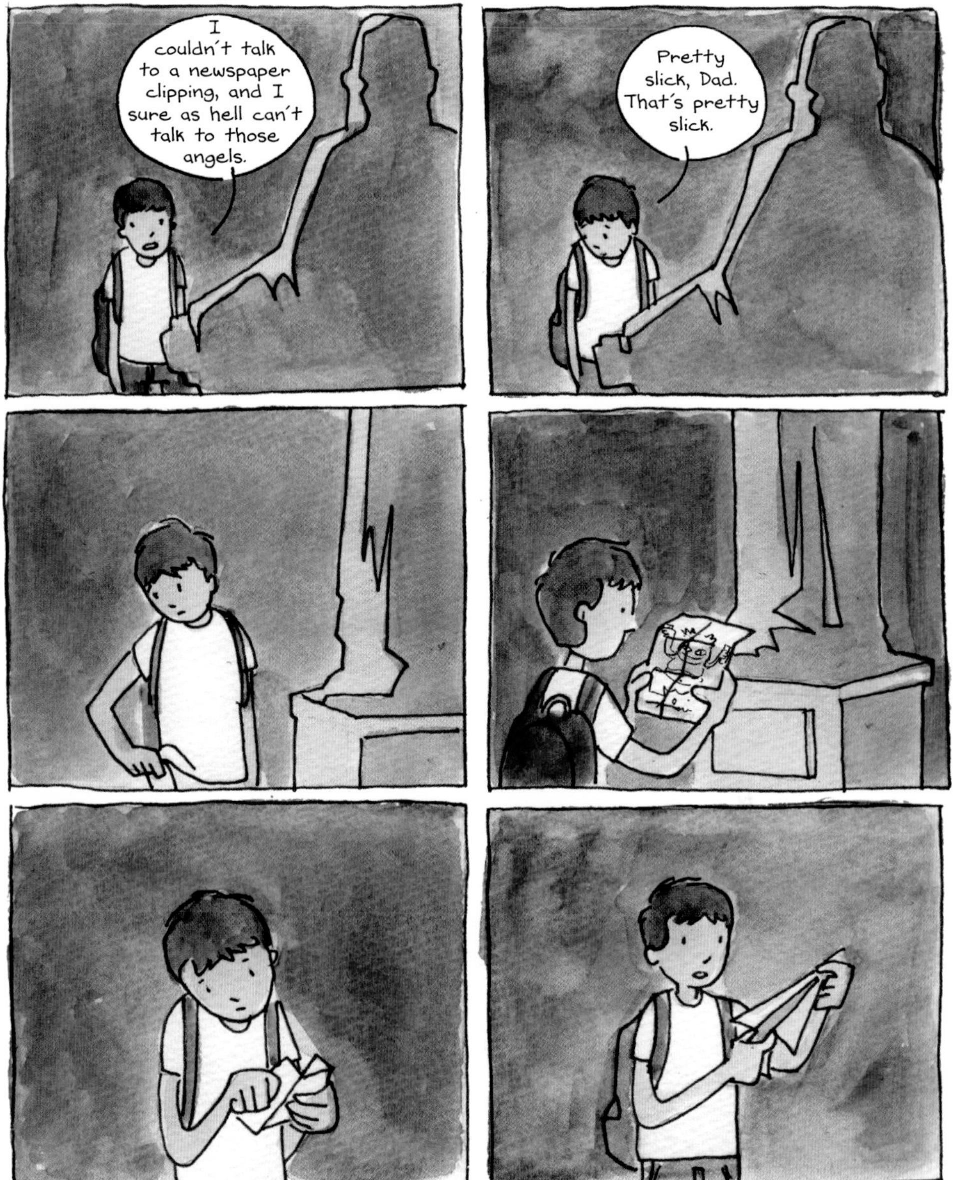
I couldn't talk to a newspaper clipping, and I sure as hell can't talk to those angels.
Pretty slick, Dad. That's pretty slick.

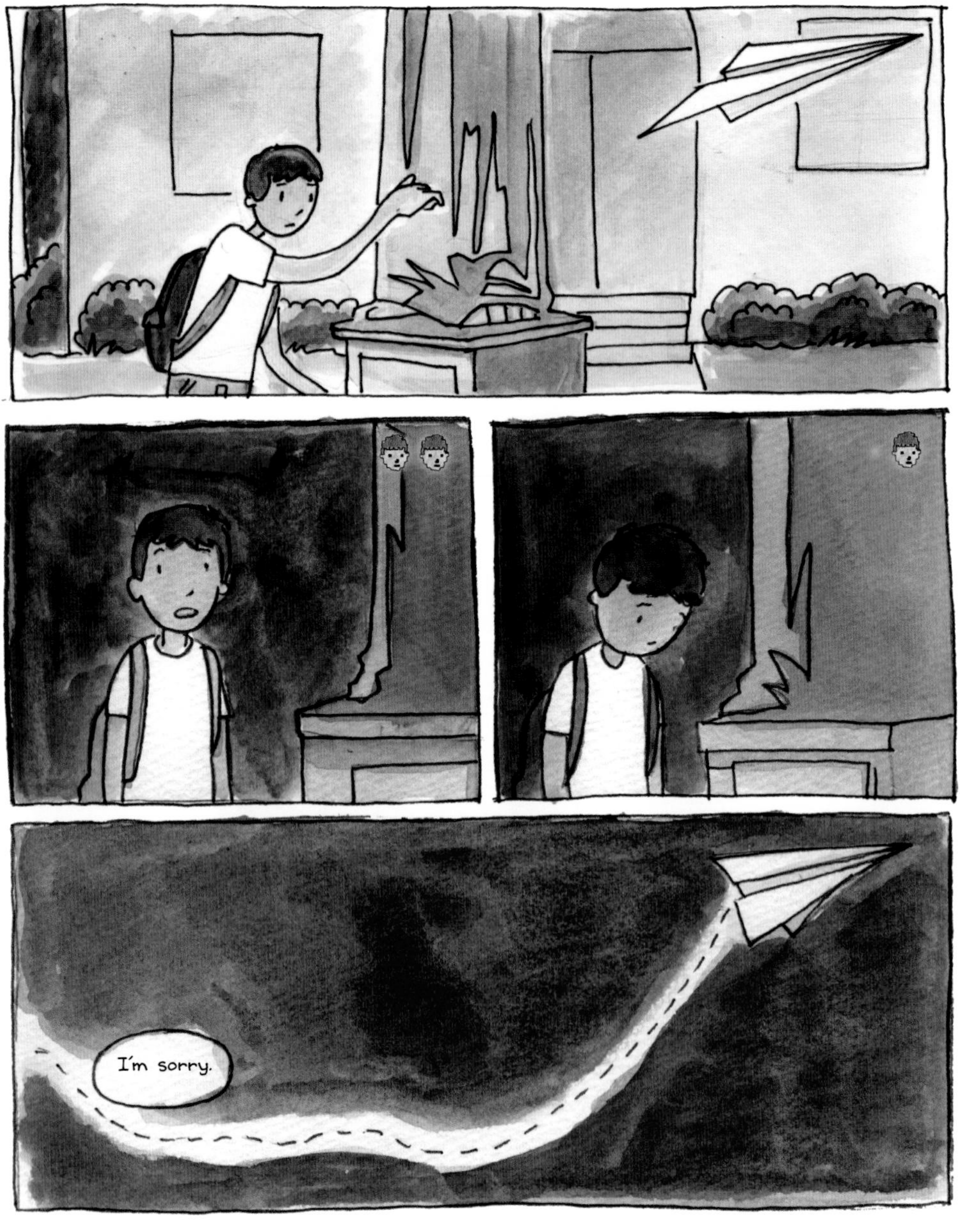
I'm sorry.

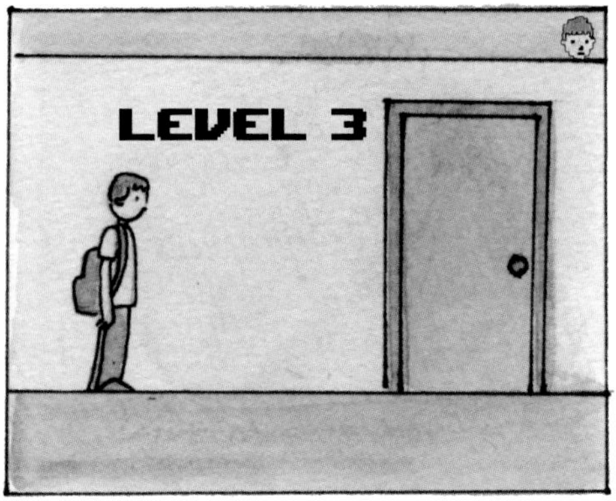
LEVEL 3

I knew exactly what I was going to say and
how I was going to say it. It was my life.
I wanted it back.

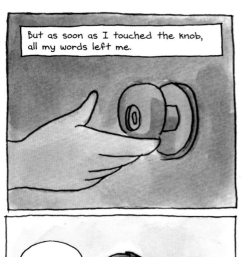

But as soon as I touched the knob, all my words left me.

Guys.

I... I...

I quit.

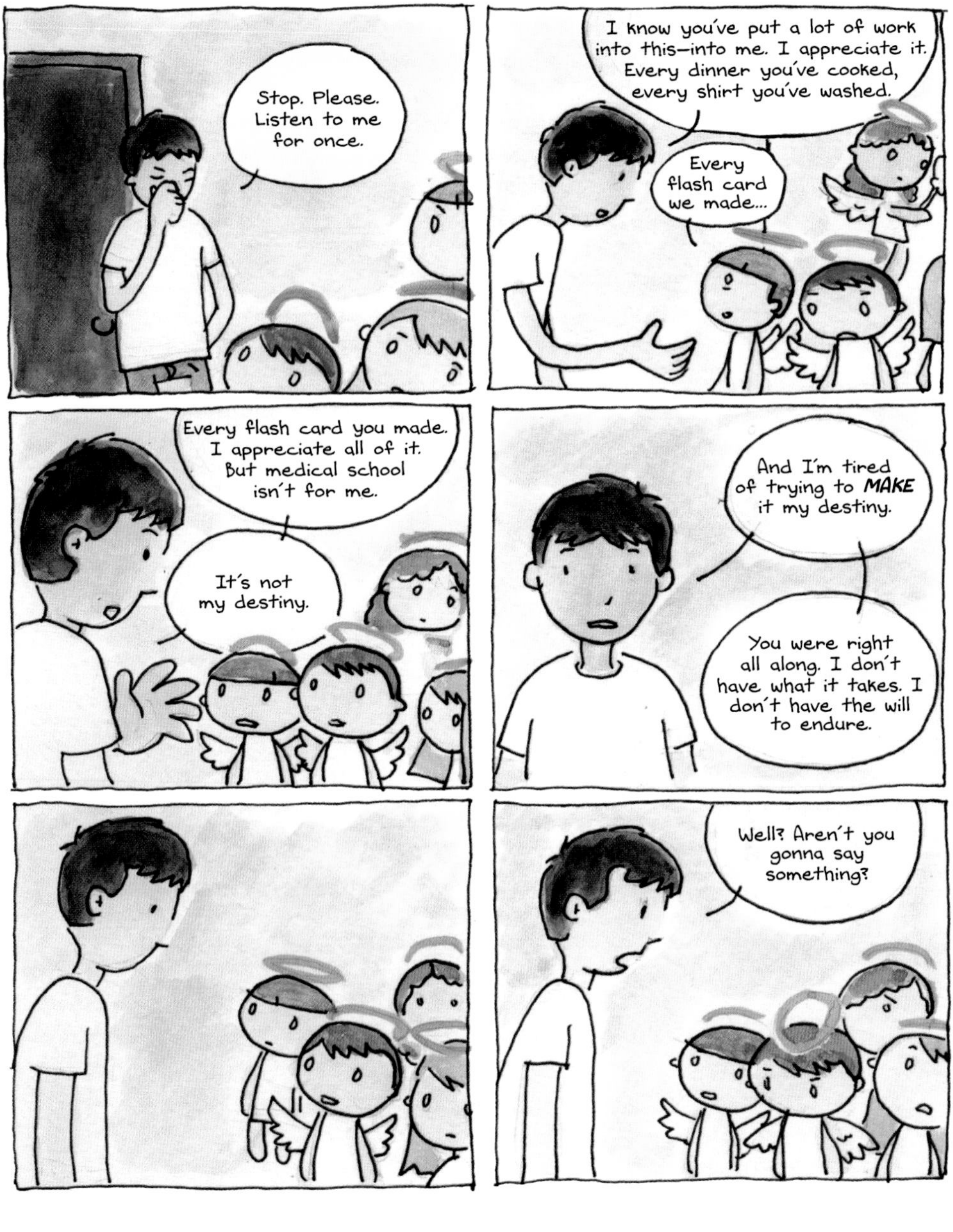
Stop. Please. Listen to me for once.
I know you've put a lot of work into this—into me. I appreciate it. Every dinner you've cooked, every shirt you've washed.
Every flash card we made...
Every flash card you made. I appreciate all of it. But medical school isn't for me.
It's not my destiny.
And I'm tired of trying to MAKE it my destiny.
You were right all along. I don't have what it takes. I don't have the will to endure.
Well? Aren't you gonna say something?

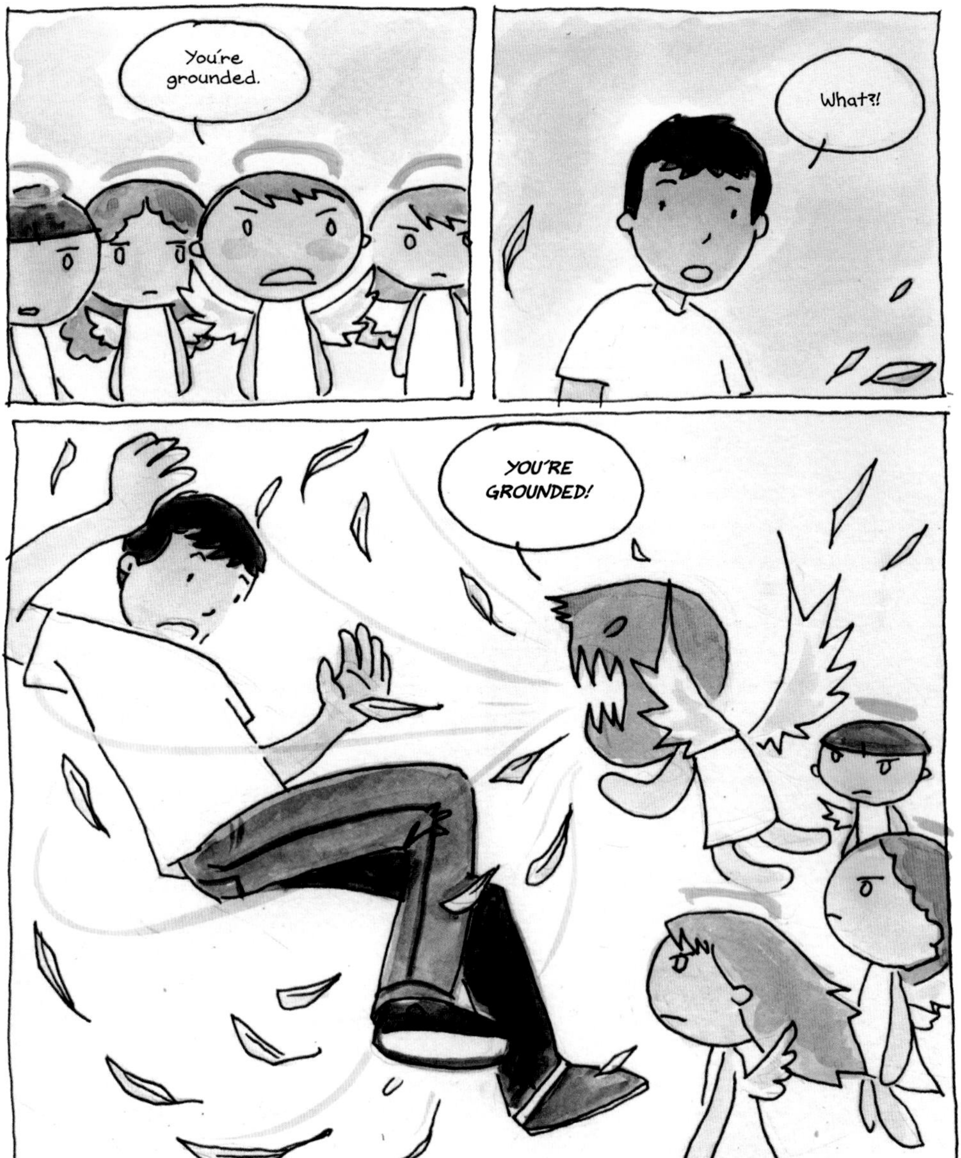
You're grounded.
What?!
YOU'RE GROUNDED!

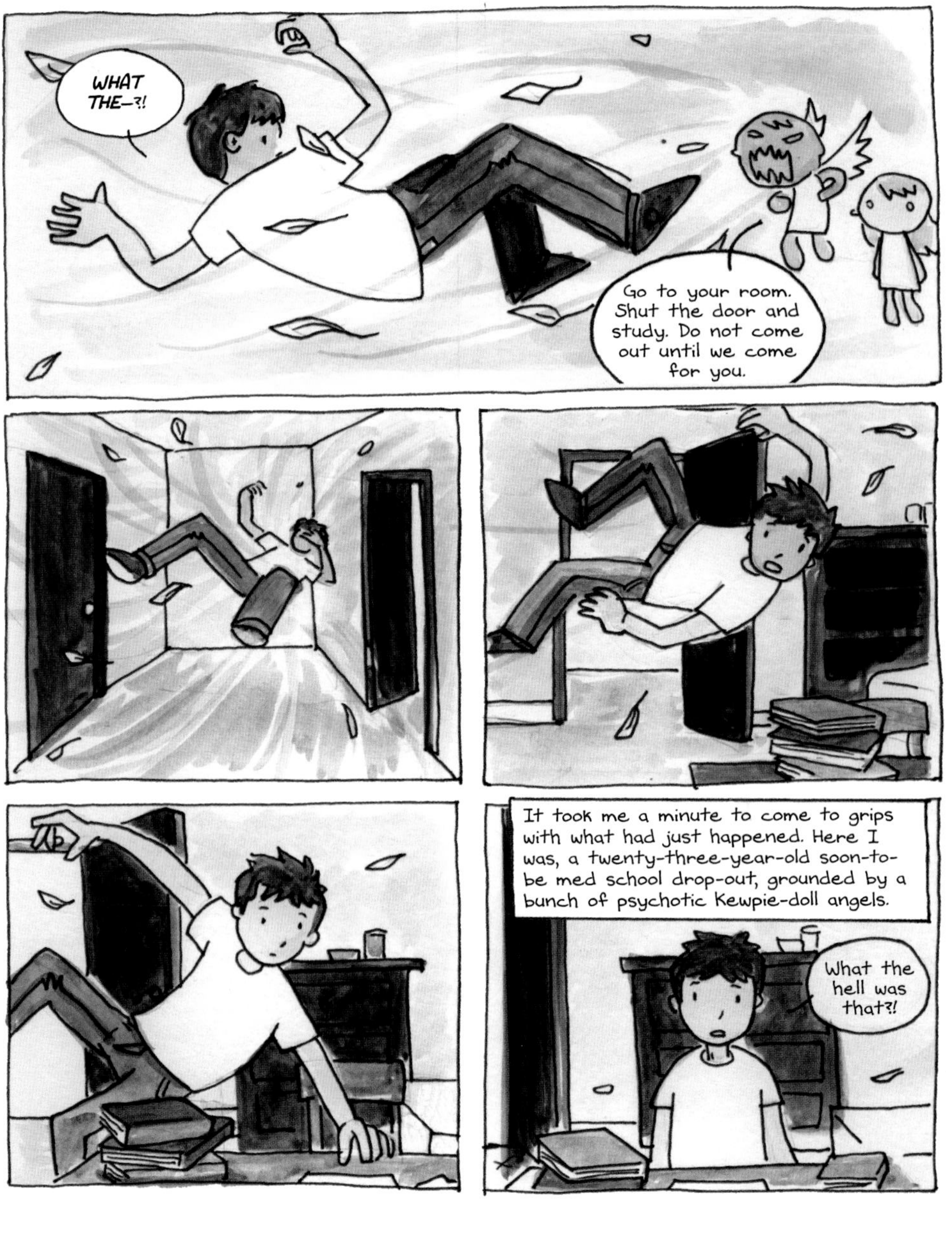
WHAT THE–?!
Go to your room. Shut the door and study. Do not come out until we come for you.
It took me a minute to come to grips with what had just happened. Here I was, a twenty-three-year-old soon-to-be med school drop-out, grounded by a bunch of psychotic Kewpie-doll angels.
What the hell was that?!

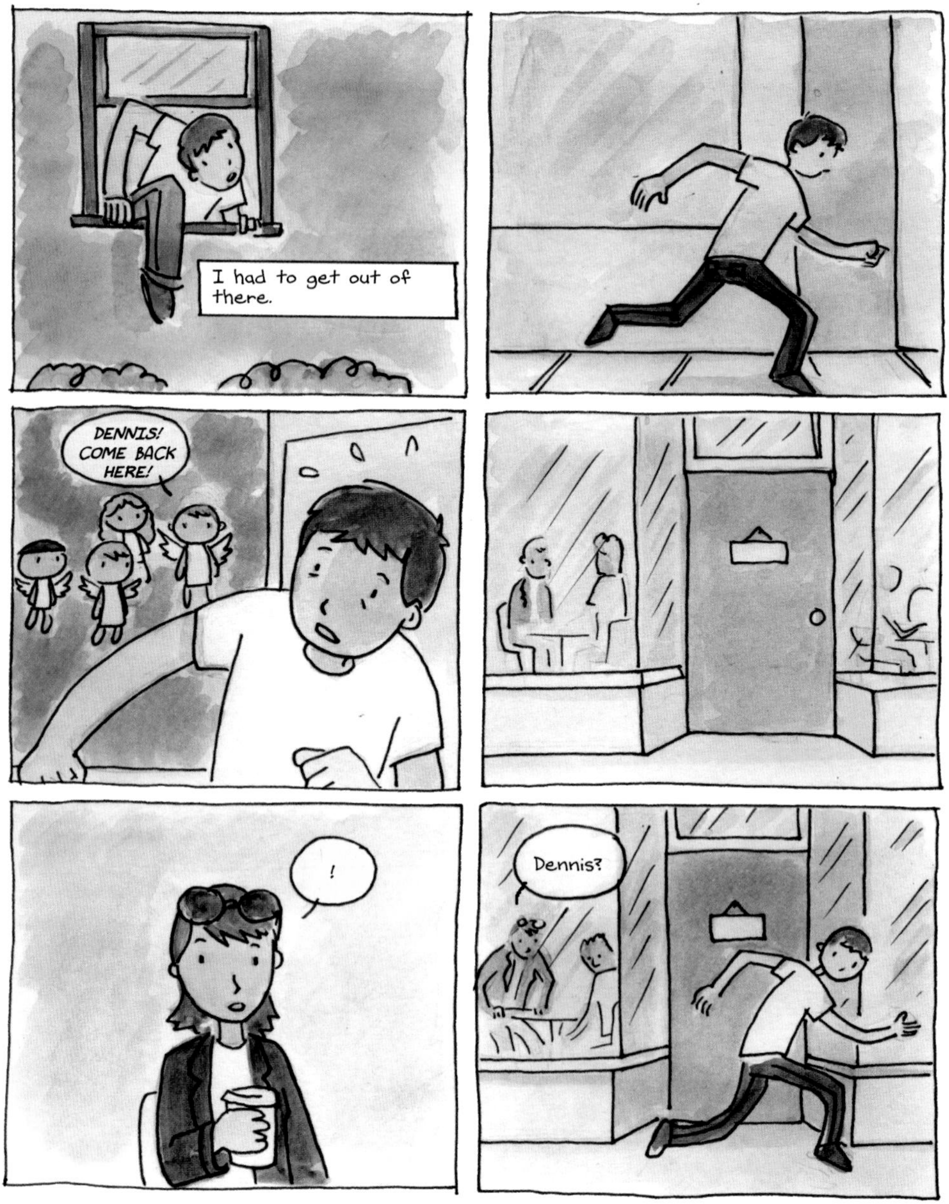
I had to get out of there.
DENNIS! COME BACK HERE!
!
Dennis?

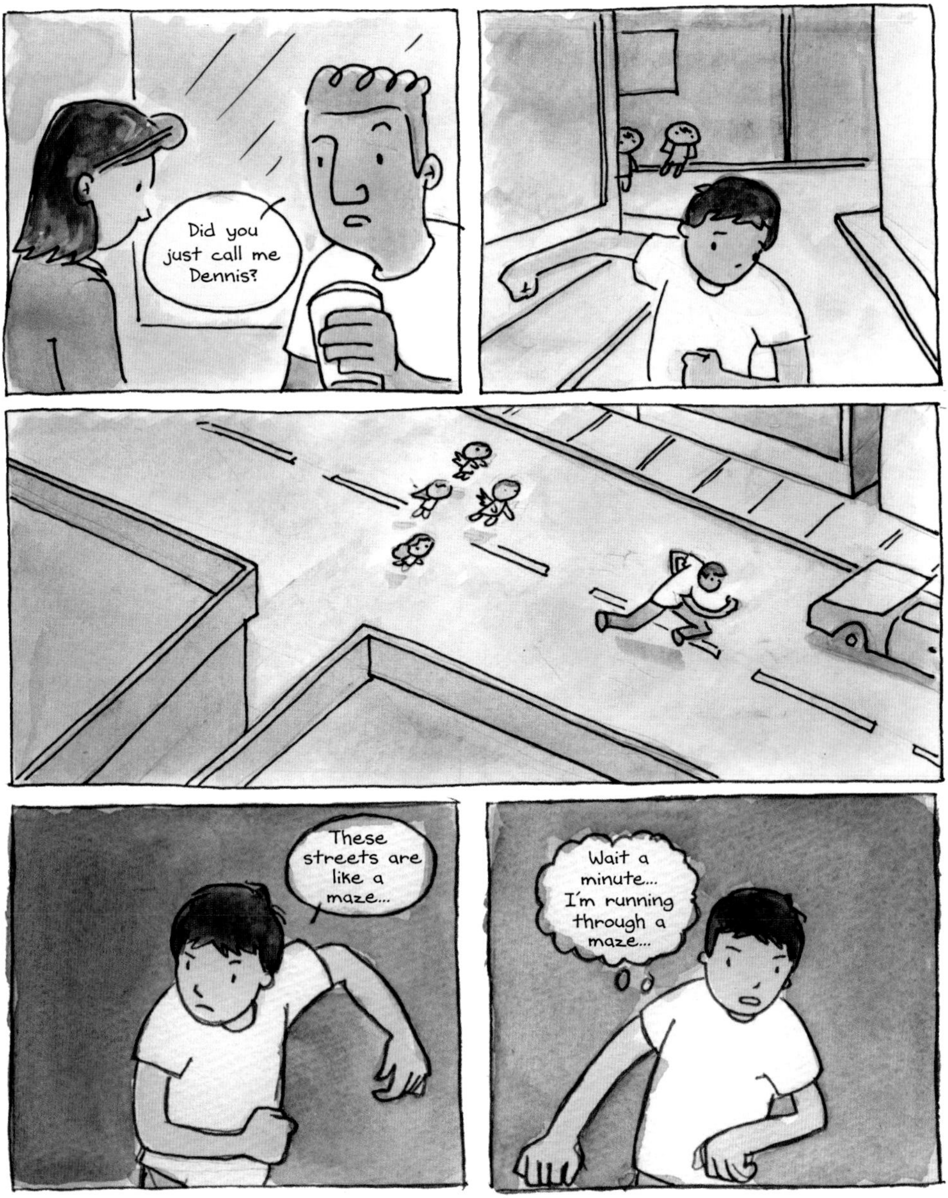
Did you just call me Dennis?
These streets are like a maze...
Wait a minute... I'm running through a maze...

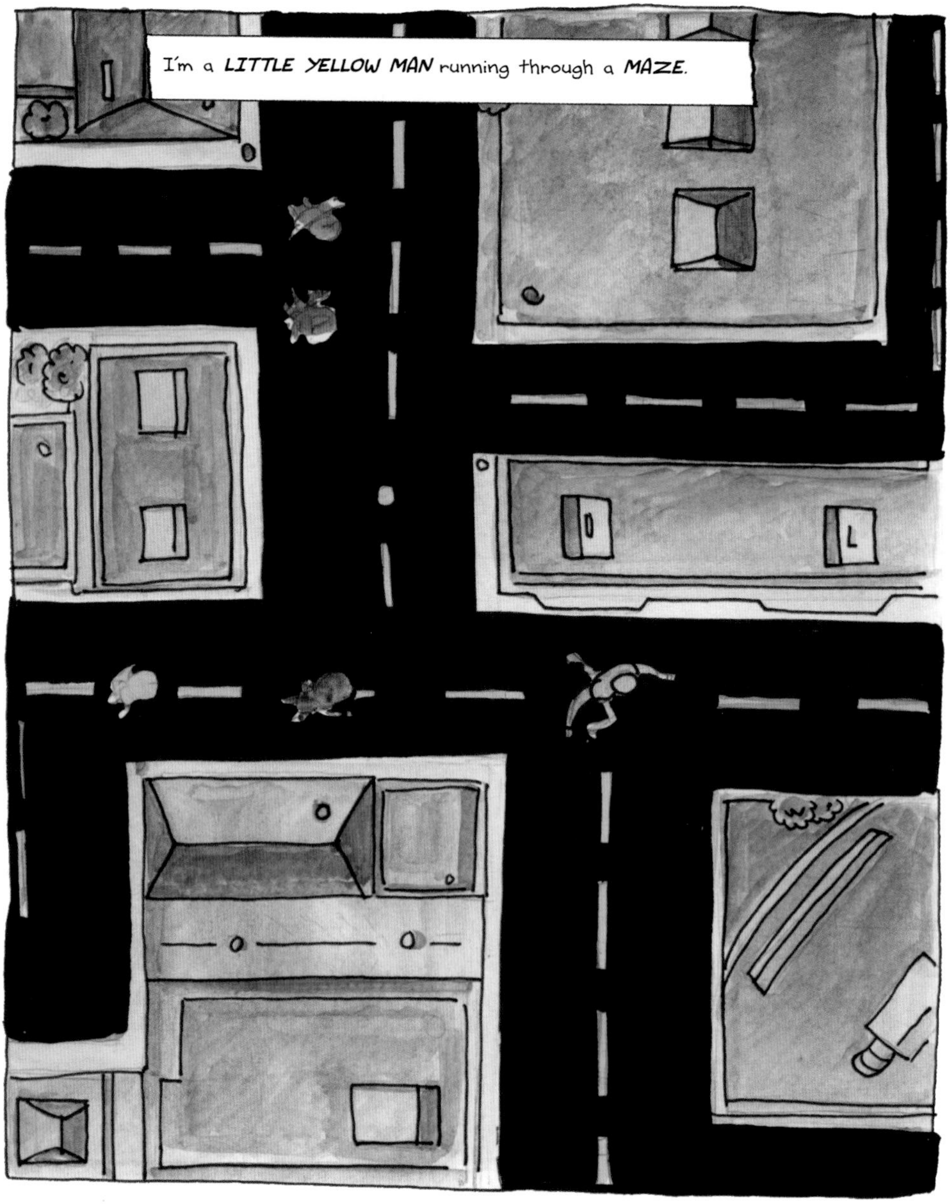
I'm a LITTLE YELLOW MAN running through a MAZE.

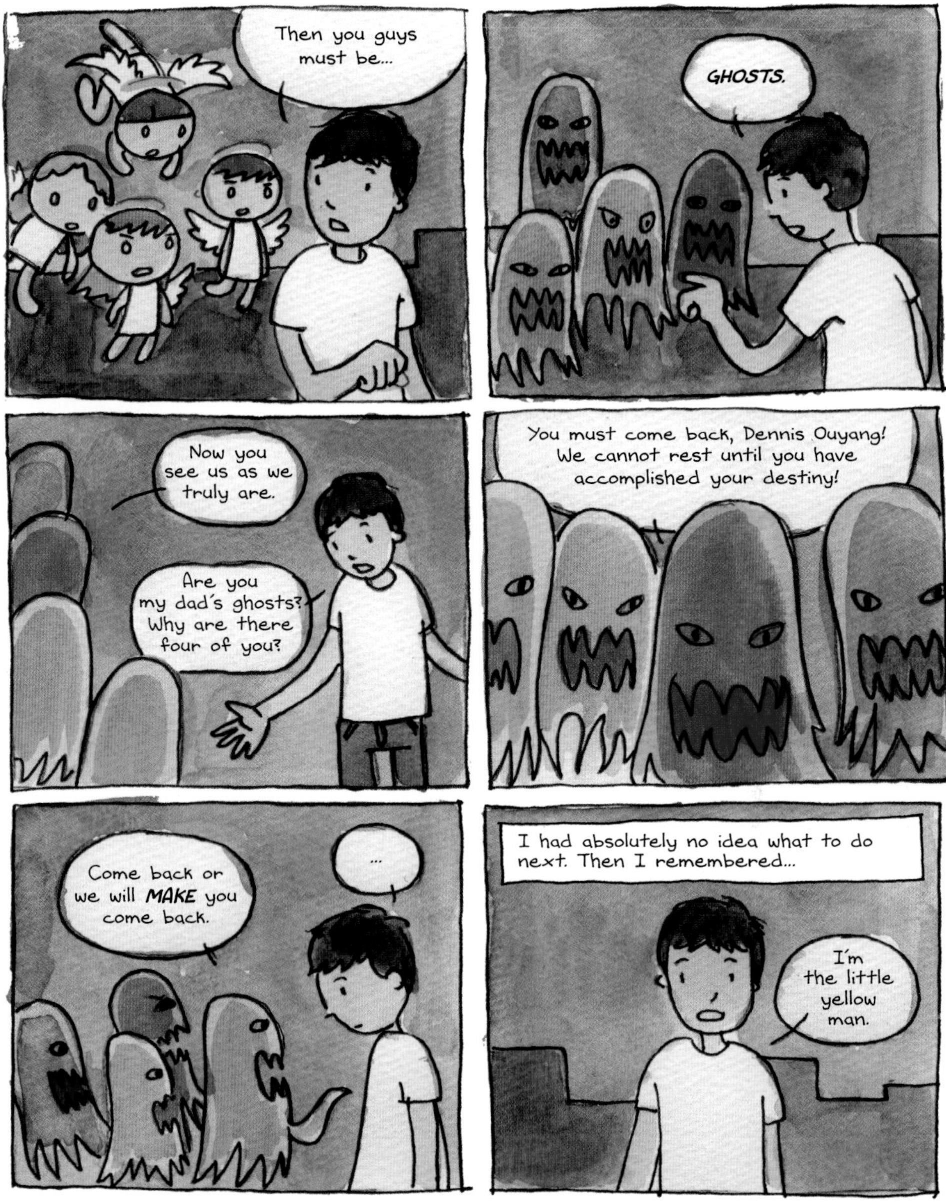
Then you guys must be...
GHOSTS.
Now you see us as we truly are.
Are you my dad's ghosts? Why are there four of you?
You must come back, Dennis Ouyang! We cannot rest until you have accomplished your destiny!
Come back or we will **MAKE** you come back.
...
I had absolutely no idea what to do next. Then I remembered...
I'm the little yellow man.

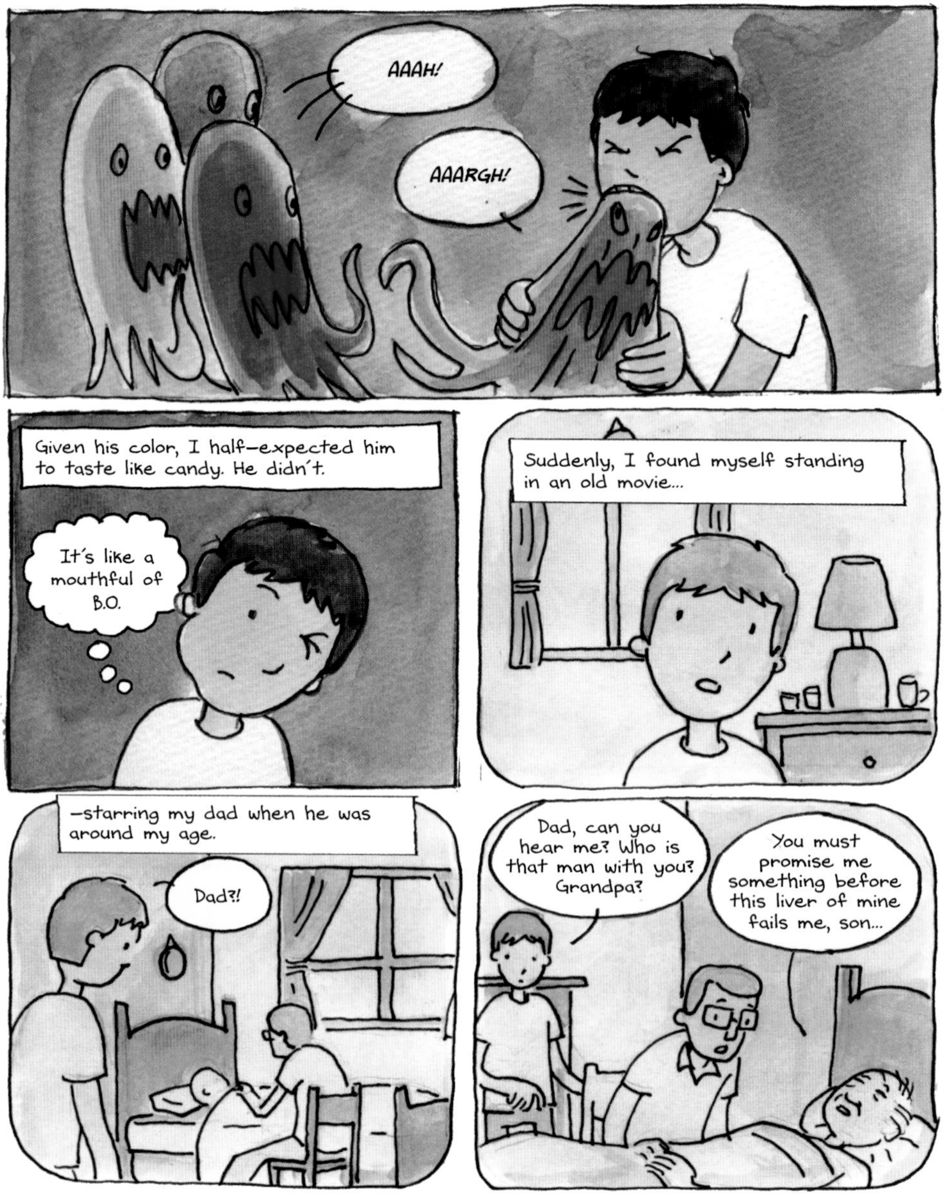
AAAH!
AAARGH!
Given his color, I half-expected him to taste like candy. He didn't.
It's like a mouthful of B.O.
Suddenly, I found myself standing in an old movie...
-starring my dad when he was around my age.
Dad?!
Dad, can you hear me? Who is that man with you? Grandpa?
You must promise me something before this liver of mine fails me, son...

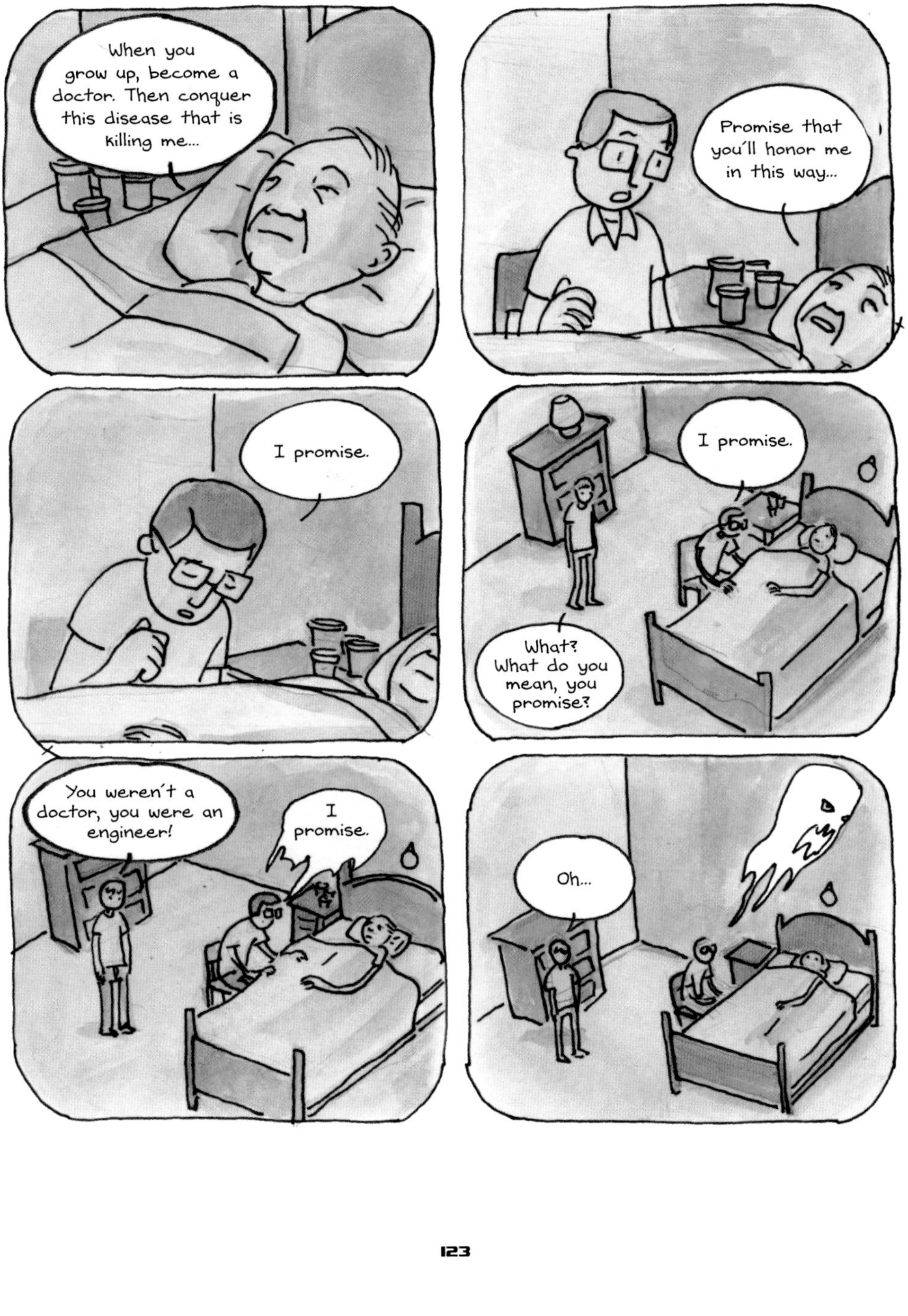
When you grow up, become a doctor. Then conquer this disease that is killing me...
Promise that you'll honor me in this way...
I promise.
I promise.
What? What do you mean, you promise?
You weren't a doctor, you were an engineer!
I promise.
Oh...

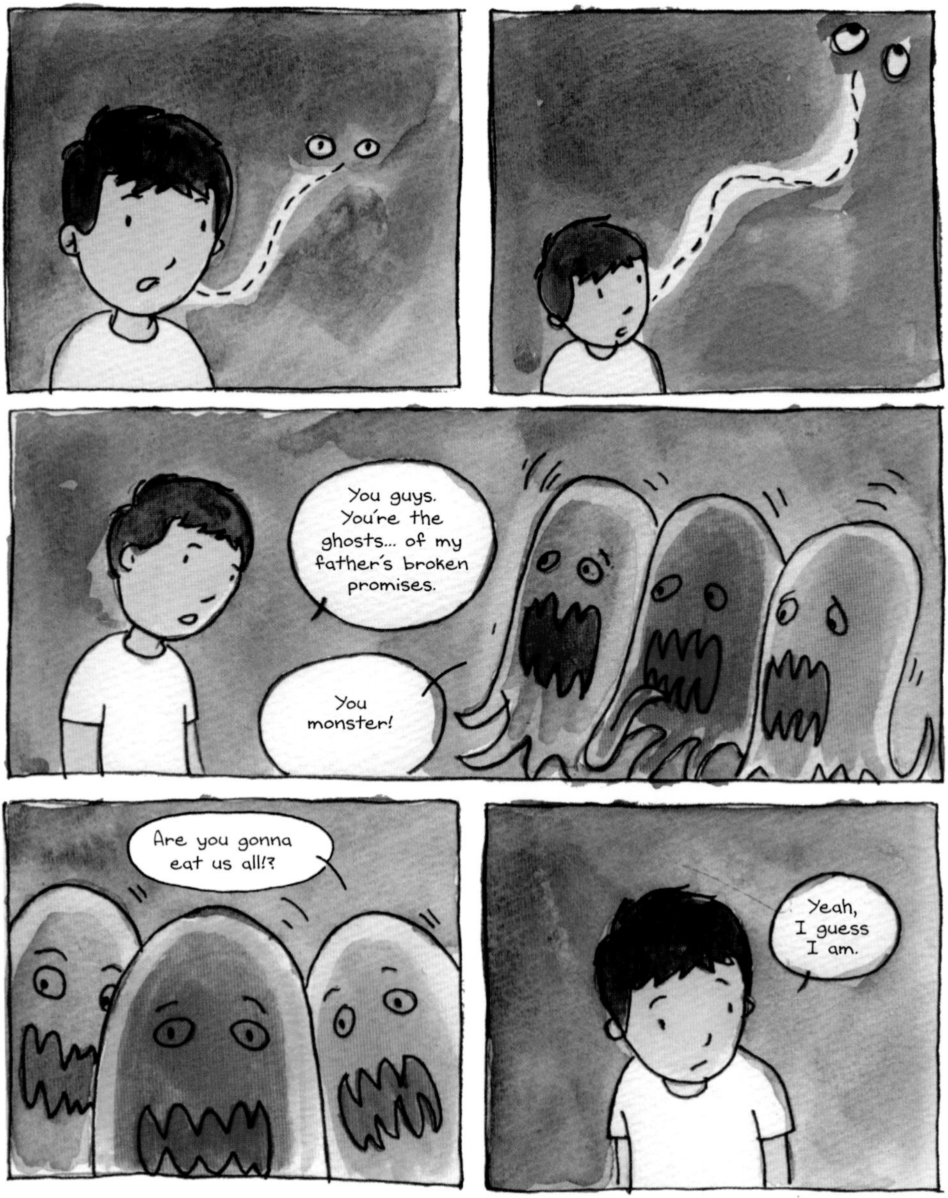
You guys. You're the ghosts... of my father's broken promises.
You monster!
Are you gonna eat us all!?
Yeah, I guess I am.

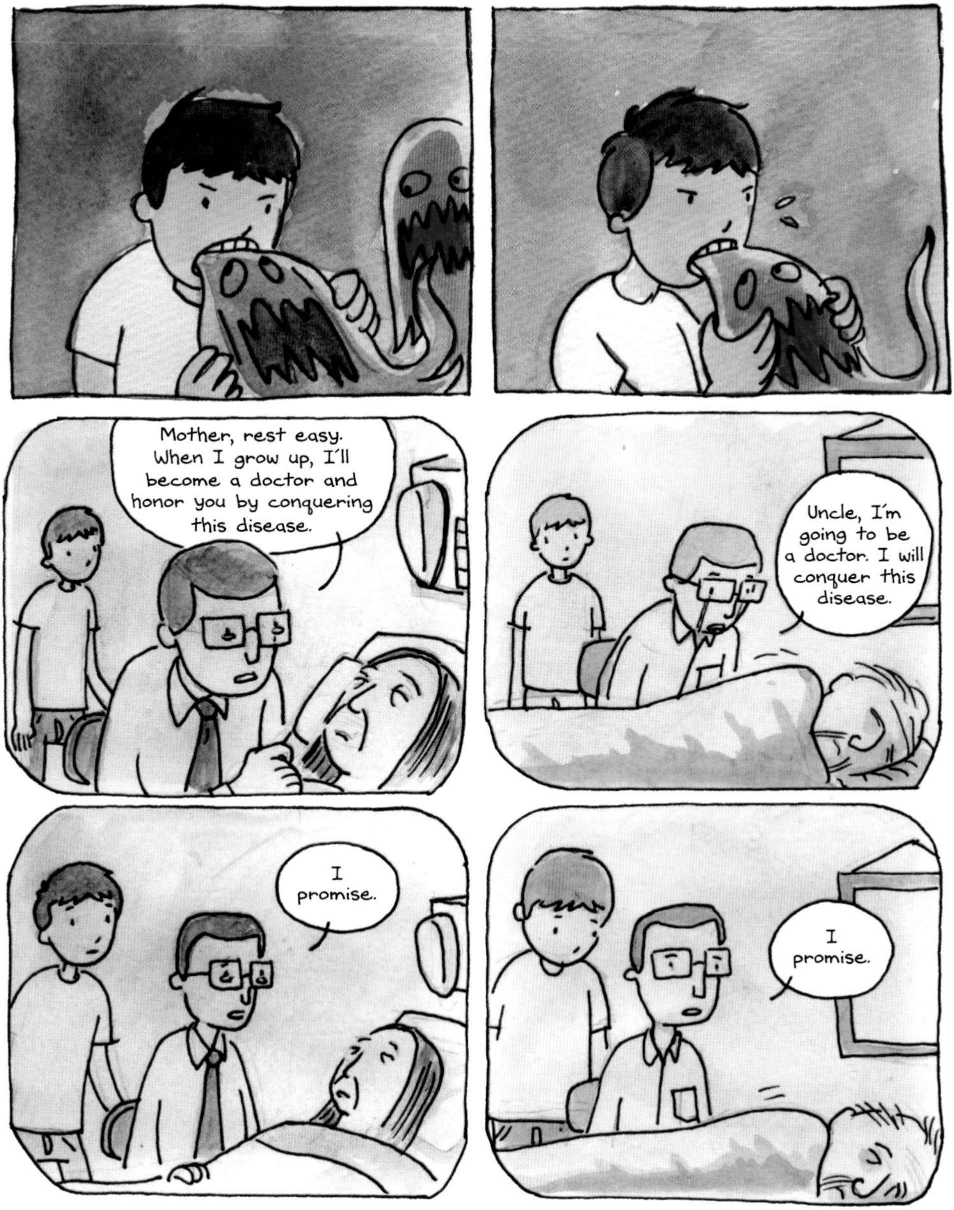
Mother, rest easy. When I grow up, I'll become a doctor and honor you by conquering this disease.
Uncle, I'm going to be a doctor. I will conquer this disease.
I promise.
I promise.

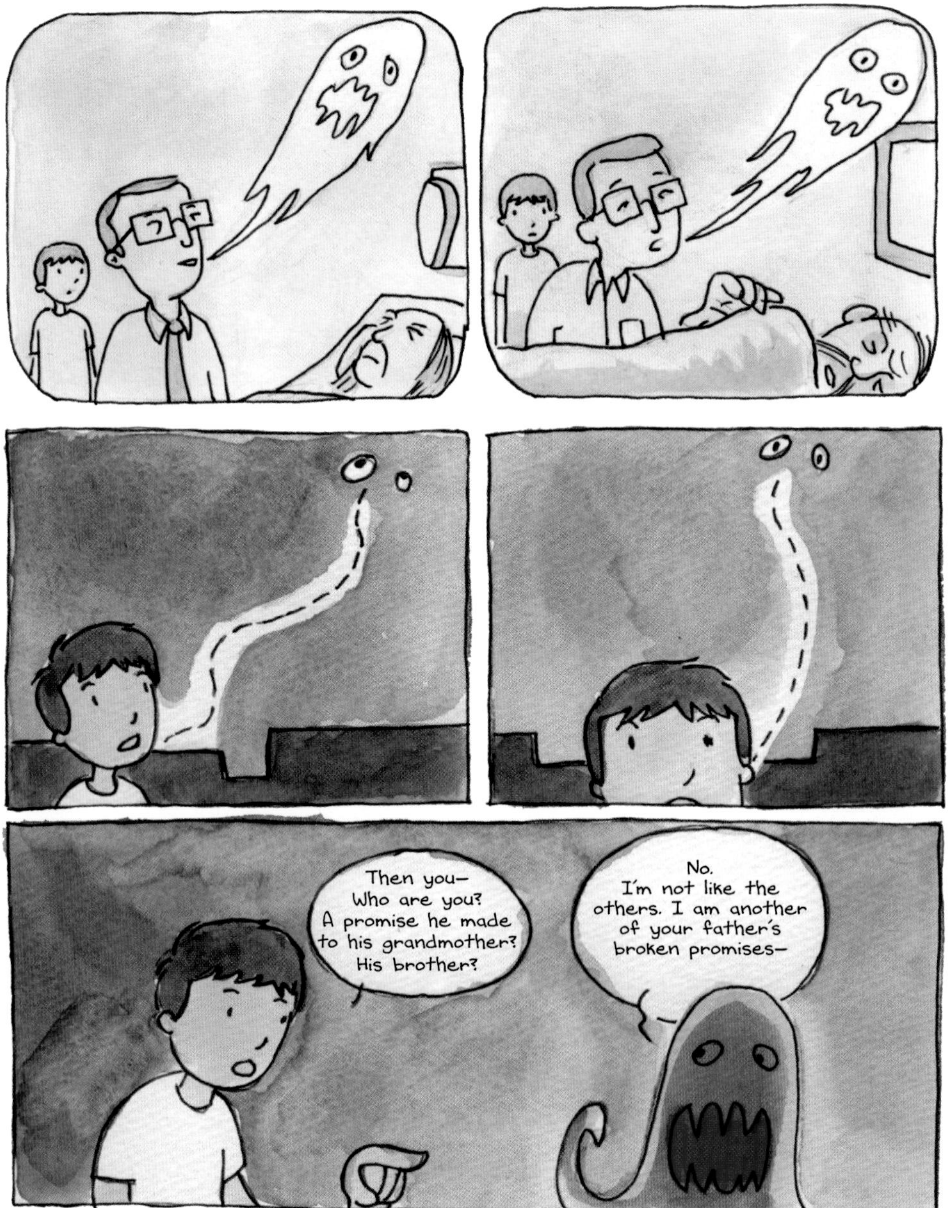
Then you—
Who are you?
A promise he made
to his grandmother?
His brother?
No.
I'm not like the
others. I am another
of your father's
broken promises—

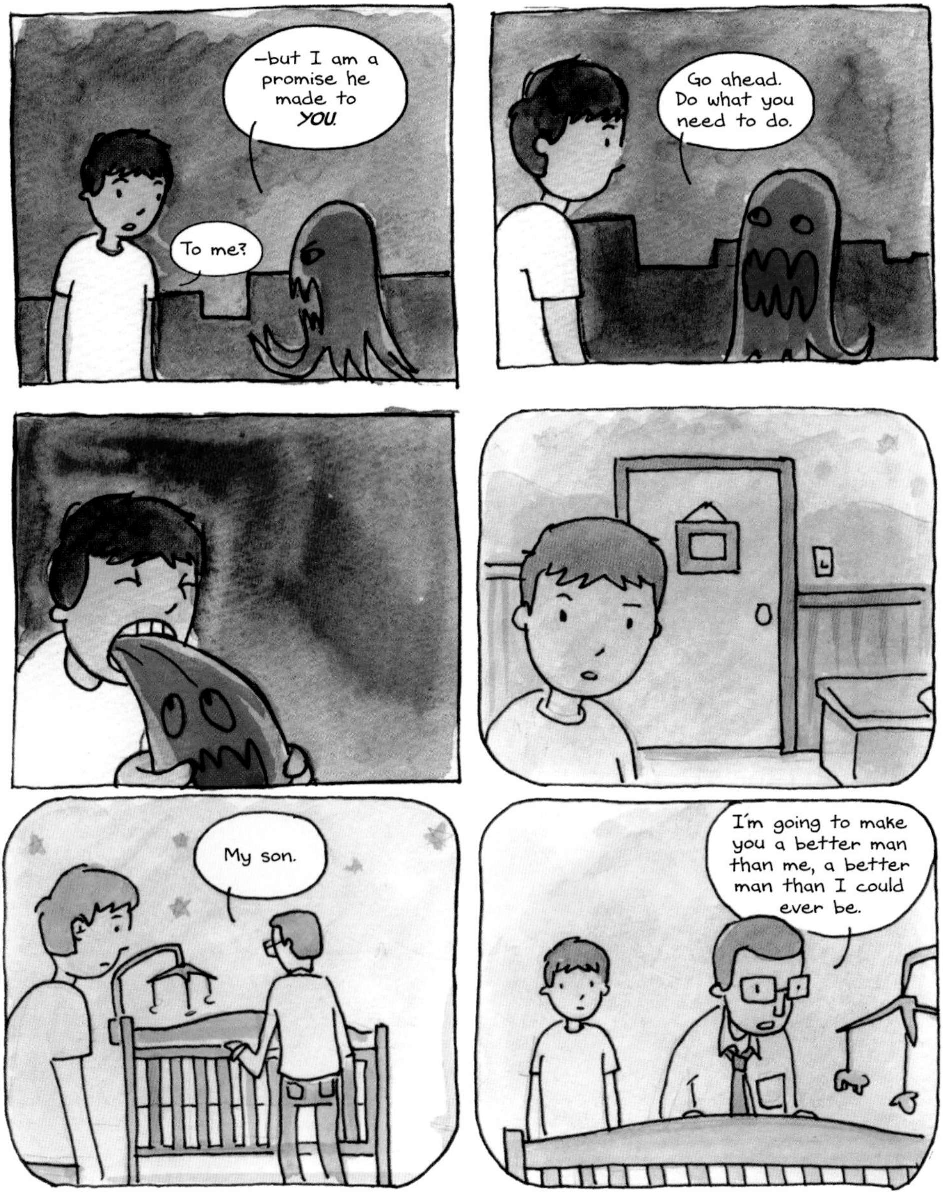
—but I am a promise he made to *YOU*.
To me?
Go ahead. Do what you need to do.
My son.
I'm going to make you a better man than me, a better man than I could ever be.

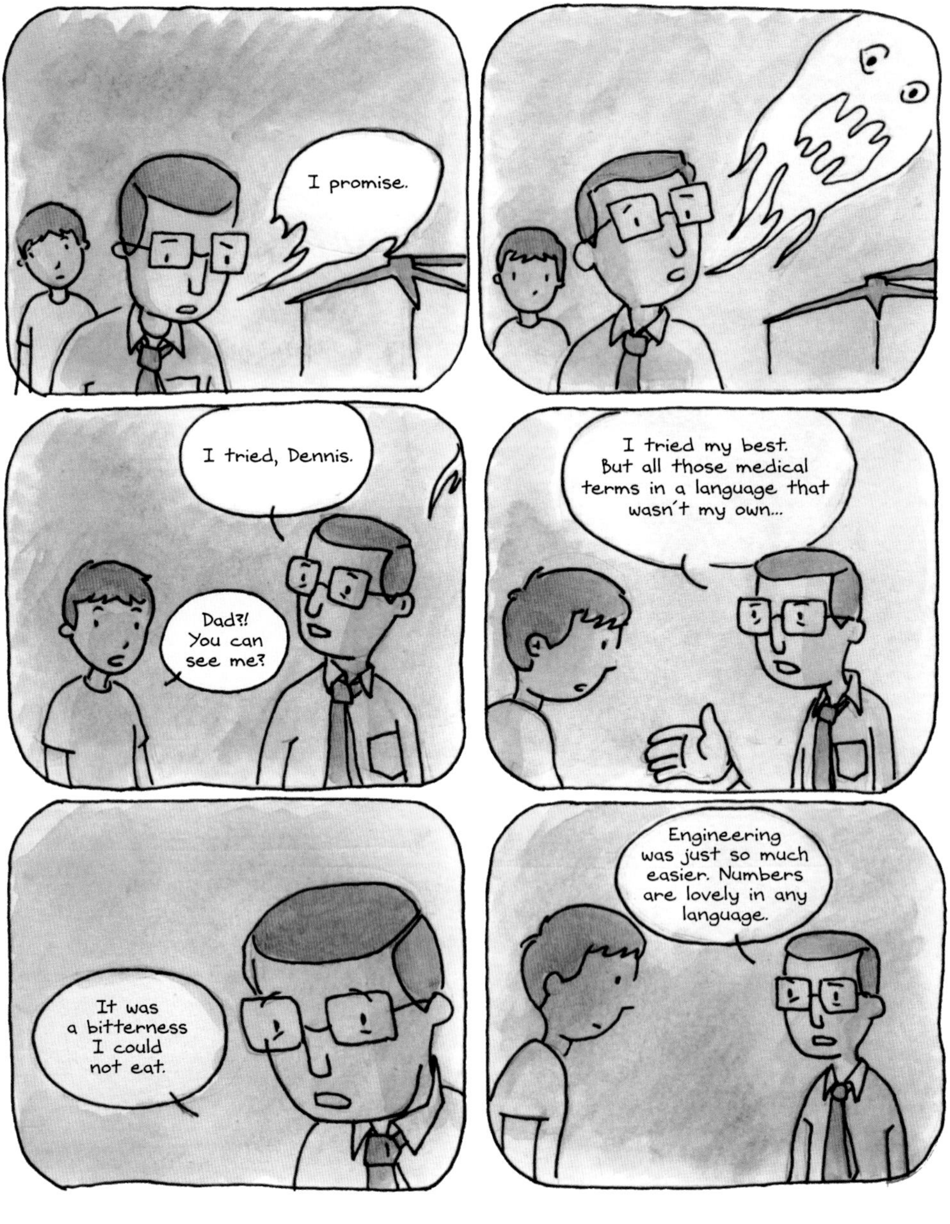

I promise.
I tried, Dennis.
Dad?! You can see me?
I tried my best. But all those medical terms in a language that wasn't my own...
It was a bitterness I could not eat.
Engineering was just so much easier. Numbers are lovely in any language.

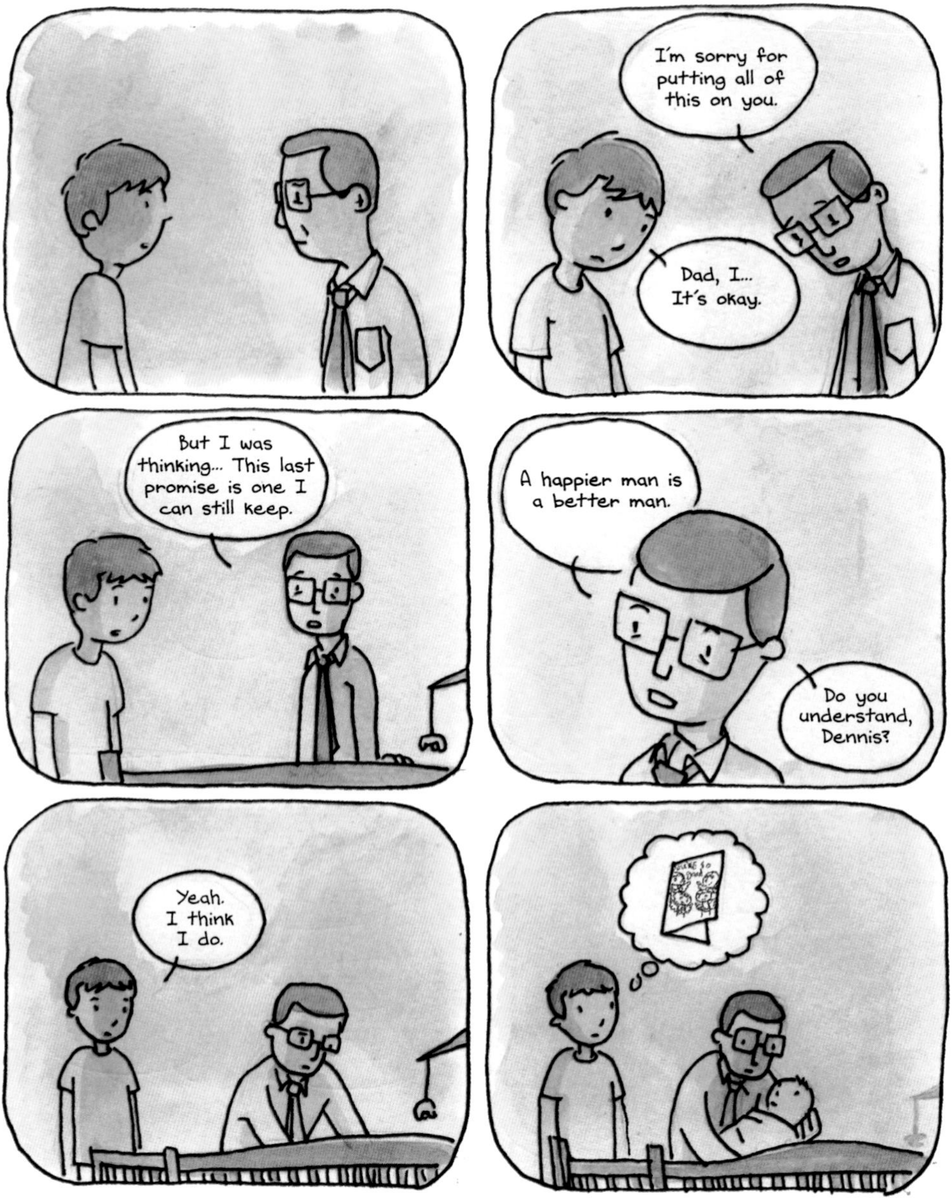
I'm sorry for putting all of this on you.
Dad, I... It's okay.
But I was thinking... This last promise is one I can still keep.
A happier man is a better man.
Do you understand, Dennis?
Yeah. I think I do.

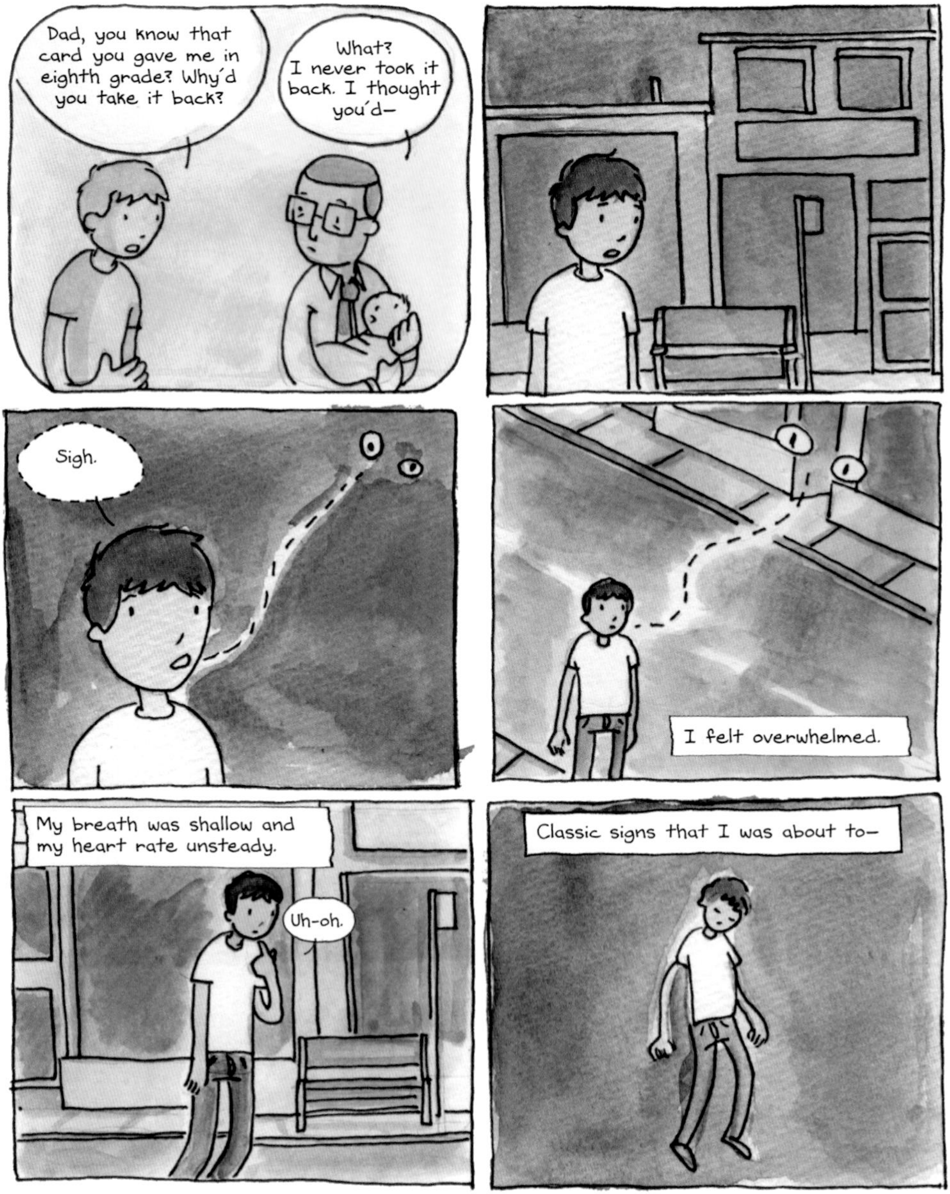
Dad, you know that card you gave me in eighth grade? Why'd you take it back?
What? I never took it back. I thought you'd—
Sigh.
I felt overwhelmed.
My breath was shallow and my heart rate unsteady.
Uh-oh.
Classic signs that I was about to—

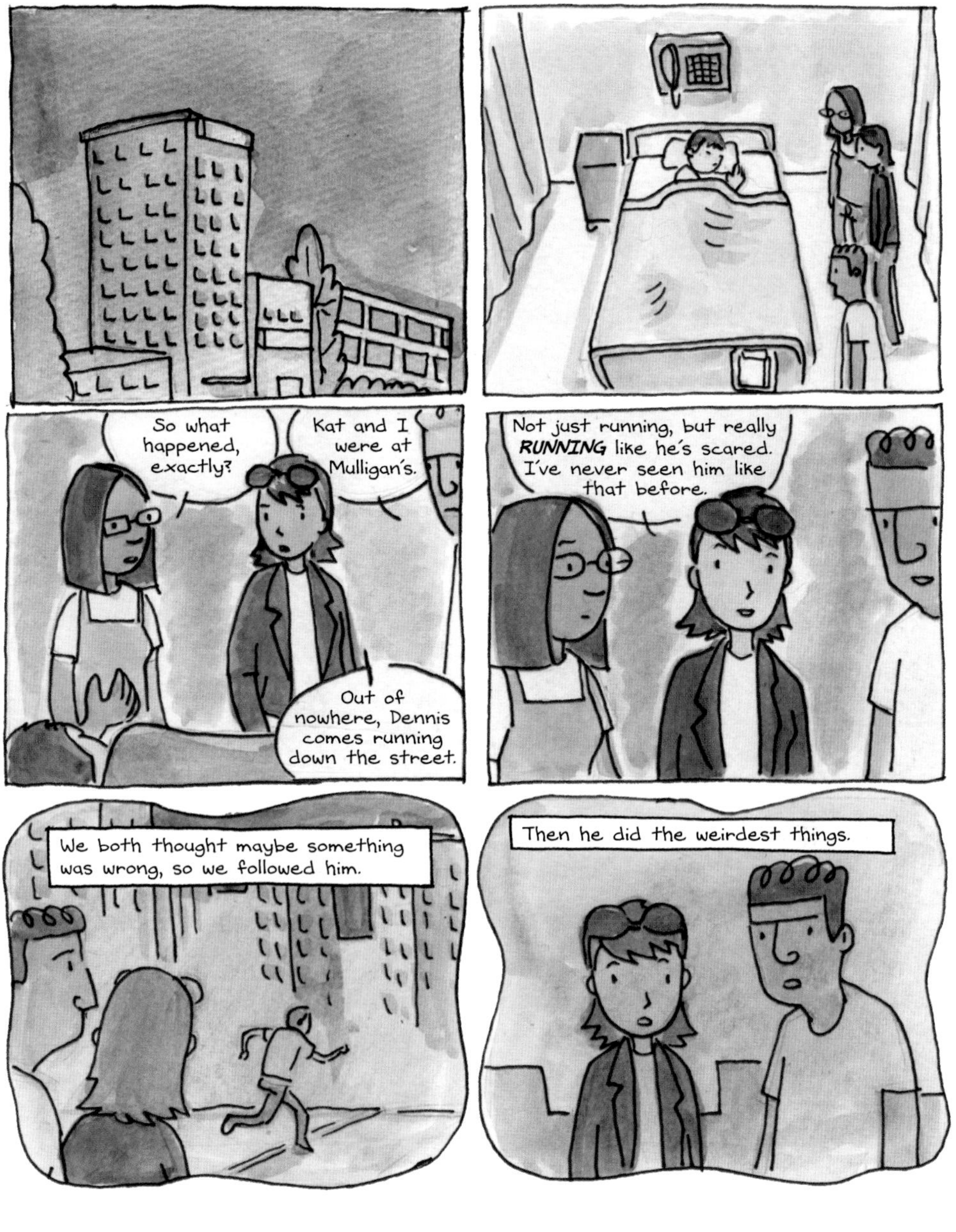

So what happened, exactly?
Kat and I were at Mulligan's.
Out of nowhere, Dennis comes running down the street.
Not just running, but really **RUNNING** like he's scared. I've never seen him like that before.
We both thought maybe something was wrong, so we followed him.
Then he did the weirdest things.

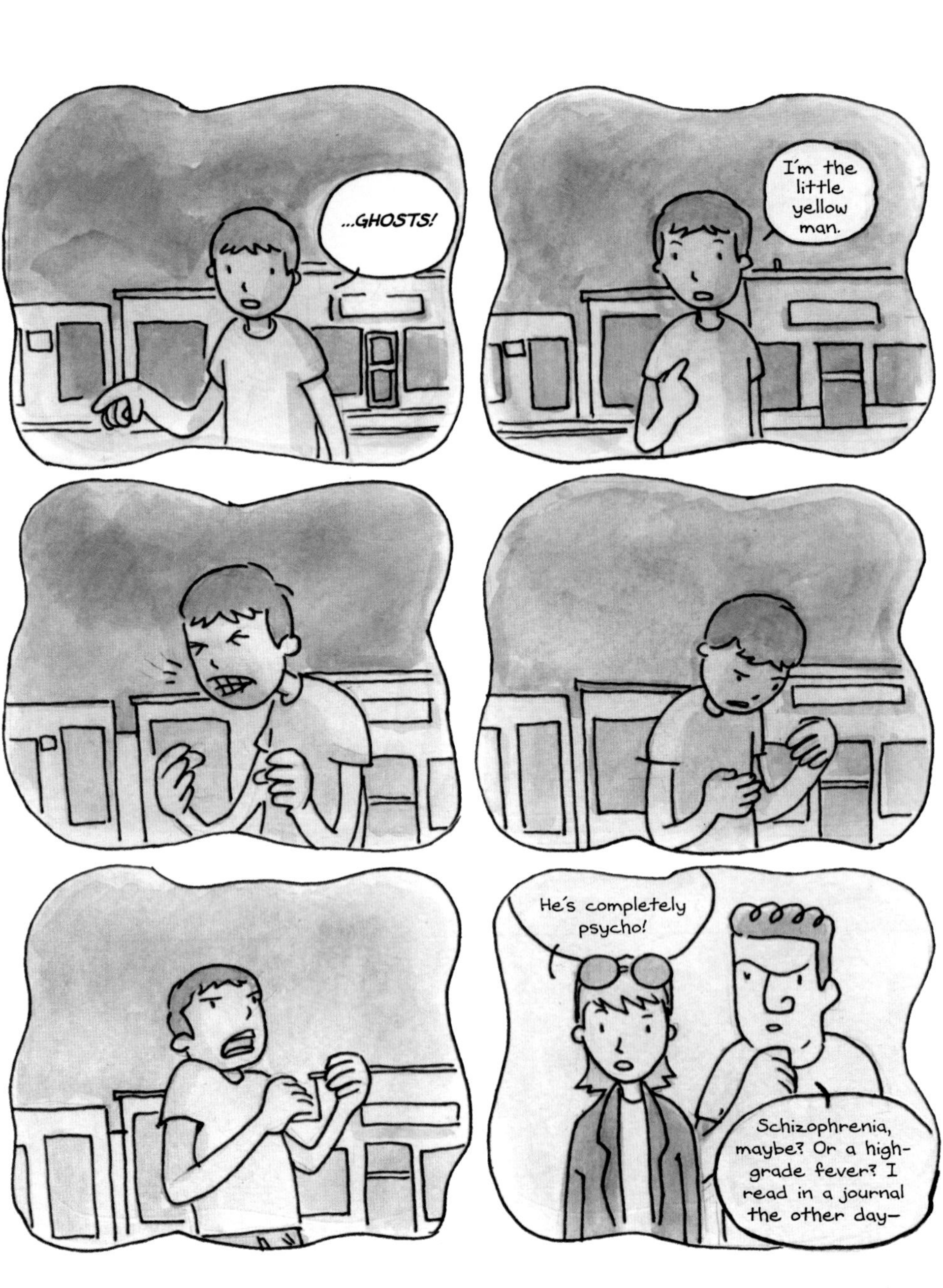
...GHOSTS!
I'm the little yellow man.
He's completely psycho!
Schizophrenia, maybe? Or a high-grade fever? I read in a journal the other day—

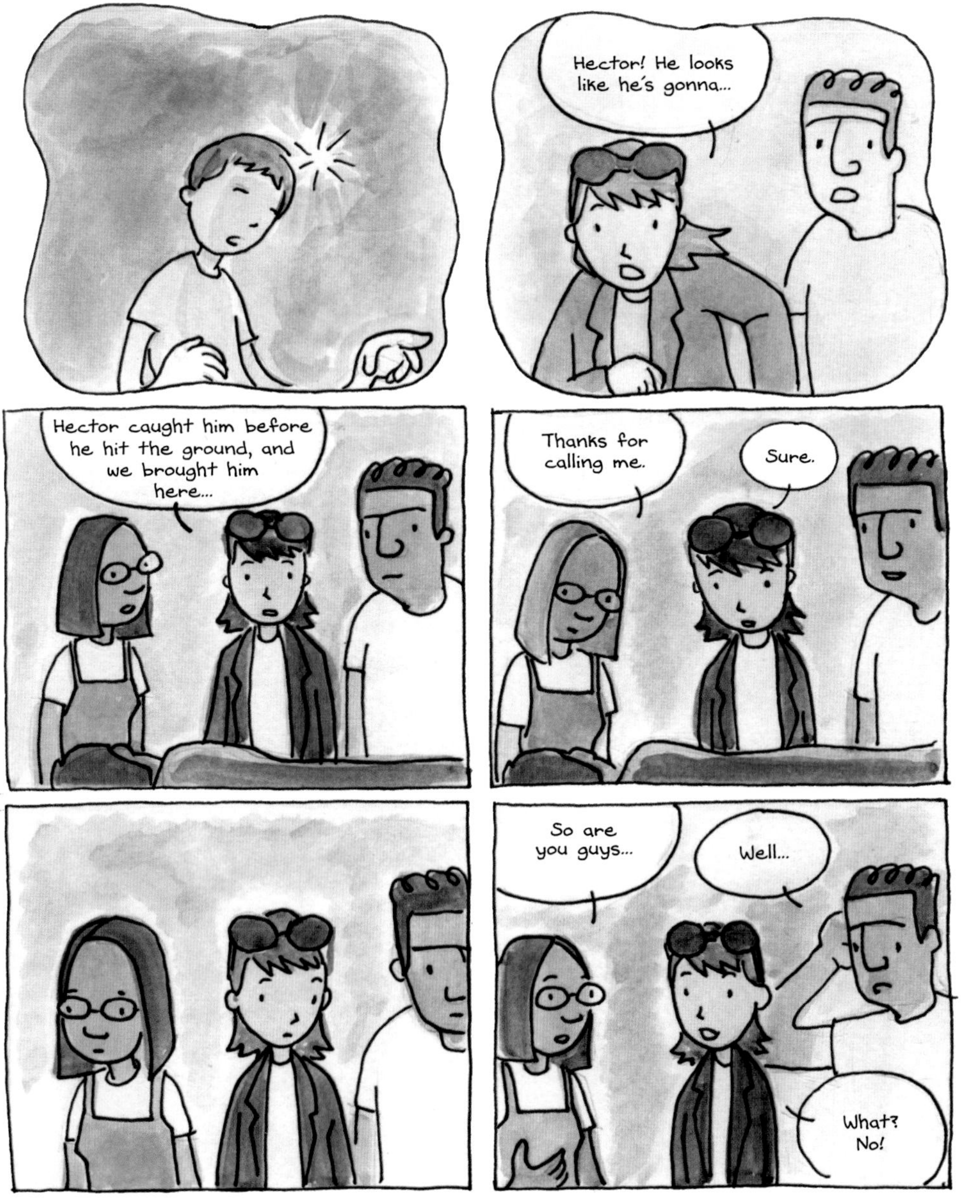
Hector! He looks like he's gonna...
Hector caught him before he hit the ground, and we brought him here...
Thanks for calling me.
Sure.
So are you guys...
Well...
What? No!

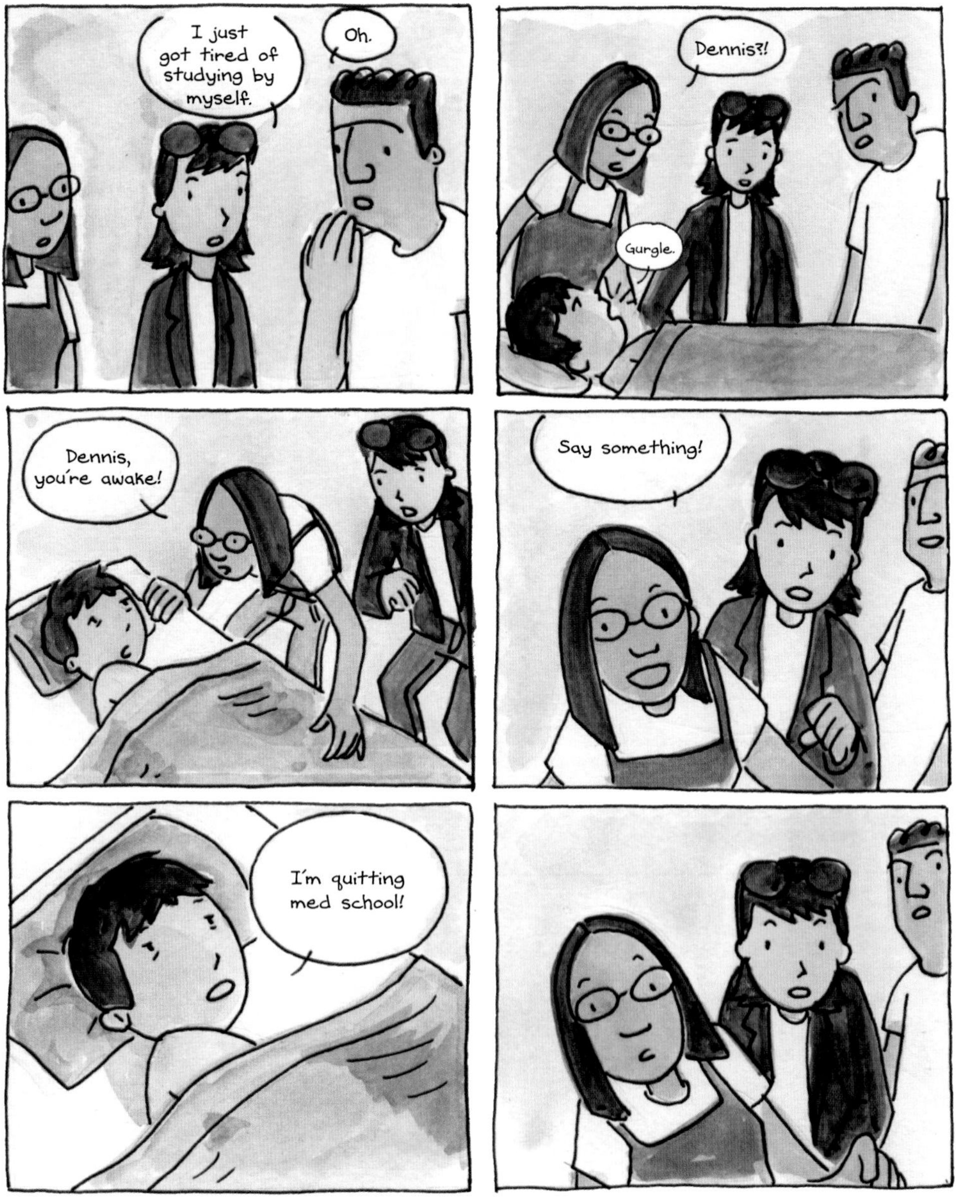
I just got tired of studying by myself.
Oh.
Dennis?!
Gurgle.
Dennis, you're awake!
Say something!
I'm quitting med school!

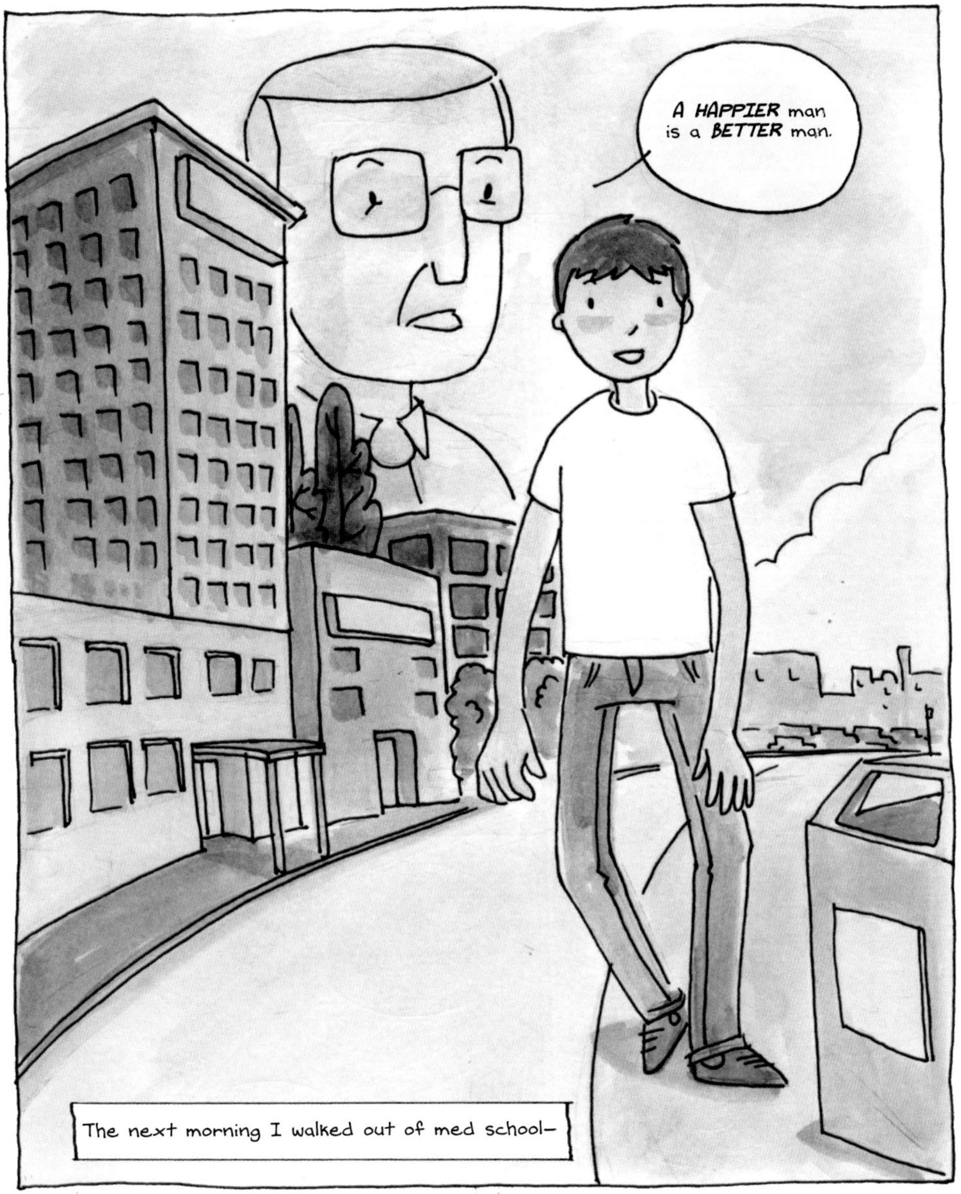
A HAPPIER man is a BETTER man.
The next morning I walked out of med school—

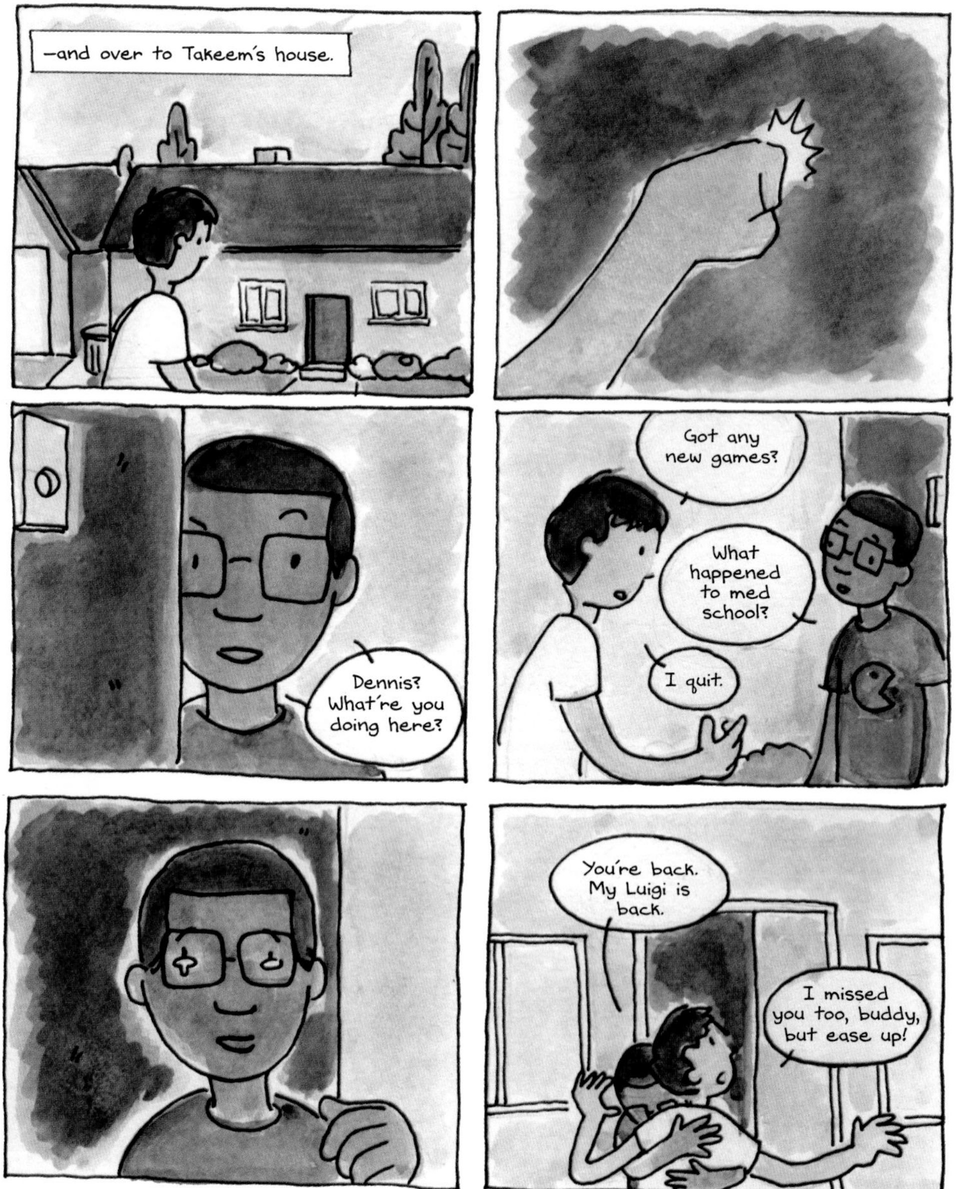
—and over to Takeem's house.
Dennis? What're you doing here?
Got any new games?
What happened to med school?
I quit.
You're back. My Luigi is back.
I missed you too, buddy, but ease up!

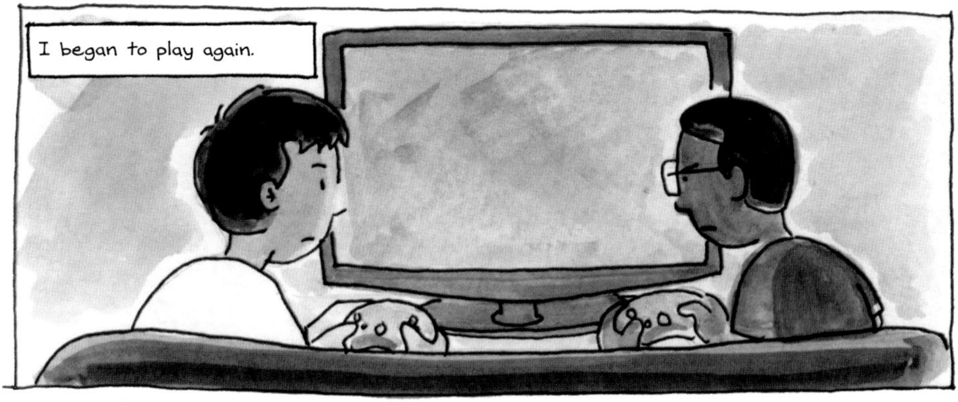
I began to play again.

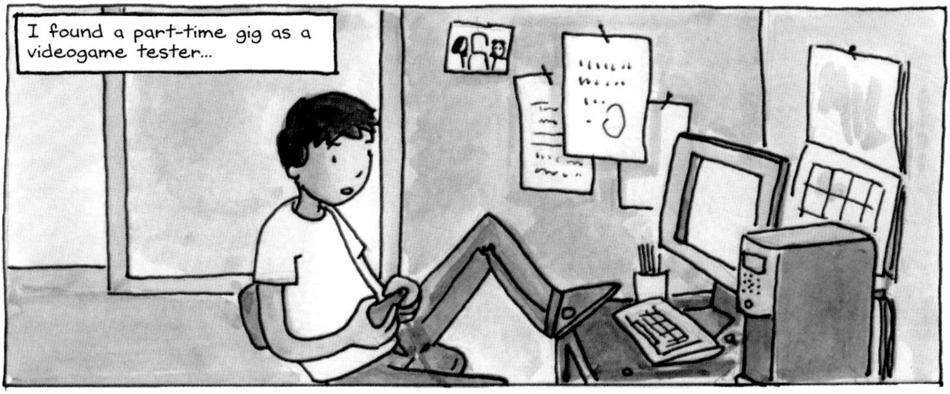
I found a part-time gig as a videogame tester...

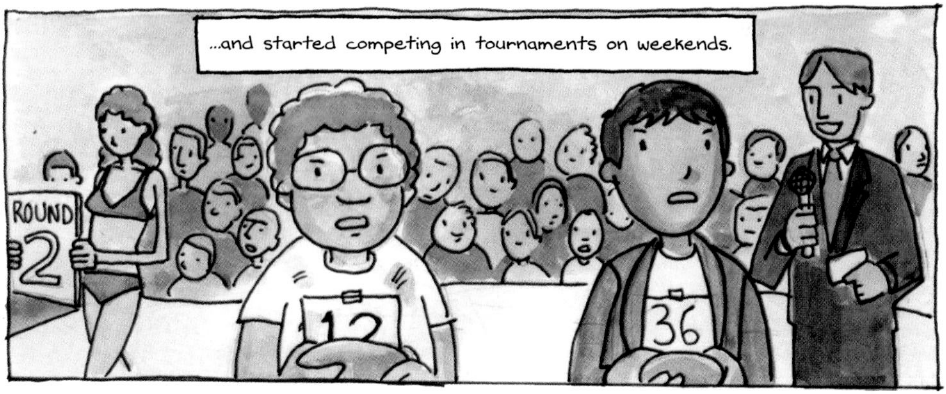
...and started competing in tournaments on weekends.
ROUND 2
12
36

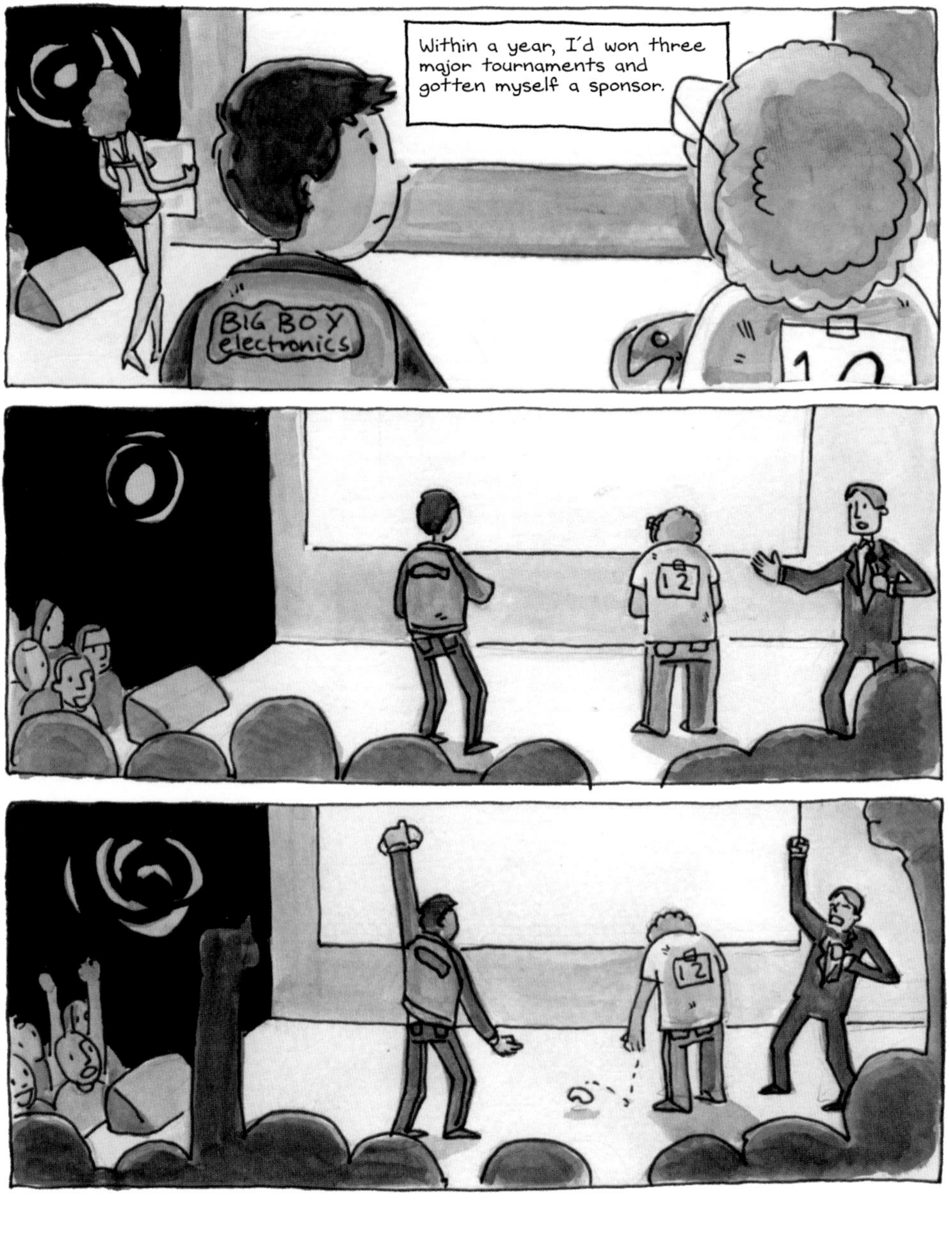
Within a year, I'd won three major tournaments and gotten myself a sponsor.
BIG BOY electronics
12
12
12

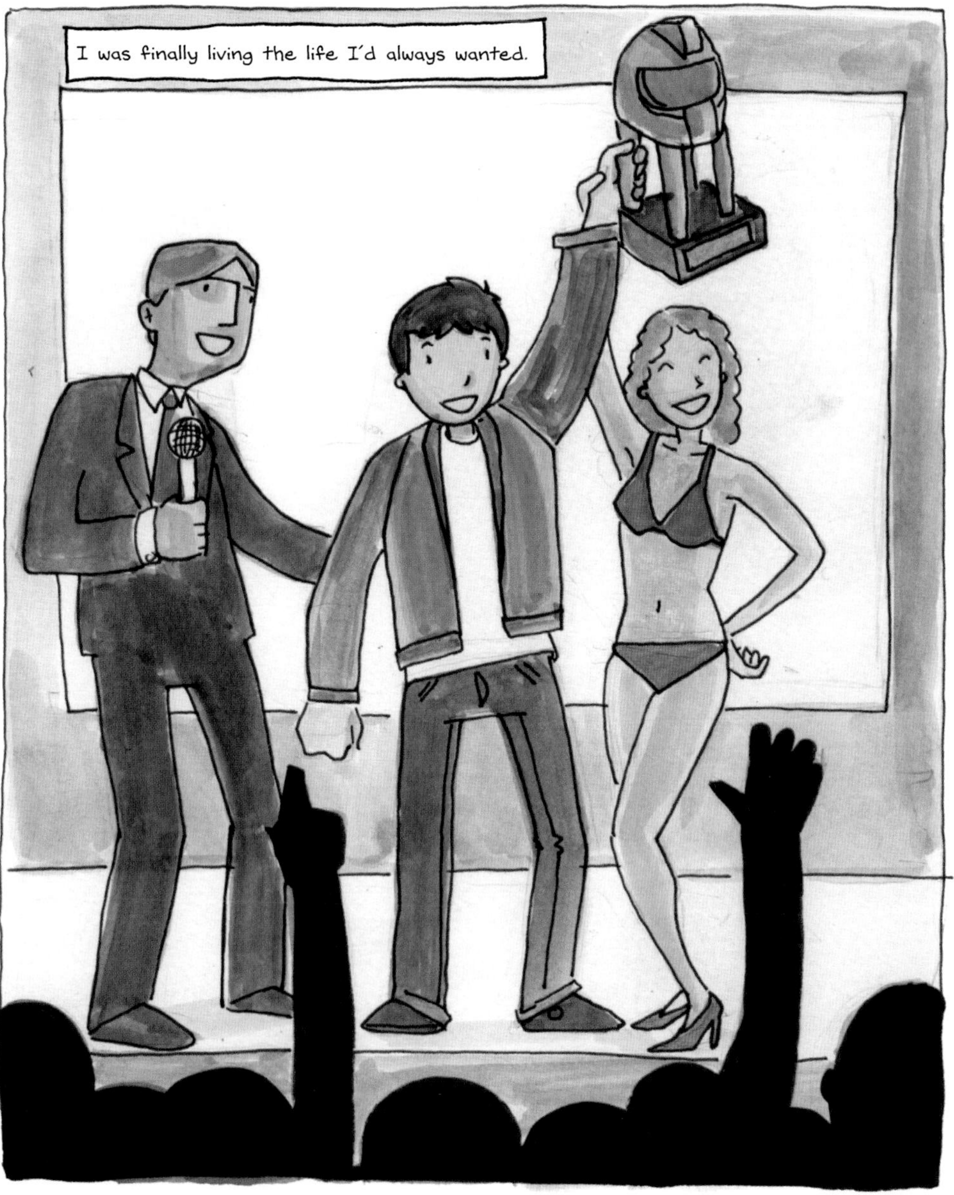
I was finally living the life I'd always wanted.

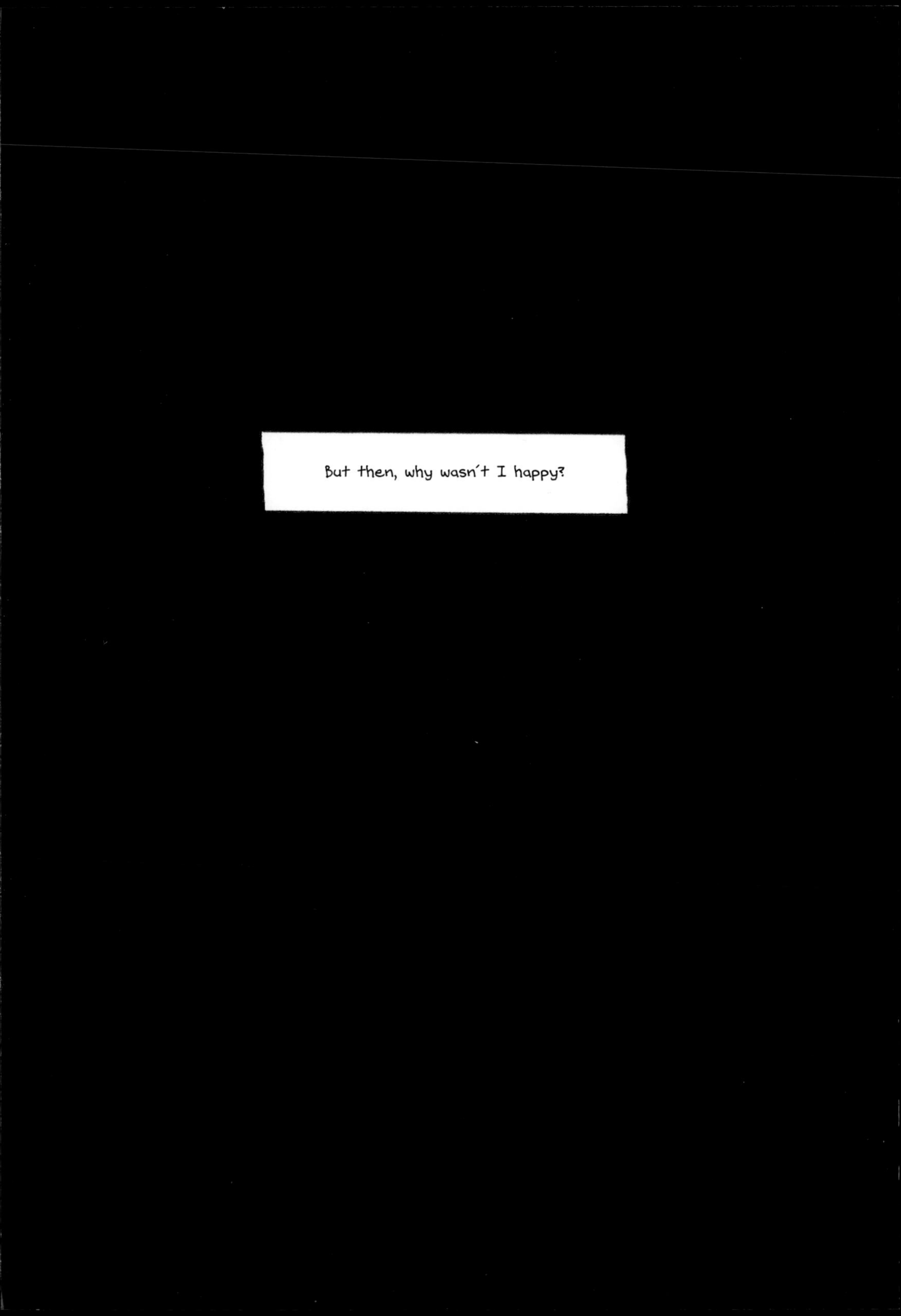
But then, why wasn't I happy?

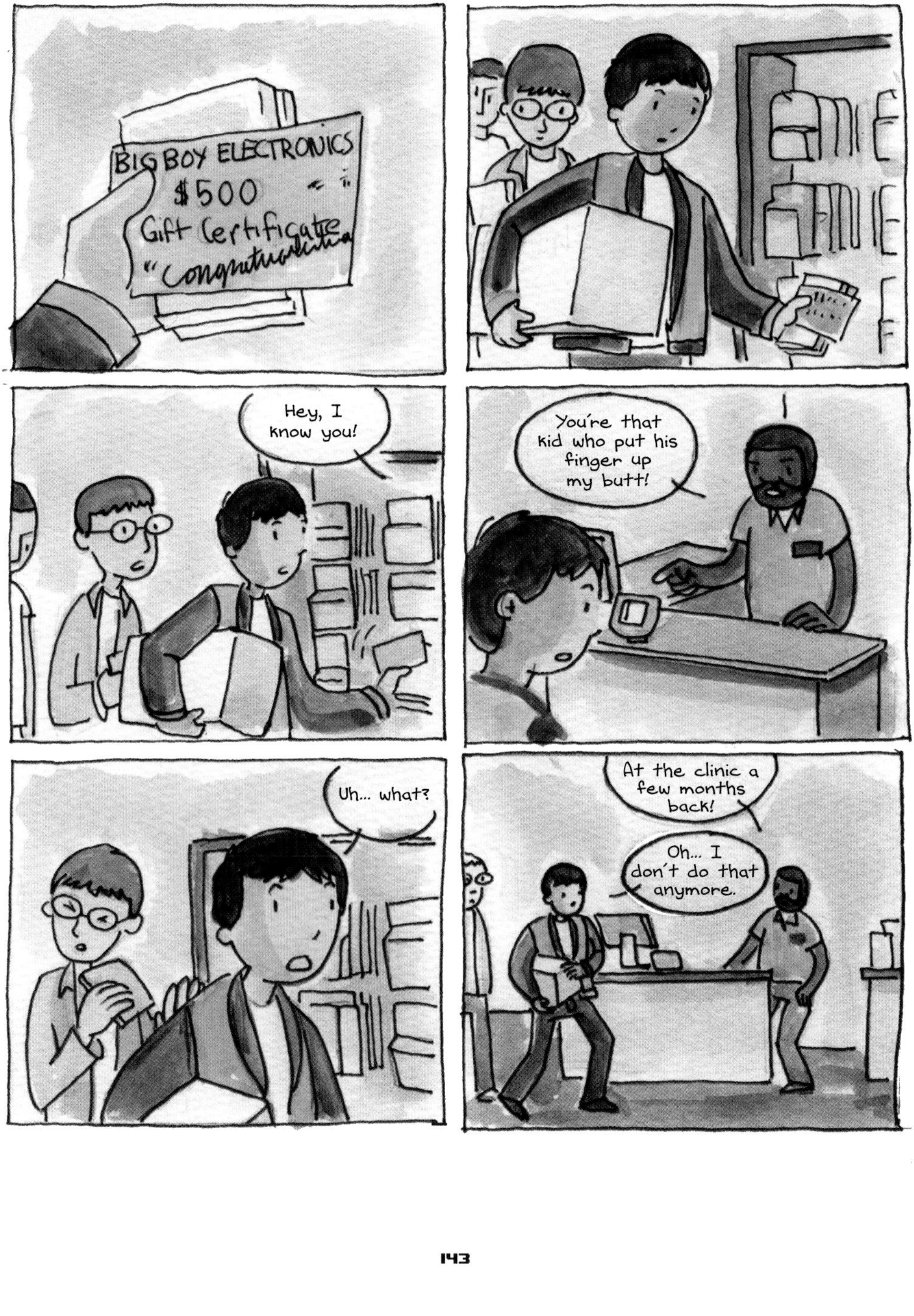
BIG BOY ELECTRONICS
$500
Gift Certificate
Hey, I know you!
You're that kid who put his finger up my butt!
Uh... what?
At the clinic a few months back!
Oh... I don't do that anymore.

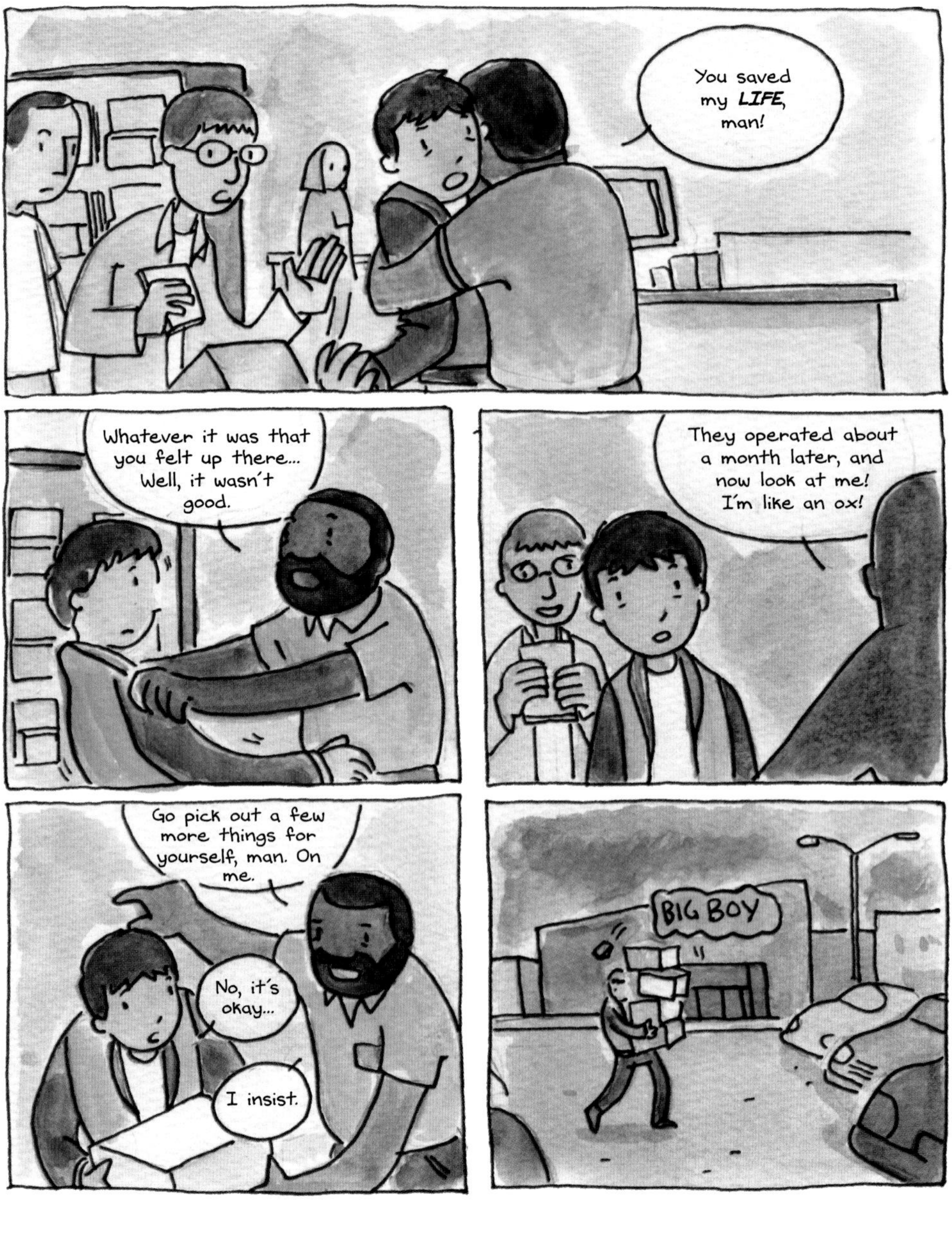
You saved my LIFE, man!
Whatever it was that you felt up there... Well, it wasn't good.
They operated about a month later, and now look at me! I'm like an ox!
Go pick out a few more things for yourself, man. On me.
No, it's okay...
I insist.
BIG BOY

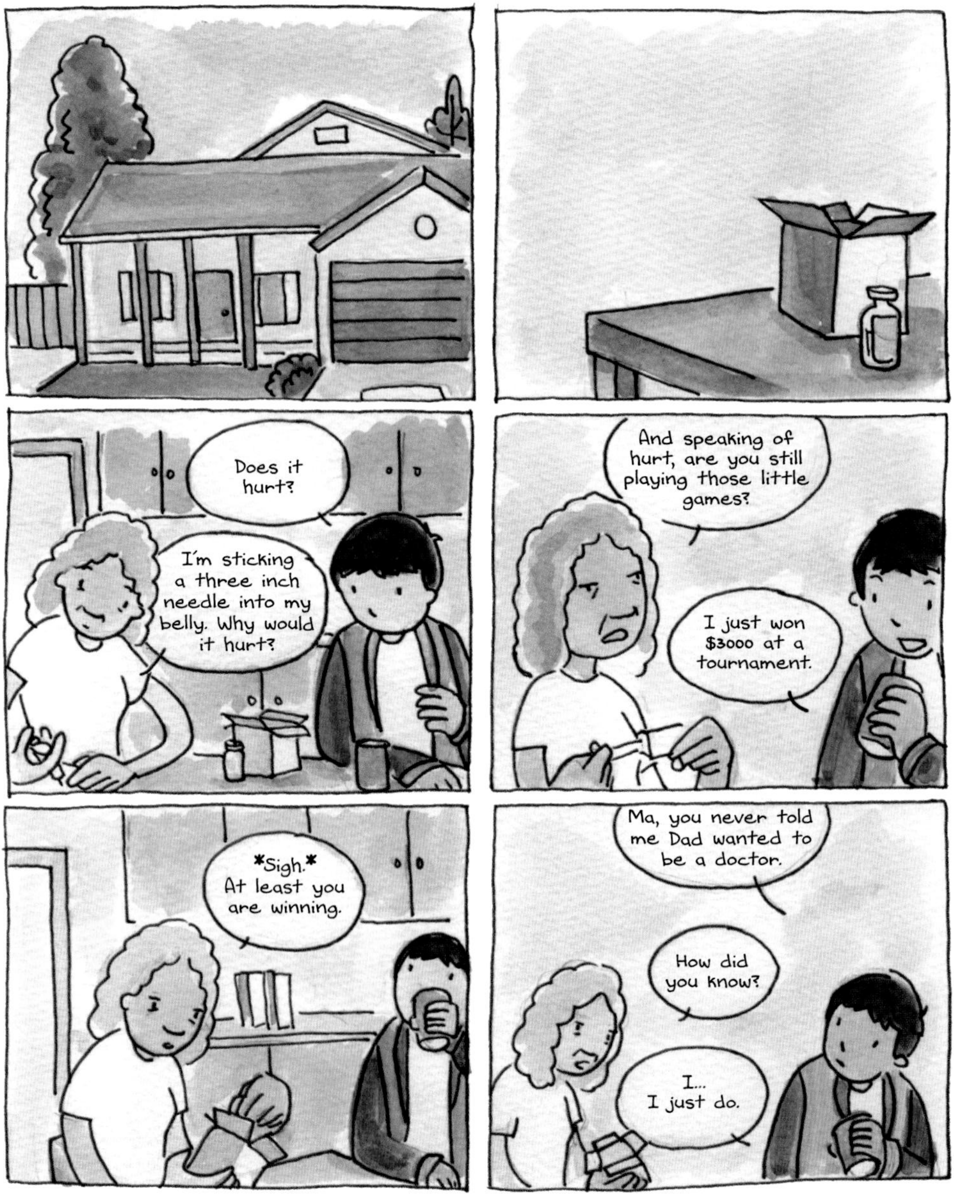
Does it hurt?
I'm sticking a three inch needle into my belly. Why would it hurt?
And speaking of hurt, are you still playing those little games?
I just won $3000 at a tournament.
Sigh. At least you are winning.
Ma, you never told me Dad wanted to be a doctor.
How did you know?
I... I just do.

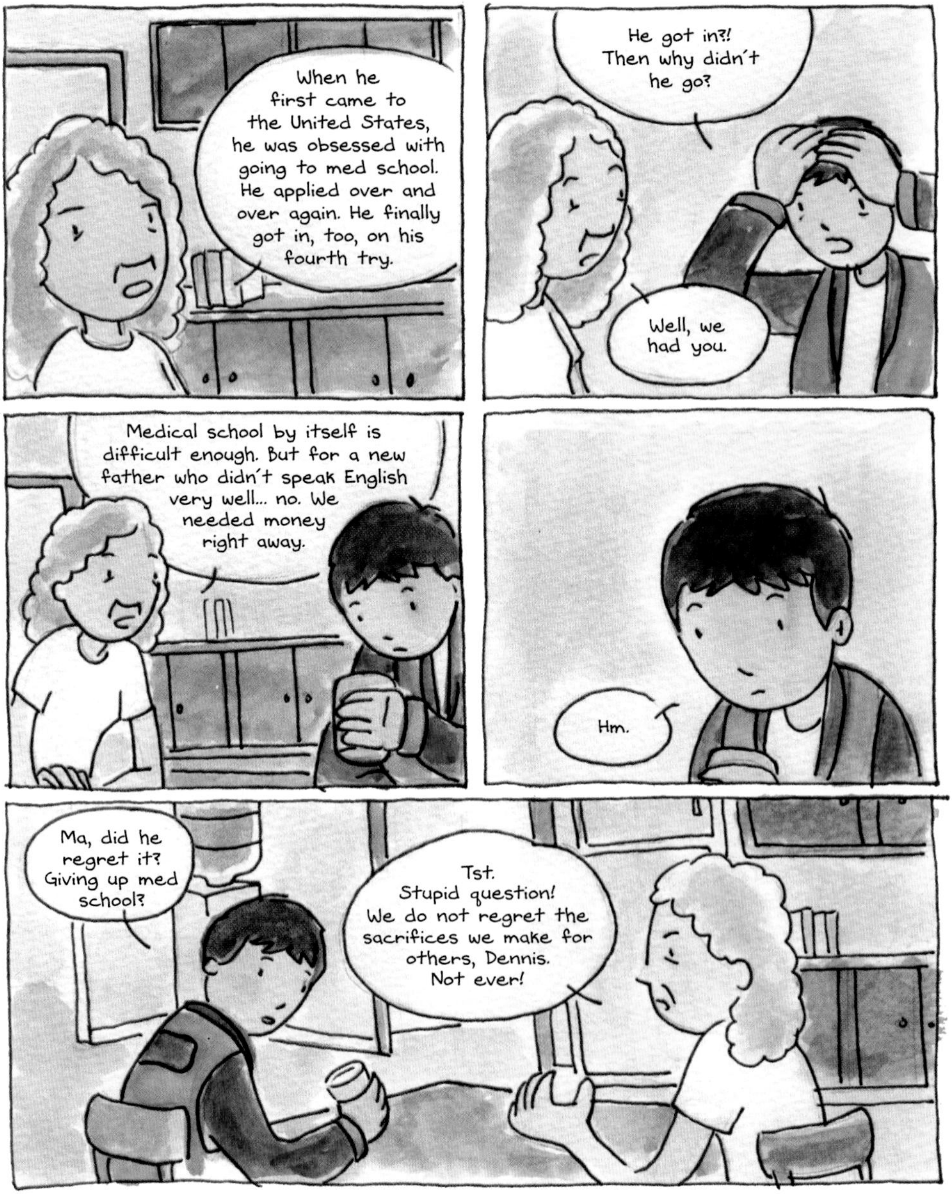
When he first came to the United States, he was obsessed with going to med school. He applied over and over again. He finally got in, too, on his fourth try.
He got in?! Then why didn't he go?
Well, we had you.
Medical school by itself is difficult enough. But for a new father who didn't speak English very well... no. We needed money right away.
Hm.
Ma, did he regret it? Giving up med school?
Tst. Stupid question! We do not regret the sacrifices we make for others, Dennis. Not ever!

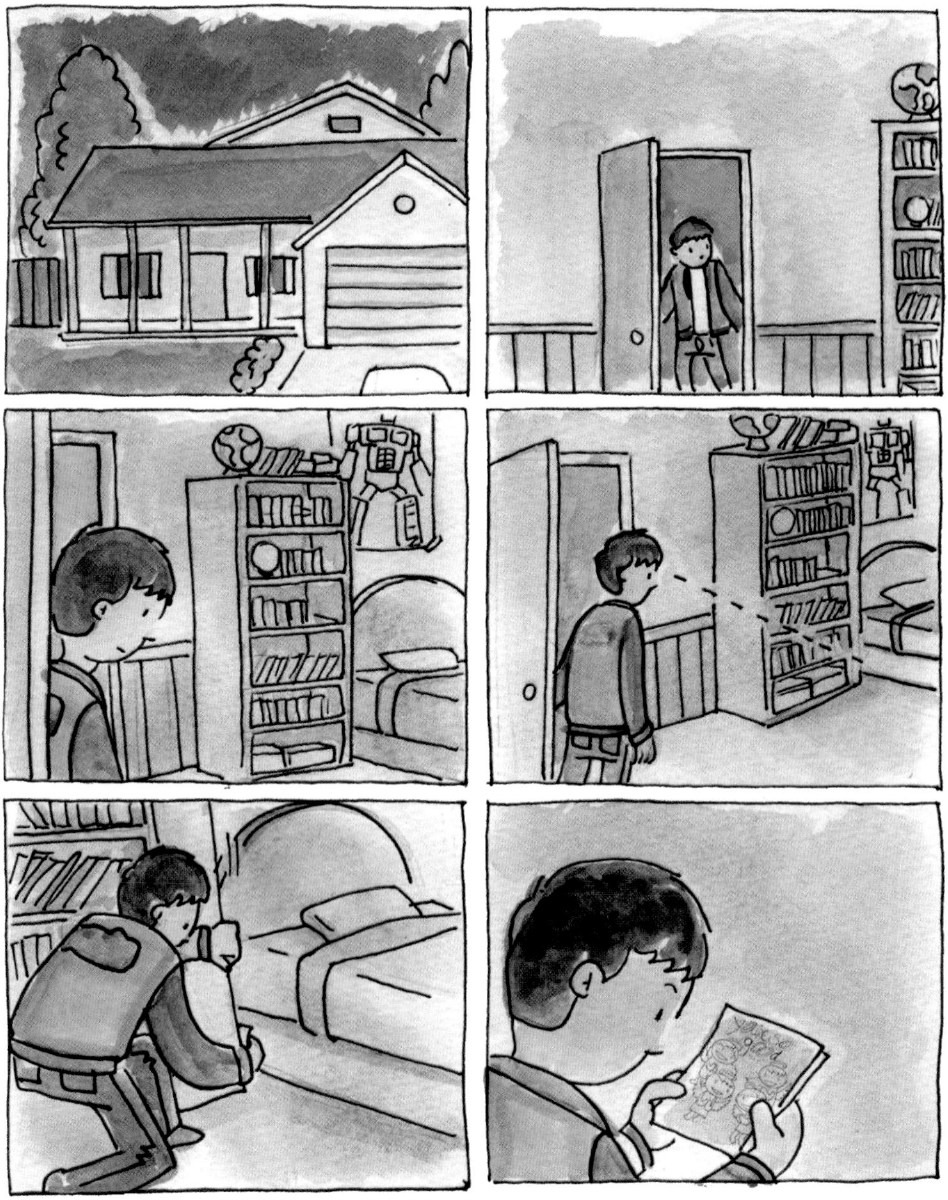

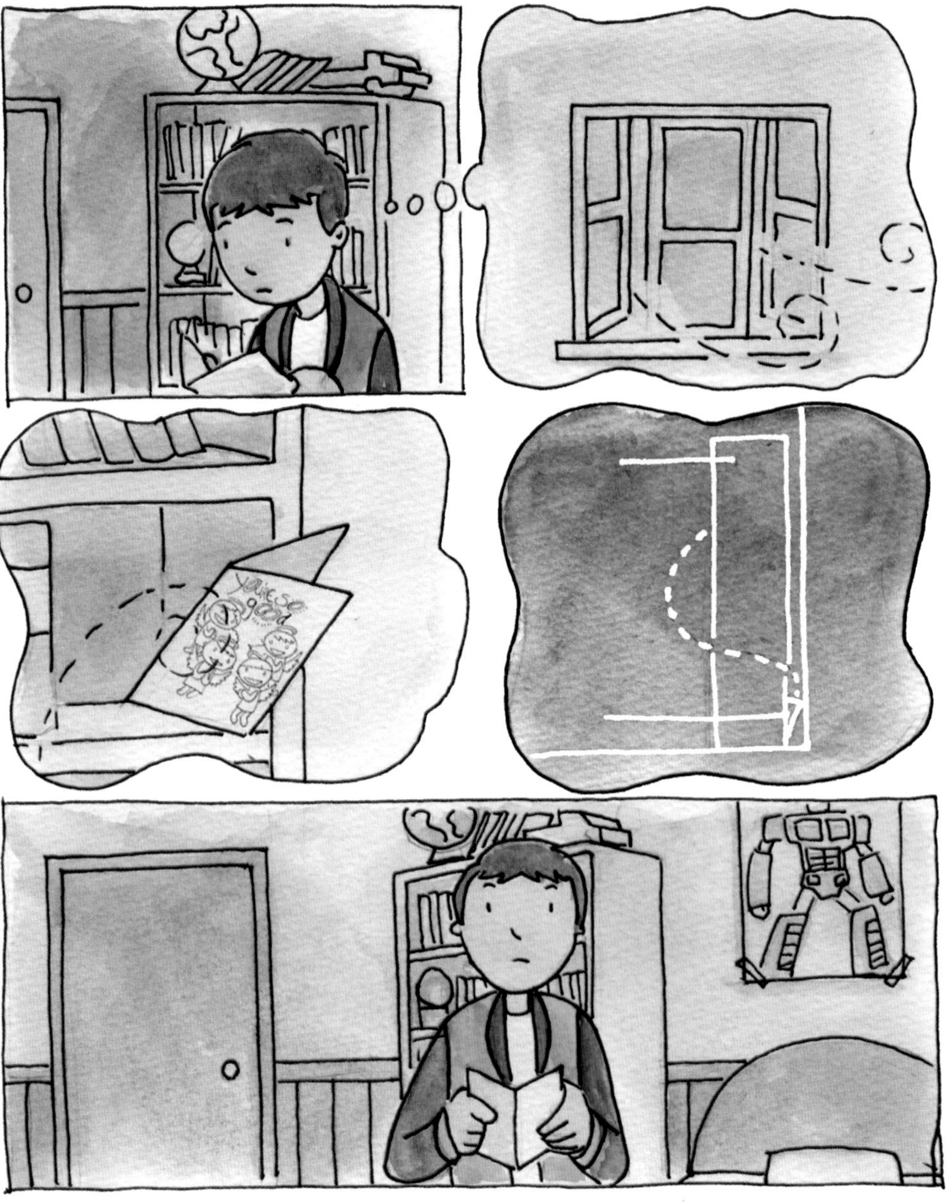
You're so good

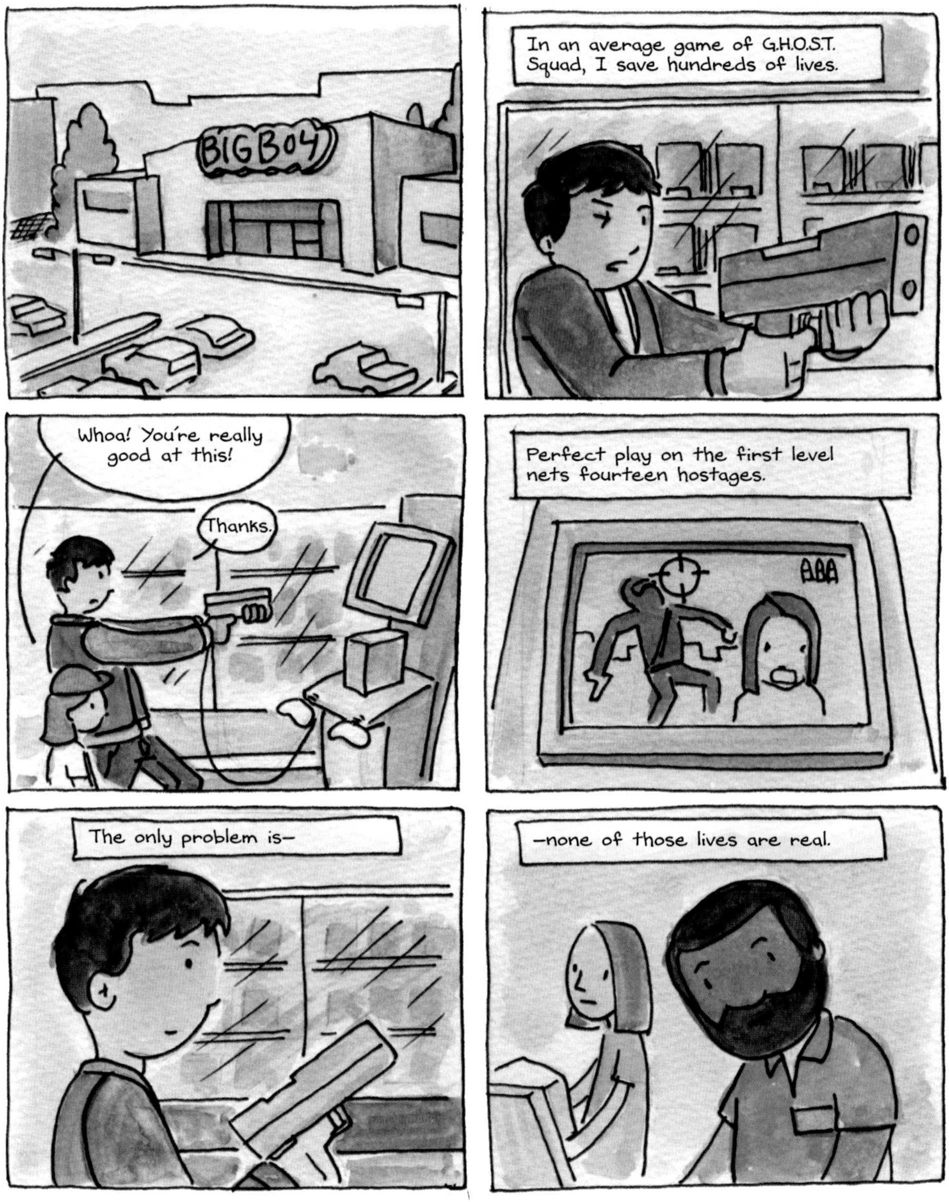
BIG BOY
In an average game of G.H.O.S.T. Squad, I save hundreds of lives.
Whoa! You're really good at this!
Thanks.
Perfect play on the first level nets fourteen hostages.
The only problem is—
—none of those lives are real.

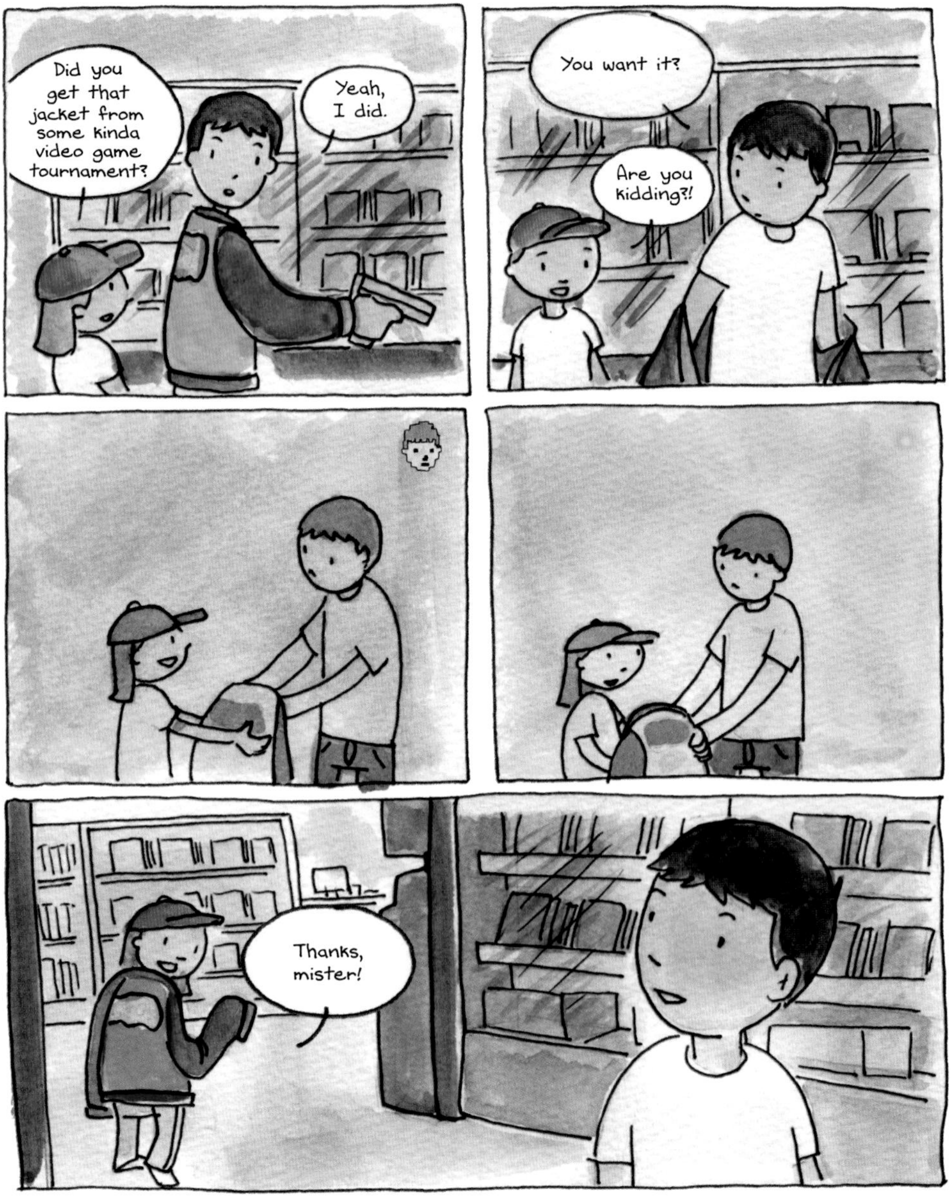
Did you get that jacket from some kinda video game tournament?
Yeah, I did.
You want it?
Are you kidding?!
Thanks, mister!

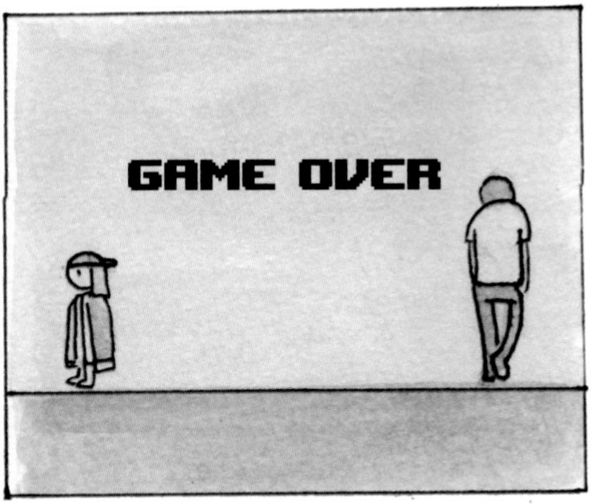
GAME OVER

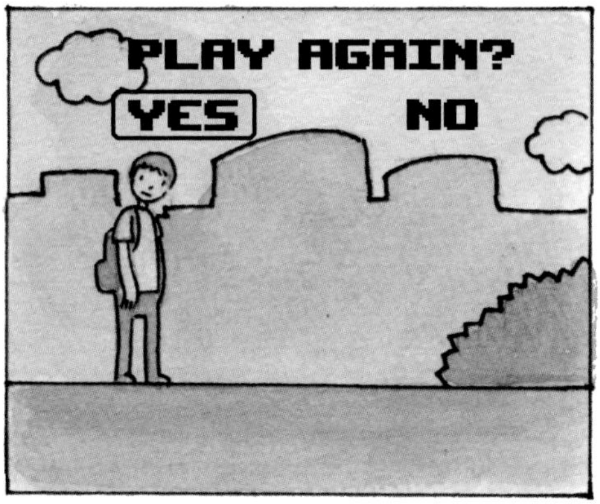
PLAY AGAIN?
YES
NO

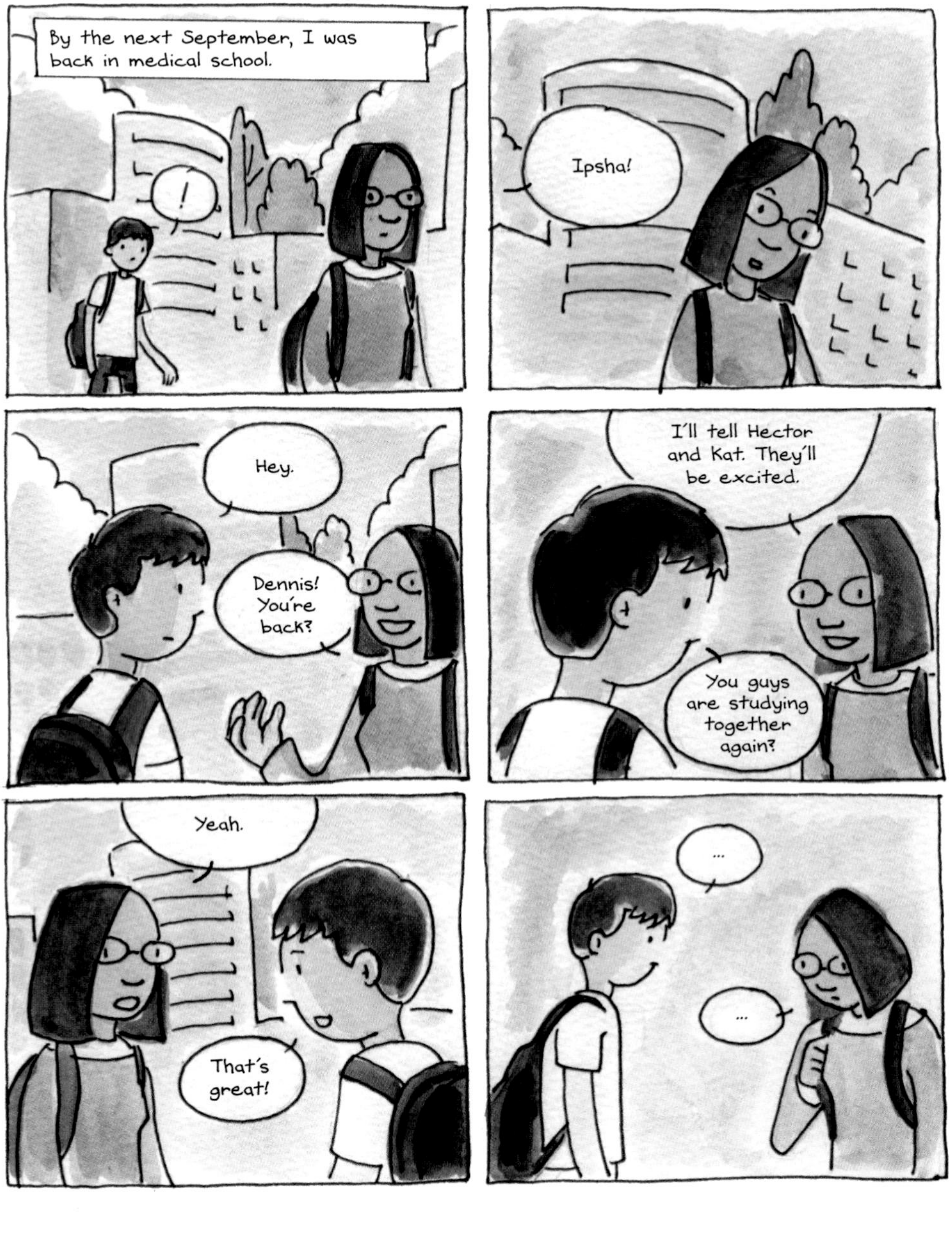
By the next September, I was back in medical school.
!
Ipsha!
Hey.
Dennis! You're back?
I'll tell Hector and Kat. They'll be excited.
You guys are studying together again?
Yeah.
That's great!
...
...

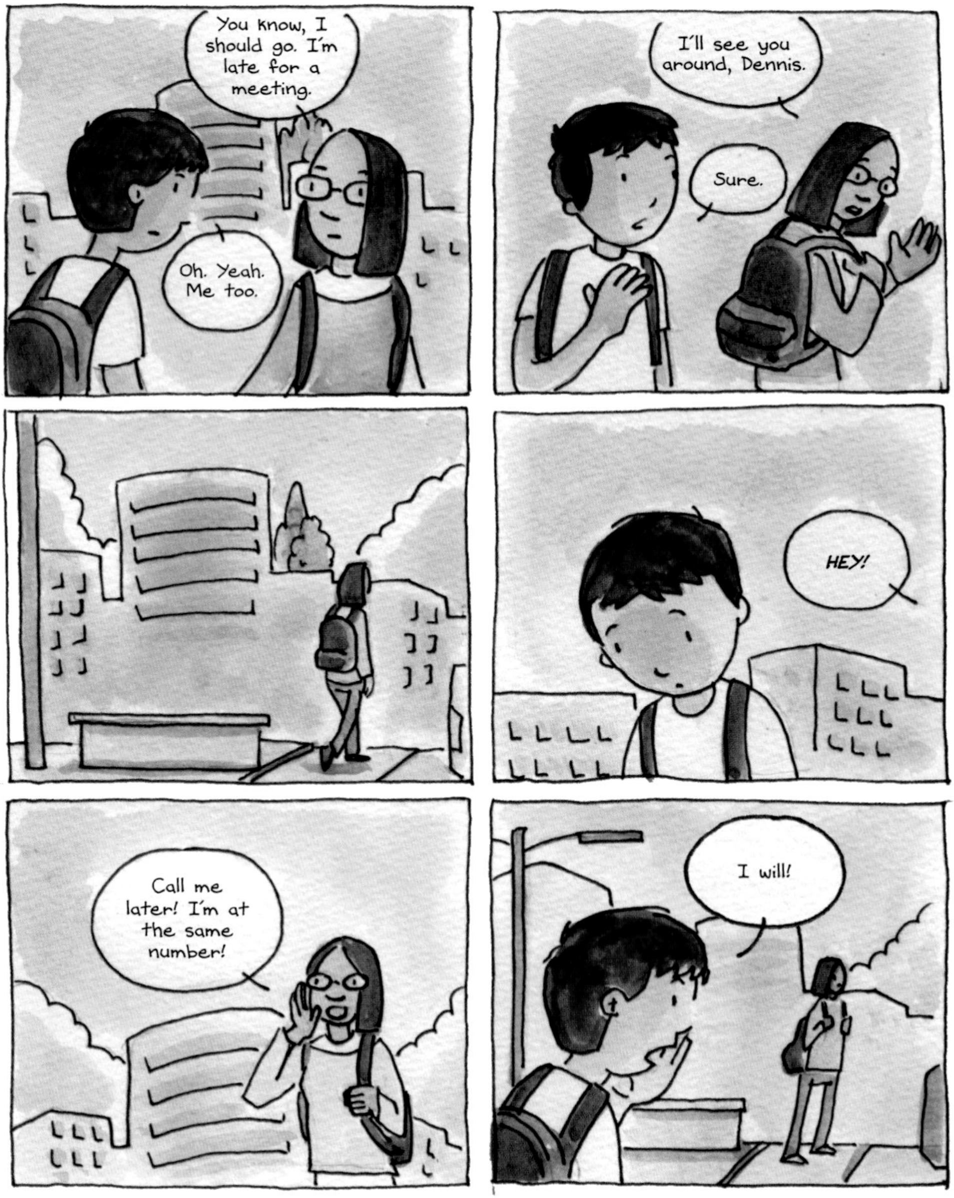
You know, I should go. I'm late for a meeting.
Oh. Yeah. Me too.
I'll see you around, Dennis.
Sure.
HEY!
Call me later! I'm at the same number!
I will!

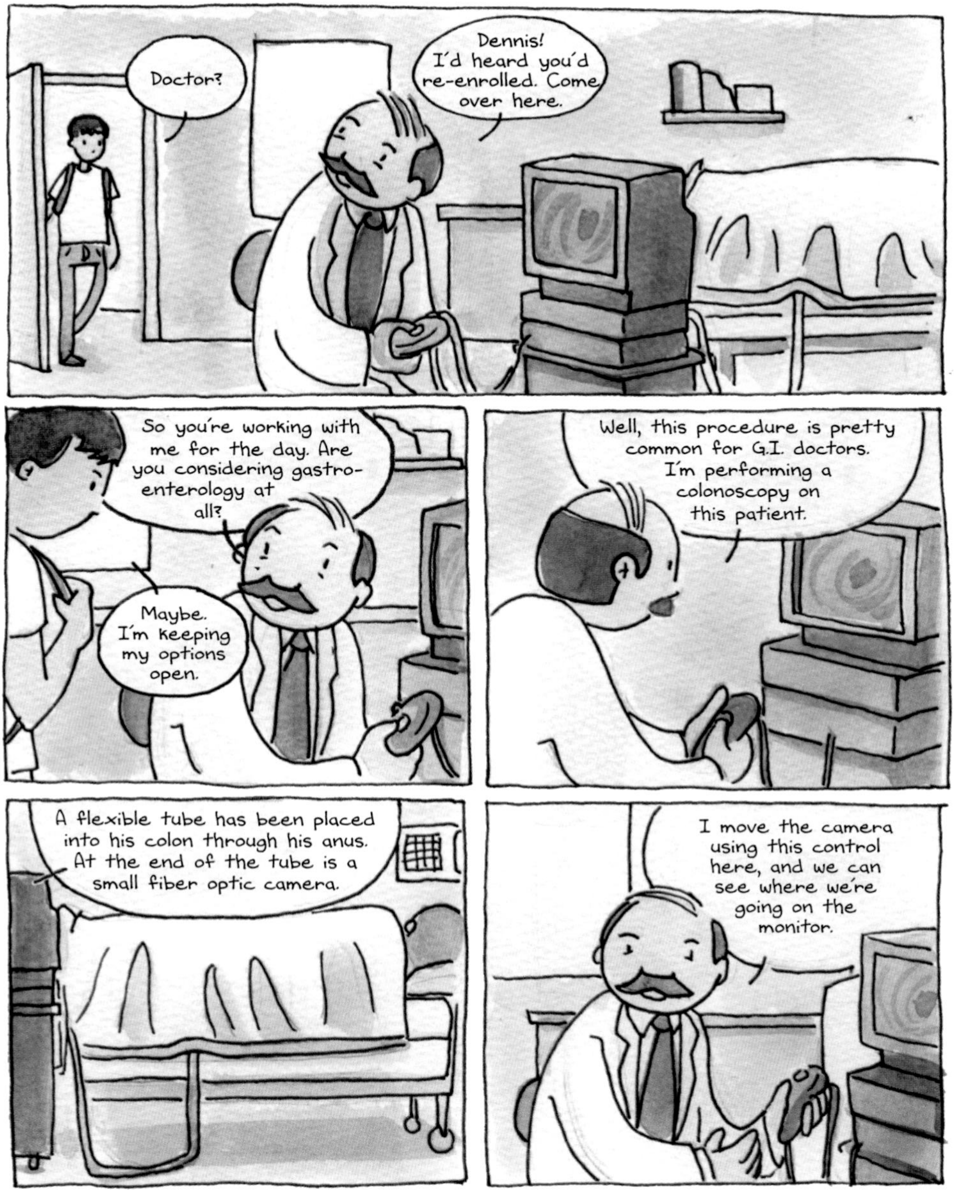
Doctor?
Dennis! I'd heard you'd re-enrolled. Come over here.
So you're working with me for the day. Are you considering gastro-enterology at all?
Maybe. I'm keeping my options open.
Well, this procedure is pretty common for G.I. doctors. I'm performing a colonoscopy on this patient.
A flexible tube has been placed into his colon through his anus. At the end of the tube is a small fiber optic camera.
I move the camera using this control here, and we can see where we're going on the monitor.

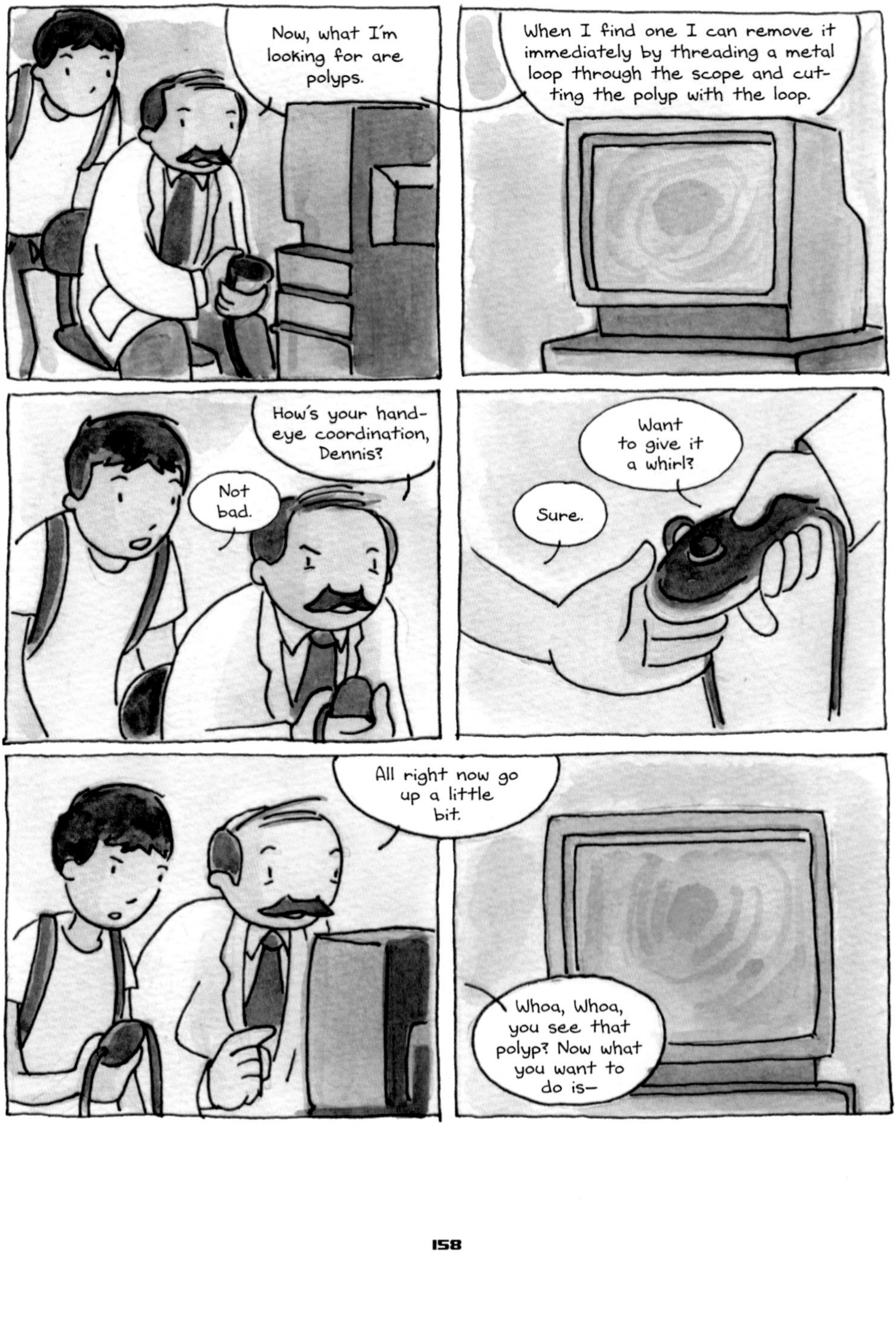
Now, what I'm looking for are polyps.
When I find one I can remove it immediately by threading a metal loop through the scope and cutting the polyp with the loop.
How's your hand-eye coordination, Dennis?
Not bad.
Want to give it a whirl?
Sure.
All right now go up a little bit.
Whoa, Whoa, you see that polyp? Now what you want to do is—

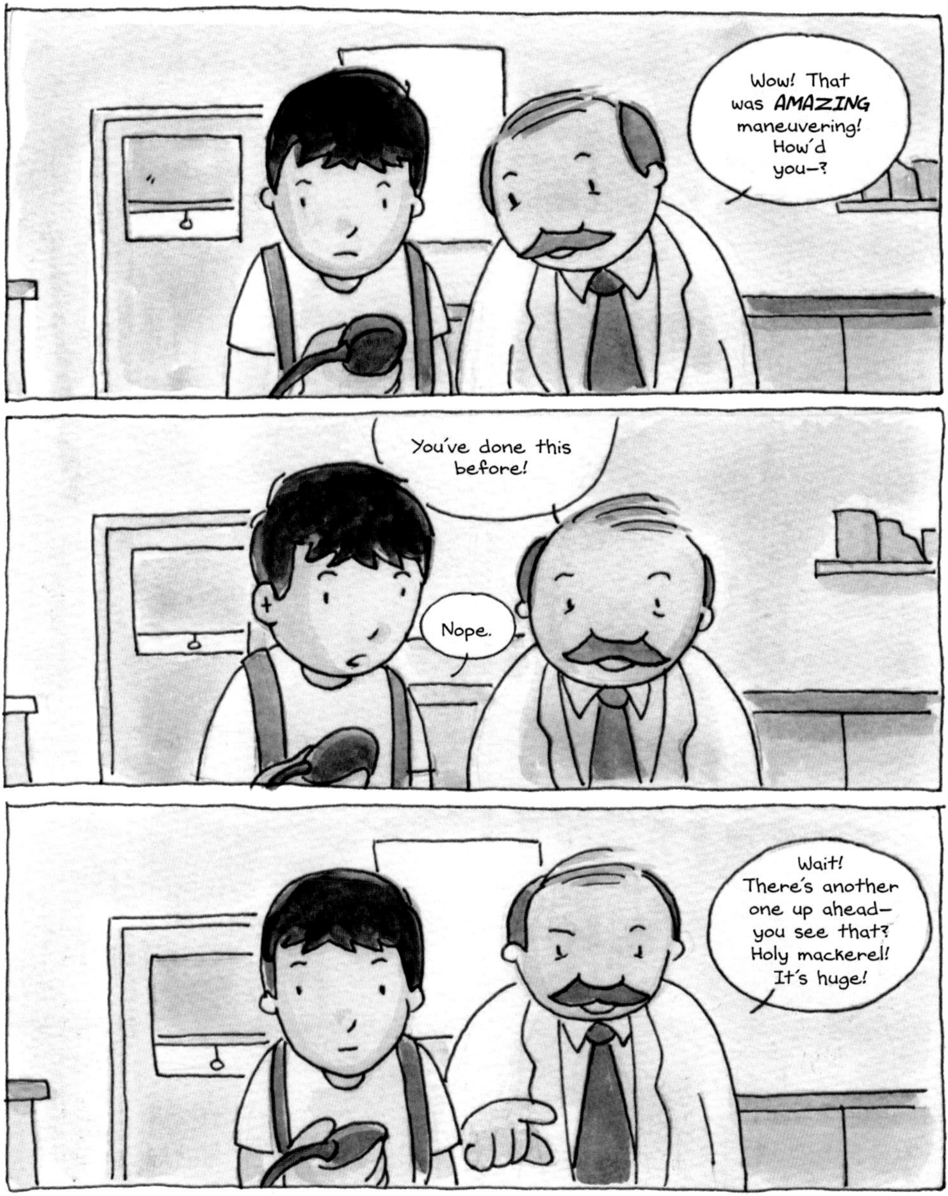
Wow! That was AMAZING maneuvering! How'd you–?
You've done this before!
Nope.
Wait! There's another one up ahead– you see that? Holy mackerel! It's huge!

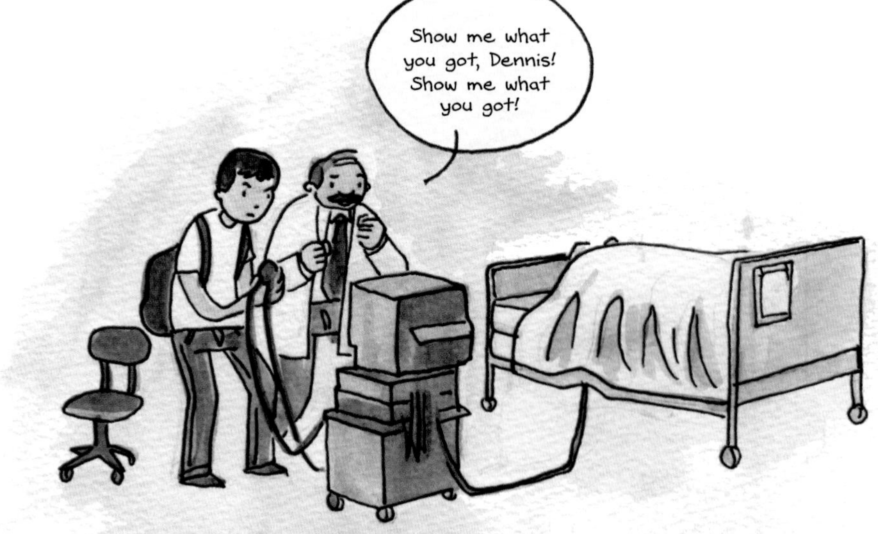
Show me what you got, Dennis! Show me what you got!